The Trouble With Love

The Trouble With Love

Jane Lovering

Choc Lit
A JOFFE BOOKS COMPANY

Revised edition 2024
Choc Lit
A Joffe Books company
www.choc-lit.com

First published in Great Britain as *Hubble Bubble* in 2013

This paperback edition was first published
in Great Britain in 2024

Cover art and illustration by Rachel Lawston

ISBN: 978-1781897874

*For my mother, Betty, who still believes that writing books
is a slightly perverse way to earn a living, and my brother David,
for his attempts to change her mind.*

CHAPTER ONE

The fridge had definitely exploded. The small squat box, now minus a corner, leaned slightly forward into a green patch of ooze, sides bulging and its front flapping from one impotent hinge. It looked like R2-D2 after a really hard night on the Crème de Menthe. I bent and tugged at the line of rubber door seal, which pinged sullenly back at me. 'What the hell did you have in there, fusion fuel?'

Megan looked at her toes and mumbled something. Her black curls fell over her pretty-pug face but I could see she was blushing by the darkening shade of the mocha-coffee skin visible between her hair and the back of her neck.

'And since when did you eat' — I held up a dripping fast-food wrapper between finger and thumb — 'this kind of stuff?'

Her mutters became more audible but more defensive. 'It was the last meal Tom and I had before he . . .'

'Stop trailing off when you talk about him as though he went off to a tragic hero's death! He's living in Wolverhampton, and he'd been two-timing you, *and* she's a topless model.' Only my best friend could keep the leftovers of the meal during which she split up with her boyfriend. Only she could keep them until they went critical, anyway. 'Oh, Meg,' I said

1

helplessly. 'If ever there was a man who'd had his chips, it was him.' I picked up a newspaper from the recycling pile and began scraping unidentified runny stuff off the floor of Megan's otherwise pristine kitchen.

'I don't know why I asked you over. I knew you wouldn't understand, Holly. You are *very* unsympathetic. I think it's because you don't get attached to men like I do.' She clasped her forehead dramatically. 'You don't know what it's like to be in love.'

'Because they're all wankers. We've discussed this and you agreed. Wankers. Fat wankers, some of them.'

'Only after Tom had left. And now I'm feeling like I'm ready for something new.'

'Yep. That would be a fridge.' I handed her the pendulous paper, replete with greasy puddles. 'I've got my own house, a great job — why the hell would I want a man hanging around wanting meals and laundry and doing botched DIY?'

'Because . . . oh, just because.'

'Great argument there, very persuasive. Richard Dawkins would love a debate with you, you know that?'

But Megan didn't reply. She was staring down at the sinus-clearing pool in the newspaper package. Her chunky-cut curls were, for once, completely still. 'Oh Holly, look,' she breathed.

'Never seen evolution in action before?' I poked the wobbly pile of fat. 'Hang around long enough you'll be able to tell it your views on love and the universe.'

'No.' She flexed the newsprint. 'This advert. Here.'

I looked.

What would you wish for? Women interested in forming a group to practise a new branch of the magic arts, get in touch. No experience necessary, just a broad mind and the desire to make wishes come true.'

And then the name Vivienne, and a phone number.

'Magic, Holl,' Megan breathed. Her brown eyes had gone all shiny and big; she looked like a little girl on Christmas Eve. 'She says we could do magic.'

'Yeah, I see the mistake you're making here.' I took Megan's shoulders and shook them gently. 'Magic. Not real. Like, oh, I dunno, the Tooth Fairy, Doctor Who and impartiality. Pretend. Something you grow out of by the time you're about' — I looked into that rapt expression and my hands dropped — 'twenty-nine. Or maybe, on current evidence, even later.'

'Don't be so . . . *pragmatic*, Holly! Wouldn't you love to wish for something and be able to make it come true? What would you wish for?' Her eyes were still unnaturally sparkly, and it made even my inner cynic go all rubbery round the edges. 'After the way Tom treated me, I'd wish to be worshipped like a goddess.'

'Wouldn't you get a bit sick of all the sacrificial blood? And then, think of being on call all the time; it'd be worse than being a junior doctor. Or a dutiful sister, which is what I am, and I have an arrangement to meet my dear sibling in twenty minutes, so I'm going to leave you with your fantasies.' I collected my jacket and bag, and went to the door. Megan was sitting on the floor clutching the newspaper bundle, which was now dipping alarmingly in the middle. Her face was all dreamy and there was a little smile I didn't much like the look of tweaking at the corners of her mouth. 'You heard me say "fantasies", right?'

'Bye, Holl.'

I shook my head as I left the flat. Megan was about as grounded as dandelion fluff on a good day. Today, with the winds of romantic disappointment whistling through her life, she'd probably left Planet Sensible for geostationary orbit.

CHAPTER TWO

Nicholas was waiting for me in the already crowded pub. 'Hey, Holl. I've got a round in, come sit down.' He took my jacket and hung it over the back of a nearby chair, next to the bloke who was sitting there. I smiled in apology and went to remove it, but Nick stopped me. 'This is our table. I asked Kye to save it for us.'

'Kye?'

The man stood, and it was a movement which went on for some time. He was tall, ridiculously tall, and had the kind of shape that is usually described as 'lithe': slim but muscular enough to give him shoulders that filled his jacket in an interesting way. 'That's K-A-I. You must be Holly.' Welsh accent. There were other things that I noticed about him too, like his hair, which was very dark and very long but drawn back to show off his cheekbones, and the single piercing in one ear which glinted whenever he moved his head. And his hooded black leather jacket, worn over a pale blue T-shirt cut low to reveal the dip at the base of his throat, the silver ring on his thumb, and those long legs wrapped in washed-out denim, so old it was nearly white. But my brain took all this in in a flash, like looking at a photograph, then ignored it. He was a bloke, that was all.

4

I looked quickly at Nick. He was bouncing around on the balls of his feet, rubbing his hands together. A good day, then. But Nick's 'good days' had a way of bringing disaster to anyone who got involved, his un-aimed enthusiasm was a form of weaponry that warring nations could exploit. 'Yes. Er, Kai. Thank you for holding the table for us. I'm sure you'd like to get off now. Back to . . .' I stared around for inspiration.

'No, no, Holl, Kai is with us. Well, with me, although not in the way that you are obviously thinking by the way you're staring. Not a couple. No.' Nick bounced a bit more, then sat down.

'Why the hell would I think you were a couple?' I moved my gaze from Nicholas to Kai, only to find that his eyes were fixed on me with a peculiar intensity, and when I met his stare I realised that he didn't only have a body that would make any red-blooded woman break stride, he had unusual eyes too. They were probably really a kind of paleish brown, but the lights in the pub made them look yellow. Nick was staring too, but that's the kind of person he was, he didn't mean anything by it. His eyes, like mine, were on the normal side of grey, although he'd inherited our father's pale skin and blond hair, so we used to tease him that if he was photographed in black-and-white he'd be invisible. I, on the other hand, got Ma's ginger ringlets and freckles, Aunt Mairi's athletic build and, from some anonymous donor to the family gene pool, the kind of mouth that always looks as though I am smiling, even when I'm not. I looked, so I was told, like Little Orphan Annie's evil twin hatching a plot.

The two guys eyeballed me until I began to feel awkward. 'What?' I sat down behind the gin and tonic.

Kai broke the silence and dropped his eyes, to stare at the scratched and scarred table and the two pints sitting stickily atop. 'Nicholas has been telling me about your job. You're a location scout? Sounds brilliant.' The Welsh accent made every word musical and slightly foreign but however sexy the voice I couldn't ignore the content.

'Nicky! You know you're not supposed to go round blurting out what I do. Remember last time? And, oh God, the time before?'

Nick looked down at his scuffed shoes. We'd never managed to get him to polish his shoes, not even with all the family nagging, and now scuffed toecaps were as much a part of my brother as his floppy fringe, huge eyes and eccentricities. 'Sorry. Sorry, Holl, but I think it's so cooooool to have a sis who drives around finding places to be in films!'

I couldn't be cross with him for long. It was completely pointless in the face of such effervescence, like sulking at a beagle. 'I know. And yes, it is cool. But when you tell people, they always think I'm some kind of backdoor entrance to the industry.' I turned to Kai. 'Look, sorry, but I don't know any movie directors or film stars and I can't help you get your script in front of a producer. I never get to meet anyone with any influence, I just scout locations. I'm only slightly higher up the food chain than the guy who makes the coffee on set. Okay?'

This got me an even-toothed grin. 'You don't know any film stars?' He picked up one pint and drank, watching me over the soapy froth.

'No.'

'Want to meet some?'

'Kai's a journalist. Knows all sorts of people. Hugh Jackman and David Tennant, people like that. You like Hugh Jackman, Holl, don't you?'

'Hey, steady boy, you'll get me into all kinds of bother.' The golden eyes turned back to me. 'Interested, that's all. No agenda.' His look was cool now.

'So, why are you and Nick . . . ?'

'Kai was doing a piece on these new drugs. Wanted to interview someone who's taking them and my doctor put him on to me.' Nick cupped his pint glass and lifted it, spilling beer as his hands trembled.

Yeah, I had my doubts about that doctor too.

'I thought you were all about the famous people.' To fit in I took a sip of my gin. The lemon slice bobbed to the surface and hit me on the nose like a fairy slap and, as if in reaction, someone behind me burst out laughing. The Welshman's eyes flicked up for a second to watch the crowd and I caught a hint — I mean, call me Mrs Suspicious if you want, but it was there, trust me — of someone used to watching, observing the crowd from the outside rather than being a part of it.

'Yeah. Sometimes. But I do other stuff too.' Now I got the full economy-pack version of the look, and I swear his eyes really were a pale gold, like a cat, or an owl. A colour I'd never seen on a man before. 'Deeper stuff, you know? Can only go so long asking all these gorgeous women if they've had work done, just so they can deny it.'

I waited for him to leer and ask if I'd had work done, but he didn't. Bastard. I mean, I haven't, but it would be nice to be asked.

'Anyway.' The body stretched out again, seemed to grow towards the ceiling. 'Thanks for the drink, Nicholas. Better be off. Deadlines, you know how it goes.' A hand went into a pocket of the battered leather jacket. 'Nice to meet you, Holly. And if you're ever looking for a gothic cottage, well, quite fancy seeing my place on screen.' He held out a card to me. 'Come over.'

'Thanks.' This, at least, managed to sound sincere. Not many people volunteered their homes; most had to be persuaded into letting some film crew muck up their lawn, scare the cat and leave traces of John Nettles everywhere. And by the time I looked up from the small-printed square of card, the lanky Welshman was gone and Nick was drawing house shapes on the table in spilled beer.

'I thought he'd be your type.'

'Stop it. He's not my type. I don't have a type. Anyway. How're you doing? Did you get the washing out that I put in the dryer at your place this morning? It needs folding as soon as it's dry or it goes all crinkly.'

Nick flicked me a sudden straight stare. It was disconcerting, from someone whose eyes usually never stayed still. 'He's a nice guy, been nice to me anyway, and you can't say that about everyone, can you? And he was interested in you, Holl, I could tell, the way he kept looking at you.'

'People always look at one another when they're talking. That's how people *are*,' I said without thinking, draining my G & T and watching his fingers fill in curtains on the little beer house.

'No. That's how normal people are.' He added a chimney and a winding plume of smoke. 'I don't look at people like that, do I?' A sudden, almost vicious flat palm wiped the outlines, scrubbed them back into the sticky pool they'd come from, then kept moving until there was nothing but a brown smear stretching between beer mats.

I reached out and laid a hand on his bony wrist. 'Hey. Come on. You're doing okay. And the new stuff seems to be helping, doesn't it? You're better than you've been for a long time.'

'Yeah, yeah.' A flick of the head and his mood changed again. 'How's Megan?'

I told him about the exploded fridge and the latest idea and he laughed until beer came out of his nose. 'Seriously? She really thinks you should join a witching group? Oh, God, Holl, do it, just for the laugh. She's so great, isn't she, Megan — it's like having this never-ending supply of fluffy kittens, and, hey, it'd be so fantastic to have you doing these like magic-y things — I can so see you and Meg prancing around naked, waving wands and chanting stuff.' He snorted again, then started sneezing. 'Well, I can't see *you* naked, *urgh*, that would just be wrong.'

'Ain't gonna happen anyway, brother dear. It takes August sunshine to get yours truly into a bikini, there is absolutely no chance of me taking even one layer off in a Yorkshire winter.'

'Wishes come true!' Nick giggled again. 'You never know, it might work. Stranger things have happened, hey, no, my bad, those were hallucinations, but you'd go along, wouldn't you? If Megan was up for it?'

'If Megan was up for it I'd have to.' Megan has all the gullibility of a toddler and all the self-protective instincts of, well, a toddler. Someone had to watch her back. Given her 36DD chest there were already plenty of volunteers to watch her front.

'So, then.' My brother leaned in close across the table, one elbow in the beer pool. 'What would you wish for? What's your . . .'

CHAPTER THREE

'. . . greatest wish?' The redheaded woman hunched towards me again and I nearly hit Megan in the forehead in my attempts to lean back out of the way. But then it was her fault I was here, so the odd black eye would be payment.

'I don't think I have one, Vivienne.'

She looked away from me now, round the crowded little room. I hadn't been able to stop myself assessing her house on a professional basis when I arrived, but there was nothing that could have featured in anything other than a sitcom based on the antics of a rural witch-wannabe. Heavy velvet curtains, incense, crystal just-about-everything and a deep, layered smell of cats, damp and sage. And as if all that wasn't enough, it was a cottage in the woods. If anyone offered me gingerbread, I'd be violent.

'Oh, come now, Holly! Everyone has something they wish for.' Vivienne tried to rally support from the other women. Apart from Megan, and to a much lesser extent me, the advert had gathered two others. None of them looked like witches, apart from Vivienne, who, with her bony chin and slightly-too-large nose, looked like a starter-hag. 'Isobel, what about you? What do you want?'

Isobel gave a squeak and vanished further into her brown handbag, where she'd started scrabbling the moment she'd entered the room. '. . . hanky . . .'

'No.' Vivienne laid a long-fingered hand on Isobel's knitted sleeve. 'When you saw my little charm in the paper. What was the wish that came to your mind?'

Isobel's immediate wish came true as she finally emerged from the satchel carrying a scrunched-up bit of tissue. 'Sorry, sorry. Allergies,' she snuffled, trying to avoid looking at the cats which were lined up along the top of an oversized piano like a collection of malevolent tea cosies. 'Sorry, what was it you asked me?'

Vivienne sighed and repeated her question. She had the sculpted face of someone with no body fat and the slightly sunken eyes of someone who worked hard to keep it that way. Her hair was the wrong side of red to be real and she wore an amazing amount of jewellery even for someone who is convinced about witchcraft. She rattled like a rain stick. 'What is the wish that came to your mind when you read my advertisement?'

'Oh.' Isobel looked at us from under her straight, brown fringe. 'I can't say.' She had skin pebble-dashed with acne and a thin, unshaped body which made her look like a teenager, although I knew she was twenty-seven because she'd said so. Twenty-seven, shy to the bone and dressed like a sixty-year-old — I knew what I'd wish if I'd been her.

Vivienne sighed again and I had a moment of sympathy. She'd obviously thought all her potential witch-trainees would be outgoing, bubbly 'Bewitched' girls with sparky wishes at their black-varnished fingertips. We looked like the Asperger's version. But then, when you think about it, if we'd been bubbly and outgoing, would we have been sitting here in this over-furnished room with a bunch of strangers, being ogled by cats? No, we'd be out there getting things to happen.

'All right,' I piped up, to spare us all the embarrassment. 'I've thought of something. I'd wish for some excitement in my life.'

'But your life *is* exciting.' Megan dodged round in front of me. 'You've got your job . . .' I pinched her hand to stop her mentioning what it was. I'd got so sick of people trying to use me to get their script in front of Peter Jackson, who wouldn't know me from a crate of peas. '. . . and your house, and your family.'

'Holly obviously feels that her life lacks a certain spark.' Vivienne leaned in again. 'Would that excitement include — a man?' When I shook my head she subsided back.

'Holly doesn't like men.' Megan piped up, and I felt the bristling interest of the group rest on me for a second. 'She only keeps them around for sex.'

The group interest deepened. 'Like, locked up?' Isobel asked tentatively, but with a prurient gleam in her eye.

Oh good God.

'No. And that's rubbish, Meg, as you well know. I've had . . . I mean, there are . . .'

'Wankers,' she supplied helpfully.

'I'm not all that good at being a girlfriend. I have a, um, difficult family situation.'

'The last one called her brother a retard.'

He'd actually called him a 'fucking retarded jizz-monkey', if memory served, but that had simply been a symptom of his wanker-hood. I'd dumped him very shortly afterwards and although he'd left my heart intact he took my mobile phone and forty quid from the kitchen drawer. It didn't exactly fill me with confidence in my ability to attract caring men.

'Um, excuse me?' The final member of our quintet put up her hand. She was a plump older lady with greying hair and ill-advised orange lipstick.

'Yes, Eve?'

'Does that mean we're going to do, you know, proper magic? Dancing round a cauldron and spells and so on? Only, I don't really *do* dancing. Was never allowed when I was younger, and I just can't seem to get the hang of it now. Can't really get my head around drum 'n' bass, or whatever

12

they call it. All sounds like saucepan lids to me. Besides' — she waggled an ankle — 'I've got a touch of sciatica, so I'm not supposed to dance. Especially not nude. My doctor was quite specific about that.'

Vivienne's attention switched instantly to her. Perhaps my non-man-related wish hadn't been interesting enough. 'No, we won't have to dance. My magic is different to that you might have heard of as being practised. When I feel that we are all, how shall I put it, *sympathetic*, we shall begin work on our wishes. My working area is over there.' She swept a long arm at the curtains.

'Behind the sofa?'

'In the woods, Holly.' Her voice went all breathy. 'Behind this cottage lies Barndale Woods, one of the last stretches of the Wild Wood, relics of trees that were growing here before man ever came to these shores.' She sounded like a voice-over from Most Haunted. 'Merely being in those woods makes one more connected to the earth-energies and that is what makes the spells more efficient, the age of the woodland and of the ground beneath.'

'Ah,' I said and nodded slowly. 'Let's just go, Meg,' I whispered out of the corner of my mouth. 'She's barking.'

'No.' To my surprise Megan stood up. 'There has to be more in this world than we understand, there *has* to.' Too late I remembered that Megan's mother had died when she was six. Meg swore that she'd seen her mum several times since her death, sitting on the end of Meg's bed and stroking her hair, which had given her a profound belief in all matters paranormal. Personally I'd rather not be watched over by my deceased relations when I was, say, on the toilet or partaking in some kinky shag-work, but I didn't suppose that you could choose. 'Science can't explain everything, and maybe there is something to magic that we don't *get* yet.'

The other women were nodding. Isobel's ironed-smooth hair tossed up and down like a horse's mane. 'I believe that too,' she said.

13

'I'm not certain,' Eve rested her forearms on her comfortably round thighs. 'But I'd *like* to believe. I'd love to think that we can make amends for wrongs we've committed in this life, in the next.'

'And what is your wish?' Vivienne's eyes were suddenly bright. If she'd had prickable ears, I'd take bets they would have gone up as though she'd smelled dinner.

'I want to meet the man of my dreams,' Eve said simply. She gave an apologetic shrug. 'I'm fifty-seven. I'm lonely. What can I say?'

Isobel raised her hand. Her knitted sleeve rolled back to reveal what looked like cat-scratch marks on her arm. 'My wish is to be someone's whole world.' It was a whisper, as though she was ashamed. 'That's all. To have someone unable to live without me.' She drew down her arm and self-consciously tugged her cardigan down to her wrist again. 'That's all,' she repeated.

'And what about you, Vivienne?' Everyone's new-found confessional status made me twitchy. 'I'm guessing you've already made your wishes come true? How did that work out for you?'

Vivienne moved across to the piano and began stroking the heads of the cats in sequence as though she was trying to get a tune out of them. 'Ah. Well, I'm . . . my advertisement may have been just a *touch* misleading . . .' A general air of incipient disappointment descended over the group and even the cats drooped a bit. 'Oh, nothing terrible, just that . . . I'm not actually an *established* practitioner of the Arts. As such. More . . . working on broadening my theoretical knowledge with like-minded souls.'

'She means she read a book once,' I hissed at Meg, who was sitting back next to me again, her eyes still frighteningly shiny, but she ignored me.

'I am perfectly grounded in the *conjectural* and academic uses of magic.' Vivienne was obviously avoiding my gaze.

'She read a *thick* book,' I muttered, but was still soundly ignored.

'And my wish is a little different.' She turned her back to us. 'My husband left me last month.' Her voice wavered a little. 'Twenty years of marriage, three children, and it all went for nothing.'

All four of us exchanged a look. No one knew what to say.

'He's gone to "find himself" apparently. Said that he needed to "question his life". To find answers.' There was a momentary savagery in her words, and the cat beneath her hand stretched its eyes in alarm. 'I suspect that top of the list of questions was "has that girl in accounts had enlargement surgery or are they natural", but he says there's no one else. Just him and his *questions*.' She almost spat the word. 'So, my wish.' Now she turned to face the room and the prominent bones of her face were highlighted by the random beams from the crystal lampshade, making her look slightly evil. 'It's that his life becomes full of *real* questions. None of this poncing about with the "where is my life going?" midlife crisis rubbish, all that "I have to look into my soul and find the eternal answer". Proper questions. And when he's been called upon to find those answers, I want him put out of his misery.'

Now we all felt uncomfortable. Vivienne had clearly been working on her wish, carefully phrasing it so that the word 'death' never featured, but it backfilled the gaps in her sentences as though her ex's corpse was already buried there.

'Not sure I'm joining up for that one.' I stood up alongside Megan. 'This is all getting a bit too focussed for me. I mean, I don't believe that leaping about in some ancient woodland is going to bring me one iota closer to any excitement anyway. Other than that briefly afforded by a visit to hospital suffering from the respiratory illness of my choice.'

Eve looked at me from under her greying fringe. 'But doesn't one tiny part of you *want* to believe that science doesn't know everything? That we might, just *might*, be able to influence things, if we want something enough?'

I shrugged again.

Vivienne narrowed her eyes at me. 'It should be an uneven number. If you drop out, we shall have to find someone else.' The anxious way she plucked at the cat's head led me to believe that this might be tricky.

'And what if it does work?' That was Isobel. With her feet tucked up under the hem of her librarian-type pinafore and her hands invisible up the sleeves of her knitwear, she looked like a string puppet, waiting to be bounced along the carpet. 'If it does, you've got excitement, if it doesn't, well, you've lost nothing, have you?'

Except entire swathes of my life, I thought. But then I caught sight of Megan's bright, drawn-in expression. Oh bloody buggery, she'd gone for it, hook, line and sodding great big goldfish, and before we knew it Vivienne might be trying to part her from fifty per cent of her income or whatever con artists thought they could get out of a woman who worked behind the counter in British Home Stores. More crystal lampshades, possibly.

'Okay. I'll play.' And, just for a blink of a second I wished my disbelief would allow itself to be suspended, let me throw myself whole-heartedly into magic and spells and life being transformed beyond recognition . . . And then I thought about Nicholas and the need to persuade him to get his hair cut and have a shave and the absolute, down-to-earth necessities of my life, and I embraced my cynicism with both arms again.

Megan hugged me, Eve patted me on the shoulder and even Isobel smiled at me from under the pony-like forelock. 'It'll be fun, the five of us. It'll be like that knitting group.'

I stared at Meg. Even taking into account Isobel's wool-based idea of fashion and Vivienne's obvious addiction to pointy things, I couldn't see one similarity between us and a knitting group.

'In that novel,' she went on, 'they share their problems and it's homespun wisdom and friendship that wins the day. That could be us.'

I really had to get her reading more erotic romance.

CHAPTER FOUR

It's been a long time since I wrote to you. Wrote real words, instead of an article about Botox or the pharmaceutical industry or some overambitious starlet on the make. How long? When Imogen finally got the message? That long ago, yeah, probably. Whenever my life changes I feel this need, this . . . I dunno what you call it, an urge to put it down on paper for you to read. So you can know who I am. Know what drives me forward, what makes me the man I am — and this is what makes me crazy, the need to communicate with you. A woman who never knew me, never wanted to know me — and yet, there's still this soul-deep longing in me for some kind of contact. So. Here I am. Again. Putting it down, scribbling these unconsidered words on scraps of paper in the hope . . . no. Not hope. Not now. In the madness, yes. In the mad belief that one day I'll get to hand them all over to you, to push them into your face and say, 'Here. This is what you did. This is the man you made.' So that you can read about the vicious highs, where I'd run as far as I could to the top of the mountain, to where the air was so thin that I couldn't breathe it any more. And then the come-down, those abseils into the dark. The pit, the abyss, where you should have been waiting. Bringing the light in.

But you weren't. Never there. No hand to hold, no comfort. So I found it where I could, and who can blame me? We all need something, we all need something to lean on, and if I pitched my desires wrong, if I made myself into something reckless and wild and put my love in a box that wouldn't open . . . well, who's going to blame me?

Been here before. How many times have I written all that — tried to explain why I want . . . why I need these letters? Words I have to write because no one is there to hear me say them.

I've pushed everyone too far, you see. Pushed and pushed and taken everything I could from them, the women who wanted to give me their lives and their hearts, and I took their bodies and their beds, and gave them nothing back. Then I took their dignity, their loyalties and screwed them all up so tight that it's a wonder any of them had a life left when I'd finished. Oh, I still see them looking, women. Giving me the once-over, checking it out, this body that you gave me. Or did you? Was it you that bequeathed me the height to look down on them all? Or the eyes that they look into and see whatever they want to, reflections, nothing true, nothing real . . .

Because you gave me the looks of a romantic, and ain't that an irony?

CHAPTER FIVE

'I've had a look through the pictures and there's nothing suitable, Holl.'

I cradled the phone under my chin and flicked through the albums on my laptop. 'Are you sure, Guy? What about number 576? That little white place? People who own it are dead friendly, there's masses of room for the lorries, and the neighbours even let you use their loo when it gets busy.'

Guy sighed down the phone, and I could picture his face. He ran a small production company on a shoestring out of Newcastle and looked exactly like someone who ran a production company on a shoestring, all cutting-edge hair design and thin-cheeked fret. 'Nah. Like I said, Holl. Looking for something different. Doesn't have to be for long; external stuff only is what I need here, establishing shots, bit of close work. Couple of days should see it finished, but the place has to be right. We're talking more . . . I dunno, gothic.'

'Gothic.' Vivienne's 'Seven Dwarves' Holiday Cottage' came briefly to mind but was dismissed. Then I remembered Nicholas's friend Kai, and his unlikely offer. 'Hold on. There is somewhere that I had described to me as Gothic Cottage. I'll go take a look, mail the pics to you if I think it'll work.'

'Thanks babe, you're a star.'

I put the phone down and located the card in my Rolodex. Just 'Kai Rhys' and a mobile number, which took me straight through to answerphone. As I put the phone down it rang again. Megan.

'Well, what about last night? What about Isobel, isn't she nice? And Eve? And that Vivienne, isn't she a scream — do you think she really does do magic in the woods? We won't have to take our clothes off, Holl, will we, I mean, it's okay for you what with you being size twelve all over, but . . . no one really appreciates how hard it is to dance topless with big boobs. All that slapping, it sounds like I come with my own applause.'

Bless her. Fifteen years I'd known Megan and the only thing that really took the shine off her incessant Angelina Ballerina cuteness was period pain and heartbreak. 'You do know that I don't believe a word of what she said, don't you?' I wandered through to my kitchen carrying the phone. 'Vivienne is deluded at best.'

'Yes, but . . .'

'. . . what if.' I finished for her. 'It's okay, Meg. I've said I'll go along with it.' And it could have been worse, she could have discovered the French cinema . . .

'Great! Only she rang me this morning, we're having another meeting tomorrow evening at six. In the woods this time. She said to bring a blanket and a warm coat. Apparently we're going to do some visualisation exercises.' Her voice went up in a little squeak. 'Isn't it exciting!'

'I thought you said it was going to be like a knitting group.'

'But you can't knit, Holl, can you?'

No, but I can bloody well visualise, and if I'd been feeling really cynical I would have told Megan what it was I could visualise, i.e. a bunch of gullible women getting duped into helping some nutjob of a deserted wife slice up her ex's designer suits. But I was taking a day off from pessimism. 'No, I can't knit. I'll be there. Six o'clock, Barndale Woods.

Anywhere in particular, or do I roam the whole hundred acres, like Eeyore on a really bad day?'

In my hand the phone buzzed.

'Text me, Meg, got another call coming in.' I switched to the new caller.

'Rhys.'

'Sorry, I think you have the wrong number.' I was about to put the phone down when I recognised the accent. 'Oh.'

'Yeah. Returning your call?'

'Okay.' I explained my — or rather, Guy's — predicament. 'So if you're still willing to put your place forward, I'd like to come and take a look at it.'

There was a pause. Right, so he'd changed his mind, fine, that happened all the time. People thought it would be glamorous to see their house on TV, until they read through all the forms and disclaimers and waivers which practically ensured that the crew could burn down your home, disembowel your children, run over your dog and wave a cheery, and unsueable, goodbye at the end of the day.

'Don't worry about it. I'll go scouting, there'll be somewhere.'

'No, no, just thinking. I'm not at home at the moment. I could be back tonight but you won't want to come here in the dark, so how about tomorrow? Fourish?'

He gave me directions. Later, when I traced them onto the Ordnance Survey map, I found his cottage was on the opposite side of Barndale Woods to Vivienne's, their houses lying either end of a connecting track. Barndale Woods was a sprawling mass of ancient forest, although the map made it look an innocent green blob, and I knew that some bits were quite inaccessible. If the track wasn't driveable, at least it meant Kai's place was close enough to Vivienne's not to condemn me to getting embarrassingly lost on foot. I could go straight from his place to meet up with Megan, for our cosy-in. Well, maybe not *straight* there; I'd quite like to get tanked on vodka before I had to meet up with the Earnest Sisters again.

I shook my head over the map. What the hell did they all think they were playing at? A bunch of grown women making wishes? I let my eyes trace the contours of the local hills. Sensible lines, *practical* lines, nothing whimsical or fanciful about them, nice and plain and solid; unchanging. If only all of life could be that impassive and sensible, that rooted in reality . . . and it hadn't escaped my attention that all the women's wishes were a bit man-centric. Isobel, wanting to be someone's whole world; Megan, wanting to be a goddess; Vivienne and her, quite frankly, scary desires for her ex. Even the outwardly sensible Eve. What the hell was it with them? I mean, yeah, okay, men were fine in their place, and I'd had a good time with quite a few over the years. They could be good company for an evening, over a meal, and then later they were entertaining for a while in bed, but anything else? Not for me. Oh, not that I'm a slapper or anything — I mean they've all known the score — but, nah, I don't regret any of it. Fun, that's what it was for, all it was ever meant to be. Fun while it lasted.

I'd realised a long time ago that the manacle round the third finger, left hand was not for me. I wasn't meant to be tied down and restricted; liked my own space too much. My lovely triangular house with its double-fronting onto the main Malton road, which tapered in an unlikely fashion to the world's only Isosceles kitchen at the back. My office, my sunny bedroom, all untainted by scattered copies of Top Gear magazine and skiddy underpants. I spent long enough clearing up Nicky's messes — in his kitchen, even the mice had mice — and, what with keeping his laundry up to date and making sure he had regular meals, coming home to do it all again would be enough to make Kirstie Allsopp run for the hills. So, since I had no desire to have children, could acquire a casual shag whenever I wanted or needed one, what on earth would I want a man for?

Besides, I travelled so much. I'd worry about who was exercising him when I was away.

I shut down the laptop and went into town to meet up with Nicholas. Since I'd done all his housework yesterday, today our designated venue was the big park down near the river. Open-air meetings suited Nick: he could run around the trees if he was having an 'up' day, or sit brooding on a bench, blurting out all the random stuff that seemed to poison his mind without disturbing other people, on one of his down days. Today he was lounging on the grass, despite the damp, eating a packet of peanuts. I spotted him from the path and tried to assess his mood before I reached him. With Nicholas it was best to know what you were facing before you actually faced it, so you could prepare, and the slouched posture could have meant almost anything, although the fact he was eating meant that this was probably one of the better days — he'd been known to go two weeks without food when his mood took a downward slide, and I'd have to tempt him to eat with treats, like a sickly cat.

'Hey!' The simple syllable told me all I needed. Or rather, the inflection. On a bad day, Nick could put a depressive tilt on 'I won the lottery'. 'How's the witching business?'

'Don't start.' I sat beside him, trying not to catch my boot-heels in the mud. 'Is that jacket new?' Wow, this was a turn up, Nicholas actually *buying* clothes. If I didn't make him change, he'd stay in his favourite outfit all the time. Seriously. *All the time*. It's cute when a five-year-old wears his wellies to bed, but when a thirty-two-year-old refuses to take off his parka, it really isn't. It was some kind of security thing, apparently.

'Yeah, well, newish.' He looked at the blazer-style grey wool. 'Makes me look a bit like a teacher though, doesn't it?'

He actually looked fragile, with his blond hair and pale eyes and even paler skin. The jacket was slightly too big for his skinny shoulders and too bulky for his frame, it made him look like Paddington Bear without the hat. 'Nah. It's cool.' I took a proffered peanut. 'So, what's the excuse for the new wardrobe?'

A shake of the head. I watched two girls, students in their Ugg boots and tight jeans, pass, turn to look over their shoulders at Nick, then nudge each other, giggling. 'Are they laughing at me?'

'No, Nicholas, they are checking you out, you daft bugger. Damn but good looks run in our family.'

'I should have got married.'

Conversational shifts were something I took for granted with my brother. 'Why?'

'Because I'm thirty-two. By now Ma and Dad should be grandparents. You should be an auntie and we should have had a big family wedding with cousins everywhere and everyone dancing to La Vida Loca with their elbows.'

I sighed and hugged his arm; padded by the grey wool, it was like hugging a lagged pipe. 'Plenty of time. You'll meet the right girl one day. What about that dark-haired lass you used to hang around with when you were just out of hospital? You went to support group together, didn't you? Whatever happened to her?'

'She was a jumper.'

'Woolly and a bit thick?'

'No.' And he mimed someone diving from the top of something high. The splat bit was very effective. 'So, I was thinking . . . when you're doing your witchy stuff, can you do a spell for me? To help me find someone?'

'What is this? You've never believed in stuff like this before — apart from that time when you thought the squirrels were talking to you. And suddenly witchcraft does it for you?'

He pulled back sharply, like a horse tugging at a rope, with his head coming up in alarm and sending his hair tumbling backwards, leaving his face exposed and little-boyish. 'Why are you angry, Holl?'

'I'm not,' I said, locking down on the sarcasm. If I got angry, Nick got scared. I'd learned to be careful about showing my emotions in front of him. 'Honestly, I'm not. I'm just confused that so many otherwise sensible people have come over all credulous and naïve all of a sudden. Is there something in the water?'

He gave me one of his sudden grins, all signs of panic gone. 'But I've never been sensible though, have I? Go on, Holl. Do a spell for me.'

'But I . . .' Useless. Pointless, even, pleading with a guy whose brain works on an alternative-sanity clause. Absolutely no good telling him that I was only going along to keep Megan out of mischief. 'Yeah, all right. I'll do a spell for you.'

'Great.' He threw a peanut up and caught it between his teeth. 'Make it a good one. I mean, no eye of newt stuff — I want a girlfriend not an amphibian.'

'Yes, Nicholas.'

'And not ugly. She doesn't have to be gorgeous but I'd like her to at least be pretty.'

'All right.'

'And if she could have enormous . . .'

'You don't need witchcraft, you need a mail-order catalogue. Shut up about women, will you?'

'Okay. Can we go to the café now, I'm hungry.'

Yeah. Why the hell would I ever want kids when I had Nicky to look after?

I parked at the end of the road that led into Barndale Woods. I looked at the state of the forestry track ahead from a professional point of view. The lorries and catering trucks would be able to manage it, no trouble, but crew with little cars like mine would have to park out on the road and walk in. As long as it wasn't too far, I thought; most of them came up from London and had to be cappuccino'd every five yards or their legs fell off. Pulling my wellies on and setting out, I looked at the track from *my* point of view. No way did I feel like walking to Vivienne's through this squicky muck in anything less than a diving suit. Better off coming back for the car and driving the long way round.

After a couple of minutes walking, the conifer belt gave way to much older woodland, dark-barked birches and squat oaks. The trees hid the sky, underfoot the track was squashy with their discarded leaves and their vast trunks muffled sound. Ahead of me a heavy-bodied pheasant clucked its way up into the branches like a panicked housewife trying to get airborne, making me jump, and I hunched deeper into my coat as I kicked my way through the drifts. 'It's about a quarter of a mile,' Kai Rhys had said. 'You can't miss it if you go straight on.'

But surely I'd gone further than a quarter of a mile by now. Had the path branched and I'd been concentrating too hard on not getting my boots sucked off to notice? I stopped walking. The bleak strip of sky visible between the skeletal tree-fingers was darkening alarmingly. Somewhere, with impeccable timing, an owl hooted and I wrinkled my nose. These woods were almost self-consciously atmospheric; I suspected that any minute now a little dormouse would run over my foot and twitch its whiskers cutely at me.

'Lost?' The voice out of nowhere made me leap forward. Was I inheriting something from Nicholas and hearing the trees talk?

'Hello?' I managed.

'What are you doing walking around out here?' The voice was no-nonsense, clipped. 'Have you lost your dog?'

'What? No.' Reassured — after all, if the trees were going to go all animate on me they'd hardly sound like a bossy upper-class twit, would they? — I turned around. 'I'm trying to get to the Old Lodge.'

'I see.' The shadowy figure came closer. He was stocky, dressed in gamekeeper-green, reddish hair poking from his head like flames. Under one arm he carried a shotgun, properly broken and everything, but the way he held it left me in no doubt that he could flip it shut and fire without thinking twice. 'It's down the track there. Between the trees.'

'Okay, thanks.' I waited for him to move off, but he stayed, still half in the shade of the trees.

'You want to be careful, being in these woods, girlie.' The light made his figure look ethereal, his green clothing camouflaging his body so that his ginger hair appeared to float above the leaf mulch. 'Dangerous. Make sure you keep to the footpaths.'

'I'll be fine.' As long as no one shoots me in the back, I wanted to add, but you don't mess with an armed guy with no noticeable sense of humour and a distinct problem with women. 'Thanks.' I added.

'Well. All right then.' He turned away, there were a few moments of crackling footsteps, and then I heard the engine of a Land Rover cough into reluctant life somewhere behind the trees. I hadn't heard it arrive, which meant he'd been standing there watching me for a while before he spoke. Sinister.

A few yards further on, the track suddenly widened out and branched off. I followed the right hand branch and the Old Lodge came into full view. I stopped and stared.

It had clearly been designed by an architect who was a full-on fan of the Transylvanian school of civil engineering. Not one spare brick was undecorated, unfestooned or ungargoyled and if there were as many fireplaces as there were chimneys then this was conflagration central. It was perfect, and I fired off a couple of quick pictures.

I went up to the front door and rapped, using the enormous wrought iron dragon-shaped knocker. After a moment the door swung open with a wheeze and a sucking sound, as though the hallway was pressurised.

'Hey, you found us.' Kai Rhys stood backlit on the threshold. He looked even taller than I remembered and, in his half-illuminated state, slightly spectral. 'What do you think? Told you it was gothic, didn't I?'

'This is gothic plus. Supergothic. Hypergoth.' I followed him into the hall and stared around. 'Oh wow, it's the same indoors.' If this building had been a person it would have been wearing six-inch eyeliner, a Buffy T-shirt and quoting Leonard Cohen lyrics.

'Come through.' Kai ushered me into a double-height, beamed sitting room, which smelled oddly impersonal, of new carpet and fresh paintwork. A fire burned picturesquely in an enormous iron grate and two sofas faced one another in front of it, but apart from those and two towering bookcases crammed with paperbacks, the room was bare of furniture. A number of large crates were dotted around the floor, one had the lid half off and polystyrene packing material hanging out.

'Are those bodies in there?'

'I'm a journalist not a serial killer. Still moving in, hence—' he swept an arm around to indicate the largely empty room. 'So, what do you think?'

'Fantastic. Guy will love it. I've taken a few shots outside for him, but could I take some in here, just for me?' I brandished my digital camera. 'I love that fireplace.'

'Sure. You'll excuse me? I just got back in from Glasgow and I've a story to file.' He didn't wait for my answer but left the room. I heard him call something but didn't hear what. I was too busy taking shots of the warring demons over the mantelpiece and the arched ceiling beams.

When I straightened up eventually, a young, blonde, and very pregnant girl had come into the room and was arranging something on the window ledge. She smiled when she saw me. 'Hey. I think it's a bit much for a house though, don't you? I mean, what's acceptable in your average chateau doesn't go down too well when you try to stuff it into a thousand square feet.' She straightened up with one hand in the small of her back. 'Phoo. Come on babes, shift over. We're nearly done.' Her accent was not Welsh, more lower Midlands.

Outside the window I could see the night had crept up on me. Damn. It would be too dark to do any more outside shots now. Oh well, Guy would have to make do with what I'd done already. After all, how many angles did he need? The place was the architectural equivalent of Marilyn Manson lyrics. 'Well, I'd better let you get on with it. Thanks for letting me see round the place, and say thanks to Kai too, would you?'

'No worries. Where did you leave your car?'

'At the top of the lane, at the pull-in to your track.'

She pulled a face. 'God, it's dark out there now, you can't walk back through the woods. I'll get Kai to give you a lift back to get it.'

'No, it's fine,' I tried to protest but I have to admit my heart wasn't in it. The thought that the fiery-headed bloke with the gun might still be lurking away in the undergrowth kept forcing its way to the front of my mind.

'It's okay. He could do with a break anyhow. And some socialisation exercises. Works too much on his own, that one. Kai!' she called through the doorway, 'Can you fire up the Jeep?'

A distant voice yelled back. 'Give me a couple of minutes.'

The girl grinned. 'See? Told you he'd be keen for a break.' She winced and put a hand to her bump. 'God, next month can't come soon enough.'

I felt obliged to make conversation, although I would rather have waited alone and taken another look at the place, maybe had a poke into cupboards, all the kind of stuff I felt a bit inhibited about doing with her in front of me. 'Do you know if you're having a boy or a girl?'

'One of each. Yeah, I know, twins are going to be hard work, but I didn't really get much of a say in the matter. Anyhow, they can't be much harder out than in, quite frankly.' She rubbed her bump.

'Why do you want the Jeep, Cerys?' Kai appeared at the top of the stairs. In contrast to everywhere else in the place, the staircase was plain wood, the newel post crying out for a series of skulls and demons and he stood out as the most decorative thing about it. 'It's not the babies, is it?'

'A lift to the main road for this lady.' Cerys smiled up at him. 'It's okay, they're staying put for a bit.'

'Good.' He put a lot of feeling into the word and I smirked a bit to myself. Typical bloke, doesn't mind doing the impregnating, but gets all huffy at the thought of his life being disrupted by kids. He came down the stairs towards us and I was taken aback again by the sunset-gold of his eyes. And his height.

'Aw, shut up you fat-faced scour-bum.' The words were severe but the tone was mild. 'Go take . . .'

'Holly,' he supplied.

'. . . Holly back to her car. I'll carry on with the unpacking.' She gave me a final beaming smile and, rubbing her back again, headed off down the hallway towards regions unknown.

'Okay. I know when I'm being sent away.' Kai pulled the battered leather jacket he'd worn in the pub off a peg behind the door and rummaged in a pocket. 'Come on.' He led the way out of the door and I noticed that even the steps leading down were ornamented with little incised gothic-type patterns.

'Whoever designed this place would not have been popular with the builders,' I said, following him round the (equally ornamented) back of the cottage. 'He must have watched their every move, to make sure they didn't try slipping in some plain stonework, for a rest. There's so much ornamentation going on that it can only be hope that's stopping the place falling apart. It must be like living in a brick doily.'

'Apparently it was designed by a warlock,' Kai said conversationally. 'There's some kind of occult meaning to the symbols. Although there's even gargoyles in the bathroom, and anyone who wants to get occult while they're having a piss has gone a step beyond the merely supernaturally-inclined, if you ask me.'

I never thought that a breeze-block 1950s garage would come as a relief to look at, but this one did. 'Hop in.' Kai unlocked the big Jeep and his legs were so long that he could step up into the driver's seat. 'Where to?'

I pointed along the track. 'Out on the road.'

He pulled a face. 'Mind if we go the long way round? There's someone I'm keeping an eye on in the woods. I'd like to check he's not lurking around anywhere too close to the house.'

'He wouldn't be a big ginge dressed like Mellors, without the sex appeal?'

For that I got a sideways look. It gave me the chance to notice that Kai had long, dark eyelashes to match his long, dark hair, and really rather nice cheekbones under some seriously journalistic stubble. 'Yeah,' he said slowly. 'You know him?'

'We've met. But anyone who carries a gun into woodland with a footpath running through it and in rapidly dwindling light is not a guy I want to encounter again, so if we see him, I shall be hiding behind the seat.'

We roiled and bounced out onto the track, heading deeper into the forest, with the headlights slicing the dark into shreds. Kai didn't speak again, except to swear briefly when a fox trotted across our path and made him brake suddenly. In the end I felt obliged to say something. 'Have you got any names yet?'

'Names?'

'For the twins. Your wife was saying it's one of each, and they're due next month? You'll really have your work cut out to get the place ready, won't you?'

'Cerys isn't my wife.'

'Partner then, if you're going to get all trendy about it.'

'She's my daughter.'

My jaw clicked as it fell. He'd got a broad grin on his face, even though he wasn't looking at me. 'But how the hell . . . ?' I turned to stare at him. 'I mean, you're . . .'

'Flattered, actually. I'm thirty-six. Cerys is twenty.' Now he turned to look at me. 'Cerys's mum and I were at school together. I don't know if you've ever been in North Wales on a wet Sunday, but there's not a lot to do, and nothing is open. Particularly the chemists'. When Merion got pregnant, we got married, disaster, of course, at sixteen. But we stayed friends, she moved to Peterborough and married Mike, brought Cerys up there. Cerys is staying with me for a bit while her bastard boyfriend comes to his senses regarding two lots of child support. So.' He lifted his foot and the Jeep slowed to walking speed. 'There you go, that's me.' He still looked amused, but now there was something more intense about his expression. 'What's your story?'

'Boring. Born in York, moved to Malton. Worked in London for a while for a production company, went into location scouting. When Ma and Dad moved to Scotland to be near Auntie Mairi, I moved back.'

'For Nicholas.' The Jeep bucked and a large branch cracked beneath the wheels. For a second I thought we'd been shot at.

'Well, not entirely. But partly.'

'What's his diagnosis?'

It always felt disloyal, discussing my brother with anyone outside the medical profession. 'He's got a few problems, there's nothing definitive. But he's coping, the new medication is great and he's started going out a bit more. I mean, I still have to keep an eye on him, pop round most mornings before I start work, that kind of thing, but . . . yes, he's definitely improving.'

There was a few seconds of quiet as the track evened out before us. Then Kai spoke, his voice very low. 'It must be hard for you.'

'And you must be a bloody good interviewer. There's the road, you can let me out here.'

'We're on the far side of the dale. I'll drive you back.'

'No, it's okay, I'm meeting some people here.' I could see the lights from Vivienne's cottage breaking through the trees. A swathed figure was going towards the front door; I thought it might be Isobel. 'Someone will give me a lift to the car.'

Kai stopped the Jeep and peered out at the darkness. 'Who the hell are you meeting, the three bears?' He tapped his thumb ring against the steering wheel. 'Nobody law abiding hangs out in these woods.'

'And you should know.' I opened the door before he could protest again, misjudged the distance from the ground and landed on my hands and knees in a fine tilt of mud and leaf mulch. It had been such a good exit line up till then.

'You all right?' Twin-beam eyes blazed down at me from the warm, well-lit Jeep.

'Yep, I'm fine, thanks.' I peeled myself off the forest floor and tried to look indifferent, as though falling was how normal-heighted people always got out of cars. 'Thanks for the lift.'

I strode nonchalantly towards the cottage for a couple of yards, then realised that I'd got huge sycamore leaves stuck to both my knees, which were flapping as I walked. I chanced a quick look over my shoulder and, sure enough, Kai was still sitting there, watching me go.

I pulled the leaves off with as much insouciance as I could manage, wiped my muddy hands down my coat and straightened my back. The headlights remained stubbornly stationary. He was going to watch me walk every inch of the way, which, I had to admit, was gentlemanly. Or maybe he had a taste for slapstick humour, I thought, as I bounced gently off the trunk of an invisible birch tree, catching my coat on a branch and ripping it all down one shoulder.

'You sure you're okay?'

I didn't turn to answer, just waved one slimy hand and tried not to break my ankle in any of the ruts. When I heard the door of the Jeep bang open I tried to hurry, but only managed to lurch into a large puddle.

'Here.' A large metal object was pushed into my hand, there was a click and sudden, blessed light. I looked down to see he'd given me a huge flashlight which was currently illuminating my immersed foot. 'Bring it back when you've done with it,' he called. I heard the door slam and this time he started the Jeep, pulled it round in a big circle, and roared away back down the track, obviously reassured that he'd done his civic duty.

God, I felt such a prune.

Vivienne opened the door to me, then stood staring. 'Holly? What happened, were you attacked?'

In the advanced lighting situation of her front doorstep I could see myself better. The flashlight had only illuminated sections of me and carrying it had meant I'd only had one hand at a time free for remedial activities, so I'd not been able to clean myself as well as I'd hoped. Or, it appeared, in the 100-watt brilliance, at all.

'The woods. The woods attacked me,' I said, with dignity, and passed Vivienne to walk into the living room where everyone was already assembled.

They stopped talking and looked shocked. 'Holl?' Megan came over. 'Are you all right?'

One of my knees was slightly grazed and oozing blood through my thick tights, my skirt had leaves all over it, and not in a pleasant-pattern way, my maroon wool jacket was flopping at one shoulder seam and my wellies squelched on one side as I walked.

'If you'd said you didn't have your car you could have got a lift with me.' Megan looked me up and down.

'I got a lift.'

'Or I could have lent you a torch.'

I held up the enormous flashlight. 'Got one.'

'So you were driven here, and you have a torch, and you still managed to get covered in mud?'

I glared at Megan. 'Apparently.'

Vivienne bustled in carrying blankets. 'We'll take these. It can be chilly in the woods at night.'

Isobel peered at her from round her handkerchief. The cats were in evidence again. 'We aren't going to be, you know, naked or anything, are we?'

Vivienne beamed at her. It made her thin mouth pouch out at the sides so that she looked as though she was attempting to swallow a leek. 'We are practising my own branch of the craft, Isobel. There is no need to go sky-clad for that.'

'So there's no kissing the devil's bum or anything like that?'

I looked approvingly at Eve. She clearly had a streak of cynicism in her which was nearly as wide as mine.

'Of course not! We are practising earth-magic, not devil worship!' Vivienne almost dropped the blankets. 'Now, come,

34

follow me. Tread only in my footsteps, for there are things which should not be disturbed abroad in the woods.'

'She's a broad in the woods all right,' I muttered to Megan as everyone filed out, following Vivienne down the garden, through a narrow gate and out into a broad ride which swept through the woodland, heading uphill.

We marched in single file, up the trackway to the brow of the hill, where the trees fell away and left the crown a bare, grassy mound. 'The only wood to suffer from male pattern baldness,' I whispered to Megan, but she shushed me, biting her lip with earnest concentration, eyes firmly fixed on Vivienne's skinny back broaching the darkness ahead of us. At the very top we all stopped and laid the blankets down over the grass-skinned mud and, following Vivienne's lead, sat cross-legged on them beneath the overcast skies. I looked out into the leaden night and wondered if I'd be able to see the lights of the Old Lodge from up here and how I'd recognise them if I could. Maybe, given all that occult carving, they'd strobe.

Vivienne's voice droned out, talking us through relaxation exercises and visualisation skills. It was all similar stuff to some of the things I'd sat through with Nicholas in the early days, when the doctors had tried to manage his problems with behavioural training. Only the November wind, making nippy little sorties through my damp clothes, stopped me from dropping into a light doze, as Vivienne had us all expanding our consciousnesses to encompass the trees, the earth and even the invisible moon. My consciousness remained determinedly human-sized, but I was feeling surprisingly peaceful, concentrating on my breathing, in out in out, my shoulders dropping from what I now realised was an almost permanent tense hunch. My neck relaxed and even my fingers uncurled and I was about as close as I would ever come to feeling one with nature, when Isobel let out a shriek.

'There's someone watching us!'

Instantly all of us were scrambling to our feet. 'Where? Did you see them?' First up, I walked out beyond the circle of blankets, scanning the treeline for movement.

'I felt it! You know, eyes boring into the back of my neck.'
Isobel gave a half-sob. 'They must have been over there, behind
us. Maybe they're hiding in the trees . . .' She was clutching her
knitted coat closely around her body, as though some kind of
assault had been attempted. 'It was a presence,' she whispered.
'You know, evil.' Her eyes were huge with panic.

'I think we ought to go back to the cottage.'

'That's not necessary, Holly. Isobel was probably visual-
ising some past event. She's clearly more sensitive than . . .'
She'd been going to say 'you', but the expression on my face
made her change to '. . . most people.'

I didn't want to scare the group by telling them that I'd
already seen one armed bloke loose in the woods tonight, and
I wouldn't have put it past Kai to be wandering around in the
dark trying to find out what I was doing, meeting people in
the middle of nowhere. 'She's probably just spooked herself.
There's no sign of anyone around now. Even if there had
been, screaming out like that, she'd have scared them off.' I
began to roll up my blanket; the others followed suit. 'But
anyway, better safe than sorry, don't you think?'

'I suppose so. But, what a shame, we were so close to opening a gateway.'

I rolled my eyes and led the way off Comb-over Hill.

Megan dropped me back at my car and I drove home,
Kai's flashlight bouncing around on the back seat. I knew I'd
have to return it, no one was ever going to call me a flashlight
thief, but I was in absolutely no hurry to go anywhere near
him again. Rather gorgeous-looking though he might be, I
thought, but only to myself. I would die rather than admit
to finding a man attractive, after all that Girl Power I'd been
talking. Wouldn't have kicked him out of bed, mind you, but
fancy him? Nah. And anyway, he might be attached. Besides,
I could always FedEx the flashlight over, when I sent all the
paperwork for him to sign to exempt Guy from any responsibility from the premature labour Cerys was going to go into
when she saw the lorries arrive.

CHAPTER SIX

I never told you this, did I? Or maybe I did, one of my earlier 'letters' might have it in but, to be honest, I can't be arsed to go back through and look. Anyway. Yeah. Point is — women like me. And I like them back, but that's as far as it goes, liking. Intellectually I know there's this one step further that I'd need to take to make it anything real, one more level of engagement, one last barrier dropped, and that's where it all gets complicated. Messy. And I can't quite do it, can't quite let them in that last inch. And, you know what? None of them even fucking notice. They think they've got me because there I am, in their beds night after night, drinking their wine and sitting on their couches discussing the state of the economy, and they think that's me. They really don't understand that it might as well be a robot lounging around their carefully interior-designed rooms, some kind of gigolo in their beds, because it's not who I am. Not inside. Because really I'm . . .

Stupid. Yeah, just stupid, whistling in the dark . . . Did I say whistling? More like pissing, pouring it all out into nothingness to help me feel better for a while. Anyway, fact is, I keep mobile where the girls are concerned. Give them a look, give them a taste of the 'me' they all think I am. The me they think they're getting to know. And then, when they're in deep and falling hard — that's it, I'm out, not what I signed up for. And I don't go clean, you know that. No 'it's not you, it's me' for this guy, oh no. When I go I leave a bad taste that will keep them from trusting for a long time.

There's not been anyone since Imogen. Think I wrote to you about her too, didn't I? When it all went shit-shaped and hit the fan like a hurricane in a slurry tank, when she found out what lies underneath the jacket and jewellery image. Yes, the real me turned up to the party eventually . . . Yeah. Not proud of it. Another one of those things about myself that I'm not proud of, along with my upbringing and my mistakes.

And yeah, so. Reason I'm writing this? I've seen the look on another girl. Sizing me up, checking it out, the leather, the earring. Measuring me up with her eyes to see if I come up to whatever expectations it is that she has for a man, raising one eyebrow at me like she's asking some question I'm supposed to have heard in some hormone-to-hormone communication that's gone on underneath all the polite chat. She's hot. That dark red hair that looks like the sun shining through a copper beech at evening, fine, pale skin. And single too, I've checked her out with her brother — in a purely conversational way, I mean, hey, I've got finesse, I've got class. Although . . . their relationship, it's not right. She's more like . . . I was going to say 'like his mother' but I'm no expert on that one now, am I? But Nicholas — nice guy, all kinds of shit kicking off in his head and some kind of issue with his sister — he reckons she prefers being single. Doesn't fall in love, doesn't get attached.

My kind of woman.

CHAPTER SEVEN

Next day I had to go to Scotland. There was a shoot under-way on the North East coast, a location I'd booked sometime earlier in the year, but a problem had arisen with the owners of the site, and Aiden the director wanted me to 'interface'.

Nicholas came along to keep me company, and after I'd interfaced — which was mostly a diplomatic exercise — I dropped him and his carrier-bag of belongings off at Ma and Dad's. Sometimes a change was good for Nicky, and I'd been a bit worried about his new-found desire for a girlfriend. If I wasn't careful and quick, and if things didn't go the way he'd got planned in his head, he might spiral into full-blown psychosis. Again. Still, the new medication — which I had triple-checked was in his bag, maybe paranoia does run in the family — was doing great things at present, and I left him waving cheerfully from their driveway, looking relaxed and happy to be there.

Then I detoured back to the shoot. Something about the intensity of Nicholas, hot on the heels of Vivienne and her home-made religion, made me want to tear all my clothes off and enter into some screaming, uncomplicated orgias-tic activity. Aiden and I had met when I'd been working in

London, we'd dated a few times but we'd both agreed that 'a relationship' wasn't what we wanted, not what we were about. Fuck-buddies, however, was a different matter, and his pleasurable version of the full-body workout was exactly what I needed right now. We spent two days 'interfacing', and I got back to Malton mid-afternoon, to an empty fridge. Because I'd known I was going to Scotland I hadn't been shopping, but now, when the post-sex hunger had only been sated by a Service Station bacon butty and a packet of Wotsits, it had become an urgent requirement.

I drove into town, shopped, and was on my way back to the car with a full trolley when I met Cerys. She was sitting perched on a bollard in the supermarket car park, looking rotund and very fed up, but her eyes brightened when she saw me.

'Holly, isn't it? Hey.'

I stopped, even though this meant that the trolley swung a complete arc around me and nearly mowed me down. 'Hello.' I didn't mean to but I couldn't help myself, and looked around. 'Kai not with you?'

'He's somewhere. I had to get some fresh air, hence . . .'

'Well, tell him Guy loves the look of the Old Lodge. He wants some more external shots, so I'll come over some time soon. No hurry, and Kai doesn't need to be there, I can just walk around and fire off some pics by myself. As long as he knows I'm going to do it and doesn't think I'm sneaking around trying to catch sight of him getting out of the bath or something!'

'Well, it's a thought.'

The voice came over my shoulder. I widened my eyes at Cerys. 'He's behind me, isn't he?'

'Yep.'

'And he heard me say that bit about catching him getting out of the bath?'

'Yep.' She was trying not to giggle.

'Ah.' I turned around slowly. Kai was leaning against a wall looking exotic in another leather jacket, and faded-to-grey jeans. The fact he was wearing dark glasses just added to the image. 'Then you did hear me say that I *didn't* want you to think that.'

'Never crossed my mind.'

'Good.'

A conversational impasse resulted. I stared at my shopping trolley, wishing it wasn't quite so full of single-woman crap. A packet of biscuits wobbled atop multi-pack crisps and the only really nutritious food, a pack of frozen steak and some fruit, was right at the bottom. I didn't really care what Kai thought of me, but some tiny little niggle of pride didn't want him to see me as an 'insta-food for one' girl.

'Why don't you come over for a meal?' Cerys must have caught a look at the Birds Eye specials crammed in the far side. 'I am so bored with my own company that I could make conversation with Fred and Rosemary West if they dropped by. Please, Holly.'

'Bring Nicholas,' Kai added. 'I need to do a follow-up on that drugs article anyhow. Need a bit more input from him.'

'Nicholas's in Scotland at the moment. Staying with Ma and Dad. He'll be back in a fortnight, so we could come then.'

Cerys groaned. 'I might have exploded by then. Come tomorrow, please. Look, I need distracting from my predicament, don't I, Kai? You'd be doing me a kindness.'

Kai pushed off from the wall. It was like someone erecting a skyscraper right next to me. 'Go on, Holly. You could return my flashlight at the same time.'

'And do your photographs.'

'It'll be dark.'

'I'll describe the place to you, then.' Cerys said, in a 'standing no nonsense' tone that boded well for her future as a mother of twins.

I finally gave in and agreed. Otherwise I was afraid they'd keep me talking until my syrup-topped cones melted. They let me go and I drove home, to find Megan camped out on my doorstep.

41

'Good, you're back.'

'Good, you're here. You can help me unpack the shopping.' I unlocked the front door and she went inside, carrying a loaf of bread while I struggled behind with four carrier bags with stretching handles. 'Don't strain yourself.'

'Vivienne says it's time to start doing proper magic.' Megan could barely contain herself. 'She says we can start our wishing spell.'

'How long have you been possessed by the ghost of Enid Blyton?' I pushed past her and started filling the freezer.

'We had a meeting while you were in Scotland.' She peered inside my freezer. 'Did you see Aiden, by the way?'

'Might have.'

'I think I might get one of these.' She wiggled the hinge experimentally. 'Your doors have never blown off, have they?'

'I've never kept a Big Mac for seven weeks. Why are you bringing up Aiden, all of a sudden?' Megan knew about Aiden, of course; keeping the fact that I'd had sex from her was like hiding Smarties from a dog.

'I think he's delish.' She took one of the apples I'd rolled into the fruit bowl. 'If you don't want him, I'll have him.'

'I do "want him", but not like that. He's happy with the whole "no strings" thing, I'm happy with it, end of. Why does that make everyone — by which I mean you, Meg — so uneasy?'

'It's not very romantic though, Holl, is it? Having a sex-only relationship?' She bit the apple. 'Don't you sometimes think it's a bit shallow?'

'Nope. Well, yes, but it is kind of the point. Shallow is good. Kama Sutra sex, no ties and *definitely* no meeting-the-family, how-shall-we-spend-Christmas talks. Fan-bloody-tastic, my dear. I recommend it.'

Megan shrugged. 'You say. So, are you on for Wednesday? Vivienne's at seven. Oh . . .' she looked a little embarrassed, and, as she'd been discussing my shag-pal without so much as a pink cheek, it must be bad. 'She's given us a list of things.'

'Things?'

'For the spell. Hold on.' Megan raked about in the pocket of her robustly tight jeans. She did look fantastically curvy in them, I had to admit. 'Here.'

I read the typed list twice. 'But this is . . . I mean, it's some kind of joke, isn't it? A horrible, sick joke?'

Megan put her head down and mumbled and her cheeks darkened.

'The nail from a demon? Frog's head? A rich man's hidden treasure? Oh come on, Meg, these are nasty. She can't be serious, she's having you on.' I scanned the list again. 'Where's she getting this "spell" from? The Boys' Own Book of Black Magic? The Beginners' Grimoire?'

'She said it's in a library book.'

'Seriously? Only if she's a ticket holder to the Library of the Damned, and she'd better not spill anything on the pages because she *really* wouldn't want to upset the librarian . . .'

'It's all stuff we need for the spell.' Megan sounded defiant, although she'd still got her hair over her face. 'Vivienne says the things have to be hard to come by or everyone would be doing it.' Now her head came up and her brown eyes flashed me a look. 'Don't you want us to have our wishes come true? I mean, you haven't even really got a wish, have you? "Some excitement", that was the best you could come up with, and do you know something, Holl? To me, your life already looks pretty exciting. You've got your own house, fantastic job with all that travelling, a family that loves you, and you've even got fucking *Aiden*, no strings attached. What have I got — a detonated fridge in a rented flat, no boyfriend, and a twenty per cent discount on curtains!'

Wow. I'd never heard her so militant. It was like being bitten by Bagpuss. Maybe there was something about Vivienne's group that was doing her good. 'Yeah. Sorry. Of course I'll come along. How many of these things do I have to get?'

'As many as you can. We all need to bring lots of stuff and duplicates are good, apparently. Anyhow. D'you fancy going out tomorrow night? If we're doing the spell on Wednesday, tomorrow might be my last night as a single girl! We could pop into York, there's a band playing at Fibbers . . .'

'Can't, sorry.' And because I still felt a bit indignant that my best friend thought my life, which she *knew* contained more shit than a laxative testing unit, was already so great, I added, 'I'm going over to Kai's for dinner.'

'*Who*? Male or female?'

'He's a journalist, lives in Barndale Woods in the most fantastic cottage.'

'Sexy?'

When I thought about Kai, all that came to mind were those golden eyes. 'He's not bad.' And then, taking pity on her, 'For an about-to-be grandfather.'

Megan grinned. 'You had me really jealous there for a second, bitch.'

And then the full-body image thundered in, and I could see those dark stubbled cheekbones, long thighs in washed-white jeans, and the way his shoulders filled out that black leather.

'Holl? You've gone pink.'

I shook my head and the image was gone. 'I think, actually, it might be quite fun to have the spell to think about,' I said. 'Phew. Yes.'

* * *

The ground was a bit drier today, so I'd inched the car down the track to the Old Lodge this time. I didn't want a repeat of the falling-in-the-mud thing and I most definitely didn't want a rerun of the meeting with the ginger guy. I glanced around, eyes keen for the dull gleam of the rising moonlight on a gun barrel, but the woods were quiet tonight, apart from the rustle of small, terrified wildlife and the imperious hoot of an owl. My headlights raked the darkness until they found the answering lights of the Lodge and I parked as closely as I could to the front door.

44

'Oh good, you came.' Cerys opened the door to me. 'And you brought wine! Fantastic.' She lowered her voice. 'He won't let me drink even a drop. Says it's bad for the babes, even though I've told him, at eight months all they're going to get is a bit relaxed. Especially as I think I'm really doing well if I drink half a glass. God, I really can't wait to have them out of there, so there's room for other things, like food and breathing. And I can relax in a chair without feeling like I'm sitting on my own lap.'

She shuffled back and let me into the hall. 'We've got the dining room straight, thankfully; I *hated* eating in the kitchen. Well, I say *we*, Kai is about as much use to me right now as a condom would be. Spends half his days on the phone, the other half on his laptop, and absolutely no percentage sorting out this place.'

I followed her into previously unseen regions, still talking. 'Anyway, only another week or so and I can go back to Peterborough. Mum and Dad will have got my flat sorted by then — my ex doesn't want to leave, but he doesn't want to pay either, so Dad's getting some of his friends to go round and then Mum's going to give the place a once-over. *Apparently*,' she raised her voice slightly when we heard footsteps on the stairs, 'I'm in no fit state to be cleaning and moving furniture and suchlike.'

'Come on now, you're as fit as a butcher's dog,' said Kai, arriving behind us in the enormous kitchen. 'Your mother was always a soft touch.'

I turned around and nearly didn't recognise him. His hair was neatly tied back and he'd had a shave, which made his cheekbones stand out more. He'd got out of the washed-out denims in favour of black trousers and a black shirt, which made him look taller, and oddly, more imposing.

'Yeah, she married *you*.' Cerys carried on leading the way, until we stopped in a room where the walls were red as blood. 'Make yourself comfortable, Holly, I'll just stand here and envy you. Kai, you can fetch the food through.' She waved me over to a leather couch in one corner. It, too, was oxblood red. The vast mahogany dining table was about the only thing that didn't look like it had been poured directly from an artery; even the carpet was red.

'It's very red,' I said, perching atop the leather.

'Oh, it was like this when we moved in. I will take bets the warlock that built the place never had a girlfriend, just an unhealthy obsession with Lord of the Rings. I mean, the little study is practically a scale model of a hobbit hole. The sofa is Kai's; I didn't want to put it in here, because it's virtually invisible, but it's the only place it fits. Still, he'll probably paint the whole place magnolia eventually.' She leaned against the sofa back and rolled her hips. 'I adore him, really I do. I mean he helped Mum out with money and everything, he's never not visited even when he's been on sort of undercover work, he even gets on with Dad. He just doesn't have much of a clue where fashion, style and normal human operating systems are concerned. Sorry, now I'm embarrassing you. Shall I open the wine?'

'Please.' I thought she was being a bit hard on Kai. He didn't strike me as being all that unsociable. Just a bit withdrawn, maybe. A little bit . . . sad.

Kai carried through a huge dish of chilli which we ate with baked potatoes. At least, Kai and I ate; Cerys nibbled a few mouthfuls then had to stand up and walk around the room to get that to go down. After that, whilst we ate plum crumble, she stood at the window and looked out into the darkness.

'No, it's no good. I'm going to have to go and lie down.' She looked towards the floor. 'My legs have started to swell. At least, I assume they have, I haven't seen them since June. God, where does all the skin come from?'

Kai jumped up, but she glared at him. 'Kai. We have a guest. Now, I realise that you are somewhere to the sociability left of "The Curious Incident of the Dog in the Night-time", but, please, for me, try and make polite conversation. We didn't invite Holly over so she could sit on her own in here while you hover around on the landing in case my waters go while I'm getting into bed. Now, play nicely you two.'

She went out and, I noticed, closed the dining room door behind her. Kai looked at me, properly, for the first time. 'I'm not that bad,' he said. 'More wine?'

'She probably worries about you.' I pushed my glass over. 'I worry about my dad, although I've no idea why; he's a fifty-five-year-old English teacher not a cliff-diver.'

'You've cause to worry about Nicholas though.' He held up his wine glass and stared through the amber liquid at the light. The wine and his eyes were exactly the same colour, I noticed.

'Sometimes.' I spun the word so that it would be clear it was my final comment on the subject, and he noted it with an inclination of the head, which brought a silence during which we both emptied our glasses.

'I'd better be off,' I said. 'Say thanks to Cerys for me, dinner was lovely.'

'Not hurrying away on my account?' He came around to my side of the table to set the corkscrew to another bottle. 'She's right, it is good to have company. I'm sorry I'm not better at it.' The cork slid out with a *plump* sound. 'Come on, have another drink. I promise I'll try to think of something to say.'

'All right.' I was in no real hurry to get home and, close up, this man was *gorgeous*. Nicholas had been right, although I'd die rather than admit it; Kai was just my type. He had an air of being very much cleverer than he ever let on, coupled with an exact awareness of himself, that was hugely sexy. There was a kind of careful casualness in the way he sat beside me and passed me the refilled wine glass, brushing my wrist with the tip of a finger as he did so, that told me he'd probably reciprocate if I wound my arms around his neck and kissed that fabulously inviting mouth. With half an eye on his reaction I licked my lips and shook my hair back. 'Have you thought yet?'

'Mmmm?' Result. His eyes travelled from my face, via my chest, to my thighs. 'What about?' And now his voice had gained that telltale raspy note that meant he was picturing me naked. Oh, this was going to be almost too easy . . .

'I don't know. Why don't you tell me what you're thinking about?' I leaned in a little closer, until I could smell the slight earthiness of his skin and feel the gentle heat of his breath against my cheek. Hardly a challenge at all, in fact. I'd have thought that *he'd* be the one to make the running, the first approach . . .

'I'm actually wondering what that piece of paper is that you seem to have dropped under your chair.' Kai jerked his head at the floor and his golden eyes held a knowing amusement. 'If it's important, you don't want to leave it here when you go home tonight.'

Oh, well played, sir! I almost broke into a round of applause at his sudden wresting of the power back from my slightly unsubtle come-on and into his own hands again. *And* he'd managed to work in a 'don't take it for granted that I fancy you' reference — I was clearly in the presence of a master player of the game, possibly someone even more practised than me. I gave a grin to show that I understood the checkmate situation, and bent down to pick up the much-folded wodge. 'It's not important, actually. Well, it sort of is, but . . . it's like . . . it's a spell. No, it's the ingredients of a spell.'

'Really? Can I see?' As he stretched his hand towards me I saw for the first time that he had long, slender fingers and the thumb ring was more of an ornament than an affectation. 'God, someone's got a sense of humour.'

The earlier pheromone-laden moment was gone, wiped out by his obvious interest in the words on the page and I found myself telling him about Vivienne, about the gathering in the woods, the earnestness of the group. He laid the paper down on the table and looked at me over the top of his wine glass, serious-faced now. His eyes had lost the challenging spark and there was something about the way he listened, something calm but almost empty, as though I had to keep giving him words to fill up the quiet space between us.

'And you all believe in this?'

'I don't. I think Eve is sceptical, but she's going along with it, I dunno why. Isobel and Megan are deep in.'

He bit his lip. 'This Vivienne, what is she? Fraud, delusional, a real follower of Wicca? Because mucking about with these things, with this kind of psychological mojo, without understanding what you're doing is asking for some serious shit to come down on your head.'

'And you'd know. As a journalist.'

'I know a lot of stuff.' A slightly loaded sentence and for a second he looked different, as though I was looking through a crack, into someone else. 'But I believe less than a fraction of it.' A twitch of an eyebrow. I couldn't tell if he was being deliberately cool or whether he was warning me off, and I felt oddly unbalanced. Tried to regroup myself by sipping slowly at my wine and focussing my attention on the glass for a moment. 'And I like you. I wouldn't want demonic forces dragging you down to hell when I've only just met you. Tell me, do you believe in anything, Holly?'

Did I? What was there to believe in? 'Why?'

'Just interested.'

'Well, of course I do. Death and taxes.' The room spun slightly. At least he'd said he liked me, so maybe his back-pedalling on the seduction scene was reversible? 'What made you go into journalism?' The change of topic just fell into my mind as though it had been posted through the gap in the conversation.

He gave me a slow stare from eyes that shone with a chilly light. 'I'm a nosy bastard,' he said and raised his glass to me. While he drank, he never took his eyes off my face but there was no sexual invitation in them now. The man sitting beside me was something other than the leather-clad game player and his look was colder, darker. Full of depths and shadows. 'Why do you ask?'

'Well, I figure, if you got married at sixteen you probably didn't go on to A-levels or University, because you'd have a wife and Cerys to support. Which means you didn't fall into it after an English degree because you couldn't think of anything else to do with it, like so many people do, so it has to have been a conscious career choice. And that means some serious thinking, because you'd have had to have gone back to studying, as an adult. You're — thirty-six, wasn't it? — and you're working high-profile stuff, so you've been in the profession a while.'

'Have you been spending your spare time thinking about my life choices?' The tone was light, frivolous, but his eyes said different, the shadows were rising now, coming closer to the surface. He didn't like this.

'Just interested.' Now it was my turn to raise a glass to him.

'What do you want, my life story?' Bitter now, I'd definitely touched a nerve and there was no hint of flirtation in his voice any more. I was oddly glad that this wasn't going to degenerate into a quick sofa-fumble because, despite myself, I was intrigued by this mercurial man. 'It's not important, none of it is.' He flicked my list. 'Now, do you want suggestions on some of this stuff?'

'You know how I can come by these things?'

'Got a few ideas. Lateral thinking, see. I do crosswords too.' Kai leaned forward over the table, arms propping his weight. 'See this one? Nail from a demon? Come with me.'

He headed towards the door and I couldn't help but follow. It was that or stay alone in a room that looked like it had been decorated in shades of O positive.

We tiptoed up the stairs, on the off chance that the overloaded Cerys might have fallen asleep. When we reached the landing, he turned right and led me along a dark passageway, panelled in heavy wood. 'This is the older part of the house.'

'What, you mean Bronze Age?'

Kai laughed. 'Despite appearances, the place was built in the seventies. Or, should I say, rebuilt. Apparently, there was something even more gothic on the site originally, but that fell into disrepair.'

'Fell into Hell, more like,' I muttered. Some of the panelling was so deeply carved that it was a wonder it was still in one piece. It looked like wooden lace.

'Here.' He opened a door. I walked in behind him, then stopped dead.

'It's your bedroom.'

'Yeah, so? Oh, come on, if I was going to seduce you, I'd hardly be discussing architectural niceties would I?'

'I don't know. What does your seduction technique normally consist of?'

It was too dark to see his face, but his voice was as unnaturally smooth as a starlet's forehead as he said, 'Pretty much the same as yours, I'd say, Holly.' He turned on a lamp. 'This is what I wanted to show you, over here.' His voice was back to its normal tone now, I was glad to hear.

The room was almost as big as the kitchen. A double bed carved out of dark oak took up a large proportion of floor space, an equally ugly carved wardrobe squatted in one corner, and most of one wall was full-length windows, outside which I could see a wrought-iron balcony. Kai was pointing at the wardrobe. 'The furniture came with the place. I've spent every night I've slept in here staring at it. Look.' He ran a finger over the wardrobe door.

'It's absolutely horrible.'

'Yep. But look, here . . .' He bent closer and I bent in too, until our heads were almost touching and I could smell his smoky, heavy aftershave. 'See? Demons.'

'Gothic *furniture*? That was one serious obsession.' We had lowered our voices as our bodies had got closer, and now we were almost whispering.

'And what's holding the panel to the wardrobe?' He turned his head and his hair brushed my cheek but his voice was pure practicality and I didn't even feel the tiniest flare of any kind of attraction now.

'It's . . . it's *nailed on*.' I started to laugh, straightening away, from the demons, from him. 'The nail from a demon! You're bloody brilliant.'

'Oh yes.' The grin was wicked. 'All we have to do is pull one out, and you're good to go.' There was a drawer at the base of the wardrobe. He dragged it open with a shriek of tortured oak and drew out a pair of long-nose pliers. 'Right.'

'You have pliers in your bedroom.'

Again the wicked grin. 'And that isn't even my secret drawer. Oh, come on, we've just moved in, there's stuff all over the place. Now, you hold the door and I'll — there, that's got one.' He grabbed my hand, unfolded it, and closed it again around the stubby little tack. 'I'm enjoying this. What's next?'

'Frog's head. Oh, but that's not so hard, there's loads of dead frogs out on the track. I'll pick one up on the way home.'

We left his bedroom and crept back downstairs, where we shared another triumphant glass of wine each, and Kai looked at the list again. 'Rich man's hidden treasure? Wow, don't envy you that one.'

I looked at him. There was a prickle in the air between us, like a static charge. It wasn't lust, that particular firework was well extinguished, even though I had the feeling that the blue touchpaper was quietly burning in another universe, but something else. Something with a depth to it that made me almost feel shy. 'Kai, would you say you were well off?'

He stopped, half way through refilling his glass. 'I'm not rolling in it like some people. But then I'm not grubbing down the back of the sofa for fifty pence either. This place is bought and paid for, my bank balance is in the black so . . . yeah, guess I'm okay. Comfortable, anyway. Why?'

'Have you got a picture of Cerys anywhere? Doesn't have to be recent or anything.'

'Yep, there's one in my wallet . . . no, Holly, you're not thinking . . .'

'Come on, admit it, she's the most precious thing you've got, isn't she?' Triumphant, I swigged my wine. 'Your treasure.

And fairly well hidden, since she doesn't even call you Dad. Rich man's hidden treasure. QED. I thank you.' And I sat down, rather more heavily than I'd intended. Damn, but that wine he kept giving me was good stuff; I was amazed I could still think, let alone tangentially.

Now Kai's eyes were positively glowing. 'That, may I say, is bloody cool thinking. I knew I was right about you.' He reached into a drawer and pulled out a sheaf of photos, spread them on the table between us and started riffling through. I couldn't help but notice . . . oh, all right, I could, but I didn't try, in fact I stared blatantly . . . there were quite a few of Kai himself, with a very pretty dark-haired woman. Who looked fantastic in a bikini. He picked out one of Cerys, pre-pregnancy, sitting on a gate looking cute, and handed it to me. 'Is there anything else?'

I looked at the list. 'Only a couple. Eye from an owl. That's disgusting.'

'No, no, I can do this one. Wait here.' He shoved what was left of the wine, and his glass, into my hand and dashed out of the door, returning a minute later with a tatty cardboard box.

'Please tell me you didn't go out and murder an owl.'

'Take a look.' While he held the box I cautiously tore off the tape which sealed it. Inside was the scruffiest, most motheaten stuffed owl I'd ever seen. 'It was here when I moved in, but it gave Cerys the creeps so I shoved it in the garage.' A moment's probing and he dropped something into my hand. 'There.'

'It's glass.'

'It's an owl's eye by someone's interpretation. Shit, this is great. Anything else?'

'Last one. The words of a king.'

There was a moment, a perfect moment, when we stood there in the hallway, thinking the same thing. Then he dropped the box, I pushed the wine and glasses onto the staircase and we both ran for the living room, jostling each other as we raced to be first through the door and over to the bookcase.

'Yes!' Kai won and snatched a dog-eared copy of The Tommyknockers from the shelf. I was halfway to The Shining, but let go when he ripped three pages out of his book and waved them in the air. 'That's it! What do we win?'

'Our wishes, I think.'

'Jesus.' He calmed down instantly. 'So, you all make a wish, do the spell and then what?'

'It comes true, according to Vivienne.'

He whistled softly and went back to finish pouring the wine into both glasses. 'Right. So a bunch of possibly psychologically-uneven women get loose in the wood and try to perform magic . . . Wow, I am going to look for something to work on in the Orkneys while that's going on. Sounds as though it has the possibility to become the oestrogen-fuelled bitch fight to end all bitch fights. Whereabouts did you say you were, again?'

'The bare hilltop on the other side of the dale. Creepy place, Isobel said she could feel someone watching when we were there last time.'

'I bet she did.' He emptied his glass. 'Look, Holly. This place, Barndale — even if most of you wouldn't know Wicca from a wardrobe, it's still not a good place to be wandering around.'

I whistled the theme tune to the X-Files. 'Yeah. There's armed gamekeepers and loony journalists for a start.'

'No, seriously.' A hand curved onto my shoulder. 'Just be careful.'

There was a sudden darkness to the mood, his image switch was complete. 'Okay, I will.'

'Right.' He flashed his wrist in front of his eyes. 'God, look, it's nearly one. Sorry, but I'm going to have to kick you out. Got an early start tomorrow.'

'Oh, yes, course. Well, me too.'

'I'll call you a taxi. Give me your keys and I'll drop your car off for you tomorrow morning on my way to the station.'

Damn, I'd forgotten about my car. Or had I? Had I secretly been hoping that being over the limit would get me invited to stay the night in that balconied room with the toad-like furniture and this amber-eyed man? Had his previous flirtatiousness really just been a knee-jerk reaction to a female presence then? It had felt like more . . . I glanced up at him and raised an eyebrow. 'Taxi?'

'I think so, yes.' The hand on my shoulder turned me firmly towards the door. 'They can normally be with us in five minutes. You wait there and I'll ring.'

That was possibly the subtlest turning down of my charms I'd ever encountered.

CHAPTER EIGHT

It would have been so easy. She was giving off all the right signals, the cute little head-toss, bit of lower-lip action between the teeth, all carefully choreographed, of course, and I had to admit that she does it well. Almost unstudied, a kind of knowing innocence about her, like she doesn't know how she's doing it but she's going to keep doing it until I go for it. But. And, oh yeah, there's a big but here, something else kicked in. We were playing the whole 'eye contact' game and it was going so, so well, point to her, point to me, it only needed one of us to take advantage and . . . And then she looked right into me. Can't describe it. It wasn't like she changed, conversation kept right along the lines it had been but . . . yeah, there's that word again. But. She asked me about my past. About what made me go into this mental whoring that I like to call 'journalism' as if that gives it any respectability, about what I am. A simple little question, nothing that anyone else couldn't have asked anywhere along the line. Any of them. Any of those thoughtless, careless women who wanted me enough to let their eyes skim the surface without their brains even trying to get underneath. For all their smart ways, their great jobs, their intellectualism, not one of them ever asked me why I did it. They were all content to let the image rule. Like they didn't want to know anything else, like they wanted me to be the man they thought I was, with nothing going on to break that image. Like they didn't want me to be real, somehow. No shitty background, no identity crises, nothing nasty to ruin the view of me that they had, as some kind of black knight, in his designer jacket and jeans, riding in over the horizon to sweep them from their lives of boring mediocrity.

It hit me hard. Oh, I covered myself, the good old bait-and-switch. Distracted her attention and got it all back to where I could deal with it, put myself back in the driving seat and never let her know that she'd done something that no one has ever attempted before — got through my armour like a tungsten carbide round. And there I was, like one of those poor bastards on the war fields, too shocked to feel pain, with all my protection rendered useless.

And she never even knew what she'd done.

CHAPTER NINE

Vivienne had pushed all the furniture up against the walls of her living room and we stood awkwardly in the bare centre, like early arrivals at a school disco. A ginger tomcat stropped against my legs and Isobel had hardly taken her face out of her handkerchief since she'd arrived. Megan looked perky, bouncing from foot to foot, a supermarket bag swinging from her wrist, containing what looked like a human head. Eve had brought a stick, on which she leaned heavily.

'Sciatica playing up this week,' she explained. 'It's the weather, must be changing.'

'Well, we're not going anywhere yet.' Vivienne motioned us to one side and we huddled in the kitchen doorway as she rolled back the dusty carpet to reveal bare floorboards on which someone had chalked an amateurish circle. 'First we must prepare our ingredients.'

She made us put our bags in the centre of the circle and then fussed around drawing symbols beside them.

'So, how was dinner with Kai last night?' Megan asked. 'I rang you around elevenish but you weren't back.'

'It was good, yes.' I didn't know what else to say. Kai and I had parted company chastely enough, with a shaken hand

and a kissed cheek, and even now I could feel the weight of his hand on my shoulder, turning me away from him. There had been a strange weakness in the gesture, as though he knew he had to do it, but hadn't really wanted to. Or maybe that was wishful thinking on my part. Or not. I still didn't even know what it was he had going on, but I wouldn't have turned down a quick bounce on that limber-looking body.

'Please.' Vivienne's voice was stern. 'We must keep our minds on the matter in hand. Now. What did you all bring?'

I confessed to the contents of my bag. There was a moment of hushed admiration. 'What, you got *everything*?' Isobel stared at me. 'The thing about the demon as well?'

'Yep.'

'I got an owl's eye from roadkill,' Eve confessed. 'Cut a picture of a frog's head and the nail from a demon out of some old Reader's Digests, and I printed out Edward the Eighth's abdication speech from Wikipedia. Couldn't think what to do about the hidden treasure thing.'

It turned out that Megan and Vivienne had also googled Edward the Eighth. Isobel had cut some pages from a Bible and was rotating with paranoia in case this affected the spell. 'I mean, *some* people believe Jesus was King of the Jews, don't they? But it won't be, sort of, counterproductive, will it? We're not *evil*, after all, are we?' Vivienne had found an article on Tutankhamun's tomb, and seemed a little bit put out that any of us had an alternative approach to the rich man and his hidden treasure.

'I got pictures of owls as well,' Megan pointed to her bag, 'And I found a dead frog in the pond in the park, but I couldn't bring myself to cut off the head, so it's all in there. No treasure though, or demon's nails.'

Vivienne rolled her eyes. 'So only Holly found all the ingredients?' I tried to look unassuming. '*Hmm*. The spell will work best for her,' Vivienne sounded disappointed that it had been me. I think she would rather have Isobel or Megan strike gold; these two appeared to be her most devoted disciples. 'As a matter of interest, Holly, where did you collect your things?'

'Most of it came from a friend of mine who lives on the other side of the woods,' I said, trying not to sound smug or as though I was implying that the others had no friends. 'In the Old Lodge.'

She hissed in a breath and the ginger cat shot from between my legs into the kitchen. Isobel lowered the handkerchief. 'The warlock's place?'

'Well, he wears a lot of black, but he's a journalist, really.'

But Vivienne had started to smile. At least, I think that's what she was doing — her mouth went an alarming shape and previously unnoticed wrinkles began to manifest alongside her eyes. 'Oh, Holly.' She sounded almost orgasmic. 'Now I know the spell will work for sure.'

'What did you do?' Megan whispered to me.

'I don't know,' I whispered back. 'But whatever it was, it must have been good.' Vivienne was now groaning ecstatically, cradling my small bag to her chest.

'Just think, these are the real thing! Oh, girls, we are going to have such results tonight!'

'Looks like she's getting results already. If her knickers start smoking, get ready to run.' Only Eve smiled at that.

A bit more chanting, a few more esoteric shapes drawn in coloured chalk — which non-esoterically came from a primary-coloured bucket with kindergarten pictures on — and we were ready to hit the hill. Vivienne was carrying a Primus stove and a large saucepan; I had high hopes of mulled wine when we got there. The rest of us carried our bags and Megan also carried Vivienne's hessian tote bag containing her offerings. Apart from King Tut, Vivienne had, apparently, a real owl's eye (I didn't dare ask if it had been parted from its owner pre- or post-mortem). Her 'demon's nail' turned out to be one of her ex's toenail clippings — yeah, she looked like the kind of woman who'd hang on to that sort of stuff. She hadn't struck lucky in the frog department though; maybe she'd been too busy trying to kiss them, and had driven them all away . . .

So, carrying the results of the world's oddest treasure hunt, we plodded up the sticky track to the open-topped hill. I carried Eve's bag, to give her a bit of a start; she struggled quite badly with the incline, even with the stick. 'You all right?' I walked alongside her, giving Vivienne a chance to go on with the Suck-Up Twins. 'It's a bit of an odd choice for a hobby this, isn't it?'

Eve smiled at me, as we paused for a moment for her to get her breath back. 'It beats watching reality TV,' she puffed. 'Or getting cats.' She inclined her head towards the toiling shape of Vivienne, today draped in wafty, floating tie-dye and looking like a woman who's fallen into a vat of handkerchiefs.

'Do you think she's mad?'

Eve considered. 'I think she's very sad. But, mad? Well, as long as no one is getting hurt. And, although it's not exactly a reading group, we've all met new people and we're getting out and doing new things, so does it matter?'

'I guess not.' I could even manage to muster warm thoughts about Isobel now. She was shy and allergic to everything and I really wanted to introduce her to a skin care regime, but she was cutely naïve and fun to be with in the same way as a puppy. I didn't know if I'd ever come around to Vivienne, but the woman had organising abilities coming out of every orifice. It struck me that she was wasted on this little 'Women's Group' as we'd agreed to call it. She should have been on Dragons' Den, giving them nightmares instead of us.

By the time Eve and I reached the summit, Vivienne had got the Primus going. She placed the saucepan on the top and tipped in the contents of all our bags, plus two litre bottles of Evian water. Then, from the farthest reaches of her bag she pulled five small notepads and pens.

'This is most important.' We all sat cross-legged surrounding her and the Primus. 'I want each of you to write your wish clearly and toss it into the pan.' She led by example, scribbling words so hard that her paper actually tore. 'Voila!'

Her page hit the now bubbling liquid and sank. The smell was evil.

'Right.' Megan leaned against her own knee and mouthed her words as she wrote. 'I . . . want . . . to be . . . worshipped — Is that one P or two? — as a goddess.' She balled the paper and tossed it in. 'I think I spelled 'worshipped' wrong, will it matter?'

There was a gluggling sound from the pan. I refused to look.

'To meet the man of my dreams.' Eve's page fluttered in.

'To be the centre of the world to someone.' Isobel's paper missed the pan on first throw and then slid beneath the now boiling surface. 'Your turn, Holly.'

I shrugged. 'All right.' I wrote the words 'to have excitement in my life', and was about to drop it in when I remembered my promise to Nicholas. 'And for Nicholas to find a girlfriend. With big knockers,' I added almost indecipherably. And then I thought of the others' wishes, their narrow-focussed deliberate man-trap setting and I bit my lip. Something inside me wanted to make sure that, even by association, I didn't get any of that kind of wish-granting.

'Hurry up, Holl,' Megan whispered. 'My bum's getting damp.'

'Ssshh, I'm thinking.' How to be completely unambiguous, to make sure that I didn't end up being worshipped, having anyone's world revolve around me and to make sure that the man of my dreams remained firmly in the world of the night-fantasy. However unlikely the event of Johnny Depp's declaration of everlasting passion might *actually* be, I didn't want to run the risk.

'Well, think fast then. These pants are new.'

I smoothed my page out along my thigh and began scribbling an amendment. 'Excitement of the right kind, not anything stupid or shallow. The kind that shows you what life is really all about.' I was about to add something about 'with definitely no men in it', but Megan wrestled the paper from my hand and hurled it into the boisterously rolling water.

'Sorry, Holl, but I don't want to get piles, not if there's some gorgeous man out there with my name on. I really can't see him getting far with the whole worship thing if I have to sit on a special cushion, can you?'

My page caused the scummy brown fluid to rise several centimetres up the inside. A grey froth overflowed and hit the Primus, causing a round of steam and a smell like the inside of a tramp's shoe. We all coughed.

'So that's it?' I went to stand up. 'Ritual over?'

'Oh no.' I didn't like the way Vivienne was looking at me. 'Now we drink it.'

The chorus of disgust almost drowned out the vague, distant sound that I'd been hearing for the last few minutes. Somewhere, out on the edge of hearing, was a humming. A vibrating, like a nest of wasps. I tipped my head on one side.

'What's that noise?'

But the other women were still being revolted, and didn't hear me. Vivienne had produced a large silver tablespoon which she dipped into the water.

'It's fine.'

'It's *boiled frog!*' Isobel looked horrified. 'And owl bits. I can't possibly drink that. I'm a vegetarian!'

It was more the thought of the toenail that bothered me. And that noise, which was beginning to sound familiar.

'It's been boiled. It's sterile. And the animal bits are all roadkill, so it's not like they died for you.' Vivienne raised the spoon to her own lips and drank. I stopped being bothered by the noise and stared in horrified revulsion as she swallowed. 'Tastes a bit like chicken.'

Megan went next, pulling terrible faces and only managing to lick the very tip of the spoon before she drew away. Then Isobel, who at least managed to get a mouthful, then collapsed retching on the grass. Eve and I looked at each other.

'After you,' she said.

'No, I insist. You first.'

Eve's mouth did its best to get away from the spoon, but she persisted. A drizzle of greasy-looking foam fell from her lips and her eyes went very round, then her throat worked like a python trying to digest a goat. 'It's not so bad,' she said hoarsely. 'Go on, Holly.'

Like Vivienne had said, it was boiled. How bad could it be? I dipped the spoon under the surface to avoid the speckled film forming on the top of the pan, and put it to my lips, trying not to look at it or smell the steam rising. It was hot. I blew on it for a second, then grabbed my nose and tipped the lot down the back of my tongue. '*Errgh*. Delicious.'

For a moment it felt as though someone had hit me on the back of the head, very hard. My thoughts fragmented and the earth shuddered underneath me, shaking itself like a wet dog before my head cleared and I opened my eyes. Isobel was still retching, Megan had her tongue stuck out and Eve was frantically draining the last of the Evian water from the bottles. 'Wow. Did anyone else feel that?'

'Fee' whap?' Megan looked down at her tongue, grimaced and left it sticking out. 'Ah dimp fee' anufin'.'

I looked at Vivienne, who had rather a smug expression on. 'Did you put drugs in this? Acid? No, that would be destroyed by boiling . . . there was something, some kind of, I dunno, hallucinogen. Very quick, very short acting.'

Vivienne shrugged. 'Not of my doing, Holly. Perhaps it was the magic you felt, the spell taking effect.'

'No, it was more . . . what the *hell* is that noise?'

Isobel managed to quell her stomach for long enough to give a short scream. 'It's motorbikes! Men on motorbikes, riding around down there at the edge of the wood.'

'Probably some kind of motocross rally.'

'Vivienne, it's *dark*. No one does motocross in the dark.' I looked where Isobel was pointing. At least three figures were visible, riding high-framed dirt bikes. Every so often one of them would point our way, but it looked as though they were holding back from approaching us. Scoping us out, maybe?

'Let's go.' I tipped the remains of the liquid onto the grass.

'But we need to cool the Primus down.' Vivienne protested.

'Look. There's five of us. Three, maybe four of them. They don't look like they're up to any good; they could be drunk, they could be high. Now, you might fancy your chances against a possibly armed crackhead, but me, I'm not so sure. Leave the bloody Primus.' I helped Eve to her feet. 'And they look like they're closing in, so I'd hurry, if I were you.'

With a little yelp Vivienne snatched up her bag and pan, and with the rest of us hanging on to one another, we flew down that hill like the witches we weren't.

CHAPTER TEN

Megan had to take to her bed with a world-class case of diar-rhoea and vomiting for the next two days but the spell seemed to have the opposite effect on me. I felt ridiculously fizzy, like someone had lit an adrenaline fuse deep in my chest, and found it hard to concentrate. Was it really magic? Or had Vivienne slipped something into the brew to make us all believe that it was? I tended towards the latter explanation, even though I couldn't see how or what, because the idea that a mouthful of papier mâché and incipient typhoid could make magic happen was too ridiculous for anyone less fluffy than Meg to believe. But. Still. Fizzy.

On the third day I went back to the Old Lodge. Guy had couriered over some paperwork and I wanted to pass it by Kai before we signed to anything, and to take a few more outside shots of the place.

'He's not here.' Cerys leaned against the door. 'Buggered off somewhere, God knows where, and here's me feeling like I'd better avoid any sharp corners in case I go bang. Please come and talk to me, Holly. I can't stand up for long, but that's all right because I can't lie down for long either, so it averages out.'

'I brought some contracts for Kai to see, if he's really going through with letting a film crew loose around here, and my camera.'

'So this is a professional visit?' Cerys gave me a 'Princess Di' coy look. 'You two didn't . . . um . . . get it together when I'd gone to bed the other night? When I woke up your car was still here.'

'Went home by taxi. Kai brought the car back next morning.' Not that I'd seen anything of him; he'd shoved the keys through the letter box and, by the time I'd got down from my office to the front door, he'd vanished. 'And anyway, you're his daughter. I wouldn't tell you anything, it would be nasty.'

Cerys slumped on the edge of the kitchen table. 'He and Mum split up when I was eighteen months old. She married Dad when I was three. So I've never known Kai as a father, he's always been more like a distant family friend. Sometimes *really* distant.'

'And he's gone off and left you on your own? With, what, around three weeks before the babies arrive?' I pulled a face.

'Yeah, well, I can phone an ambulance like a bitch.' She got up again. 'Put the kettle on, Holl, will you? I'm gagging for a coffee but I'm busting for a wee first.' She waddled off into the downstairs bathroom but carried on our conversation through the closed door. 'So you can tell me anything about Kai. I won't judge you. Well, I can't, I'm the stupid bint who got pregnant with twins by a tosser.'

'There's nothing to say, Cerys, honestly.'

The flush sounded and she appeared again. 'You're not going to hurt him, are you?'

'Hurt him? I'm more likely to damage myself.'

'I've never really got what's going on with Kai, y'know.' Cerys weebled through the door towards me, hands pressed into the small of her back. 'I know he and Mum had me very young, but I don't reckon that's what's behind him being so totally weird.'

'Is he? Totally weird?' I spooned coffee into two mugs and tried not to think about what form this weirdness might take, whilst disturbing images of various sexual peculiarities tiptoed through my mind. This involved imagining Kai naked and more coffee sprinkled over the worktop than hit the mugs.

Cerys made a dismissive motion with one hand. 'He's always a bit . . . I dunno really . . . he doesn't really *relate* like other people. It's almost like he's acting a part instead of living.' She gave me a shrewd look. 'Oh he thinks he's so clever and so straight, but I can see through him like an ultrasound scan. Oh, God, listen to me, I've become completely baby-centric. Shoot me now, Holly, please, before I start talking about giving birth to the sounds of whale-song instead of the ninety-decibel screaming I've got planned.'

I rested a hand on the top of the kettle switch and fussed with the plug to occupy my hands and give me a reason to avoid her eye. Was that it? Was that why I felt so ambivalent about this yellow-eyed Welshman, because he wasn't behaving in the ways I expected? 'Aren't we all, a bit? Acting a part, I mean, pretending to be normal and ordinary while we've all got stuff going on underneath — isn't that the only way we can carry on without spending all our time in tears or therapy?' I turned back around to find that Cerys had an eyebrow raised and her mouth twisted into a prematurely motherly expression.

'Sounds like you and he are going to get along fantastically,' she said, and the parental tone of irony was noticeable. 'Just, you know, be careful. Of yourself, not just him. He's a bit of a . . . not a bastard, not really, but a bit . . . careless, I suppose. He had this one girlfriend, Imogen, 'bout a year ago I suppose, and she was lovely, really sweet and she and I got on and everything, but that all fell apart accompanied by some fairly serious yelling.' She shrugged. 'She wanted him close, and he doesn't really *do* close.' A hand rubbed the bump in concentric circles. 'He does screwing though, I've heard him.'

'Shut up. Enough.' I poured boiling water onto the coffee. The rising steam made me think about the spell and I

68

had to smile at the ridiculousness of it. Yeah, I'd wished for excitement. What had I got? An enormously pregnant young woman telling me about her father's sex life, and a best friend who could heave for Britain. Oh, how thrilling.

'Have you seen the weather forecast?' Cerys took her mug. 'Storms and snow and all kinds of stuff on its way, apparently.'

'Oh, that'll be my excitement for the year then. Nothing like getting trapped in your house for four days and then flooded out when all the pipes burst. Wonderful.' I hadn't, after all, specified *good* excitement, had I?

'Yep. These babies had better hang in there, otherwise they'll have to airlift me out. With a jumbo jet. Does it often snow up here? In Peterborough we really like snow because we don't get much of it, but everything grinds to a halt if we get so much as a sprinkling.'

'It does snow, but we're used to it. And it's not usually feet of the stuff, just enough to make life bloody awkward. Talking of which, I'd better pop outside now and do the pictures Guy wants.'

'I'll stay here. I'm drip-filling my bladder.'

I went outside and did some close-up shots of the front porch and some of the general location, then wandered out along the track until I could fit the whole of the Old Lodge in a single frame. As I locked off the last picture, someone spoke close to my shoulder.

'You've been hanging around Dodman's Copse haven't you?'

Instinct increased my grip on the camera, but I turned around. 'What?'

'Hill on the far side. We've seen you.'

It was the ginger-headed bloke, this time seconded by a thin man with what looked like a joke moustache. They were both carrying shotguns, and the thin man had a brace of pheasants, dripping blood, by the feet.

'It's a free country.' I couldn't tear my eyes away from the dead birds. Their eyes were bleeding, surely shot birds don't drip blood from the eyes? 'And we're not doing any harm or anything.'

Joke-moustache looked me up and down. 'Depends what you *are* doing,' he said. His voice was less classy-twit and more gravelly-bastard. 'We seen you, all of you, sitting up there, chanting.'

'Oh bollocks. Chanting's not against the law. We're a women's support group,' I added, keeping one eye on those guns.

The men exchanged a smile. 'That's what you're calling it these days, is it?' Ginger-hair took a step closer to me and I took an involuntary step back, which made him smile even more. 'Look. She's scared.'

'She should be.' Joke-moustache raised his gun, clicked it closed and fired into the sky. I'd never been so close to a discharged firearm; the noise was tremendous and I covered my ears, albeit too late. When I managed to unscrew my eyes and lower my hands, the men had gone. Melted away into the woods, leaving only the smell of cordite and a tiny patch of dripped blood staining the brown and yellow leaves of the trackway.

Cerys was at the door. 'Holly? What's happened? I heard shooting, are you all right?'

'Yes.' To my horror I felt the tears of shock begin to prick my eyes. 'It was . . .'

'Oh, Kai's back.' The Jeep jounced into view coming down the track towards us. I couldn't hear the engine of the Land Rover and I could only hope that ginge and his skanky friend weren't standing behind an oak tree watching his arrival.

'Hi.' The long legs unfolded onto the forest floor. 'Holly? What's happened?'

I managed to breathe through the desire to throw myself at him and blurt that I'd been scared of the big men with guns — it was a little too romance-heroine for me.

'Someone fired a gun,' Cerys supplied.

I could have mistaken the quick look Kai gave me, but I didn't think so. 'Was it our auburn-headed friend?'

I nodded. 'And a thin guy with a moustache that looked like it came out of a cracker.'

'*Fuck.*' Kai turned to go into the Old Lodge, slamming his hand down on the porch rail. 'Thought I told you to stay clear of him.'

'No. If you remember, *you* were staying clear of him, and I said that was all right with me. You've warned me off just about everything else, but you never mentioned him.'

'Well he . . . what do you mean "just about everything else"?' He turned back to face me, rolling his hand along the rail so that his rings tapped.

'I'm going for a lie-down. This is all getting way too heavy for me, and being that I weigh roughly the same as Albania, that is going some.' Cerys hauled herself into the hallway, pausing to give me a quick wink over her shoulder as she went.

'Holly? What did you mean?' Kai stayed where he was.

'Well, the woods and stuff.' My voice sounded a bit feeble and my eyes still stung.

'Stuff?'

'You.'

He dipped his head slowly and looked at me. It was like being stuck in a binary system, those twin-sun eyes. The stubble had renewed itself, but looked artful, as though by a freak of nature his beard had some kind of designer pattern. 'Get in the Jeep.'

'I beg your pardon?'

He twitched his head towards the olive-grey vehicle. 'In.'

'What, get into a car with a bloke who seems to think ordering women around is the way forward for polite society? I don't think so.' The shock was draining from my system, leaving me feeling a weakness I would never show. The anger covered it up nicely.

Kai closed in. Put a hand on my elbow. 'Look. My daughter is up there.' Eyes traced a way through the open door and up the stairs, then returned to mine. 'And if I know Cerys, she's listening to every word we say. You don't want to have this conversation thrown back at you any more than I do. So get in the Jeep.'

'Why? What are you going to say?'

'Get in the Jeep and find out.'

I finally complied, and he got in after me, starting the engine with a sudden, ferocious amount of throttle. The wheels spun, gained purchase and then hurled us forward, narrowly missing a tree which probably qualified for Ancient status. 'Where are we going?' I'd barely managed to get my seat belt done up.

'What do you want me to do, Holly? Throw you down on the ground and have sex with you?'

'God. Way to be cold-blooded about it, Kai.'

'I sent you home in a taxi instead of taking you into my bed, was that what you meant? *That* was warning you off me? You've clearly not been on the receiving end of many real warnings.' He jolted the Jeep around in a semicircle. We were off-road, deep within the forest, parked at the bottom of a deep depression filled with birch and oak leaves like snow-drifts. 'So, you fancy me and you reckon I should reciprocate?'

'It felt like reciprocation the other night.' I kept staring out of the windscreen at the sporadic leaves that floated from above like broken kites.

'It . . .' he bit off whatever the end of that sentence might have been. 'We were playing, that was all. Teasing. I'm sorry if you read more into it than was intended.'

'Look, forget it. I've just had a guy set off a shotgun next to my head, I'm not thinking straight.'

'Too right you're not.' To my surprise he sighed deeply. 'Did Cerys set you up for this? Holly, my daughter knows nothing about my life, whatever she might think and whatever she might have told you. It's . . . difficult. I'm not . . . I like women . . . I like *you*, but I'm not in the right place for any-thing right now. We had a bit of a game going that night and, yeah, okay, I admit it, it did cross my mind that the evening might have ended differently but . . .' His accent strengthened for a moment, then he gave another sigh and leaned back in the driver's seat, using one hand to push the hair off his face. 'Wrong time, wrong place.'

'I wasn't looking for a proposal, Kai. A good time would have done.'

A steady stare and a shaken head. 'It felt . . . yeah, wrong, that's all I can say. Like — jeez, can't believe I'm saying this — like something would have been spoiled if I'd taken you to my bed.'

I remembered him chasing around his house looking for spell items for me. He'd been fun then, charming and outgoing, no sign that there had been anything awry. Now here, he seemed locked-down, wary.

'I think you're scared.'

'Really.' Fingers tapped the wheel. 'And what of?' He was doing that calm, listening thing that he'd done the other night, too. Waiting for me to show myself.

'Well, you seemed to be quite happy to give me the come-on right up until I asked you about yourself, and I think it freaked you out. So maybe you're afraid *because* I asked, after all, if you never give anything of yourself, then how can anyone actually get close to you, hey? Like . . . yes, like friends. Do you have any friends, Kai?'

He turned towards me and slowly closed his eyes. 'Well. Score one for the apparently superficial woman.' When he opened them his pupils were huge. It turned the golden irises into pale rings around the darkness, like eclipses. 'Holly.' The chill of his ring bit the warm flesh under my chin as his fingers touched my face. '*Holly.*' His voice was a whisper now, very Welsh, my name brushing against my own lips as he brought his mouth to mine.

I knew I was being played, knew this was to keep me quiet, almost to buy me off, but as soon as the kiss started I didn't care. He tasted of cucumber and mint, his teeth grazed across my upper lip and I could hear nothing but his breathing, feel nothing but the heat rising in me. Then, as suddenly as it had started, the kiss was over, he pulled away and put his head on his arms, resting on the steering wheel. 'And that's all you get.'

'Wow.' I said, when I could trust my voice. 'Well. That's one hell of a waste of a sexy body.'

'Yours or mine?' Now he sat up, shaking his hair off his face, and I started to laugh. He joined in until we were both rocking with laughter, steaming up the windows of the Jeep with it and probably disturbing every hibernating creature for a hundred yards.

CHAPTER ELEVEN

Megan lay on her sofa looking wan. She'd managed to dispense with the bucket but was still a bit touch-and-go.

'I brought you some more Lucozade.' I unpacked the shopping on her table. Her dependency made it a bit like dealing with a female version of Nicky. 'And some ice cream for when you feel a bit more like eating. Oh, and some more toilet paper — has that stopped yet?'

'I feel a bit better today.' She struggled up onto one elbow, fighting her way free of the duvet which enclosed her. 'And you didn't even get a bit queasy?'

'Nope.'

'I must have got some of the frog.' Going pale, she lay carefully down again. 'I think I might need the bucket back, actually.'

'Do you want me to call the doctor?'

A brave shake of the head. 'It's passing. So, what's the news from the big, wide world? Anything happening? Heard anything from the others?'

'Vivienne left a message, there's a meeting tomorrow night for us to compare notes. But I'm going to ask that we stay in the cottage. I mean, stuff the bloody rituals, there's blokes out in those woods with guns. Not very nice blokes at that. Oh, and the weather forecast is horrible for the beginning of next week. Snow and stuff. You're in the best place, all snuggled up in here.'

There was suddenly a terrible clattering, clanging noise from the little yard outside the flat. 'That's that bloody dog again.' Indignation drove a little colour into Megan's cheeks. 'I can't find out who it belongs to, but it keeps on going through my dustbin. Holl, please would you go out and make sure it hasn't dragged all that horrible grease down the yard again? I don't think I could stand the sight of it all reappearing . . .' She blanched and took some deep breaths. 'Please,' she repeated.

I went out of her flat and down the two flights that led to the locked back door out to the yard, where the residents of the four flats kept their bins. Also their old bicycles, radiators, prams, mattresses and anything else that was too big for the bin and too broken to sell. I unlocked it with Meg's huge old-fashioned key and stepped outside where the wind hit me like pins, tiny sharp points digging into my skin even in the relative shelter of the enclosed area and little bouts of hail bounced around my ankles. I looked around. A six-foot wall ran all round the yard, topped with broken glass which had yet to deter a peeping Tom, although it gave the residents an illusion of security, and the only way in was through the locked door. It smelled of old fat, bleach, and sour damp.

I saw the dog eventually, cowering behind a wheelie bin, with a mouthful of newspaper, and a guilty expression. It was a big dog, almost Alsatian-sized, but there its similarity to any recognised breed ended. It had one ear up, one ear down, a bit of backcombed string for a tail and a dirty brindled grey coat like something which had failed to sell in a jumble sale. I tried speaking to it, but it huddled even further back, obviously terrified, and showed me its teeth, with a desperate look on its face, as though its mouth was growling without the brain's permission. I relocked the door and went back upstairs.

'It must belong to someone in one of the flats,' I said, thankfully getting in front of the gas fire. 'Probably someone who's out at work all day. I should call the RSPCA if I were you, it doesn't look very well cared for.'

'And had it been through my bin?'

'It was eating newspaper, but without closer examination I couldn't tell if it was yours.'

Megan sighed. 'I'll just have to wait until I'm feeling better then go down and clear up after it. I wish people wouldn't do this, we had two feral cats down there which used to fight under my window at three in the morning. Turned out that they belonged to the guy in number two, that weird bloke who wore women's skirts at the weekend.' She propped herself up again. 'Will you give my apologies to Vivienne? Even if I'm feeling better, I don't know if I'm going to be strong enough to make it tomorrow night.'

'You want me to go on my own?'

'The others will be there, won't they?'

'Yes, but—'

'You have to report back, Holl. Tell Vivienne about the effects of the spell. Have there been any effects?' she added, almost wistfully. 'Anything exciting happening?'

'About as much as you've been worshipped.'

She sighed. 'Oh dear.' Big kitten-eyes looked at me over the duvet. 'I really hope all this hasn't been for nothing. I mean, it's such a tiny wish, isn't it? It's not like I've wished to marry a billionaire.'

'Have you been reading those Mills & Boons again?'

'Might have.'

'I suppose we should think ourselves lucky that you only want to be a goddess then. You could have wished to be carried away by a sheikh. And you'd never get a horse up those steps.'

'You have no romance, Holly Grey, you know that? Anyway. I tried to ring you this morning but you weren't answering. Where were you, not with that grandad again?'

'Kai? Yes, I was, actually.' I began to blush faintly at the memory of his kiss and I think my eyes might have glazed over.

'Woah, Holl, you didn't! You've not added some pensioner to your shag-pile? That's disgusting.'

I slumped on the floor, being careful to avoid the bits where her sick-bucket had sat, and told her about the Kai situation. Or, at least, I told her that I was trying to get the Old Lodge contracted for Guy as a location, and that Kai was thirty-six with a pregnant daughter. I left out all the stuff about gold-coloured eyes and leather-jacketed lean legginess and the kind of disconnected personality that hated personal questions; a woman who's spent the last three days on the toilet with her head and bum being interchangeable, did not need to know any of that.

'Oh well, if it's work,' Megan lost interest and we spent the rest of my visit discussing daytime television, which she'd had plenty of opportunity to study.

I spent the next day with my laptop and camera at the seaside. A company in London wanted a suitable location for a 1920s detective series, set by the sea, so there I was, huddled in my best down coat and still freezing, sending live-feed pictures down the line to some coked-up executives in a nice, warm city office. Standing in the wind was like being carved and little slivers of hail prodded my cheeks into numbness, while the boys in the production office kept getting me to move another hundred yards along the cliff, to show another angle of Scarborough which they could have got from the tourist brochure.

Finally the light went and they decided to 'think about it', so I drove straight to Barndale, where at least Vivienne's cottage was warm.

Eve was sitting on the sofa already when I got there. Two cats were jockeying for position on her lap and she and Vivienne were indulging in a very unwitchy pot of tea and plate of scones.

'Ah, Holly.' Vivienne fetched down another cup, which was nice. I was so frozen that I wasn't sure I could hold it. 'Did you bring Isobel?'

'Was I meant to?' I folded my hands around the cup for the warmth.

'Not really. But she lives near you and her car was in getting a service, so I wondered if she might have asked for a lift.'

I shook my head. 'I've not been home since this morning. Working.'

'She self-harms, you know.' Eve spoke over Vivienne's shoulder. 'Isobel. Because of her skin problems. She says she feels ugly all the time, so she cuts her arms to feel better.'

Now I felt like a shit for not offering someone a lift when I didn't even know they needed a lift in the first place. 'I could go back and look for her,' I offered, reluctantly groping behind me for the still-damp coat.

But then we heard the growl of Isobel's old Isuzu truck drawing up outside. I sat down again with relief and then wondered what they said about me when I wasn't there. Did they discuss my great job and lovely home or did they spend their time picking to pieces the fact that I didn't have a regular boyfriend? *Hmm.*

'Sorry I'm late, had to pick the car up.' Isobel sat beside me. 'Megan rang, said she's still feeling poorly.'

Everyone looked at me as though it were my fault. In fact, they eyeballed me as though I was responsible for every act of civic nastiness in the previous fifty years. 'What?'

'Have *you* had any results from the other night?' Vivienne looked at the scones as she spoke.

'No, not really. I did feel a bit squitty on Friday, but I think it was the prawn sandwich I had for lunch.'

'Vivienne means positive results, from our . . . little experiment,' Eve explained. I looked at her properly for a moment and wondered. She'd wished to meet the man of her dreams, but she'd not done anything practical about it, like getting a good haircut or buying some trendier clothes. No. She'd teamed up with a deserted wife, a girl who cut her arms to escape the miseries of acne and loneliness, a woman who thought love was like the romance novels and me, someone who didn't believe in Mr Right and was content to shag her way through lots of Mr shut-the-door-on-your-way-out. That was weird behaviour, however you looked at it.

'Well, a bloke did fire a gun next to me.' I reluctantly conceded that this was probably the most exciting moment in the past week, although it hadn't exactly been the fun event I'd been expecting. The huge adrenaline rush that had been Kai's kiss was none of their business. 'But he was a gamekeeper. Or something.'

'So. No, you know, thrilling things? Nobody whisking you away to the Côte d'Azur for a weekend?'

'Not so's you'd notice. Anyone else getting anything?'

The other three shook their heads.

'Maybe it didn't work,' Isobel said. 'I don't mind, really. Being part of this group has been so good for me, being able to get out and chat and do something other than sit at home with Mum and Dad watching wildlife shows. If the spell doesn't ever work, I still feel like I've gained such a lot.'

I rolled my eyes. Any moment now and they'd start embracing and calling each other 'sister'.

'Well, *I* think it's damn shabby. And I blame you, Holly, I really do.' Vivienne snatched the scones away, into another dimension probably.

'Hang on, how is this *my* fault? I only came along to keep Megan company. I didn't even have a proper wish!'

Isobel and Eve also interceded on my part. 'Perhaps there was something wrong with the spell?'

'Yes, could the wording have been wrong? Were we meant to put our wishes in like that?'

Vivienne shook her head. Her cropped hair was showing root growth, I noticed, about half an inch of brown sprinkled with grey was lying along her parting. The vivid red hid it well but she'd not had her hair done in a while. 'My part was perfect. It must have been some of the ingredients that were wrong, and, Holly, you supplied the major part of them.'

My teeth ached with the urge to say 'but it's all just *pretend*. Magic isn't real.' They completely believed their own fabrication, and it would have been useless to point out that we'd used photographs and computer printouts and surely *that* wasn't in the spirit of any branch of magic.

'Okay, well,' I said into my cup, 'I did my best.' Maybe it was because I'd had *fun* getting all the bits and pieces that it hadn't worked. Perhaps it all had to be dark and joyless and rocking on the edge of the razor blade between sanity and talking squirrels to be properly occult.

'And we haven't really given it very long, have we?' Isobel-Pollyanna went on. 'I mean, we're supposed to be channelling earth-energies into our wishes, well, at this time of year earth-energies must be a bit low. I think we should wait a while before we write it off. Maybe do some more visualisation up on the hill?'

'No,' I said quickly. 'I mean, let's let the bad weather pass first. I can't be the only one who doesn't fancy sitting in six inches of snow with nothing but an IKEA blanket between me and anal frostbite.'

Eve shuddered. 'I'm with Holly. Let's wait and see.'

Vivienne twitched her long nose. 'Well, if that's the opinion of the group.'

We all nodded vigorously, and I checked around for the scones.

'All right. But we can really only spare a short while before we have to link ourselves in to the rhythms of the earth mother once more. We can't ignore her and yet expect her to bend to our dominion.'

Ah, bollocks, I thought. But it's hurting no one. And she's providing scones. So I joined in the nodding, and refilled my cup while they were all hugging.

CHAPTER TWELVE

So, yeah. Drug article done and posted, not exactly Pulitzer prize stuff but it makes a point and makes it well, I reckon. New product, mostly untested but useful results so far, launched on kids with problems so complex that . . . hey. Nothing to do with this, with us. It's just . . . gods, sometimes I wish I could show you what I do. Hold up something I've done that's made a difference, changed something. I wish I could tell you how I've sweated and hung in for something because I *believed* in it . . .

Part of the problem, I guess. I want you to know me. I want someone to know me, not to take this outer shell as gospel but to get through, to understand . . . and you can't. You never will. But now I know, that's what's behind so much of what I do, why I drive them away with my behaviour, my bastard act; I want someone to make the effort, to put the work in — I know that now. And it's because of her, because of Holly, when she started plugging in to some kind of weird psychological shit, me not wanting anyone to get inside my head — that kind of crap. Okay, yeah, like I said before, her asking . . . it threw me for a loop, y'know? Like it was the first time I realised that no one was interested in my hopes, my dreams, and it took this girl with her Merlot hair and the kind of stare that you normally see on something nocturnal, it took her to . . .

And I couldn't take it. Scary, huh? That thing I want so much from another person, that thing I wanted from you and could never have, that understanding? Because, I guess, so much of what I've done has been so shitty that the only way to deal with it is to pretend that it's how I am. Not a conscious choice made to keep people distant when I judge them unworthy, but something that I can't help. Something I can blame you for: if you were here I wouldn't be like that. If you'd . . . nah. I've judged you and judged you so many times in my head. Found you guilty, condemned you, I've argued with you and pleaded so hard that I'd cry in the night and . . . No more. It is what it is, and I am what I am. And what I am is a coward, a sad, vindictive heap of terror. I don't deserve understanding. So I cut her loose. Killed it. Who needs someone giving it the full MI5 treatment, trying to drag your background out of you when all you want to do is kill the dark, not illuminate it. I don't want light, not now. Afraid of what I'll see perhaps, if someone holds the light up to my face; what might be operating now behind these eyes? Nah. Just prefer the shadows, me, where I can watch and wait and listen, pick up the tail-lines of stories until I can follow the scent back to the origin and then blow it all open for anyone to read about. I've got a good life here, things running nicely, all under control. I'm cool, it's all fine. Yeah. It's all fine.

CHAPTER THIRTEEN

And then things got weird.

Well, no, first things got cold.

The wind swung round to the north, and while it had felt like having stitches in your face before, now it felt like it was inflicting the injuries which would need stitches. 'It's like being attacked by Edward Scissorhands,' as Cerys put it, during one of her ten-second outings. She was so huge she couldn't get behind the wheel of the Jeep any more and had to be driven by Kai with the passenger seat back as far as it would go. She wound the window down and called it 'getting fresh air'. The news had come through that her flat was taking rather longer to get straight than it should have; apparently her tosser was some kind of second cousin to the many wankers I'd dated, and had trashed the place before eviction took effect. Cerys had spent a morning swearing and then resigned herself to staying with Kai until just before the twins arrived. It was going to be touch-and-go, but she reckoned she'd be back home in time for the labour twinges.

Kai behaved as though he'd never kissed me, as though the whole of that strange time in the Jeep had never happened. He behaved, in fact, as though I were a friend of Cerys's, and rarely hung around when I went over. If I spoke directly to him he'd answer me politely enough, but I never saw those unusual eyes light up with pleasure or amusement the way they had the night we'd searched for the spell ingredients. He behaved now like a man who's carrying his entire life in an invisible suitcase strapped to his back, weighed down and weary.

And then it really got cold. A week after my visit to Vivienne's, it started to snow. Brief flurries at first, then settling, until a couple of inches lay underfoot. It was picturesque, and everyone started predicting a white Christmas, never mind that it was a month away. Then it got grubby, the buses ran late and trains were cancelled and everyone got annoyed.

And then . . .

Cerys and I were lounging around in the living room at the Old Lodge. Guy had postponed the external shoot he'd been planning until the weather improved, so we'd been cheated of the promised sight of Jude Law prancing about in the warlock's shrubbery, and Cerys was feeling peevish.

'Ow. The doctor says they're lying back to back in there.' She prodded her bump. 'I bet the boy is hogging all the covers.'

'Not long to go now though.' I kicked the footstool over so she could put her feet up. 'Stay in touch, won't you? Facebook me or something. I really want to see pictures of the twins when they arrive.'

'You'll be the first. Well, after old sulkyboots.' She nodded at the ceiling; Kai was upstairs in his bedroom. We heard his footsteps pacing up and down every so often.

'What's he doing up there?'

'Working, I guess.'

There was a particularly loud set of footsteps which ended with a bang, as though Kai had kicked something over. 'Do you think I should go up? Check he's okay?'

Cerys raised her eyebrows at me. 'Oho, my dear. Are you sure you don't have a case of the hots for the lanky one?'

I sat back down. 'Don't be silly.'

There was another crash from overhead and Cerys leaped up. 'Ow, he's making the twins jump. And that feels uncomfortably like being possessed, so please would you have a word, Holl? I'd go but by the time I get up those stairs these two will be teenagers. Ask him to keep the sulking down, or whatever it is he's doing.' She turned on the TV. 'And this is on to cover the sound of anything you feel like getting up to, but I warn you, if you come through that ceiling I won't be responsible for my actions.'

'Cerys?'

'Yes?'

'Shut up.'

I walked quietly up the stairs and to the door of Kai's room, tapped and waited. The striding footsteps stopped, there was a pause as though he was trying to decide whether or not to answer, then the door flew open and he stood in the doorway, staring down at me.

'What?' He sounded annoyed. No, more than that, wound up. Tight.

I said the first thing that came into my head. 'God, you're tall.'

'No, you're short. Now, if that's all,' and he went to close the door again.

'Is something wrong?' The winter afternoon light barely penetrated this far into the House of Goth, but reflected from the snow it managed to edge its way up the landing as far as his eyes, which gleamed amber. His face was pale and pulled thin over his cheekbones, he smelled of sweat and damp laundry and his hair looked unbrushed. 'We could hear you stomping about.'

Another long pause. He was staring out onto the landing but he didn't seem to be looking at me. It was as though another person stood between us, like a ghost he didn't want to acknowledge. Then he closed his eyes and stepped back inside the room. I took this as invitation and followed.

'Close the door.'

I did so, then my heart sped up. What was he about to do that he didn't want Cerys to hear? He had his back to me,

86

staring out of the long window, over the balcony ledge and into the forest beyond. His fingers tapped against the glass.

'Kai?' Using his name felt strange. Almost as though I shouldn't, there was some taboo on calling him anything. 'Would you like me to make you a drink? Cerys has got the kettle on almost permanently down there.'

He didn't turn round. By the snowlight his skin looked almost blueish pale. 'I need . . . something. Something else. Something even I don't recognise.'

'Are you all right?' His voice was wrong, strained, and his shoulders dipped and curved inwards as though to hold something invisible closer to him. 'Kai? Is there anything wrong?'

His nails tapped the glass again. The tiny noise rang into the quiet like a solid thought. 'I had a letter,' he said finally. 'This morning. I don't know what to do.'

Then he did turn round, his body a streak of darkness against the window. My heart gave an uncomfortable squirm inside my ribs at his shadowed expression. 'What kind of letter?' I asked. 'Oh, the kind that's written on paper, I suppose, sorry. Just, you know, thinking with my mouth open again.'

'It was . . .' Kai moved away from the window and folded down onto the edge of the unmade bed, sitting with his arms on his knees, head in hands. 'It was someone looking for me.' A bitter kind of smile. 'I don't know. What's got into me? Why do I have the urge to tell you anything at all about my life?'

I shrugged. 'Because I'm here?' There was that smell of dampness again, as though he'd put on wet clothes, a sour, uncaring sort of smell, and not only was his hair unkempt but he didn't look as though he'd showered today either. It was so far from his normal, careful, image that I felt my heart writhe. Something was very wrong with this man, something soul-deep. 'And you don't have to tell me anything you don't want to. But, you know, growing up with Nick . . . I'm a good listener, Kai, and I'm used to hearing terrible, scary stuff. And I know that letting it out of your head can help.' I gave a quick smile, remembering. 'Thoughts lose some of the power to hurt if you share them.'

'Was it hard? Having a brother like him?' Kai was looking at the floor, twisting the thumb ring around and around, screwing it up and down over his knuckle. The question sounded unconsidered, as though the answer didn't matter as much as simply keeping me talking.

'I love Nick. However he is, however hard it might be, he's my brother. And I've never really known him any other way.' I took another step closer to the bed, noticing the way the pillows were bunched and distorted and the covers twisted; last night had obviously been a very restless one. 'And I've also learned to keep things to myself, if that's what's worrying you. Our parents are very . . . They don't . . . they don't really *understand*. They think that Nicholas . . . that he's only got to take his medicine and not let things get on top of him and he'll be fine, so he can't tell them some of the things that he . . . So, if you need to talk to someone, I know about keeping things to myself, Kai.'

A short laugh. 'Thing is, you see, I don't think I know how to talk to someone. I . . . I don't *share*, Holly. I don't let people in. Since Merion and I split it's just been me, no one else to worry about and I like it like that. Oh, there've been women, but my relationships have all been short and intense. But mainly short. And now — now something has hit that's so bad, so *hard* and I could do with someone, and there's no one, you know? Shit.' He lowered his head and cupped his hands around the back of his neck. I could see the quick rise and fall of his chest under his shirt as though he was struggling for control of himself, but his voice was steady when he carried on speaking. 'What have I been doing so wrong all these years?'

I came further into the room now, and perched my bottom along the edge of the stumpy dressing table. A sudden, short pain dug under my ribs as I remembered some of the rambling, confused conversations with Nicky, some of the thoughts and doubts that he'd shared with me, that I couldn't share with anyone. A pain and responsibility that I had to carry. Had to. Because he was my brother. I knew how it felt to need to talk . . . 'I don't know, Kai. I don't think there's anything so wrong in not wanting attachments. Keep your life clear and uncluttered and take your fun where you find it, that's my motto.'

'But what about when you wake up one day and it's not fun any more? What then? What about when you think "shit, I need to talk about this" and there's no one there to listen?'

'*I'm* listening.'

He rubbed both hands over his face, tiredly. 'I know. And maybe it's that, maybe because you had Nick and I had no one that makes us the same, gives you some kind of . . . I am going to regret this, I know, but I'm so . . . it's all got confusing and I can't make sense of what I think, what I *feel*.' He glanced up and I noticed for the first time how shaded and tired his eyes looked, how pulled-down his whole face seemed, as though fifty thoughts fought for his attention at the same time.

I stopped perching on the edge of the table and sat back properly. 'I'm here,' I said quietly. 'If you need an ear, I'm here, Kai.'

'Yeah.' An outbreath, long and hard and carrying a decision. 'This goes no further, right? And definitely not to Cerys. Well, definitely not to *anyone* but especially not her. No, no one is best, let's say no one.'

'All right,' I said, trying not to sound impatient.

'Okay.' And Kai stood up. 'What? I'm only six foot four, it's not like I'm a freak or something.'

'Sorry. It's . . . you look different today. More . . .' I'd been going to say 'attractive' but I didn't want him to start thinking I really went for the unwashed, unbrushed, unshaven thing. It was rather that he seemed more approachable, more *real* somehow. '. . . tall,' I finished feebly.

'Here. Read this.' He fetched a letter from the dressing table and thrust it into my hands. Then, as if he were afraid to look at my face while I read, he took himself back to the window and stared out again.

The letter was from a private investigation agency. It asked Kai to confirm to their address that he had been born 'on or around 15 September 1976' and handed in to a hospital in Caernarfon.

'Handed in? What, like a parcel?'

'I was found in a bus shelter, I was about four hours old and wrapped in a copy of the Daily Mail.' He tapped the window glass with his fingertips again. 'You don't grow up with a warm feeling of being loved with that sort of background.'

I was about to say 'I can imagine', but then realised that I truly couldn't. 'And you think this letter . . . ?'

'I suspect it's my mother, trying to find me.' He turned around again and started up the pacing. 'I was adopted, lovely couple, farmers on the coast. Couldn't have kids of their own so they gave me everything, all the love they'd had bundled up all those years . . . and then, when I was ten, they died. And then the fun started.'

'Fun?' I watched him rub his face again. There was so much not being said, it almost outweighed the words.

'I was fostered. And with these—' he waved a hand to indicate his eyes, 'a lot of people thought I was the son of the Devil. Oh, don't laugh . . .'

'For fuck's sake, Kai, laughing is the last thing on my mind.'

'No. I suppose not. It sounds so . . . so parochial, so stupid and rural. But at that time, up North, it was all very Chapel, very religious. They really believed in the Bible and all God's works and so the Devil was the downside. I had a lot of foster carers try to beat Satan out of me. Oh, not all of them, some of them were fine, but it was hard, you know? I'd lost the only parents I knew and . . .'

I nodded so as not to break his flow.

'So. Merion and I ended up in the same foster home. Both fifteen, both desperate for something to hold on to. For a while we held on to each other, then to Cerys, but it wasn't enough, not for either of us. She's okay now, she's got Mike, she managed it, the transition to a proper life, trust, *hope*. Me, I still can't do it. You were right, you know?'

I had to clear my throat. 'About?'

'All that stuff you said about me deciding to be a journalist. Went to University when Merion and I split up, got my degree in journalism, ran off to be a hotshot story-digger. Exposing the bad stuff, the warped people, the twisted logic. Oh, I've done my share of the celebrity stuff but what I'm best at? It's showing the world up as pure hypocrisy.' He scribbled a finger against the bedside table as though composing another exposé in the dust. 'For every selfless act there's a dozen evil ones, for every dolphin saved there's ten kids shot on the streets. You see enough of that, Holly, you realise that there's no place for love and romance and all that crap, you learn to be hard, to take what you can and not to expect any kind of a future.'

'But what you do, it helps to make the world a better place. You don't just see it, you make others see it too. And you're very good at it.'

An eyebrow raised. 'I see. You followed my work to expose the child slave trade in Chad, did you? Or was it my undercover work that led to the jailing of a Serbian drug overlord and the freeing of the underage girls he'd been prostituting?'

'I googled you.'

'Right, yeah. I can see how that would be easier.'

'Sorry. But life ran the way you wanted it though. You were . . .' I cleared my throat. I was trying to track his emotions, to understand how he felt, and I was becoming aware that, somewhere in the middle of me, was a big black hole into which the understanding fell. 'You're happy, aren't you? And now you're freaking because the woman who dumped you in a bus shelter might want to get in touch? Isn't that overreacting a bit? You can always say no.'

'For thirty-six years I've wondered, Holly. What did I do that was so bad she had to abandon me like that? *Am* I the son of the Devil?' He stopped, and his pacing had brought him right in front of me. 'Who am I? And what made me so unlovable that she wrapped me in a fucking newspaper?' A deep breath. 'Yes, you were right, talking helped. Now bugger off.'

I stared at him. 'Are you really a complete bastard, or do you just get off on imitating one?' Then I cringed inside. *The guy has laid himself bare, now he feels shitty. Taking it out on you is the only thing he can do.* 'Sorry.'

'No, you're right.' A shaky hand raked through his hair. 'Now you can see why all my relationships have been so short. I'm a bastard.'

'But it was deliberate, wasn't it?' There was that hole again, less black now, more of a mirrored surface. This man was so like me that it hurt. *Keep them distant, keep them from loving you. Protect yourself.*

A shrug. 'I'm a high-functioning disconnected personality. Work alone, live alone, and when people get too close . . .' he dropped his eyes and considered the carpet as though it held the answer to universal mysteries, 'behave so badly that they get the message.'

'But why didn't you tell anyone? If you'd explained, or even *mentioned* your past, women would have cut you some slack.'

'Right. So, they'd have caught me in bed with their best friend and thought "oh, he was an abused child, it's nothing personal", would they?'

I stared at him. 'You did that? With someone's *best friend*?'

'Yeah. Quite a few times.'

'With the same best friend? Or different ones?'

He tipped his head on one side. 'Oh, there were lots. And other stuff too. I . . . I *hurt* people, Holly. And I have enough self-awareness to know why I'm doing it, but I still do it, still drag them in and then . . .' He stopped. Slapped the bedside table so that dust jumped and a water glass hit the edge of a lamp with a high-pitched clink.

I stared at his somewhat skanky appearance. 'Blimey, there's loads of women out there complete pushovers then. Or do you have some kind of strange power of suggestion?'

The sun had faded now and we were lit only by the reflection on the snow. It was an odd golden light which accentuated his eyes and the atmosphere felt strangely heavy, as though we moved through something semi-solid, something which slowed our responses into deliberation. 'Yes.' He leaned in, touched my hair, his eyes never leaving mine. His hands were cold but even icier was the touch of the silver ring which almost stuck to my skin as his fingers drew my face in close. But his mouth was warm as it came down and it tasted of lust.

And I knew what he was doing. Recognised that need to block real life out with sex, to hide from the big and the scary and the sheer *perpetuality* of the ruthlessness and the guilt, behind physical reactions. It was how I got through the days, after all. His tongue flickered against mine and his teeth slid gently over the soft skin on the inside of my lower lip, raising an erogenous zone I hadn't even known I had. One of those long legs slid between my thighs, bringing his body in so close that I felt the bones of his hips against my flesh and the firm length of arousal around my navel.

It felt slightly weird to be inside the moment whilst knowing what was behind it all, but, dear God, he *was* gorgeous . . . I kissed back, reaching up until I could put my arms around his neck, pulling him into me, thigh to thigh and lip to lip, my body held against his chest so hard that I could feel his heart racing and the faint tremble of his ribs as he breathed in. He smelled musky and the taste of his mouth was pure sex.

He moved, trying, I think, to touch bare skin, but the movement unbalanced us. We toppled backwards, landing on the bed in a tangle of legs and arms and hair; I was underneath suddenly, lying on a duvet which smelled of his skin, staring up at his chest. From the way he was gazing down at me his usual blocking technique wasn't working for him this time — his expression was all distress and confusion.

'Well,' I said, to hear a normal, human sound.

'Well indeed.' He rolled off me, and lay flat on his back. His eyes looked a bit unfocussed. 'I'm sorry.' A flick of a look, 'I shouldn't have done that.'

I was breathless. 'Where did it come from? Not that I'm complaining, you understand, just . . . it was a bit intense.'

'Habit, I guess. Use sex to block everything else out. But I usually try for at least a little subtlety, not that . . .' He waved an arm, struck wordless. 'It was like pole dancing.'

'It was from where I was standing,' I said, and giggled. 'I bet you're really something with your clothes off, Mr Rhys.'

'Ha. Of course I am.' He turned towards me. 'I guess I was — I dunno. Overwhelmed by the moment? Uptight and in need of some contact? Because when you're using your body, you don't have to use your mind, and I really don't want to think at the moment.'

'Well, I'm here,' I said, almost as an instinctive response and then bit my tongue as the realisation blossomed slowly through my mind that I didn't want to be something he used to block everything out. Knowing what he was trying to do had blown my own life open in front of my eyes and left me staring at the wreckage.

'Yeah.' A fingertip traced the contours of my face. 'You are.'

The line we hadn't yet crossed trembled in the air between us. Part of me wanted to throw myself over, let gravity take me down, but that part was pure habit and the part that was looking down from above and starting to understand the suffering of this man held me back. There was a sense that something was changing.

'But this isn't what you want.' My voice sounded hoarse, dark, unlike me.

'No.' His hand fell away to rest casually against my hair.

'Thanks very much.' I didn't move away though.

'What I said just now, about short, intense relationships. And how there's nobody when you need someone. Understanding . . . I'm having a major rethink about it all, about my life.'

'Whilst lying on a bed with a woman.'

'As you say.' He smiled gravely. 'Still working on the fine details.'

'Well.' I sat up, trying not to let my inner confusion show. 'At least something has been resolved. God, I know I wished for excitement, but it could have been a bit more . . .'

'You wished for what?' He grabbed the change of topic and ran with it. 'Is this part of that spell thing you were making?'

Cautiously, waiting for the laughter, I told him about our wishes. 'Mine was for excitement. And, you have to admit, that was pretty exciting. So, maybe, that was my part of the spell working out for me.'

'It was really *that* exciting?' Kai propped himself up on one elbow. 'God. You should see me on a good day.' His legs stretched over the side of the bed and he was up, standing beside me, looking down. 'Come on.'

'That bastard streak really does run wide in you, doesn't it?' I complained, but I'd felt it too, our moment of closeness was over.

'It wouldn't be right, Holly. I think you felt it too, didn't you? That whatever we did here, it was never going to be enough to stop . . .' he cupped his hands over his eyes and bent his head into them for a second. 'When . . . just as I kissed you I saw your expression . . . You haven't always wanted it either, have you? You've gone along with it, played along with men . . . blocking stuff out. Hiding from the hurt but never managing to connect . . . and I don't want that from you. Not just to block out something . . .' He stopped talking and turned his face as he let his hands fall. 'I didn't want that,' he finished.

'Unfinished business,' I said, trying to lighten the mood and swinging up to stand next to him. 'Well known for causing impotence.'

'Cheeky mare.' He leaned past me to turn on the lamp, but carefully avoided touching me. 'Did I feel impotent to you?'

I didn't dare look at him. He'd felt anything but impotent pressed against me on that bed, and I was beginning to feel a touch ashamed of my response. *Why, though? He'd been offering, I'd been willing . . . hadn't I?* I hesitated a moment, driven by an impulse that was strange to me and then touched his arm. Not for the sake of touching, not to try to rekindle his interest in my body, but simply as a gesture of support, an attempt to comfort. 'Kai . . . it will be all right. Whatever you decide, it will be the right thing for you.'

This time he looked at me and I saw his eyebrows rise. 'You've got a lot of faith in me for a woman who hardly knows me, haven't you?'

'You seem to have made the right choices so far. Just don't let fear make you jump the wrong way this time.'

He gave a ragged laugh. 'Right choices? Yeah, that'll be why I'm sitting here in a house that looks like Aleister Crowley's weekend retreat pouring my heart out to a woman I've just met who has every right not to give a tuppenny shit about my life.' His voice was low and bitter. 'Right choices all down the line, Holly.'

I had to lift the mood. I knew how it worked, this kind of thing, and it circled downwards into scariness really quickly. Had to make a joke . . . 'Anyway, maybe you can get it up but you can't use it.'

I moved past him to get to the doorway, flinging the door open to surprise Cerys, about to knock.

'I'm going to pretend I didn't hear that,' she said. 'In fact, I'm going in for hypnosis tomorrow to get it wiped from my mind. Holly, your mobile's been ringing and ringing down here, on and off for the last twenty minutes.' She held out my phone. 'If someone's that desperate . . .'

'Probably Megan, calling from work to tell me British Home Stores has got a special on cushions again,' I said, looking through my Missed Call record. 'I've got no idea why she thinks I'd be interested.'

But it was my parents' number, in Aberdeen. I dialled it, and my mother answered immediately. 'Holly! You're there.'

'Well, actually I'm over here,' I said jokingly, but worried by her tone. 'What's up, Ma?'

Cerys and Kai looked at one another. He shook his head gently at her, I couldn't guess what she'd been about to say.

'Is Nicholas with you?'

'No.' Ridiculous, I know, but I looked around in case he might have been. 'He's with you. Isn't he?'

'He . . . he's stopped taking his medication. Yesterday he got a bit . . . oh, Holly, it was bad.'

I stared at the phone. Stopped? But he'd been so settled, so happy on them. 'Are you sure he's not . . . forgotten or something?'

'He'd been fine up until the day before yesterday. Then he just seemed to . . . have one of his moments, you know how he gets overexcited about things, a bit . . . silly. Anyway, he and your Dad had . . . words last night, and he went off. I thought he'd come in later and gone to bed, and we were out all day today. I thought he was sulking, you know how he can be, but when I went to call him for tea, he wasn't there, and then I thought . . .' her voice wavered. 'His mobile is switched off. I thought he'd be with you.'

I couldn't get my head around this. Nicholas definitely had enough meds with him, so why would he stop taking them, just like that? I mean, usually I phoned him or saw him every morning to check that he'd taken everything, but, surely, Mum would have made sure while he was up there . . . ? I had a moment of cold guilt. I'd virtually forgotten about Nicky while he'd been away; out of sight, out of mind . . .

'He might be trying to get here, Ma. I'll go and look in the usual places, don't worry. He'll probably be in in half an hour, starving hungry and terrified of the dark, if not with you then with me.'

I reassured her several times that Nicholas, even on one of his worst days, could manage to transport himself safely, then hung up. Cerys and Kai were watching me and they followed me down the stairs to the kitchen.

'I'll go and drive around,' Kai said. 'Do the local train station and the bus station and then try York. Cerys, you co-ordinate.'

'I can't ask you to do that.' I dragged my still-damp coat from the back of the chair where it had been steaming gently in front of the fire. 'It will be fine, he . . .' I swallowed the terrified lump in my throat. 'I can find him.'

Kai's hand intercepted my attempt to pull my coat on. 'It will be easier with two pairs of eyes,' he said evenly. 'We can cover twice as much ground.'

'Yes, but . . .'

'You need help, Holly. For fuck's sake, take it when it's offered.' Despite the urgency of his words his tone was still light and careful. 'And like you said earlier . . . I'm here. I'm offering.'

I hesitated, but the wind drove another fierce flurry of snow against the window and I gave in. 'I'll go up to the dual carriageway, in case he's hitching in,' I said. 'He might have got dropped off.'

'If I find him,' Kai paused, starting down the stairs, 'is there anything I should do?'

'Get him somewhere safe and call me. It's okay, Cerys, he's thirty-two.'

'Thank God, I thought you'd lost a child!' She clutched her heart. 'So he's a bit fragile, Nicholas, yes?'

'You could say that.'

We parted on the step, Kai to get the Jeep out, me to drive the treacherous ten miles back to Malton to search all the main road junctions. As he swung into his jacket and palmed the keys, I put a hand on his shoulder.

'You really don't have to do this.'

He looked at me darkly. 'I want to. And I can't sit here worrying about that letter. Looking for Nick will give me something to do.'

'Well, thanks.'

A pause. 'I guess sometimes we all need help. Let's just find him, Holly.' And then, as the night swallowed up his shape, 'Holly?'

'Yes?'

'I don't think any of this is the kind of excitement you wished for, is it?'

I turned my back and headed for the car.

CHAPTER FOURTEEN

I drove faster than was safe, terrified that Nick would have started travelling, got caught up in one of the many things that were liable to take his attention from the task in hand, and decided to sleep rough. The temperature was plummeting below freezing and the wind kept beating snow on the sides of my little car; even Ranulph Fiennes and his huskies would have gone home to bed on a night like this.

There was no sign of Nicholas. I drove up and down the motorway for a bit then parked in the Service Station and rang his mobile again, but it went straight to voicemail. I rang the flat he shared with several other lads, but no one was there either. As I was about to pull back out onto the almost deserted dual carriageway my phone rang and I snatched it up, my heart thundering. 'Nicky?'

'No, it's Kai. Are you all right?'

'Cold and my tyres seem to have lost all grip. You?'

'I'm in York, waiting for a train. Someone thought they saw a guy who looked a bit like Nicholas on the platform at Berwick getting on a train headed south. Where are you?'

I told him, clutching the steering wheel so hard that my fingers went grey. 'How did you find out about Berwick?'

'I put the word out. Being a journalist has its advantages, sometimes. The staff on Berwick railway station are very friendly, you know.'

'God, I hope it's him.'

'So do I. Look, the weather is pretty diabolical, why don't you get back to your place. One of us on the roads is enough tonight. It's getting dangerous and I've got the Jeep. Your car doesn't have four wheel drive, does it?'

'I consider myself lucky that it's got four wheels.'

'Then get home. There's nothing to be gained by being in a nine-car pile-up, and I'll keep looking until even the Jeep can't handle it any more.'

'Thank you.'

I heard the smile in his answer. 'That's all right. This is nicely distracting, if you know what I mean,' and he hung up.

I drove very carefully back to my house, where the heating was battling to keep the draughts at bay, drew the curtains and cried for a bit. I couldn't bear it. Couldn't bear the thought of Nicholas somewhere out in the cold, alone and confused. Or the awful sorrow that I'd seen on Kai's face at the idea of his birth mother trying to find him after thirty-something years. And a little bit of introspective horror at the realisation that what I'd really and truly felt on hearing Nicholas had disappeared, was *relief*.

I rang Megan on the house phone, leaving my mobile where I'd see its flashing Incoming Call light.

'Hey, Holl. Isn't it a filthy night? The snow is nearly over the top of my window ledge. I've got the phone in bed, it's the warmest place.'

A little bit of tension went out of me at the normality of her chat. She might not be the most practical person on the planet, but Meg was always there for me. 'Yeah, it's disgusting. I've got the heating going full blast and it's still chilly in here.'

'You remember that dog from the yard? It's so cold, and I didn't like the thought of him being out there with no shelter, so I let him into the passageway.' She spoke quickly, and I knew she was lying.

'He's on your bed, isn't he?'

'Well . . . Holl, he's so thin and so sweet, and I offered him a tin of stewing steak and he ate it so fast, I'm sure he's been starved, and I gave him a bath and he looked so grateful,' she said in a rush. 'I'll find out who he belongs to when the storm dies down.'

'Right now I'd settle for a mangy dog,' I muttered.

'Sorry?'

'Nothing.'

'Oh, and Vivienne wants us all over at hers tomorrow morning at nine, if the roads are clear enough. She said that it's time for us to perform some devotions, or something like that. To get the spell to start working.'

'Do you think the spell knows that there's two feet of snow lying? Don't you think it might cut us some slack?' I looked out into the darkness. The main road, which lay outside the front of my house, was empty. Every so often an enormous truck or snowplough would barge its way through the deepening snow, but there was no regular traffic and cars were parked up where my neighbours had got home early. I felt a lurch in my stomach. 'Anyway. I might see you there, if I can dig my way through.'

'The ploughs are out. Roads will be clear by morning.'

'Okay. Look, I'd better go.' Nicholas might be trying to get through on the landline. Or Kai. 'Stay safe.'

'You too, Holl. Oh, look what he's done! Get *down*! Or sit, or something . . .'

I checked the phone. No one had tried to ring. I went to the front window and stared out at the misleadingly soft whiteness. People died in this stuff. They lay down and they froze, or their cars went off the road, or they . . .

My mobile rang. Kai didn't waste time on pleasantries. 'I've got him.'

'Oh thank God.' I was afraid I might cry again. 'Where are you?'

'Back at mine. I picked Nick up, then went on to his doctor's, got him some emergency meds. By then we were nearer here than your place, and the roads are getting so bad I thought I'd better come back. You know, with Cerys and everything.'

'No, that's . . . it's fine. Is he . . . ? Can I speak to him? I ought to come and get him.'

'Don't worry about coming. He was pretty strung out when I got to him, but the doc gave him something and he's asleep now.'

'Oh, Kai.' I swallowed. I wanted to say something else but my throat seemed to have swollen. 'Kai.'

'Hey,' and his voice was soft. 'Everything's okay. Go to bed Holly. You can fetch Nicholas tomorrow, but don't hurry, wait until the roads are clear. He's fine here.'

My heart was calming down now. 'You are brilliant, Kai Rhys.'

A smile in his words. 'Yeah, yeah. See you.' And he put the phone down.

I had too much of the adrenaline of relief to want to sleep. I decided to watch TV for a bit, so I wrapped myself in a fleecy blanket and snuggled down on the sofa. There, life wasn't so bad, was it? My brother was safe, I had a plate of toast, warm toes and some trashy programmes, it was going to . . .

What was *that*?

It came again, an insistent kind of tap-tapping. I looked around the room. Was the snow leaking in through the roof? But I was downstairs. And besides, it was a harder, more brittle sound. I tweaked the curtains open to look out onto the road again. 'Holy shit!'

Outside my window was a dark shape, arm raised, making scratchy little noises against my front window. It was hideously misshapen, hunched and deformed, with a hooded head that looked far too big for the body. I stood, frozen, looking out at it as, very black against the white snow, it raised the arm again.

And this time it pushed back the hood and showed me its face.

'Aiden? *Aiden?* What the hell . . . ?' I dashed to the front door where Aiden, swathed in layer after layer of coat, fleece, scarf and really stupid hat, met me. 'Why didn't you just knock?'

'I didn't know if you had company.' He stamped his feet free from snow and took off an upper layer. 'I didn't want to intrude.' He nodded towards the street. 'Drove down this afternoon.'

I stared at him. He came into the house and was peeling off more and more layers, like an Ann Summers version of pass the parcel, and had got down to jeans and T-shirt. 'Stop now. Why are you here?'

'I wanted to see you. Wanted to talk.' He threw himself down on the sofa and stretched out. 'Okay?'

'Um,' I said, staring at him. Aiden was good looking in a put-it-on-the-mantelpiece way, small and fine-boned like an oversized china figurine. That had been the attraction, his looks. That, and the fact that he'd been delighted to meet a woman who wanted nothing more than the undivided attention of the contents of his jeans now and again. I'd never asked for dinner or flowers, or even for him to keep in touch — it was easy enough to find him when I wanted to, Scotland not exactly being coast-to-coast with film directors, whatever the tourist board might want you to think. I was surprised he'd managed to find my house; he'd only been here once, passing through on his way to London and stopping off for a night of, as I remembered it, the kind of sex you had to change the mattress after. Looking at him here, staring at me from under his dark-blond hair with a blissed-out expression, I wondered if, maybe, I'd been wrong to keep it going this long. 'Tea?' was all I could think of to say.

'I've brought whisky.' Aiden groped behind him in the pockets of the shapeless coat and brandished a couple of bottles.

I frowned at him. 'You know I don't like whisky.' I'd told him so often enough when we'd last met, but he suddenly seemed to regard whisky as absolutely necessary to all Scotsmen. Could have been worse, could have been haggis. 'What's wrong with tea, anyway?'

'Hey I spent the last five hours freezing my bollocks off in a car. Tea is not going to cut it. But if it's what you want . . . all the more whisky for me.'

When I went through to the kitchen to put the kettle on, he followed, like a restless dog. 'This is new?' He picked up my carefully colour co-ordinated toaster. 'Nice. Yellow to match the walls.' He unscrewed the top of the whisky bottle and started tipping it to his mouth.

'So, how come you're here?' I turned my back to him so he couldn't see my face. I was still shaken by his arrival.

'Like I said, I want to talk.'

'But, you were in the middle of filming!'

'We wrapped early.' He sounded confused for a moment. 'Not sure how, things were going to hell when you came up. But everything seemed to . . . click, somehow. So, I had these days free, and, I dunno, got to thinking about you.' He came up close behind me and wound his arms around my waist. 'Thinking about you a lot.' His mouth nuzzled my hair, then down to my neck. 'Next thing I knew I'm in the car, half way down the motorway.'

'But the snow,' I turned around in his embrace and his mouth rose to meet mine. Aiden always had the knack of pressing all my buttons, even if he did taste of Glenmorangie.

'It's only round here. Forty miles north, there's nothing.' He spoke against my skin. 'Forget the tea, Holl, let's go to bed.'

I must admit the clinch with Kai that afternoon had left me with a lot of spare desire sloshing about, and the relief that Nicholas was safe added to that. And once Aiden slid his hands up inside my shirt, it all got added to by his own particular appeal. 'Okay.'

'Why did you really come?' It was snug in my bed, listening to the lack of sound from outside. Even the neighbourhood cats didn't feel like fighting in this weather, and the lad from two doors down, who usually came home at three a.m., engine revving, had clearly decided that tonight was not the night to be cruising the streets in a souped-up Micra.

Aiden's eyes were very dark. 'Told you.' His fingers were tracing along my arm, raising little hairs. 'I wanted to talk to you.' Our faces were very close together, sharing the same pillow. The other one was on the floor somewhere, bounced from its moorings by vigorous sex, along with a set of handcuffs that Aiden had brought with him. I'd kept a hold on the duvet; this was no night for naked sleeping.

'You keep telling me that. But you haven't said anything apart from "oh God, do that again" since we got up here.'

'Maybe that's all I wanted to say.'

I smiled. His hair was fanned out behind his head so he looked less like something you'd want as an ornament now, unless your decorative tastes ran to debauched satyrs. Which they might, I'm making no judgements here. 'Want to say it again?' I slipped my hand down his torso, sliding it over the scatter of lighter hair that lay across his belly.

He grabbed my wrist. 'This whole shag-buddy thing. I think we should stop.'

'Ah. Right, noticing you waited until *after* we'd fucked like rabbits to say that.' I shook his hand off. 'A phone call usually suffices.'

He didn't smile. 'Holly, the other day . . . I suddenly realised my feelings for you had changed. I think I want more.'

'You *think*!' I sat up and freezing air shot under the duvet like a frightened ferret. 'Well, wouldn't it have been a good idea to be *sure*, before you came all this way?' I looked down on him, sprawled beside me, skin still flushed with sex. He *was* gorgeous. Why was every molecule in my body dumb with panic?

'Yeah, it was really weird, like, kinda romantic. There I was last week, middle of the afternoon and I'm just sitting in my van mid-shoot, minding my own business and suddenly . . . it was like the earth shifted, y'know? And I realised I wanted us to have a chance to be together. Properly, like a couple. That's why I'm chucking it all in. Giving up on the film stuff. Thought I'd get something round here, maybe an ad agency in York would take me on, with my background. Move in, take it from there.'

Now panic wasn't the word. Mindless, wordless terror was more like it. *Last week? When we did the spell? Oh, please, no . . .* 'But, Aid . . . we don't really know each other.'

'Know you well enough.' A lazy smile spread over his face. 'We could get married, d'you fancy that? Big white wedding. I saw your church over there, bit posh but it'd suit.'

'Hold on.' There had to be a TV show behind this. One of those that sets you up and films your inevitable downfall? 'Firstly, we've hardly ever had a conversation before, I think you've just spoken more words to me in one night than in the last three years. Secondly, yeah, the sex is great, fabulous, but there's more to a relationship than good sex, Aiden. And thirdly, I don't want to get married.'

The smile was still there. Wasn't he *listening?* 'Aw, come on, Holl. Give it a try. We make a cracking couple. All right, maybe marriage is a way off, but couldn't you stand coming home to this every night?' He waved an arm to indicate the bed and the tumbled bed things. 'Perfect antidote to workplace stress.'

'There's someone else.' I'd blurted out the words before I'd even thought them. 'Another man.'

Aiden frowned. This simply drew more attention to his sculpted cheek bones. 'But you're here, in bed with me. Where's he? Nowhere, that's where.'

'No, you don't understand. We're not sleeping together. But . . . he and I . . . it's . . .' And the memory of Kai, intense eyes and long body, came sweeping through. 'It's something I can't describe.'

'Och, Holly.' The smile was back. He really was very pretty, Aiden. Pretty and *bloody* persistent. 'But I can be indescribable too you know.' Fingers crept under the covers. 'And I'm here, you're horny — let's see how we go, shall we?'

Okay. So, attempt one to talk him down, epic fail. But . . . oooh, it had its compensations.

We woke next morning to almost clear streets. The ploughs had spent the night keeping the snowfall under control and although the pavements were heaped and cars were quite often blocked in by huge lumps of ice, driving itself wasn't a problem. My first thought was of Nicholas, and I rang the Old Lodge, the phone being answered by a slightly testy-voiced Cerys.

'It's still *dark*, Holly. *I'm* only up because I just performed my twenty-third trip to the loo and I'm waiting for my medal. Honest to God, I never knew there was that much liquid in the human body, I should be desiccated to the size of a walnut. And your brother isn't awake yet, probably won't be for a few more hours to be honest — when Kai brought him in he was so out of things that he thought I was you. I know drugs are supposed to be bad for you, but anything that makes a nine-month pregnant blonde look like a matchstick-skinny redhead is something I want to start taking as soon as possible.'

'So Nicholas is still in bed?'

She sighed. 'Yup. Come round mid-morningish. By then Kai should be up too and I should have passed my entire body-weight in fluids, so we can chat properly. Okay? I mean, I'd stop and chat now, but I think I might have to go to the loo again.'

Aiden pressed himself against my back and began whispering into my ear, and I barely had time to hang up in a civil way, but at least he made me breakfast when I told him I had stuff to do. He seemed to think it was work — which I suppose meeting up with Vivienne was, in a warped kind of way — and that this was a sign that I was already adapting to his moving in. 'I'll get my stuff shipped down,' he said, pouring fresh coffee from the machine I'd had since I moved in and never unpacked. 'My furniture can go in storage, until we can find a bigger place.'

I forced my boiled egg down a dry throat and reminded myself that this was Aiden McCullough, the Scottish Spike

Jonze, sitting here opposite me. Scourge of many a set, known for his exacting standards and his starlet shafting; at twenty-six still a wild child with a penchant for bondage and walking off set in high dudgeon. And he wanted to *marry* me? I'd only have been slightly more surprised if Barack Obama had popped up in my living room, told me Michelle was history, and how about a quickie before the next press call.

The freezing air of outside was the sweet air of freedom to me. 'I'll wait up for you, if you're gonna be late back,' Aiden called, waving me off, wearing only my dressing gown. 'But don't be too long, don't want these to get cold.' He shook the handcuffs and grinned his old, sexy grin as I fled for the car and starting digging it out with an energy borne of the dread that he might get dressed and try to come with me.

Vivienne looked a bit surprised to see me, which was perfectly understandable, it was only eight thirty. I sat in her living room on the, thankfully well-padded, couch, drank tea and jittered.

'So, you think the spell should work *faster*?' The cup rattled as I put it in the saucer. It had been one hell of a night. 'I think I might die.'

Vivienne raised her eyebrows. 'So it's working for you?'

I thought about Aiden and his sudden declaration. 'Well, I seem to have rather more excitement than usual, yes. Although some of it is pretty horrible.'

'Then you should have thought to wish for something a little more specific. I mean, some people's idea of excitement is a show at the theatre in Scarborough. It's not really the spell's fault that it doesn't know what you find exciting. What were you expecting, torrid sex?'

'Got that.' I thought of Aiden and gave a, not completely horrified, shudder.

'Death?'

Nicholas's disappearance had certainly made me scared that he was dead. 'That too.'

'Oh, I don't know then. A man who wants to take you away from everything and shower you with gifts?'

'Yes, and that.' Although I wasn't entirely sure it was gifts that Aiden wanted to shower me with. He still seemed to think that we could build a relationship entirely based on never getting out of bed.

Vivienne's eyes widened until I could see her rather inexpertly applied eyeliner. 'Well, I suppose it's only natural that the spell would work best for you. You supplied ingredients from the warlock's house, after all.'

'Is there a way to make it stop?'

A big tabby cat was eyeing my lap. I gave in and leaned back, but it sniffed at me in a generally disapproving manner and settled on the back of the sofa. 'Stop? Why would you want it to stop?'

'See above.' I closed my eyes. A night with Aiden rarely contained much sleep and I must have dropped off because the next thing I was aware of was Isobel and Eve arriving together in the Isuzu.

'Gosh, you must have been up early,' Isobel came in first and immediately started to sneeze. 'Damn.' Her head disappeared into her oversized handbag as she began the frantic search for a tissue. 'I ought to start keeping them up my sleeves.'

I gave her cardigan, Laura Ashley frock and old-lady ankle boots the once-over. 'No, don't,' I said.

Eve came in, limping. She'd lost a little weight, I thought, and changed her lipstick to a more flattering pale pink. She and Isobel seemed to be on opposite ends of the self-improvement see-saw. 'This cold plays havoc with the sciatica,' she said. 'Horrible.'

'Ah, Holly, you're awake.' Vivienne rattled in with a refreshed tea pot. 'Did you have a nice snooze?'

Of course everyone then looked at me as though I was about a hundred. 'Late night,' I explained.

'Torrid sex,' Vivienne put in, with a face that seemed to indicate that torrid sex was only one step up from ritualised buggery. 'Holly has been complaining about the results of the spell.'

The other two piled in, talking simultaneously. 'Results? You think there's been results?'

'What sort of results? I've not had anything yet. You are lucky, Holly.'

'Why would you complain? I'd settle for the milkman smiling at me.'

'*I'd* settle for the milkman's *horse* smiling at me.'

I waved a feeble hand. 'Let's just say that excitement isn't as exciting as you might think.'

There was a sudden commotion outside the cottage, and cats went flying round the room with their ears flat to their heads, like furry bullets. The cat flap rattled like a saloon door, and Megan entered, being dragged along by a grey panting creature with more teeth than I'd ever seen on display in a mouth that didn't belong to something in the Winners' Enclosure at Ascot.

'Oh my God, Little Red Riding Hood's gone native.'

'Don't, Holl. I didn't like to leave him all cooped up on his own. He needs a walk, and I thought, if we were going up the hill anyway . . .' The big grey dog sat in the middle of the room, scratched, and looked pleased with himself. 'I'm calling him Rufus.'

A lone cat, less adept at reading an atmosphere than the others, wandered in. There was a brief moment of total confusion and when it sorted itself out, I was standing on the sofa holding the teapot above my head. Isobel had a cat clinging to her shoulder like a Halloween witch costume, Eve had been shunted into a corner and Meg and Rufus were hurtling around outside the front door with her shouting 'Stop it! Down, boy!' ineffectually. Rufus, I noticed, was grinning. 'I'll keep him out here for a while,' she shouted, completing another circuit of the small front garden. 'Try to tire him out a bit.'

Isobel sneezed and the cat fell off. 'Perhaps . . . some fresh air?' she snuffled.

'Wait, I need to collect our workshop ingredients,' Vivienne bustled about looking as though she was doing something really important. Maybe she was, but I wasn't really convinced, after all, the spell seemed to have worked big time and we'd used some decidedly unorthodox make-dos for that. It hardly seemed necessary at this stage to have exactly the right shade of red for our broom handles.

Eventually, when Vivienne was satisfied, we set out for the hill. Eve stayed behind to keep the fire banked up for our return, pleading sciatica. I wasn't convinced. Her breathlessness seemed more than mere unfitness and her limp didn't look entirely sciatic either, but if she wanted to keep to her story, who was I to blow it out of the water?

Megan went first, dog-propelled. Isobel and I wandered up through the snow more slowly. There was no track, other than the double-skid marked out by Megan and Rufus, and the snow was deep enough to cascade over the tops of our boots.

'So, nothing happening for you on the "centre of the world" thing?' I asked.

She shook her long, chestnut hair. She had lovely hair, I noticed. If only she'd get a prescription for some antibiotics for the acne and wear something that didn't look hand-knitted by an elderly spinster, she'd be quite pretty. 'Nope. I did think that a man was looking at me in the library the other day.' She sighed.

'Well, that's a start.'

'No, it turned out he'd lost his glasses and thought I was his mother.' Another sigh. 'Maybe nothing will happen. Ever. And I'll stay here, living in Malton and working in the hospital, and spending every evening with Mum and Dad telling me how I should join a club to meet more people . . .' She sounded angry. Or as angry as she ever sounded, which was not very.

'Look, the spell seems to be working for me and I wish it wasn't. So don't worry too much if nothing happens, it looks like nothing is the better option.'

Isobel shrugged under her ugly knitted coat. 'I'd just like something to compare nothing to. I've never even . . . you know, with a man. I've only been kissed once, and that was by mistake.'

'By mistake? How can you get kissed by mistake? Did he fall onto your face?'

She smiled. 'It was dark. He thought I was someone else. Story of my life, I suppose.' She looked around the hill top. 'I hope those men on bikes won't come back.'

'It's broad daylight and there's two feet of snow. I don't even think you can ride a motorbike in snow, can you? And we'll see them coming for miles, the air is so clear.'

It was, clear and ringing with cold. The distant moors stood like white shoulders shrugging into the bright blue sky and a circle of rooks blew above the hill like a smoke ring. 'Are we bonkers do you think?' Isobel asked in a quiet voice. 'Doing magic and wishing for things we'll never have?'

I gave her a quick, awkward hug. 'At least we're doing *something*. Oh look, Megan is slowing down. She's going to be really fit by the time she finds that dog's owner.'

Meg and Rufus bounced to a collective halt at our usual spot. She looked sweaty and breathless, her top had come untucked and she'd had to start carrying her hat. Her gloves were scattered with snow where she'd kept tripping over and the snowline was somewhere up near her thighs. '*Sit*,' she insisted. Rufus grinned again and started digging. 'I think he's part lurcher.'

'More like part wobbler.' I patted the grey head and then had to wipe my hand on my jeans.

'He's a bit sticky. I don't know why. But he's very good natured.'

'I can see that.'

Vivienne joined us and got her breath back. 'Here. Candles. Push them into the snow, then light one each.' We managed, eventually, to get the candles to light. They kept toppling over in the snow and extinguishing themselves with sad little hisses

113

but we persevered until a small ring of fluttering flame punctu-ated the hilltop. 'Now this.'

'What is it?' I stared at the bag of dark liquid in Vivienne's hand. 'It looks like blood.'

'It . . . well, yes, I suppose it is, *technically*.' Vivienne actu-ally looked a little ashamed.

'*Technically?*'

'It's from the butcher.'

The bag swayed from her fingers. It seemed unnaturally swollen, as though the blood inside was treacle-thick. 'From his shop, or him personally?'

Vivienne ignored me and poked a hole in the corner of the bag, using the result like an icing pen to draw dark crim-son circles around each of the candles. When the snow was ringed with gore she stood back and nodded satisfaction, like Delia Smith finishing off a Gothic Christmas cake. 'Now.' Out came the notepads and pens again.

'We don't have to make another potion, do we?' Megan anxiously tried to juggle her notepad and Rufus's lead. 'My system has only just got back to normal.'

Rufus ate her pen.

'No. We write our wishes down and then use the smoke from the candles to send them skyward.'

'Like writing to Father Christmas!'

'Yes, Megan. Exactly like that.'

I wrote my wish but decided that sending it skyward might draw fate's attention to me even more. So I balled it in my hand and gave it to Rufus, while everyone else was burning theirs, and as their smoke plumed upwards, my wish went the opposite way, dribble-assisted.

'Your candle burned white,' Vivienne observed. 'It's a sign that your wish is near completion.'

It was actually nearer digestion, but I couldn't say that. I nodded and tried to look wise, and like someone who was in possession of a nearly-completed wish. And then I wished that

I'd wished my wish *was* completed, but it was too late because Megan had taken my pen.

'And now let's join hands, close our eyes and make a silent appeal to the earth to grant us what we wish.' Vivienne groped for my hand. I held hers loosely, sure that her palm was still slightly tacky with blood, with Megan's left hand in mine. She was still holding Rufus's lead, so her hand kept getting tugged away. Isobel gripped Megan and Vivienne's spare hands and we all closed our eyes. Far away I heard seagulls calling and the sound of snow falling from overloaded branches in the wood beyond. Underfoot it creaked and whistled and fell into my boots with occasional inrushes which dampened my socks.

'Feel yourselves,' Vivienne whispered, and I tried, unsuccessfully, not to giggle. She opened one eye and glared at me. 'Feel yourselves rooting into the earth, as part of the planet. Experience the cold, the snow, the wind. Hear the voices of the beasts, for they are part of the natural order.'

Unfortunately, just then our domestic part of the natural order let out an enormous, deep bark which made us all jump. I opened my eyes to see Rufus standing outside our circle of joined hands, straining his lead to its furthest extent and staring over the crest of the hill. His hackles were up.

'What . . .' I had time to say, before the Land Rover came out of nowhere at us and everything got a bit Scooby-Doo. Rufus ran towards it, barking hysterically, and a dog the size of Rufus barking hysterically is not something you want to get in front of. Megan yelled and tried to grab his lead, but he slipped it through her fingers and took off, heading almost under the wheels.

I looked up at the Land Rover and saw something jutting from a window. Something black and slightly shiny.

'They've got a gun!' I yelled, dashing forward to grab at Megan, but missing as she ran after Rufus. 'They've got a fucking *gun*!'

Isobel and Vivienne looked frozen. They just stood as the Land Rover drove in a wide circle around us with Rufus in, well, dogged pursuit, still barking. The windows were dense with water vapour, but I was sure I could make out three figures inside, a driver, a passenger and . . . oh God, this sounded so ridiculous, an armed man. They were vague, smeary shapes, and all seemed to be wearing dark clothing.

'Get out of here,' I pulled at Vivienne until she looked at me. 'Get down the hill. You too, Isobel.'

The Land Rover performed a sharp turn, slid several yards and then came back at us. Rufus slithered, trying to turn as well, but skidded out of the circuit, paws raking at the snow for purchase as the driver gunned the engine and drove between Isobel and me, cutting us like a herd of cattle being prepared for a roping.

A window wound low. 'Satan's whores!' a male voice shouted. 'We don't want your kind here. Go take your demon lovers and your black bitch and get out of Barndale!'

Black bitch? I opened my mouth to ask what the hell they were talking about, and then realised they must mean Megan.

I found I'd ducked, which was ridiculous, since guns can just as easily aim downwards. 'It's a free country,' I screamed back. 'We're not doing any harm.'

The Land Rover came to a halt. Now I could see inside through the wound-down window, three men wearing full-face balaclavas and baseball hats, like hoodies on a skiing holiday. The one in the passenger seat was holding a shotgun loosely out of the window, finger resting threateningly on the trigger. 'We *said* we don't want your kind here. It's not open to debate.'

Okay, they wore disguise, but there was no disguising the voices: it was Big Ginge and the Moustache Master. The other man, the one with the gun, didn't speak. 'So, what, you kill people you don't want in your woods? You must have bodies stacked up to the rafters.'

We'd not been shot yet, that was my thought. They were trying to frighten us. All right, they were doing a good job there.

'Don't.' Megan had managed to grab Rufus by the collar and was using all her bodyweight to drag him along. 'Don't antagonise them Holly. Let's go.'

'Yeah, you listen to your playmate,' sneered one of the balaclavas. 'Even the wog has more sense than you.'

I'd faced down all sorts of people in the past. People who'd made wisecracks about Nicholas's behaviour, about my procession of men, there wasn't an insult I hadn't heard. 'They're bullies. How dare they try to drive us out, we're not doing anything wrong.'

I looked over at Vivienne and Isobel. Vivienne was shocked a blueish pale and her make-up stood out on her skin. Isobel looked frozen in mid-flight, half turned to head down the hill but obviously not wanting to leave us alone.

Then the Land Rover door opened. The guy with the gun jumped lightly down onto the snow, gun still held forward, fingers still wound near the trigger. Rufus growled but didn't bark; I think that was because Megan had him in a headlock.

'Do you want us to show you what happens to girls who don't do as they're told?' His voice was soft, but it wasn't only the fact he was wearing a mask that made him threatening, it was his whole body. The way he stood as though he had absolute control of the situation. 'Naughty girls get punished,' and he swung the gun up casually to hip level, pointing at Rufus. 'And the Devil's whores get what whores deserve.'

Now was *so* not the time to give him a lecture on the rights of women. I leaped away from him and ran, heading down the hill and hoping the others were following. Rufus took his cue from me and broke into a gallop, Megan overtook me half way down the hill on a bow-wave of snow. Isobel and Vivienne slipped and slithered behind me, I could hear their silent panic in the way they refused to let the snow impede their progress and leaped through drifts that had been detoured on the way up.

'Ring the police,' I gasped as we broke through Vivienne's door and huddled together in the living room, one eye on the window in case the Land Rover had followed us down.

'What on earth . . . ?' Eve came in from the kitchen, comfortably aproned and motherly, carrying the teapot like the antithesis of what had just happened.

'For starters, three men in a Land Rover waved a gun at us. Threatened us with . . . well, he wasn't offering an evening at the cinema and boxes of Maltesers, was he? And one of them called Megan . . . well, a name.'

Vivienne leaned forward to catch her breath. She didn't even raise a murmur at Rufus climbing onto the sofa. 'And what do we say when the police arrive? We were taking a stroll up on the hill? We left the candles there. It wouldn't take a detective genius to work out we'd been performing magic.'

'Yeah? It's not forbidden in the Court of Human Rights, you know. So, we lit a few candles, big deal. We didn't sacrifice babies and shag a goat, did we?'

Eve limped over and pushed a hot mug of tea into my hand. 'I understand what Vivienne is trying to say, Holly.'

'Well I wish I did! In what universe do men get away with threatening women?'

'Holly.' Eve patted my hand. 'If we ring the police and tell them that three men in a Land Rover had a shotgun and called you names . . . well, I hate to say it, but this is the countryside. And people go out shooting all the time. All *we* can say is that three unidentified men made threats. And if you are absolutely *sure* that it wasn't poachers warning you off . . .'

'If they were poachers, then . . .' I suddenly thought about the men lurking in the woods near the Old Lodge, and the brace of pheasants, dripping blood. 'I suppose they could have been. But they knew about the spells.'

'They'd been watching, I'd guess. Judging the right moment to have a go at you. Out here poaching is a way of life for some people.'

'Yeah, right up with hare coursing and incest.'

'But you see what I'm saying? It could open a whole can of worms if you report it. Poachers guard their patch. They were warning you off so you couldn't see anything which might get them identified.'

'But . . .' I looked around. Everyone was nodding. 'But, Meg. You heard what they were calling you.'

Megan rubbed absently at Rufus's scruff. 'What, "black bitch"? God, Holl, I get worse than that behind the counter in British Home Stores. You should have heard what this woman said once, when we didn't have the pelmets that she'd ordered. Bloody hell, I thought she was going to sell my ass into slavery or something.'

'But you aren't even . . .'

She sighed. 'Dad's Nigerian, Holl. Get over it.'

Vivienne came over, smoothing her hair into place. 'And the police might get a bit curious about those candles, they could ask some awkward questions about exactly what we were doing up on the hill. Do you really want everyone to know that you practise witchcraft? Everyone you work with? Your family?'

I sat down beside Rufus. 'It's all a bit of fun. People will understand that, won't they? That we just got together for some chanting and mucking around with a few spells?'

She looked at me, slightly sadly. 'But there was blood. We used blood to concentrate the spell . . . I can't believe I was so *ridiculous* . . .'

'But it was only animal though, wasn't it?' *Please God, Vivienne, say yes . . .*

'Of course. But can't you see the angle that the newspapers will take, that we were fornicating with The Master, drinking blood and dancing naked under the full moon.'

I glanced dubiously out of the window. 'In this?'

'All right, maybe not the dancing naked thing. But you see what I mean? Would you find it easy to get work if that's what people thought you did in your spare time? Because I don't want to jeopardise my wish by having that kind of reputation.'

'Nor me,' Megan piped up. The tea and warmth had made her skin flush. 'They scared us, that was all.'

'No, that wasn't all. They *threatened* us. With a shotgun. That goes a little bit beyond the Hammer House of Horror scary, it goes into the outright terrifying category.' I looked around the room. All the women were looking somewhere else. Isobel and Megan were making an unnecessary amount of fuss of Rufus, Vivienne was stirring her tea with undue attention and Eve was poking the fire. 'So you all think we should forget it?'

'Not *forget* it. Ignore it. Be more careful in future, perhaps. More circumspect, certainly. Maybe find somewhere else to perform the rituals.'

'No,' Vivienne looked up at that. 'It must be Dodman's Hill. That traditionally has the most earth-energies; it's on a ley line, and we need all the power we can muster to get the spell to work.'

'Oh come on! What's more important, some so-called magic or the possibility of getting our heads blasted off by a rapist wannabe?'

Their silence spoke for them, but then Vivienne piped up. 'Don't forget, Holly, just because the fulfilment of your wish has left you disappointed, the rest of us are still waiting. No one here wants to do anything to prevent the working of the spell.'

I shook my head. 'You're all bloody insane,' I said, and walked out.

CHAPTER FIFTEEN

I drove round the outside of Barndale Woods to get to the Old Lodge. The track down which Kai had driven me through the middle of the woods looked as if even a Jeep would struggle to get down it now. Pockets of snow lay, broken by bare stretches where the trees grew so close together that even snowflakes couldn't get between them. It gave the ground a skewbald look. I parked on the road and trekked the quarter mile in.

Cerys came to the front door, breathless and led me through to the kitchen, where Nicholas and Kai were sitting eating toast together, looking remarkably domesticated. 'And here we have the males of the species,' she announced in a bad David Attenborough imitation, 'conducting their bonding session with food prepared by the female.'

'You offered.' Kai spread Marmite on another slice.

'I offered Nicholas toast, not you.'

I pulled out a stool and sat next to my brother. 'You had Ma and Dad quite panicked yesterday.'

A quick flick of his head. 'You aren't angry with me, are you Holly?' He'd snatched the toast up and was cradling it against him as though unsure if I would allow him to take another bite. 'I don't want you to be angry . . .'

I forced my voice to syrupy consistency, although Kai was frowning at me. 'No, not angry, of course not. I was worried, that was all. Why did you stop taking your meds?'

'I just wanted to see. Wanted to check that they were working and to see what life felt like without them.' He looked remarkably normal this morning, slightly more fey than usual in clothes obviously borrowed from Kai, judging by the number of times the legs of his jeans were rolled up. He began eating the toast again, little snatched bites, like an animal that's just been released from captivity and isn't quite sure how long the freedom will last.

'Not voices again, telling you to stop?'

'No. More like . . . you remember when the OCD cut in big time? That kind of compulsion, like I couldn't *not* not take them.' He smiled, his grey eyes tired and slightly drugged. 'I'm sorry I freaked you, Holl. I was pretty freaked myself. I got this itching under my skin to be back here, that's why I got on the train.'

A hot urge to smack him rushed down my arms. 'I knew I should have put a note in with your packing to get Mum to double check you were taking them!'

He spread his hands wide in an expression of bafflement. 'Sorry, Holl.'

Cerys rolled her eyes. 'For God's sake, Holly.' With difficulty she hoisted herself onto the stool at Nick's other side. 'How old is he?'

'Nick? Thirty-two. Eighteen months older than me.'

'And you did his packing? Were you some kind of doormat in a previous life?'

'He didn't ask me to.'

Kai pushed a mug of tea at me and pulled a face. 'I think Cerys is trying to say . . .'

'Shut up Kai. I can talk for myself. I think you baby Nicholas, Holly. Surely there's nothing stopping him packing his own suitcase? I mean, being mentally a bit kah-kah doesn't

122

prevent you from checking you have clean underwear, does it?' She turned to Nicholas, then frowned. '*Does* it?'

Nicholas hadn't even broken eating-stride, even though her voice was bordering on the tetchy. If *I'd* spoken like that, he'd have been halfway to locking himself into his bedroom before I'd got as far as 'suitcase'.

'Well, no. But I like to keep an eye on him. Make sure he's taking his meds, that kind of thing.'

'Why?' Cerys stared around Nicholas at me.

'Why?' I repeated stupidly.

'Yeah. Why? Demonstrably he doesn't always take them, but that's up to him, isn't it? Surely, by checking up on him all the time and mummying him, he's never having to rely on himself for anything.' She looked at Nicholas. 'Do you often not take your drugs?'

'Not . . . really.' Nicholas swallowed the last of the toast and began picking at the table top. 'I mean, sometimes I don't take them because . . . well, just because. But it's nice, really it is, Cerys. When things get bad it's scary and I can't . . . can't always see my way out. Holly talks to me and makes sure I don't do anything stupid.'

Cerys looked triumphant. 'Well, don't you think that might be the reason you can't get a girlfriend? Because the role is already taken by your sister? And, I notice, we've just been talking about you and you haven't even *thought* to say "oy, I'm sitting right here, you know".'

'It's nice here,' Nicholas suddenly announced. 'It's like real life.'

'Doesn't get much realer than this,' Kai agreed. 'I'm off to Leeds. Anyone coming? Cerys?'

'Oh God, no. I can't bear the thought of having to sit down for an hour. Anyway, Nicholas and I have decided to watch Jeremy Kyle and heckle, haven't we?'

Nick slipped down off his stool. His borrowed T-shirt hung nearly to his knees and made him look about seven. 'Yep.'

Kai looked at me. 'Holly? Trip to Leeds?'

'I ought to get home and get some contracts in the post.' Then I thought of Aiden, lurking around my house with his laptop full of wedding lists. 'Although I probably could take some time off.'

'And I'd like the company.' He stretched and I tried not to notice his flat stomach become visible at the gap between jeans and shirt. 'We'll be back by lunchtime. Anything happens . . .'

'Yeah, yeah, I'll call the hospital. Don't worry, Nicholas can take care of me.' Cerys put her arm through my brother's. 'We'll spend the day in front of the TV yelling at the white trash, okay?'

Nick gave her a look that only fell a little short of adulation. 'I've never watched Jeremy Kyle before. I haven't got a television,' he said.

'Oh, you're in for a treat then.' She dragged him through to the living room, leaving Kai and I standing together in the kitchen.

'Do you really think I mother him?'

Kai shrugged. 'Honestly? Yes, I do. And I notice that you modify your behaviour around him. How long's that been going on?'

'You and Cerys don't understand how he can be. He needs someone to make sure he pays his rent and gets to the hospital for check-ups and stuff. Otherwise he'd float along, and then he'd have one of his bad days and . . .' I shuddered. 'And he doesn't like confrontation, or shouting,' I finished.

Kai pulled the battered old jacket on. 'Have you ever thought about what it's doing to you?'

I stopped, caught in the act of licking crumbs off my moistened finger. 'To *me*? It isn't doing anything to me. I'm just helping my brother to cope, that's all.'

He made a complicated face, raised eyebrows and twisted mouth, all without meeting my eye as he did up the jacket. 'You seem very good at not showing emotion, and I'd guess he's trained you into that. Even when . . . remember when that guy fired over your head? When I turned up you were obviously shocked stupid and halfway to screaming hysterics, but you wouldn't let go, wouldn't break down, even though it was only Cerys and me there, and we wouldn't have minded. You force yourself not to show anything in case Nick gets upset, and suppressing feelings like that isn't good.' Another twisted mouth. 'Trust me on that one.'

'All right, Freud.'

'I'm serious, Holly. You look after Nick at the expense of yourself, and that's wrong.'

I pulled my shoulders up around my ears, felt the ever-present tension down my spine. 'He needs me.'

'Have you ever given him the chance to cope alone?'

I stared at him. 'What, you mean cut him adrift?'

'No, no. I mean keep a watching brief from a distance. Check up on him, by all means, but do it over the phone, or meet up every few days. You see him every day at the moment, don't you?'

I shrugged. 'Mostly.'

'Well, like Cerys says, maybe that's stopping him from taking responsibility for himself.' He held up a hand to forestall my complaint. 'It's okay, Holl, I know. He's genuinely ill, he can't and shouldn't be expected to function like everyone else. But there are support networks you know, for people like Nicholas, it doesn't all have to fall on your shoulders, and maybe letting other people take over a bit will help him too. They can guide him into more independent living and thinking, so that he stops expecting you to pre-empt his moods and troubles.' He stood still, hands on the worktop. 'Although, of course, it would mean that you'd lose your excuse.'

'What are you on about now?' He had his back to me so he couldn't see my carefully prepared expression.

'You know.'

'Do I? God, I'm doing a good job of not letting myself in on my own thoughts.'

125

Kai turned. 'You use Nicholas to keep from having to build a real relationship. You encourage his dependence on you so that you can put him first, leaving, I must say, anyone else out there in the cold. Sex is so much easier, isn't it, Holl, than having to try?'

'There speaks the voice of experience.'

He gave a half-shrug and pushed his hands through his hair. 'Yeah. That's how I know. Don't leave it too long though, to let someone in. You could find yourself like me, deep in the shit with no one to talk to.'

'You've got me,' I said, small-voiced.

'Not really I haven't, have I?' He stepped closer, put his hands on my shoulders. 'You've locked yourself away from everyone to save your brother from anything that might upset him. I know how it feels, Holl, to not let things out, to keep secrets and be afraid of consequences, but I'm starting to . . . Look, it's fine to allow yourself to fall. You don't have to always be in charge, Holly. If you let yourself go, you might find something else comes in. Some *real* emotion. Or have you spent so long keeping everything calm and *un*emotional that you don't really know how that's meant to go, *hmm*?' He dropped his hands from me and moved away, casually, tucking them into his jacket pockets.

I sighed. I was a bit too tired for all this psychoanalytical chat this morning. 'Okay, Kai, give it a rest,' I said. 'Will Nick be all right here this morning?'

'Goes without saying, he can stay here as long as he likes. He's really hit it off with Cerys, and I think he's been a bit lonely in that flat of his. Blokes he shares with think he's a weirdo, you know that?'

No, I thought, I didn't know that. And I saw him *every day*. Perhaps they were right, seeing so much of Nicholas wasn't doing any of us any favours. I'd got too close to be able to see any changes in him. 'Okay, thanks.'

'Although, she'll be back off to Peterborough in the next couple of days. Merion rang and the flat is just about back to normal.'

'Oh. I'll miss her.'

'Yeah.' Kai looked around the multi-gargoyled kitchen, which was clean and contained piles of ironed shirts. 'Me too.'

On the way to the Jeep I told him about the men in the Land Rover with the shotgun and he froze.

'Shit, Holly.'

'I said we should have reported it but the others . . .'

'Were right. Don't go getting involved on this one, Holl. I told you to stay clear of that place, didn't I?'

'Yeah but, you were doing all International Man of Mystery at the time. Why should I stay away from anywhere I want to be?'

'Because of men with guns? Just a suggestion.'

'Yeah, but . . .'

'What is it with you? You're threatened, then run off the hill and all you can think of is how indignant it makes you? Why not concentrate on how dead it could make you?' Now he bent to unlock the Jeep.

'Who are they?'

'Get in the Jeep.'

'Not until you tell me who they are.'

'Holly, I'm going to Leeds. Where I have to be. You are coming along for the ride. Which you don't have to do. You refuse to get in and I'll drive away without you, all right?'

'Oh for heaven's sake.' I got in, but flouncily, so as not to let the side down. Kai looked across at me. The dark of the garage made him look saturnine and inscrutable, he had his hair scooped back so his face seemed to be all eyes. 'What?'

'Are you really not scared?'

'No. Leeds isn't that far and you're not a bad driver.'

'Of the guys on the hill.'

'This is Yorkshire, not Deliverance country. As far as I'm aware, armed gangs of vigilante yokels don't have the right to shoot unarmed walkers.'

'They might do it anyway.'

'What, for the hell of it? Nah. They're trying to be big scary men. Probably got one testicle between the lot of them, and they breed pit bull terriers or Rottweilers, so they can go out with them on short chain leads and feel like Real Men.'

Kai put his foot down. 'What does that make me, then? I haven't even got a guinea pig.'

Muddy snow sloshed up the side of the Jeep. 'Oh you must be a Real Man, you wear a leather jacket.'

'That noise was my ego going down the drain.'

'And shag women's best friends.'

'Ah. I was hoping you'd forgotten about that.'

'Where in Leeds are we going, anyway? They've got some brilliant shops, there's a Harvey Nicks and everything.'

Kai's expression went a bit twisted. 'I'm going to find this PI. Find out why he's looking for me, find out who sent him.'

I watched him drive for a bit. The Jeep pulled like a fresh horse so he had to keep both hands on the wheel, but he didn't need to hold it as tightly as he did. 'And what if it *is* your mother?' I kept my voice gentle. 'Do you want to meet her?'

'I thought about finding her the day Cerys was born. She was a grandmother and she didn't even know it, and I thought then she didn't *deserve* to know. But then when Cerys got pregnant and I thought, what if she'd decided to go away and have the babies and not say anything? How would I feel, my own daughter having a life like that and me not knowing?' He shook his head. 'I don't know. Curiosity is a bitch.'

'I'll come with you, if you want.'

There was a moment's silence, then a hand came off the wheel and grasped mine in a quick clasp. 'Thanks.'

Fighting the urge to wind my fingers through his, I kept my eyes front. 'So. Will there be time to go to Harvey Nicks do you think?'

'You just spoiled a moment there, d'you know that?'

'I'm not sure I need any more moments. My life seems to consist of moments. And, hey, have you noticed how there's hardly any snow now? Aiden said that it all seemed to be centred around Malton, and looks like he was right. We're, what, twenty miles away and it's only a scattering.'

Kai raised an eyebrow. 'Aiden?'

'Look, you've got your shagging-of-the-best-friends, I've got Aiden.' I remembered Aiden standing on my doorstep, priapic in my M&S dressing gown. 'Can we not talk about him.'

'Is he part of your wish-come-true excitement?' He had both hands back on the wheel now, and his eyebrows drawn down together in a frown, although he hadn't looked at me.

'I don't know. No. I didn't wish for anything like *that* kind of excitement.'

'And what kind is that?'

'The kind that comes with handcuffs, thinks sex is enough to make a couple compatible, and has suddenly taken to drinking enormous quantities of whisky,' I said faintly.

'That's exciting, is it?' Kai swung the Jeep into a turn. 'Sounds more like an overgrown teenager to me. Does he slam doors and shout "whutevah!" when you disagree with him? But then, I've been there too, I'm not one to talk, particularly with the "enormous quantities of whisky" thing.'

'You don't look like a drunk to me.' My voice was even fainter now.

'I'm a journalist, Holly, not a saint. In fact, I think journalism is the antithesis of sainthood, but I don't drink so much these days. Getting older, you see. Whisky gives me a headache.'

'Right.'

A sudden, unexpected smile. 'What? Did you think I was all squeaky clean, teetotal and dedicated to doing good?'

'It's just . . . all your talk about exposing frauds and freeing underage girls . . .'

'Vodka'd out of my head when I started out,' he admitted cheerfully. 'But I hadn't had much of a life up till then. I was growing up and getting away from everything I'd ever known, which was pretty much mountains, sheep and occasional beltings, so I did go off the rails a bit. I've calmed down a lot now.'

'Oh. Good.'

'Well, I don't want to set my grandson and granddaughter a bad example, do I?' He leaned closer, across the handbrake. 'Not if there's anyone watching, anyway.'

'Are you winding me up?'

He laughed. 'Maybe. A bit. It's just that you've only ever really seen me here, with Cerys, being grown up and responsible. I'm only thirty-six, Holly. I'm not ready for settling into Grandad things, all mint humbugs and dodgy knitwear . . . I'd like you to see me a bit more as I am.'

'Oh yes? And how is that?'

He thought for a while, tapping the silver thumb ring against the steering wheel in a salsa rhythm. 'Actually, now I come to think about it, I'm not entirely sure.'

'Well then.'

The office in Leeds was in The Headrow, city centre, not the lock-up on a trading estate that I'd been expecting. It was surprisingly salubrious and, while Kai proved his identity to the satisfaction of the smartly dressed receptionist (another surprise, I thought all PIs worked alone and the dames were strictly decoration), I read Country Living magazines. It was like a private health clinic.

Eventually a door opened and Kai was ushered into another office. He motioned at me to stay where I was, but I could see he was shaking as he went inside.

I chatted to the receptionist. It's always been part of my job, getting on with people, and I long ago learned that the quietest, most overlooked people are often the ones with the story to tell, particularly when they are the ones that open the mail and answer the phone. Her name was Laura and she'd been doing the job for five years, and when we'd got over the fact that I didn't know Brad Pitt or Johnny Depp, and she'd got out the biscuit tin, I found out quite a lot more about the letter Kai had received.

'All done over the phone,' Laura dunked a chocolate biscuit. 'The lady didn't want to travel.'

'So, when did she get in touch?'

'Dunno. Quite a while back, I think. You'd have to ask Donald. I talk to so many people who are looking for someone . . . It's sad sometimes. I mean, Donald is good, but . . . you can hear it in their voices, they know the person never wants to speak to them again, but they still want him to find them.'

'And it's Kai's mother?'

Laura wrinkled her nose. 'Can't tell you. Sorry. Confidentiality and all that,' she said in a voice loud enough to have been heard in the adjoining office, but followed it by nodding vigorously until the top of her biscuit fell in her tea.

I looked at the closed door. The silhouetted dark shape that was Kai was visible through the frosted glass. He looked hunched, as though he had his head in his hands.

'Poor bloke,' I said.

'Tasty though.' Laura grinned at me. 'You two . . . you know, a couple?'

'No,' I said. 'He's a friend. Well, sort of. His daughter and I are friends, he's . . . Do you know, I'm not sure what he is?' Yes, he'd kissed me like he'd wanted to rip my clothes off, and although we'd not got down to the horizontal tango we'd certainly managed more than a few steps of the vertical rhumba.

'I see. You're, like, the nanny.'

Before I could correct her misconception, the office door opened and Kai came out looking as though someone had yelled in his face. He was holding a folded piece of paper.

'Let's go, Holly,' even his voice was pale.

'Good luck,' Laura whispered. 'And don't forget, they *always* fall for the nanny.'

I could feel Kai shivering like a wet dog. As we walked through the crowds to get back to the car he kept stopping, turning his head, following people with his eyes and after a while I worked out that he was watching parents with children.

Mothers, specifically, pushing overloaded buggies or chatting to toddlers whose normal wide-eyed overactivity had been pushed to almost unbearable levels by the Christmas lights hanging overhead and the Santa-laden shop windows.

I touched his arm. 'You all right?'

'I don't . . . shit.' A tear found its way down one cheek and he smoothed it away with the sleeve of his jacket. 'C'mere.'

In a narrow alleyway between two shop doorways, I took the paper he handed me. 'What is it?'

He shook his head, closed his eyes and breathed deeply. 'Read it.'

It was a photocopy. Carefully neat, with very faint lines ruled across the page.

To my son, I don't even know what they called you but in my head you were always David.

I don't expect you to understand anything about my reasons for trying to find you. I don't even think I have the right to tell you what those reasons are, but I know that if you're reading this letter, I have at least got this close to you and that means more to me than I can ever say.

I love you. I never stopped loving you, and I think about you every day. Please, if it is possible for you to forgive me to any extent, let me see you. Once, that's all I ask. I realise that distance may make this impossible but even a photograph would help.

My darling David, you are ever in my thoughts.

Your mother.

I looked at Kai. He was still very pale and his eyelashes were spiky with moisture. 'What do I do, Holly? *What do I do?*' The poised, hard, journalistic facade was gone, cracked into a million pieces with the splinters reflected in his eyes. He hugged the leather jacket around himself and stared down at his feet. 'I don't even know what I feel now. I hated her so much all those years, and now *this*,' he flipped the letter I still held. 'David,' his voice was cracked and far away. 'My name was David.'

132

'Come on Kai.' I grabbed his hand and pulled him out of the alley. 'Let's go home. You need to think about this properly, and here is not the place.'

Jerkily I led him back to the car park. He still kept stopping to look at mothers, staring to such an extent that one or two gathered their children to them, halting their pre-Christmas wonder with a firm grip around wrists and glaring at Kai. He didn't even notice the animosity, just switched his stare. I had to almost drag him past two pregnant girls enjoying a shared pasty outside the bakers', his head swivelled as we drew level to keep them in eyeline.

'Fuck off, you fucking weirdo,' one of them called as he gazed at her swollen middle, shoving its way between the curtains of her unbuttoned coat.

'Come *on*.' I tightened my grip and increased my pace until by the time we reached the car I was panting. 'Do you want me to drive?'

'No. I want you to . . . just be here, Holly. It's knowing you're here that's stopping me falling apart right now.'

We drove back to Barndale. Kai was driving on automatic pilot, accurately but too fast, and when we hit the snow-belt again even the Jeep was struggling to cope with the combination of speed and frozen road. I didn't dare say anything, he was lost in his head and I had to trust that he'd got enough experience in these conditions not to kill us both. 'Put the radio on,' he said after about ten miles of silence, and made me jump. 'Apparently there's weather warnings going out for more snow.'

It was so off-topic that I had to get him to repeat what he'd said. 'Seriously? You've got all this on your plate and you're worried about the *weather*?'

He looked at me slowly and I winced as the Jeep slid a few yards. 'This has always been on my plate. Always. You never forget it, Holly, that your mother didn't want to know you, couldn't bear to have you around even for a few days. She didn't even *try* . . .' His knuckles whitened on the wheel and he was silent for a few seconds. 'If it comes in to snow again, I'll need to go and pick up some supplies. We're nearly out of bread and tea, and Cerys . . .' another second where the only sound was the roar of the four wheel drive chewing its way through the diesel, 'you know she likes her toast.'

I put the radio on without another murmur. We sat through a selection of 70s hits and they seemed so out of place, so inconsequential that I went to turn it off again but Kai stopped me. 'Please,' was all he said, so I left it and tried to ignore Marc Bolan and the Bay City Rollers chanting about their great loves.

The forecast came and surprised me by being far more localised even than the York station usually gave. 'North Yorkshire is predicted very high winds with more snow, giving rise to structural damage and disruption on the roads. Police are warning motorists not to travel if it is not essential. Local businesses are closing early and everyone is being told to stay at home until the storm has blown itself out, around teatime tomorrow.'

'Teatime?' I frowned at the radio. 'That's not very precise. I mean, I often have tea around sevenish, but Megan likes hers at half past three.'

Kai gave a weak smile. 'Split the difference and expect it to stop around quarter past five.'

'And it's only our area. Normally storms like this go right up the east coast.'

'Maybe this is more of your excitement.'

'Still not the sort I really wanted.'

'Then what did you want?' His question echoed Vivienne's. 'What did you have in mind? If it wasn't Nicholas going AWOL or your man turning up, or ferocious snow storms, what did you want?'

I shrugged. Couldn't think of anything to say.

Kai dropped me, without another word, at my car. 'Are you sure you'll be okay?' I hesitated with my key to the lock. There was a wildness in his eyes that I didn't really like the look of, the look of a man who wants to destroy something and might destroy himself if nothing else presents itself.

'I need to think.'

'Yes. You do. Maybe talk to Cerys . . .'

He cut me off with an angry gesture. 'No. Cerys knows nothing about this. Merion and I . . . we kept it all from her, never wanted her to think she'd been conceived just to get us out of the shit-pit we were in. I mean, to a certain extent she was, but . . . no. Not Cerys. And especially not now, with the twins so near and everything.'

'Okay.'

He revved the Jeep engine. 'But thanks for being there.'

'Any time, Kai. And if you need me, you know where I am.'

He nodded, back in his own private world again, and sent the Jeep leaping between the two huge elms which guarded the entry to the track through the woods. I wondered for a moment about following him, collecting Nicholas and heading home to sit out the snow storm. But then I remembered Aiden, and decided that, all things considered, Nicholas was better off where he was.

To delay the Aiden moment, I went home via Megan's.

'Have you *seen* the weather forecast?'

'Well, I've heard it.' I took the tiny portion of sofa that Rufus wasn't occupying. He raised his head from his paws and gave me a toothy stare but let me sit down.

'They're saying there'll be trees down and drifts up to the roofs and no one will be able to get out of their houses.'

'They always say that. Every winter. And what happens? Two branches come down, we get three inches of snow and the trains don't come north of Doncaster. Every year, Megan.' I patted Rufus's long back. He wagged his tail and nearly knocked me off the sofa. 'Have you found his owner yet?' With a slow yawn and a stretch that elongated him so far that he was almost next door, Rufus got up and went over to Megan. He laid his head in her lap and looked at me as though I'd suggested she have him put down.

'I've . . . asked around.' Meg plonked a kiss on the hairy nose and Rufus gave me smug eyes. 'But I was thinking, he was soooo thin when I brought him in, and he had fleas and everything — whoever owns him can't have looked after him.'

'You're going to keep him, aren't you?' I looked around at the tiny flat. 'Perhaps you could train him as a carpet. Or just use his hair.' I wiped my hand on my trousers again. Rufus wasn't only slightly sticky he was positively adhesive.

'I might look for a place in York so I can get home at lunchtimes and walk him, a basement flat, so we'd have access to a garden or a yard or something. It's great you know, Holl, going out with Rufus. Everyone stops to chat. They all ask what breed he is, which is a bit awkward so I think I might make one up, but I've been for a drink with two guys so far who got talking to me while we were out with our dogs. Admittedly, Rufus tried to eat one and screw the other one, but he's so good natured nobody really minds.'

'Rufus tried to screw a guy?'

Megan giggled. 'His *dog*, silly.' She stood up and headed for the kitchen. With a sigh, Rufus followed her as though he was attached by string. 'Anyway, I'm going to go to bed, snuggle down with some DVDs and let the storm blow itself out.' She came back in with a packet of biscuits and sat down again.

'Meg, those guys on the hill today. They weren't playing games, you know.'

She gave me a cautious look. 'I know. But going to the police . . . like Vivienne said, they'd be all over us for what we were doing up there.'

'We could, you know, *lie*.'

Rufus, sensing her wandering attention, came back and rested his gigantic head in her lap, conveniently close to the biscuits. He dribbled, in an attention-seeking way. 'But what could we say?'

'We could go and get the candles for a start. Scrape up the blood, so there's nothing to find. Then, I dunno, just say we were out for a walk. Walking Rufus, or something. And these guys attacked us in a Land Rover. Without any signs that we'd been doing magic, it's the men's word against ours, and we weren't the ones going armed.'

'Weeelllll,' Megan cast a dubious look at the window. The sky was darkening rapidly. 'I suppose we *could*. But not tonight, not with the forecast.'

'No, not tonight. But maybe tomorrow, or the next day. Get up there, clear up any sign of spells, then ring the police, tell them we were so shocked it took a couple of days to get round to reporting it.'

'Maybe.' Whilst Megan was busy eyeballing the sky, Rufus stuck his head in the packet and gobbled half a dozen biscuits, one eye on me to see if I was going to stop him. When I didn't, he grabbed the packet in his jaws and hurtled off into Megan's bedroom, where we heard him leap onto the bed, and then the crunchy rustling sound of the entire packet, plus wrapping, heading down the gullet of a big dog.

Megan didn't even get up. 'I'd better take him out. He always . . . well, after he's eaten he gets quite . . . and I've already changed the bed once.' She pulled her cute, furry coat off the back of the sofa. She looked like Fozzie Bear in it, and the big hat with earflaps added to the fluffy-bunnikins appeal. No wonder men got talking to her when she was out with Rufus; she would look like a child being dragged away by a man-eating wolf.

'Right. I'm off . . . home,' I said slowly, waiting for her to invite me to come along. But she didn't.

'Okay. Well, we're off to Brambling Fields. There's a lovely guy there who has a greyhound, and he and Rufus enjoy chasing each other. He's so nice, really adorable, all blond and sort of spiky. Great sense of humour.'

'And you can't say that about many greyhounds,' I muttered.

Since I couldn't put it off any longer, I went home.

CHAPTER SIXTEEN

You know I managed to kid myself that you were dead? That maybe you'd died giving birth and no one had told me, or that you'd been unable to live with what you'd done and ended it all?

Because I was there when Cerys was born. Wasn't meant to be, of course, not much more than a kid myself, but when she started coming and it was too late to get Merion to the hospital . . . well, I stayed, held her hand while some woman we'd had to shout at from the window came in and sorted things out. And so I held Cerys, seconds old, face all screwed up as though this world was the nastiest thing she'd ever seen. Held her, covered in blood and mucus, the colour just coming to her limbs, watched her take her first real breaths and make her first real noise. I held her and I cried.

Because I saw what it cost Merion to give birth. How it hurt. How she had to work and pant and push that baby out of her body; the pain and the blood and, oh yes, the swearing. And despite all that pain, her first thoughts, her first words were for her baby. 'Hello, love' she said. 'Hello, my little girl'.

All that suffering, and she could love immediately. She was consumed with it, wanting to hold Cerys, whispering to her, words even I wasn't allowed to be part of. Mother and child, together. And I was nowhere. So, afterwards, while Merion got cleaned up and this lady made her a cup of tea, I stood and I held my daughter as she squirmed and yelled in my arms, treating me like no more than some weird bloke who'd wandered in to her life; feeling gravity for the first time. Wanting her mother, wanting the person who'd carried her for nine months, wanting the familiar smell and the comfort. Wanting what I'd wanted for sixteen years.

Hadn't known I wanted it until I was ten. Had my parents then, not birth parents but that hadn't mattered, they'd been all I knew, all I loved. And then — they were gone, you were gone — they hadn't wanted to go but you had. You'd left me on purpose. And there was Cerys, crying for her mother, and Merion, who would hardly let go of her long enough to get washed . . . and me. Whose mother hadn't even held him long enough to leave an impression.

And now I know that you didn't forget. I have to rethink what I thought about you all these years — you loved me. Does that make it better or worse? Did you think of me with that kind of half-pleasurable pain that I get when I think of some of the women over the years? Had to leave them, no other way, but the sense of freedom made it worthwhile, that terrific, buoying sense of not having to consider another human being's feelings any more. Of being my own person. Did you enjoy it, the way I did? That self-flagellation that gives you the shudder, remembering what you did, hoping and wishing until it's real in your head, that it all turned out well. For the best.

And then you come shouldering your way back in, trying to hand me a guilt I never wanted.

Suddenly, sex isn't enough, it won't blot it out any more. Can't use heat and friction to drive you away as though you're some kind of evil spirit to be kept at bay with fire and light. And when sex isn't enough — what else is there? What steps into the breach? I need something I don't understand, something I'm not sure I can recognise, something that will soak up all this confusion and anger and turn it to the good. Another hand to hold.

Someone. Her.

CHAPTER SEVENTEEN

Aiden was still there. I could tell from outside. And from the flickering inconsequential nature of the light I could see from behind the curtains, he'd either lit candles or set fire to the tablecloth.

'Great, you're back.' He was dressed, for which I was very grateful, but in leather, for which I wasn't. A tight black shirt clung to his upper body like a shaved monkey and the trousers were probably measurable on the Richter scale, judging by the noise they gave off when he moved. I had the feeling he thought he looked really sexy. 'I got takeaway. Chinese suit you?'

Okaaaayyyy. And yes, while it *was* nice to come home to dinner and a lovely man . . . there's something rather clinical about a guy who orders in takeaways and then meets you at the door in leather. A bit like, he's acknowledging you need to eat (to keep your strength up for the contents of the leather) but can't actually be bothered to cook anything. I mean, there were ready meals in the freezer, he wouldn't have had to strain himself. But still. He'd thought a bit.

'Thanks. Chinese would be great.'

He'd fetched all the candles I owned and put them in the living room on saucers. He'd even found the obscene one that

Megan had brought me back from an Ann Summers party, where she'd won it for being the most straight-laced attendee. Unfortunately, this had now burned half way down, and the result was anything but sexy. 'So. How was today?'

I took the proffered tinfoil container and fork — washing up was also clearly not on tonight's agenda. 'Tough.' I wasn't going to say anything else, but the image of Kai's confusion was burned into my brain. 'Went to Leeds with Kai.'

'Right. That's your man, isn't it? The one you're just . . . seeing?'

'Yes. Aiden . . .'

'D'you think he'd like to come out to play?'

'Actually, I have no idea.' I thought about Kai and his confessions about drinking too much and wild living and then wondered how I could have thought anyone like him could be otherwise. 'But I . . .'

'Maybe we should give him a ring, I'm feeling like a bit of the hard stuff.' Aiden sucked on a bit of lemon chicken and winked at me. 'Oh, and I downloaded some possible wedding venues onto your laptop. Take a look.'

He genuinely didn't see any dichotomy in discussing wedding plans and almost simultaneously proposing a three-some with another guy. Maybe there were women out there for whom this was a huge turn on, all I know is, I wasn't one of them. And he hadn't even given me the chance to say so.

'Aiden. We need to talk about this.' The takeaway was really good though, and I hadn't realised how hungry I was. 'After dinner.'

'Seen the weather forecast? Tomorrow's going to be really *mental*. How about we spend the day in bed?' Aiden undid the top two buttons of the leather shirt and scrumpled up his hair, 'It'll be *cracking*.'

'There's more to life than self-indulgence.' I wondered how Kai was. How he was feeling, whether he'd come to any decision yet. I wanted to phone, but decided to leave him alone, give him a chance to think.

'Och, I give great hedonism.' Aiden grinned at me. 'Why, what else would you be doing, on a day when it's not safe to go out?' He dropped his lemon chicken and gave me a kiss that went on longer than was decent, then stood up to reveal the leather trousers straining with something longer than was decent. 'In fact . . .'

'Aid, I'm knackered.' I fought to keep hold of my prawn balls. 'Can't we, I dunno, watch TV for a bit?'

'After. Aw, c'mon, babe. You never wanted to watch TV when you visited me on set, did ya?'

I was too tired to fight him. Besides. You know. Those trousers. And he was *stunningly* good.

* * *

During the night the wind rose. And kept on rising, somewhat similar to Aiden himself, although the wind slapped the roof-tops not buttocks and moaned in chimneys not in a baritone.

We did get some sleep. We must have done, because I was woken by the phone ringing.

'Leave it,' Aiden groaned as the wind hit the side of the house with a smack and *whumph* that made the windows rattle like teeth in a punched mouth. 'They'll go away.'

But they didn't. The phone rang on. I crawled across to look at the display through blurry eyes. 'OL? Who's OL?'

'How the fuck should I know?' Aiden burrowed deeper under the covers. 'Lie still, darlin', you're letting the cold in.'

There was an almighty bang from outside as something blew into something else. It sounded like wood on metal. Snow was strafing the windows, more solid than fluffy, and the wind had started howling like a thwarted animal. It was still dark outside, but, in this weather that didn't mean much, it could have been any time from six to breakfast.

'Old Lodge!' I sat up suddenly and Aiden groaned again, pulling the duvet tight to his body. I snatched up the phone. Did Kai need me, after all? 'Kai? Is that you?' But at the other end no one spoke. The line between us sounded hollow. 'Cerys? Nick?'

Still no answer, just the sea-like sound of an engaged phone line, and if I listened hard I thought I could hear breathing. 'Is it the babies? Are you in labour? Where's the guys? Where's Kai?'

And now a change in the tone. If I really strained I could make out the word *come*, repeated with a breath's pause in between. 'Shit. I'm on my way.' I hung up and struggled from under the covers. 'I've got to go out. Someone's in trouble.'

'Fuck 'em.' Aiden reached out a long arm and grabbed my shoulder. 'You can't go out in this, Holly. Listen to it.'

As though prompted the wind roared down the street like a teenage driver in a Porsche.

'I *have to*.'

'No, you don't.' The duvet was thrown back to reveal Aiden in all his naked glory. And he was quite glorious, although a little absence would have made my heart grow fonder, also my tender places a little less tender. 'Come on.'

And Kai's words echoed through my brain. Was this it? Was this what I had to look forward to for the next twenty-or-so years, until I found myself too old and tired to indulge in the sexual carnival tricks? Rampant guys wanting no connection other than the purely plugged-in kind? I tried to extricate myself gently. 'Aid, all this. You and me. It can't work, you know it can't. We're not compatible.'

'Sure we are.' He wouldn't let go of me, kept trying to drag me back into the bed.

'But what if . . . what if, for some reason, I can't have sex? Like, say, if we have babies or something and I have to have a bit of time off?' I pried his fingers off my arm.

'Hey, that'd be no problem. After all, there's always some chick up for a good time until you were ready for it again.' He grabbed at me and managed to unbalance me backwards onto the bed. 'How about I show you what I learned in Morocco? Or, tell you what, I could come with you, find out if this Kai is my cup of tea. No point in dragging the guy in if I don't fancy him, is there?'

I thought of Kai, his desperate, broken look yesterday. Needing someone. And there I'd been, perpetually trying to seduce him into bed, wanting no more connection than the plugged-in kind. Stupid. Shallow. I closed my eyes slowly. 'Aiden. What part of the word *no* is it that you don't understand?' When I opened my eyes I saw the handcuffs we'd let fall onto the floor again. I picked them up.

'Oh yeah, you are such a tease.' Aiden watched me fasten one around his wrist. 'You want it as much as I do, don't you?'

I snapped the other half of the cuffs onto the wrought iron headboard. 'I don't think there's an untreated sex maniac anywhere who wants it as much as you do, Aiden,' I said. 'Look, I'm sorry, but I don't think you're rational at the moment, and I really do have to go.'

He pulled against the cuffs but they were real and solid and so was the bed. 'So, you're gonna come back and do me, that right?'

I sighed. 'I'll see. The key is on my key ring, so don't even bother ransacking the bedroom for it. I'll let you out when I get home, don't worry. I'm not going to leave you to starve to death or anything.' I shoved a mid-sex snack of crisps that we'd left beside the bed and a glass of water over to him. 'Now, behave yourself.'

I dressed in two pairs of woollen tights under jeans, three T-shirts, a sweater and my warm coat, plus wellies. Outside it was a little lighter but day was still struggling to dawn past a pus-yellow sky and the air was thick with wind. When I opened the front door it was instantly whipped out of my hand and slammed back against the wall, cracking the metal knob in two with the force of it.

The air stung like lemon juice. Snowflakes bit my skin and the wind made keeping my eyes open almost impossible. It was stepping out into sensory overload. My body was tugged and driven, this way and that, I could hardly draw breath and all the while the wind yelled and shrilled into my ears. It took me five minutes to get to my car, and it was only parked three yards from the doorstep.

A few hasty minutes scraping and shovelling and blowing on the keyhole, and I was in, where at least the wind and snow stopped hitting me. Instead, they hit the car, which zigzagged across carriageways, bouncing gently off the banked snow on either side and then swivelling around on the icy road surface until I was no longer sure whether I was driving in the right direction. The only fortunate thing was that there was hardly any other traffic. A couple of cautious tractors, front ends loaded with feed for distant sheep and cattle and a four by four with skis tied to a roof rack edged past my random trajectory; we all gave each other weak 'are we stupid, or what?' grins as we ricocheted by.

It took me an hour and a half to drive the ten miles and when I slowed down near the entrance to the wood I saw that one of the huge elms had blown down and the trackway was blocked to vehicles. But that was okay because the snow lay so deeply along the track that I didn't think I would have been able to drive down it without hitting a gigantic rut and grounding completely. I steered the car to roughly where I imagined the kerb to be and touched the brake. A jarring skitter told me that the ABS was doing nothing to stop us and I jammed my foot down hard in a panic, causing the back end of the car to swivel around. The car rotated in its own length, shying the width of the road like a horse imagining something truly terrible in the opposite hedge, then hit something under the snow with a huge bang which threw me against the steering wheel hard enough to make me swear.

When I got out I could see the car listing dramatically to the left, the whole of the undercarriage buried in snow up to the hubcaps. By now I was half-blind with ice crusting on my eyelashes, and right this minute I didn't care what was wrong with it. I was more concerned with getting to whoever needed my help.

I locked the Renault against car thieving yetis and battled my way into the wood. At least once I'd got under the trees the wind couldn't get to me. It was too busy working the treetops, forcing the fingertips of branches to rake the sky and all the while sounding like an incoming tide. I plonked on through the snow, and even though I tried to avoid drifts, I only managed to avoid the obvious ones and kept dropping into patches which went up to my waist.

There was no sign of the Ginger Menace. I guess even psychos stayed at home in front of the fire on days like this. I dug my ungloved hands deeper into my pockets, hunched my shoulders and struggled on, sweating under my clothes even as any exposed bits of skin puckered and screamed against the cold. At last the Old Lodge came into view as a golden light streaming out across the snow from the kitchen window, a single plume of smoke rising from the chimney. There was a newly chopped pile of wood outside the door on top of which a robin perched. It looked like a jigsaw box lid.

The robin stared at me aggressively as I knocked. At first no one came, then, after I'd readdressed the door with extreme prejudice because I was bloody freezing, Kai appeared.

'Holly?'

'No, the fucking Christmas fairy,' I stamped my numb feet. 'Please let me in. The wind keeps trying to force snow up my nose. I'm going to be the first person to drown whilst standing chatting.' And then I laughed a hollow little laugh.

'All right, Missus Brittle.' Kai stepped back and I almost fell with thankfulness into the warm hallway. 'What's up?'

'Up?'

'Yeah. Why are you here? It's God-awful o'clock, Cerys isn't even out of bed yet and your brother is watching CBBC.'

'But you rang me.' I peeled off my coat, sweater and the first of the T-shirt layers. 'A couple of hours ago. At least, I thought it was you, the line was all weird and faint.'

Kai shook his head. 'Like I said, Cerys is asleep and I'm fairly sure Nicholas's been nowhere near the phone, not when

The Sarah Jane Adventures omnibus has been running since six thirty. Unless Cerys has taken to sleep-phoning and, bearing in mind it takes her half an hour to get out of bed, I shouldn't think so.'

'But . . . I drove through this!' I waved an arm at the window where the snow, illuminated black, was swirling past the window. 'And now I've wrecked my car!' A thin prick at the back of my eyes as shock tried to make itself felt past the chill factor.

'Come and have some tea.' Kai went through to the kitchen, but I diverted and popped my head around the living room door.

'Hey Holl.' Nick was hooked over the sofa watching TV. 'Children's TV is really good.' He was just sitting, not even fidgeting. There must be something calming in the air here.

'Did *you* ring me?'

His eyes never left the screen. 'No. What, you mean today? No. I'm watching this, it's meant for kids but it's brilliant.'

'Yeah, well, far be it from me to try to compete with a Dalek.' I went back into the kitchen, gently kicking shut the door to the living room as I passed.

Kai was plugging in the kettle. 'By the way, Holl,' he said with his back to me, 'thanks for yesterday.' There was a careful casualness about his tone that told me not to ask any questions, to dismiss his thanks as an idle recognition of my taking the morning off to accompany him.

''S okay,' I replied, trying to mirror his casual tone.

'You . . . you were great.'

'I didn't do anything. I was just there.'

'Yeah. Which is more than I had a right to ask from you.' His hand, I could see, was tight on the kettle handle, and the other was bunched in front of him. 'You *cared*,' and now his voice was a hoarseness only just audible over the bubbling rattle of the boil.

'Well, you seemed to need . . .', and then, to change the subject, because there was an air of deepening emotion in that

147

room that I couldn't deal with in wet socks, 'are you *sure* you didn't ring? This place came up on the number ident.'

He shook his head. 'Maybe the weather has shorted something out.' He picked up the handset from the kitchen dresser. Looked at it, listened to it and then shook it gently. 'Looks like the lines are down now anyway.'

'Well, if you don't want me, maybe I ought to go back. I've left Aiden . . .' I grinned to myself. 'Well, he's not going to be a happy bunny if I leave him for too long, put it that way.'

'Uh huh.' Kai put a mug of tea down on the table. 'No way am I letting you go out in this again. Listen to it, it's getting worse.' The incoming tide had suddenly become a running flood, the wind booming and cracking in the treetops and even making it down to ground level now, where it sent snow whirling and crashing like insubstantial, and rather bad, waltzers.

'Oh God,' I said. 'Aiden.' I turned back to look for my coat again. 'I *have* to go, Kai.'

'No.' His voice was absolutely definite. 'You are not going anywhere. Not now. And anyway, I thought you said you'd wrecked your car?'

'Lend me the Jeep.'

'Can't. There's a tree down across the garage doors. I made a start on chopping it up, but I've only done some of the major branches, there's a whole trunk to go and I am not going out again until the weather sees sense and calms down.'

I looked out of the window. The snow was making a sound like fluttering birds. 'I have to do *something*, this could go on for hours.'

'Ring your friend? Would she go round?'

'Phones are down.'

'Mobile?'

I held mine up. 'No signal.'

'No, mine neither. Mast gone in the wind or something.'

'Besides, Megan hasn't got the handcuff key.'

'The . . .' Kai rolled his eyes at me. 'Holly. What have you done?'

148

So I told him. I didn't even edit out the leather trouser incident. 'But, Kai, I honest to God don't know what's got into Aiden. We've never . . . there's never been any talk of making anything permanent, we've never watched TV together or gone anywhere . . . it was always just the sex. And I thought he was all right with it, and then he turns up on my doorstep swearing undying love and a permanent hard-on and talking about threesomes and banging other girls like we've agreed it all!'

'And now he's handcuffed to your bed.'

'He was going to come with me. And take a look at you.'

'At *me*.'

'With a view to seducing you into bed with us.'

Kai stared at me, then started to laugh. He laughed until he spilled his tea. 'And whose idea was *that*?' he managed to say eventually.

'Aiden's. I told you, threesomes, blokes, girls, he's a bit obsessive.'

'God, that's cheered me up.' Kai rubbed his face. 'Oh, and for the record, Holly, I'm a strictly one-on-one guy.' He grinned and raised an eyebrow and I came over all flustered for a moment and had to change the subject.

'Vivienne,' I said suddenly. 'If I can get across the wood to her cottage, she might lend me her car.'

'We'll have to walk,' Kai nudged my tea closer to me. 'So drink that down. You'll need to be warm inside as well.'

'Don't. That sounds like something Aiden would say.'

He looked at me, suddenly serious over the scrubbed table. 'I don't want to be anything like Aiden.' His eyes were dark, almost brown this morning, hollowed with tiredness and shadowed with something else, something deep.

'Kai . . .'

'The other day, up in my room. You remember?' He stretched out a hand across the table and touched my cheek. His fingers were warm from the tea mug. 'I'm tired of the games, Holly. Tired of the lies and not facing up to myself.

149

And now, all this, my past coming out of the woodwork . . . I want . . .' His voice trailed off and he started to concentrate very hard on the tabletop.

I let the silence sit for a moment. 'What do you want?'

'I want something more. Not just a body to fuck and a face to go out to dinner with. Something settled, something to rely on. Somebody in here.' He tapped his forehead. 'Where you are.'

'I'm . . .'

'Ssshh. This is just me, just what I've been coming up with. Your input — welcome, of course but — I wanted to lay it on the line for you. You are the first woman who's been there for me, Holl. Not wanting anything, not in it for the glory or the perceived glamour or wanting to be seen with a guy who's made his name . . . for me. Just me, as I am. I know you've got your own demons . . .'

'Have I?'

'Oh yeah. I just think you're too close to see them, that's all. To you they look like normality but to everyone else . . . But I want to be there when they start to become visible; there for you. For me, it's all or nothing now.'

He stood up and I stared at the lean length of him. Wondered what the hell it was that *I* wanted. 'Kai.'

'Tell me, Holly. Tell me what it is you feel. What you think is happening here with us.'

'I don't . . . I don't know. You're . . . just so . . . *so* . . . When I turn round, there you are, and you keep telling me things about myself, about Nicky and the way I am and all that, and there's all the' — I made a rather feeble wave of my hand — 'leather and stuff, and it's like you're built out of solid Understandium or something and . . .' I ran out of words and all that came out now, was breath.

'Yeah,' he said, coming over to where I sat. 'Yeah, I know.' Long fingers drew me up and his mouth came down so that we met in the middle in a kiss that warmed me more thoroughly than the tea had.

The kitchen door opened, and behind Kai's shoulder I saw Cerys appear. 'Oh,' she said. 'I guess you want some privacy.'

'You guess right,' Kai said without looking at her. Looking, in fact, right into my eyes, down, through to my soul. 'Shut the fucking door, Cerys.'

'All right, all right,' I heard her grumbling as she dragged the door closed, then the muttering as she joined up with Nicholas in front of the TV.

Then Nicholas's yell of, 'She's *what?*'

Kai and I grinned at each other. His eyes were softer now, and his mouth had lost the sardonic upturn it perpetually wore. 'God, I want you,' he said very quietly.

I cleared my throat. 'Short and intense, wasn't it?'

A slow nod. 'I have the feeling that it's going to be pretty intense, yes. But I think that you want something else too, now.' He was still gazing down into my eyes. I felt the orbital tug of his stare. 'Tired of the games?'

'I don't know. I don't want to marry Aiden, I know that much.' Cautiously I reached up, touched his cheek. It was sharp with stubble and his bones seemed very close to the surface. 'But my life is pretty good, apart from that. I don't know if I'm ready for someone . . . for *you.*'

He laughed, a sudden rip through the calm air. 'Yeah. I guess I deserve your uncertainty. There's still stuff you need to work through, I can't make decisions for you, Holl. Like I said, from the outside it's obvious what's been going on, but you need to arrive at that conclusion for yourself. You need to arrive at your own destination.'

I let my hand fall. 'But for now I'd better try to get to Vivienne's. Aiden might be desperate for a pee and that's a new duvet. What are you doing?' Kai was wrapping a scarf, that looked as though it might have been knitted by Cerys — or at least someone with more enthusiasm than ability — around his neck.

'I'm coming with you.'

'You don't have to. I'll be fine, I'll follow the track. Even I can't get lost following a track five yards wide.'

'You can in snow. Hold on, I'll get my coat.'

I looked at Kai, pulling on a ghastly overcoat and tucking the scarf down inside it, his hair stringing along the collar. He was different. How different I wasn't sure. But his whole appealing, sexy, insightful, slightly crazy thing was definitely causing a major shift in my relationship paradigms. And, damn if my nipples weren't chafing too.

We wrenched the door open and stood for a moment on the apocalyptic threshold. 'Bloody hell,' Kai stared out into the blind whiteness.

'You don't have to come,' I said again.

'You can't go alone. I don't want your frozen body found huddled feebly at the root of a tree. It'd be too much of a cliché.'

'Kai,' Cerys appeared again, in the hallway this time.

'We won't be long. Stay here with Nicholas.'

'No. I mean . . . ow.'

'Ow?' I looked at her. 'Is this ouchy, or mortal pain time?'

Cerys gave me scared eyes. 'At the moment it's ouchy, but I think this is it, Holly.'

'Sit tight. Phones are down here but we might be able to call from Vivienne's.' I patted her hand. 'You'll be okay.'

Kai looked at both of us. 'What on earth are you on about?'

We rolled our eyes at each other. 'Your daughter is going into labour.'

'What!' He nearly skidded down the steps. 'Now?'

'Er, Kai . . .' Cerys waved at her enormous belly. 'Don't tell me it's come as a shock.'

'But . . . I mean . . .' Kai looked from me to Cerys, then back again. 'I should . . .' he performed a little pirouette on the spot, obviously trying to be in two places at once. 'This . . . Holly, we could stay here . . .'

'We're going to need an ambulance.' I was torn too. Cerys was obviously scared and in need of comforting, but she was most definitely going to be in need of obstetric assistance as well. Twins, I knew, could be awkward. 'I'll go to Vivienne's, Kai, you stay here.'

'You can't go alone, it's too dangerous. How about if *I* go?'

'Vivienne's not going to let some bloke she's never met into her house. She's not stupid.'

We all stared at each other for a moment. Then Cerys made the decision. 'Both of you go. It might be a false alarm, and we're going to look totally mental if we all sit in the house and I'm still here going "ow" in three days' time. And even if it's not, labours take *hours* and Nick's here to look after me.' She paused, and rubbed her back. 'Just.. Holly, you will come back, won't you?'

'We'll both come back,' Kai said firmly. 'It's Yorkshire. Bears aren't going to eat us, you know.'

'I meant . . . I want Holly with me. If the twins are coming, now, here, I want Holly there when they arrive.'

'Gosh,' I said, pleased. 'All right. I'll ask Vivienne to drive over to my place, and get straight back.'

'Go and sit down,' Kai said. 'Don't . . . I dunno, jump off any tables or anything.'

'Okay, boss.'

He nodded. 'Still ought to hurry though.'

'Oh yes.'

The cold took our breath away and the wind took it even further. Stepping out onto the track was like being punched by feathers. I put my head down and walked, Kai in front acting as a partial windbreak. He'd jabbed his hands into fists and swung them as we went, using his bodyweight to carve a way through the spiralling snow and I plodded on behind, exhausted after the first half mile. Every time I looked up there was a Kai-shaped hole in the air in front of me, I walked into it and he made a new one. Trees were down all over the place, several across the track and we had to divert through rapidly accumulating snow to get round them, and the walk began to feel endless.

After a mile or so, he stopped and turned around, his face nothing but a nose, two eyes and a bearded chin poking through a veil of rapidly melting flakes. 'Not far now,' he said. 'You okay?'

'Think so,' I gasped back. 'You look like Frosty the Snowman.'

'I'm pissing wet through. I hope this Vivienne is in, because if we've come this way for nothing I will be dropping your name into the next article I write on antisocial behaviour.'

But through the trees I could see the light spilling from Vivienne's cottage. 'Just be careful. Vivienne is like the Wicked Witch of the West without the redeeming characteristics.'

'That good?'

'She's trying to get her husband to kill himself.'

'Charming.'

'Literally, in her case.' I staggered towards the front door and rapped on it firmly. There was going to be no case of anyone collapsing with hypothermia from no one hearing the knocker.

A curtain twitched and a few seconds later Vivienne appeared in the doorway. 'Who is it?'

''s me. And my trusty Sherpa.'

'Good heavens, Holly. What on earth are you doing here?' She was clutching the front door to her, probably to prevent the wind whipping it open, but it gave her the air of a spinster in a bath towel. 'This weather is awful, isn't it?'

'Yes,' I said through gritted teeth, 'it is. Can we come in?'

Vivienne held the door open and, like two polar explorers, Kai and I stomped our boots free from snow and walked in.

Isobel was sitting on the sofa. 'Hello,' she said, somewhat nasally. 'Did we have the same thought?' I watched her eyes widen as she looked Kai over. Due to the fact that his jeans were soaked and clinging to his legs and he'd unbuttoned his coat to reveal an equally wet shirt, I wondered if she thought all her wishes had come true at once.

'This is Kai. Kai, Isobel and Vivienne.'

Everyone shook hands. 'I came to make sure Vivienne was all right, alone out here in a storm like this,' Isobel said. 'And even the Isuzu didn't like the hill much.'

'Is your phone working? Kai's daughter is in labour. Twins. We need an ambulance. Oh, and a guy in handcuffs needs letting out.'

Two sets of eyes went moon-sized. 'Golly,' said Isobel faintly. 'That spell is really working for you, Holly, isn't it?'

'You don't know the half of it.'

We checked Vivienne's landline, all the mobiles and even her broadband link. All down.

'Shit,' Kai screwed his eyes shut. 'Cerys.'

'I'll go.' Isobel stood up. An otherwise invisible cat slunk away from under the sofa. 'It'll take too long to drive right round the outside of the woods to pick your daughter up, but the Isuzu should be able to get back to Malton, if I take it steady. I can get to the hospital and at least send a midwife out to you.'

'That would be great,' he gave her the smile at full wattage and I watched her notice his eyes.

'And, could you go round to my place, please? There's . . .' I coughed. 'There's a bloke, um. He's, well. He's . . . Aiden, nice guy but, um. Naked. Handcuffed to my bed. Probably a bit annoyed, by now. Could you, um . . .'

'I can't make up my mind whether you hate me or like me very, very much.' Isobel pocketed my keys. 'Tell me where your house is.'

I gave her my address and she started putting her coat back on. 'Vivienne? Do you want to come with me? You could stay with my mum and dad. They've gone all "Blitz Spirit" and all the neighbours are round playing charades.'

Vivienne shook her head. 'I'll stay here. This will all be over soon. Besides, I'm waiting for *news*.'

Isobel raised her eyebrows at me. 'What sort of news?'

Vivienne gave a secret smile. 'Yesterday a friend rang. My husband . . . *ex*-husband's company has gone into receivership.

He's bankrupt.' Her tone suddenly ran up the gleeful scale. 'Isn't it *wonderful?*'

'We'd better get back,' Kai sounded a bit affronted by Vivienne's viciousness. Maybe he thought she'd start on him next. 'My daughter, you know.'

'She must be *awfully* young,' Vivienne looked at him with her head on one side. 'Is . . . you know, is the father on the scene?'

'Yeah, he's building them a Stickle-brick house, and as soon as he's potty trained they'll all live together in it.'

'Holly . . .' Kai poked me with his elbow. 'We'll be off then.'

'I'd better go too.' Isobel pulled her knitted coat from under a cat. 'Are you sure you'll be all right, Vivienne?'

While they were making their farewells, and after I'd instructed Isobel to put my keys back through my letterbox once she'd released Aiden, Kai and I dragged our damp coats on again and started out into the snow. It was even harder this time because we were walking into the wind and it found every pre-soaked crevice and dug its nails in.

'Come on Holly.' Kai stopped to let me catch up.

'Oh sorry, am I holding you up?' I panted. 'That'll be on account of me being normal sized and you having legs that can step over fallen trees.'

'I'm worried about Cerys.' The wind boomed and roared like a train passing three yards away and the rest of his sentence got lost.

'First babies take ages to arrive. And second ones too, if you ask my mum; I think she wanted to put me off ever having any of my own. Apparently she nearly split in two.'

'Yes, well, Cerys isn't an amoeba.' Kai set off again. 'And if Isobel can't get through to the hospital . . .'

'Don't worry, I bet you Cerys'll still be in early labour this time tomorrow.' I tried to copy his easy jump over a snowdrift but landed unceremoniously half in it. Snow seeped into my underwear. 'It might not even be labour, she might just have indigestion.'

'I *knew* I should have sent her back to Peterborough,' Kai groaned. 'I don't have any baby stuff.'

I rolled my eyes at him, although he probably didn't notice because my eyebrows had icicles, and plodded on.

As it happened, I was one hundred per cent wrong about the indigestion thing. When we finally struggled back to the Old Lodge, Nicholas was hovering in the hallway. He'd obviously had his face pressed to the front window waiting to catch sight of us, there was a big smeary mark where he'd been blowing on the glass.

'Cerys is . . .' he said, and then performed a complicated mime which seemed to indicate that she was struggling to lift a very heavy weight. 'In her room.'

All three of us dashed up the stairs. Kai and I stripped off soggy outer layers as we went.

'Where the fuck have you been?' Cerys was crouching on her bed, knees drawn up to her belly. 'Is the ambulance coming?'

Kai and I looked at each other. 'Yes,' I said firmly, before he could do the fatherly thing and tell her the truth. After all, it wasn't a lie, more of a time-dependent falsehood. 'How are you doing?'

Nicholas rubbed the bit of her back he could reach, as she rolled and gyrated her hips. 'She keeps making really weird noises.'

As he finished speaking we got a practical demonstration, as Cerys rose suddenly onto all fours and let out a huge groan, which went on far longer than I would have thought she had breath for. 'Oh my God,' she said, collapsing back onto the bed again. 'I thought there would be pethidine. Or morphine. Instead I'm going to give birth in a house where there isn't even any *aspirin*.'

'The doctor is on his way,' I crossed my fingers behind my back. 'Make yourself comfortable and he'll be here before

157

anything happens.' I started eating her glucose tablets. I was going to need all my energy, and some of someone else's.

'Comfortable!' Cerys gave an outbreathed *kkkkrrrrrrrrr* kind of noise. 'I haven't been able to make myself comfortable since June.' Then she did the rising groan noise again, which went on even longer this time. I looked at her bedside clock.

'That was only a minute or so.'

'What?' Kai was looking a bit helpless and lost.

'Between contractions. I've got a feeling . . .'

'Fuck the ambulance,' shouted Cerys suddenly. 'I want to push!'

I stared. Nicholas bolted for the door. 'We have to boil water,' he said, grabbing Kai by the shoulder. 'Boiling water. I just watched an episode of Tracy Beaker with birth in, and that's what they had to do.'

'When Cerys was born, they told us to boil scissors? And string?'

'I'm having twins, Kai, not a fucking parcel,' Cerys said, between gritted teeth.

'For the . . . you know, cord and stuff . . .'

'Look . . . just go and boil everything you can find, all right?' I said.

'Don't leave me,' Cerys had hold of my hand. 'Holly, please don't leave me. I can't do this, I can't . . .' She suddenly broke off and her eyes bulged. 'Oh God, oh God . . .'

'Right. Looks like all those hours spent watching *Call the Midwife* might have been useful after all. You two, get shifting.'

The two men went through that bedroom door so fast that there were scorch marks on the frame. I heard them rush down the stairs, Kai saying, 'and I remember there being a phenomenal amount of newspaper involved,' and then Cerys was gripping my hand so tightly that I heard the little bones begin to grind.

'Holly, they're coming,' she whispered and suddenly she was panting and heaving like a bogged horse, and all I could do was hold her hand and, when it came to it, run round to the other end, catch the first baby as it slid out onto the bed. Fortunately she was so astonished by this that I could take thirty seconds to dash down the stairs, collect the newly-boiled scissors and string, sustaining third-degree burns in the process, and rush back to tie and cut the cord.

And then I stood, with a blood-and-mucus-covered baby in my arms, splattered with seven kinds of gore, and laughed. 'It's a boy.'

'I know that,' Cerys gave me a preoccupied smile. 'He's . . . oh, no, not again . . .' and there was more pulling and pushing and sweating and his sister joined us.

I cleared the babies' mouths and noses. They were both breathing, becoming a more healthy colour and had started to unscrew their faces enough to cry. 'They're fine,' I said, passing them to their mother, who was staring at them as though she couldn't believe it. 'Fine. Healthy.'

'Big.'

'Well, they look a good six pounds each, maybe a bit more.'

'From this end they both weighed at least as much as a sack of potatoes.' Cerys relaxed back onto the pillow. 'And were covered in barbed wire.'

'I'll call the boys up,' I headed for the door but she stopped me.

'Can I . . . you know, could you help me sort of clean up a bit first? Kai not so much, but Nicholas — I don't want the first time he sees me non-preggers to be this kind of outtake from Saving Private Ryan.'

So I helped her get sorted, changed the bed, and used the mysterious newspaper to wrap and dispose of the placentas, rushing up and down to the kitchen past the two men, who glued themselves to the wall whenever I ran past, like teenagers caught in a slasher flick. Eventually Cerys was what she considered presentable, and the babies were wrapped in two clean towels. Their faces poked out of the bundles looking slightly surprised and a bit aggrieved at having arrived in such a precipitate fashion.

Then I left her to show the babies off to her father, while Nick and I made lots of tea, so as not to waste the rest of the boiling water.

'You're shaking,' he observed.

'It was scary.' Then Kai came downstairs. I took one look at his face and pushed a mug into Nicholas's hand. 'You take her up some tea. Find out if she's got any names yet.'

As soon as Nicholas left the room, Kai started to cry. He stood in the middle of the kitchen, closed his eyes and let the tears roll down his face, unchecked.

'Hey.' I put my arms around him and gave him a hug. 'Kai.'

A trembling breath. 'Oh God, Holly.'

'It's okay. Everything's fine, mother and babies doing well.' I fought the urge to join in. The full shock had worn off now and left me weak.

'I have to meet her now. I have to know . . . Cerys is up there . . .' his voice faded and he scrubbed the back of a hand across his eyes. 'I have to know if my mother felt any of that for me. Because, if she did, and she still gave me up . . . Why? If she felt one-tenth of what Cerys is going through, then how could she have done it, what was going on that was so terrible that she couldn't keep her baby? And *four hours old*. The blood wasn't even dry.'

He collapsed onto a stool at the table and cupped his face in his hands.

'She must have had her reasons.'

Yellow eyes fixed mine. 'Maybe that's what I need. Reasons. Or, I guess, it may be excuses — everyone thinks they're doing things for the right reasons, don't they?' A look that maybe meant more than the words said. 'It's this uncertainty I can't deal with. Either she wanted me but couldn't keep me, or she never wanted me in the first place — and seeing my daughter, up there, her face . . . even though those babies are, what, five minutes old? Cerys would kill for them already. How could . . .' a small, choked cough, '*how could she leave me?*'

'Then get in touch. Ask her.'

He shook his head and dark hair curtained his face briefly. 'I'm so fucking scared.'

'What's the worst that can happen?' I touched his shoulder. 'Honestly. Hasn't the worst already been done to you?'

'She could tell me she was glad to give me up. That I was some bastard's bastard, that she never wanted to be reminded of him and certainly not by having to bring up his child.'

'You read the letter. Did that sound to you like a woman who was glad to have given you up? Because it sounded to me like she's tortured herself every day since you were born for the choice she made. And, yes, I saw Cerys when the twins were born, I was *there*, looking in her face when she saw them for the first time and I'll tell you this, the woman who gave you up? She *hurt*, Kai. And if you can stop her hurting, just by seeing her one time . . .'

'You're right.' He rubbed his face. 'No, you're right, of course you are. I'm being a coward.' He laughed a thin laugh. 'Stupid. When I think of some of the things I've done . . . and this is such a small thing.' He was very pale, or maybe that was the light bleaching the colour from his skin and eyes. I still felt flushed and pink from the trek through the snow and the subsequent events. 'Such a small thing,' he repeated.

There was a cacophony of feet on wooden stairs and Nicholas launched himself into the kitchen. 'Zac and Freya. The twins. Zac and Freya, Cerys says.'

'You're a grandad,' I said quietly to Kai under the sound of Nicholas extolling the twins' virtues. 'Congratulations.'

'Yeah, I am, aren't I?' He made a clear effort to pull himself together. 'Sod tea, who wants champagne?'

'You have champagne in the house?' I grinned at him.

'Always, Holly, always.'

'Posh git.'

'Well, I never know when I might win another award. Get the glasses, Nicholas.'

'If you're drinking down there . . .' A faint voice percolated through the floorboards, '. . . just remember who did all the work, and bring up a glass for a new mother.' One of the babies squawked and she instantly lowered her voice, 'or you can all die horribly. Your choice.'

CHAPTER EIGHTEEN

Humdrum cut back in. The wind dropped from gale force to merely breezy and it stopped snowing, Kai went out to chop up enough tree to get the Jeep out. A doctor and midwife arrived, covered in snow to the eyebrows after having had to walk from the road, and were disappointed to have missed the delivery, but they checked Cerys and Zac and Freya and they were all announced to be fit and well. I was congratulated on having done such a good job of midwifery, which I accepted modestly even though all I'd really done was to catch. More tea was drunk, Nick went back to children's television, and I went up to sit with Cerys for a bit.

'You were great, Holly.' She was feeding Zac, Freya lying beside her still wrapped in her towel like a papoose. 'So calm and organised.'

'I was terrified,' I admitted. 'But you took it like a pro.'

Cerys did the 'soft faced' expression of a Madonna. 'I wish you were my mum,' she said, eyes on the babies.

'But you've got a mum in Peterborough. And by all accounts she's a lovely lady.'

Cerys looked at me now. 'I know that. I didn't mean *that* mum, I meant . . .' and she jerked her head at the door, 'with him.'

'I can't be a step grandma, I'm only thirty. Think of my image! I'd have to get a perm and learn to knit and keep a hanky in my cardigan pocket. And I've only just learned that oral sex trick with the ice cubes, it would be a waste.' I ate some more glucose tablets. Strawberry flavoured, and nicer than Nicholas's tea.

'Don't mention sex, please. I can't even bear to think about going for a wee.' Cerys kissed the baby's head. 'I thought you and he had a bit of a thing going the other day, in fact, when you came to the door — his *bedroom* door and don't tell me you were doing a crossword — you both looked very flushed.'

I thought about my purely visceral reactions to Kai. The way my stomach jumped when he smiled at me, and the tingling of outlying regions when he kissed me. His implicit confession that he, possibly, more than liked me. 'It's all very innocent. We like each other's company, that's all.'

'Yeah, right. Now who sounds like a granny? "Liking someone's company" is what you say when you want a shag but he's not playing ball. Do you want me to put in a word?'

'And then I'll have to kill you.'

She gathered the babies to her. 'Oh, think of the poor motherless orphans.' I fought the temptation to throw a pillow at her head because I didn't want to upset the twins.

I went to go and look for Kai. The sounds of chopping had stopped, so I was presuming that he'd cleared the garage doors, although with the trackway blocked at the road end we were going to have to rally through the woods to get out. Not wanting him to feel that I was chivvying him along by watching over his shoulder, I crept quietly out of the kitchen door and down through the snow towards the garage. There was a huge pile of logs, Kai's jacket and a large circle of trodden-down snow, but no sign of Kai himself. I peered through the garage window and the Jeep was still inside — well, dur, otherwise there would have been car tracks in the snow, not just footprints.

I looked closer at the footprints. I could see where one single line of prints came from the house to the fallen tree and around either side of the logs. But there was another line of prints. Smaller, deeper. Coming in from the woods which lay away to the east of the Old Lodge, meeting up with Kai's prints, and then two sets making their way back under the trees, the way the first set had come.

I should have called out. Should have made my presence known, but I didn't, and I didn't know why. No, I did. There was something about Kai, something that told me he didn't only swim with minnows, he hunted with sharks. A darkness, an intensity. Something, and I hated to admit it, that I didn't quite trust. I followed the double line of footprints, treading carefully on the compressed snow they'd left and trusting to the noise of the wind to cover any telltale crunching sounds.

And there they were, Kai and the ginger man. Ginge was talking, voice low, checking over his shoulder regularly and I dropped to the snow on my stomach, relying on the heaps that were snow-covered bushes to keep me hidden. Kai was leaning against a tree, arms folded across his chest, looking at ease, relaxed. Every so often he would interject in a low-key way but Ginge was definitely doing most of the conversational work, his voice rising in a peevish whine. I couldn't make out the words and I didn't dare creep any closer because there was a pheasant in here with me and any movement I made would send it stumbling into heavy flight, and possible discovery. I eyeballed it and silently dared it to react. It stared back with empty-eyed avian insanity.

Finally the men reached whatever consensus they'd set out to. I saw Kai give a deep shrug and Ginge threw his arms wide as if to indicate the whole forest, then he turned on his heel, in a surprisingly military way, and strode off into the trees with his bright hair flaming onto my retina even as he vanished into the dark.

Kai stood a while longer, staring after him. Then he shook his head and pushed himself away from the tree, walking back out of the shelter of the woods and towards the garage again. I stayed crouched until I was sure he was gone. Then I took a big circuit through the woods, so as to approach the house from the other side and not be seen by Kai.

When I circled round he was lugging the final log onto the pile outside the back door. 'There you are,' he said.

'Yes, here I am. Can you get the Jeep out now?'

He looked at me steadily. 'Yeah, I could, but I was going to suggest you stay here tonight. You don't want to risk running into your naked man until he's had time to calm down, do you?'

'It's all right, I can handle Aiden.'

'I don't think you understand.' Kai looked down at the packed snow by his feet. 'I'd like you to stay. Here. With me.'

Despite it all, there was still a little jump inside me at the thought of staying, a momentary hotness that welled through me thinking of his rangy body stretched out next to mine, the touch of his fingers across my body. 'Thanks for the offer, Kai, but I'd really like to go home now. And you're going to have to get into town to pick up some supplies for the twins — Cerys only has enough newborn nappies for a couple of changes each.'

'Holly?' He closed the remaining snowy space between us. 'Are you okay? You look very pale.' He reached out gently and tucked a strand of hair behind my ear. Or at least he tried, my hair was damp with melting snow and fell back out again.

'Just a bit shaken. I've never delivered a baby before.' I tried a smile which I think might have looked a bit scary from the outside. 'And there's Nicholas, I mean, he can't move in here with you, he'd be swapping a dependence on me for one on you. And he'll need to get to the doctor's to get checked over after that episode the other day.' I felt rather proud of that rationalisation.

'Suppose.' But he didn't move. Just stood, staring down at me from his lean height, eyes assessing me with a cool, yellow gaze. 'All right,' he said at last, 'if you're sure.'

'If you drop me in town I'll pop to the garage and tell them about my car. They'll have to tow it in, I guess, and I'll have to sort out a rental in the meantime. I need that car for work.'

'Hey, you can always call me if you need transport.'

'Thanks.'

We stood a bit longer in the snow. Away in the woods a bird began to sing into the clear air and an overloaded branch snapped with a crack like a leg break. 'Holly.' Kai put a finger under my chin and tipped it, forcing my eyes up to meet his. 'This isn't the end, you know that don't you?'

'What?' I couldn't look away from that tawny stare, whether it was the peculiarity of colouring or something in the way he touched me, I was stuck, fixed in the amber of his intensity.

'When Cerys goes back to Peterborough, I'm not going to stop wanting to see you.' He'd come right in close now, face bent to mine, almost touching my lips with his. 'Not going to stop wanting you.' His breath was warm against my frozen cheek, I couldn't tell if I was still breathing, couldn't tell if my heart still beat — in that moment I didn't care that he hadn't told me about his association with Ginger man — I wanted him to kiss me. My whole body was pulling forward, straining against my bones to try to get closer to him.

'Kai . . .' I ached all over with the loss of the innocence I'd had earlier. Now I knew he wasn't the superficially happy, deep-feeling guy I'd met, he was some dark stranger of the kind my mother would have warned me about if she hadn't been so busy telling me dire tales of childbearing. He was made of secrets and lies and there was so much behind that strange stare that I couldn't even guess at.

'Yeah, you're right. Better get the Jeep fired up. Don't want to have to try to navigate our way out of the woods in the dark, not when there's trees down all over the place.' Kai let me go, a casual finger brushing down my cheek as he did so, touching my lips before he stuffed both hands into his pockets, hunched his shoulders and yanked open the garage doors. 'If you're sure you won't stay?'

Now was my chance to back down, to fall into his arms, his bed, his eyes. I could just sleep with him, couldn't I? I mean, it wouldn't mean anything. His body had that alluring hardness to it, he had a great face, good muscles and I could imagine lying underneath him in the dark, feeling his hair stroking me, his fingers teasing me . . .

Hold on. Shut up. Aside from the fact that he was fraternising with men that even *he* had warned me off, I didn't know what I wanted from Kai. I mean, *yes*, the sex was almost certain to be an all-night sensation, but. He wanted something more. Wanted *me*, all of me, and . . .well, there was Nicholas to think of and . . .

No. This minnow was staying well clear of the sharks, thank you very much.

'Yeah. I'm sure.'

'I'll go get the keys then.' With a shrug he turned for the house. 'Oh, I'll tell Cerys you'll be round tomorrow, will I?'

'I . . .' I wanted to say no, but then I had a rethink. 'Yeah. I've got to come over anyway. I told Vivienne I'd get rid of the evidence up on the hill.'

There was the briefest change in his stride there. If I hadn't been looking for it I wouldn't have seen, but he'd almost stumbled. 'Holly, I've told you, it's dangerous up there.'

'I'll be fine. I'll go as it's getting light, really early so no one will see me. I have to collect the candles and stuff. The snow should have just buried them where we left them, so I'll only have to dig for a bit. Won't take me five minutes.'

He looked as though he was going to say something else, half turning towards me with a peculiarly intent look on his face, but he must have thought better of it because he swung away again without saying anything else. I watched his long stride head towards the Lodge and wondered to myself, *where do you really stand, Mr Rhys, with the woman you say you want, or the man you pretend to hate?*

In the Jeep, Nicholas bounced and chattered, filling the silence that had fallen between Kai and I, and it was the first time I'd ever been grateful for my brother's condition. I sat, head turned, the view spooling past unregistered as I wondered about my reaction to Kai. About what the *hell* was going on with him that made me want to kiss him and at the same time be a very long way away. About why I could feel his body heat despite the chasm between us, and why nothing felt the same any more.

The Jeep jerked around a corner and I saw his reflection in the window glass glance my way and open his mouth as though to speak, think better of it and switch his gaze back to the road, as Nicholas's monologue branched off and became random. I half listened to my brother spilling words to some story that had no beginning and no end, found myself judging his tone to see whether he was spiralling up or down, biting my tongue so that I didn't say anything that he might take as criticism or anger — a reaction so permanent that I hardly even felt myself do it any more. What had once been a conscious, thoughtful consequence had become second nature . . . when had that happened?

The car had stopped and Kai was waiting, engine ticking. 'Right, Malton garage. This is your stop,' he said, as though he was repeating himself. 'Holly?'

'I . . .' I shook my head. Nicholas had already bounced down onto the pavement, still talking and I bit down hard on my inner self for wanting to shout '*shut up and let me say goodbye*'. 'Thank you for driving us back.'

'You seemed to think it was important.' He was looking over his shoulder, judging the oncoming traffic, not meeting my eye. 'I'll maybe see you.'

And as he dropped the clutch and manoeuvred the big car out into the road, I wanted to shout after it, something that would fetch him back, but any words that came to mind felt second-hand and meaningless.

CHAPTER NINETEEN

Okay. Now I really don't understand. If you aren't a selfish bitch who thought a baby would just inconvenience her, hold her back, drag her down while she was so keen on climbing whatever corporate ladder she found herself on — then was it me? Something you saw in me, or saw in the man who fathered me, some kind of hovering vice, circling around and waiting to manifest? Were you ashamed? Did you think that I was going to turn out a bastard, a user; some carefree prick who thought of women as his own personal playground and fuck the consequences? Or was there something else . . . ?

Because my daughter . . . your granddaughter . . . she made a mistake, got pregnant by some fly-by-night dickhead whose attitude to parenthood was pretty much as a hit and run. But she had something you didn't. Courage. And now she's lying there with her babies in her arms and the best fucking future that I can give her, to make up for what you did to me.

Y'know how I said I could see when she was born how much giving birth must have cost you? Well, I saw in her face today how much it would cost to give up those babies. Could hardly even get them off her for a cuddle, she was hanging in there as though I was going to commit murder . . . And I come back to it. Either you didn't care, pushed me out and left me to whatever fate came along, or you cared and gave me away anyway . . . And what could make any mother do that? What *happened* to you?

I've done well, all these years, on my own. Never needing anyone. Because that's my control. If they don't know who I really am, they can't hurt me, y'see. All they can do is drag their nails down the outside of that wooden statue that they think is the real me, that hollow man with no heart to touch, no soul to steal. And all the while the real me is . . . where? Hiding, untouched where they can't see. And now I've met someone. Someone like me, who's built herself a shell to keep the world from hurting her. Oh, she thinks it's just words but . . . I know how it goes. I understand. And I wanted to be there for her, to help her to see that the way she chose to live her life has damaged her, made her into someone hard, someone who thinks they shouldn't care. And I wanted to be there when she finds out who she really is, underneath it all, when she finds her heart and soul, when she stops hiding. I thought . . . I really thought it was something good, something to build on. A new base to create a new life on, something solid and real. But she pulled, bailed on me. Guess she saw through to the far side, to the man that I am deep, deep within, the monster that I'm afraid is the real me now. And maybe it's better that way.

And now, what? What's in it for me, digging it all up, all those things I've buried good and deep, all the thumpings and the dark cupboards, the taunting and the nights spent with the Bible weighing me down so I couldn't sleep to try to force the Devil out of me . . . when what they should have asked was — if they forced the Devil out, what did they force in instead?

171

CHAPTER TWENTY

Aiden was waiting when I eventually reached home. He was sitting, perched with one buttock on the sofa arm, and he looked nervous. The washing machine was going and the handcuffs were lying on the table, as though he had dissociated himself from any bedroom goings-on.

'Holly . . . .'

'Yes, I know, and I'm *really* sorry about having to send a total stranger to let you out but . . . I didn't know when I'd get back.'

'No, it's okay. It's me who's sorry.' He shifted about a bit. He was wearing ordinary clothes, I noticed, not his usual 'strip me, whip me' gear but a plain white shirt and slightly baggy jeans. 'This is never gonna work, babe.'

Then I saw his holdall, packed at his feet. 'What isn't?' And for the world I couldn't tell you if my heart lifted or sank. 'Aid?'

'It's weird, like something kinda *shifted*, almost like I was in some dream or something, y'know? When you went, and I was here, waiting, all stoked and ready for action and then . . .' he shook his head, almost dazed. 'I fell asleep for a couple of hours and when I woke up my head just cleared, and I thought, "what the fuck am I doing here?"'

Right at the time I was with Kai. Realising that maybe, just *maybe* he and I might be more to one another than either of us had expected . . .

'*I* realise now that I can't stay here with you, I need to be free to take whatever work interests me — being based with you would be restrictive, tie down my creativity.' And he picked up the bag. 'Sorry, babe. If you're ever up my way, come and see me, but I'm afraid' — he stood up, swung the bag casually up onto his shoulder — 'a permanent relationship is not what I'm after.' A quick kiss grazed my cheek and, with the air of a man newly released from prison, he sauntered out onto the chilly pavement.

I closed the door behind him and started to giggle, although a lot of the laughter was a bit shocked. Wow. It felt as though I'd gone through all the stages of a relationship and its breakdown in a kind of time-lapse photography way. And then I stopped laughing. Wasn't that how it *always* went for me? And a tiny chill crept up my spine and whispered into my ear that all this had happened since we'd done the spell, Aiden being overcome with desire for me, a desire which had vanished as fast as it arose when I realised that Kai was . . . was . . .

Was the man I wanted.

I opened all the windows, despite the chilly air, trying to get the breeze to drive all traces of Aiden out of the house. The living room still smelled of Chinese takeaway and burned-down candles, there was a foil dish smooshed into a flying-saucer shape and dumped on top of the TV and a forgotten single sock behind the sofa. I dropped it all into the kitchen bin, fetched clean laundry from the cupboard in the hall — Aiden had put all the bedding on a hot wash cycle — and remade the bed. The place felt like mine again. Quiet, yes, after the frantic activities of today, no tiny babies crying, no heavy footsteps thumping up and down the stairs, no shouts for tea from the kitchen. But mine. The way I liked it. Silent. Empty.

Lonely.

I did some work on my laptop for a while. The local weather had put anyone off wanting any location work from me lately, so I just had paperwork to catch up on and a company in Bath wanting a large 'typically Northern' house for some grim drama they were casting. I found myself staring at the screen without registering the words I'd typed on it. Seeing, behind the Word document, a kind of glowing after-image of Kai's face, that yellow-eyed focussed intensity that he'd had when he'd asked me to stay. The serious, slow way he looked at me, as though he was waiting for me to come to some realisation, his questions and observations about my life and friendships . . . About Nick.

What did he see when he looked at Nick and I? Devoted sister, caring for her brother? Or something else, something darker — something I wouldn't even let myself think, except sometimes, when it snuck through and had to be excised from my brain like a bad idea?

I could see my own face now, words shining through my cheeks and eyes and highlighting my skin. *Was he right?* Did he know how I really felt, underneath it all? Why I kept everyone at arms' length? Not because I couldn't make room for them in my heart, but because I was afraid that they would see through my caring and into the guilt that lay inside, that they might ask the question I was terrified even to think to myself — *why, exactly, did I do it?*

I stared out of the window as my mind cantered round and round the realisations. Outside, in the late dark, the snow had turned to rain and the thaw was in progress, accompanied by the meltwater drip from gutters and the slushy swish of tyres on the road.

There was a tap on my front door. 'Holly?'

I hesitated for a second as my thoughts overlapped with reality, but then realised that I couldn't make my brother suffer for my introspection. 'Hi Nicky.' I let him in. 'You don't often get all the way down here.' Nicholas's flat was at the top of town in a dingy area where they didn't mind his rent money being provided by the Benefits agency.

'I wanted to talk to you.' He looked around. 'And have you got any food?'

'Dual-purpose visit then.' I ransacked the freezer and put two pizzas in the oven. 'What did you want to talk about?'

'They were right, you know.'

'Who were? Not the voices again, I've told you, voices in your head very rarely have good ideas.'

'Cerys and Kai. They were right about me getting dependent on you, not looking after myself because I knew you'd sort me out.'

'Okay.' I said slowly. To give my hands something to do, I laid the table.

'So I've decided to leave.'

I stopped, one hand still holding forks. 'You've *what*? Where would you go?' And then the horrible, sick-making spurt of relief, quickly covered by the plaster of despair, *and if you go, what do I have left?*

'Look, Holl. I hate my life.' Nick leaned over the back of the sofa, it made him look like a fey male model. 'I've pretty well resigned myself to never being able to get a proper job round here. I can't get away from myself, I'll always be Mrs Grey's difficult son, the one with the problems. If I go somewhere else I can start again.'

'But, I repeat, where would you go?'

'Peterborough.'

'*Peter* . . .' My voice was all squeaky. 'What, you mean with Cerys?'

'Yeah. We've been talking. On Facebook. She's got a three-bedroomed flat, she needs a bit of help with the twins, she said I could stay with her in exchange for a bit of mother's helping and doing housework and stuff like that. Maybe get a proper job eventually.'

'But . . .' I waved a fork weakly, 'your meds?'

'They have pharmacies in Peterborough. Doctors too. But, like you said, these new meds seem to be working out for me. I know I . . . up in Scotland things got a bit strange, but I didn't take my stuff then.'

'I'm just amazed that, as the new mother of twins, Cerys has had the time for all this chatting and hanging around on social media,' I said, to distract him from another monologue on how, sometimes, he got the feeling that his drugs did nothing more than paralyse him and blunt his feelings. I'd sat through that explanation more times than I cared to remember.

'Think Kai had the babies. He's been staring at them a lot, she says. But, listen Holl. Things Cerys said make sense. About sometimes everyone needing a bit of help and nothing to be ashamed about and all that. And that all made me realise . . . I used to think that the meds evened me out too much, took off my edge, but now I know they make life easier for me. I like myself more when I'm on them. I won't not take them again, Holl, I promise.'

'Oh.' It was all I could say. I could smell burning cheese.

'So, Kai's driving us down in a few days, when Cerys has got used to the twins. Thought I'd better tell you.'

'Are you and Cerys . . . ?'

Nick grinned a wicked grin. It was such a 'guy' grin I had to smile back. I didn't think I'd ever seen him do that before. 'You've got a mucky mind, Holly Grey. Cerys and I are just mates. Friends.' He shot me a furtive look. 'Like you and Kai. No sex please, we're too busy being busy.'

'What's that supposed to mean?'

'Aw, come on. You stand a much better chance with Kai if I'm not around. I know he's not a wanker, he's a nice bloke, and . . . you can give him your full attention when you're not worrying about me.'

'And you think I won't worry about you in Peterborough? It's not the Other Side, Nicky, it's only a hundred miles or so away.'

'Yeah. Are we eating now? Those pizzas smell funny.'

I'd bent down to the oven when a thought struck me. 'Oh my God. Nick.'

'I *told* you they smelled funny.'

'No. I . . . you and Cerys. Remember your wish? The one that I had to make for you when we did the spell?'

'Think so, yes.'

'You wanted a girlfriend. With enormous tits.' We stared at one another, then started to laugh. 'Well feeding twins is better than implants. And she's a friend who happens to be a girl.'

'I got my wish. And what about you, what did you wish for?'

'I don't even want to think about it right now.' I plonked the pizzas onto the table.

'Kai really likes you.' Ignoring the cutlery, Nick picked up his slice of pizza in his fingers. 'I've heard him talking to Cerys about you. Like he was really fond of you. And you like him, don't you? Your eyes go all big when you look at him. And you stare at his groin a lot.'

'He's about nine foot tall, his groin is the only bit I can see without binoculars.' I tore a massive bit of pizza off to cover my embarrassed confusion.

'I'm going to miss you.'

And I'm looking into a big blank space where you've been for all those years. 'Yeah, well I'll miss you too.'

'No you won't. You'll be able to have a proper life, not always have to be looking after me. Like Cerys said, I'm thirty-two, you shouldn't have to be looking after me, I can look after myself.'

'No you can't. Look at that time with the pigeons.'

'No, I can. I *should*. I've done too much leaning, too much letting you cope when I should have been trying to manage everything myself. I *know* I'm not normal, that my mind doesn't work the same way as other people and that I have to be careful and take the meds and not get overtired . . . but I still screw up, Holl, because I know you'll pick up the pieces. If I go to Peterborough — well, I can't lean on Cerys, she's got her hands full, *she* will need *me*. I think that's what I need most, Holl, to be useful rather than just the weird tit who talks to walls.'

He was right. Of course he was. It was just that . . . I'd spent the last twenty years looking after Nick. I wasn't sure I knew how to stop.

We finished the pizza and he went back to his flat to start packing up his things. Since his things consisted of a duvet and pillow, two cardboard boxes of clothes and a stuffed badger that he'd found on a skip and refused to be apart from, I hardly thought it would take the next few days but, hey. I'd stopped interfering. And I couldn't believe, really and truly that it could be that simple. That he could just decide to go, pack up, and leave, this man who'd needed me to remind him to change his underwear and brush his teeth until he was twenty-five.

I slept long and deeply, uninterrupted by a self-absorbed film director with a permanent erection. So many women, I mused, waking up next morning refreshed and unsticky, would have killed for a man like Aiden. I would have ended up killing Aiden.

I got dressed and got in the hire car that I was going to use while my car sat in the garage and got poked. A lot of men in boiler suits had sucked their teeth at it already, and come to what I was going to call an overall consensus that the axle was snapped. The hire car was smaller than my Renault but newer and didn't have crisp packets all over the floor. I drove it across to Barndale on the squishily slushed-over roads, while the rain continued to wash at the edges of the snow, eroding it back gradually into lumps that looked like half-sucked sweets, discarded along the margins, and the banks of ploughed snow wore down to weirdly topiarised shapes, sculpted by the running water.

I struggled and waded up the hill like a simple, if somewhat masochistic, early morning sightseer. It was, after all, a lovely day. The dawn sky was Renaissance blue in the gaps between the rain clouds and apart from the fact that the ground was covered in a layer of rapidly liquidising snow, it could have been summer. Only cold, of course. Leaves, curled like ammonites, blew across the hilltop, somewhere a dog barked and a sheep coughed. Rooks cleared their throats overhead, their finger-wings combing the sky and the air was as clear as a mirror.

Hands in pockets, I sauntered to the bare hilltop. The snow still lay thickly up here, and footprints and tyre prints were translucent trails nibbled into it, showing where someone had been creeping around since we'd been up here performing psychological warfare on our sanity. The site of our ritual was bare, though, just a blank, white sheet of virgin snow which had blown around, so the surface was only inches deep, but drifts sulked around the trees like onlookers driven back from a juicy accident. Trying to look innocent and just-out-for-a-walk, I began to stomp and rake through the snow with my boots, stirring the smooth surface into a battlefield of tread marks and kicked-up piles.

The first candle turned up surprisingly easily. With an almost invisibly fast glance around to make sure no one was spying, I bent down and dug it out of its snow hole. It froze onto my skin, hard and oily like a dead man's finger and I shoved it quickly into my pocket with a shiver. One down, three to go.

I kicked snow innocently for a bit, getting more vicious as I became more frustrated. Eventually I was sending torrents of snow from each boot cascading up over my head and I nearly sprained my ankle twice from kicking unexpected small rocks. I must have looked like the video-nasty version of Walking in a Winter Wonderland as I brutally belted another footfull of snow which fell in a frozen shower onto my head and shoulders. 'Bloody *bloody* things, where are you?' I muttered.

'They're here.' A voice from near the treeline made me jump. 'If it's these that you're looking for.'

Leaning against a tree and swinging the three remaining candles from one hand, stood a man. Something about his voice and arrogant stance were familiar.

'Can I have them, please?' I moved towards him, down off the shoulder of the hill and towards the wood, holding out my hand. 'They belong to a friend.'

'I know.' The man came properly into view. He was quite attractive, trendily long-haired and nicely shaped under an unimpressive grey duffel coat. 'The witch.'

Then I recognised him, but of course by then it was too late to back up. Of course, he would have known we'd come back for the evidence . . . He must have taken the candles almost as soon as we'd gone off the hill, and the snow had covered his tracks. 'You're the guy with the gun from the other day.'

An acquiescent tip of the head. 'Which, I think you'll notice, I never fired.' His accent wasn't local, more southern. Well-spoken but without the braying edge of the Ginge.

'Bully for you.' My teeth were clenched so I'm not sure he heard me, which was probably just as well. 'Can I have my candles now, please?'

'No.' Now the voice did have an edge. I think it might have been menace, but I'd never really *been* menaced before, so I wasn't sure. It could, of course, have been outright rudeness.

'But they're mine.'

'Now, let me see. If I give you the candles, you'll . . . *hmm* . . . what would *I* do? Well, I'd probably go round and blow the living hell out of anyone who'd got in my way, but then you're *not* me, are you? No, I think, if I held these' — he swung the candles again — 'and if I were a woman, convinced of my utter rightness and permission to behave as I wanted, I would go to the police. Tell them that some nasty men scared me.' He put on a stupid, simpering voice for the last bit. 'And there was me and my black girlfriend, out for an innocent stroll. Am I getting warm?' He raised his eyebrows and I fought my face not to let it react. 'And then the plods would be stomping around, asking stupid questions, getting no closer to the real truth of the matter which is,' he lowered his voice and now the menace was unmistakable, even to me, 'that some bitches were playing with Satan on the hill. Dancing with the Devil. Conjuring evil spirits with the use of blood and offerings.'

'That's bollocks!'

'No. That's women for you. All tits and lies.' He moved away from the tree, towards me. I didn't know what to do, I was on the rising ground of the slope so he had to move uphill to get to me, but I didn't think I could move fast enough to get away on the snow-packed ground. He was wearing big tyre-treaded boots and I'd only got wellies on. Leopard print ones. 'And you did do witchcraft.'

'It's not witchcraft. It's a bunch of women playing. Pretending.' Despite myself I took half a step back.

'So you didn't do spells then?'

'No!'

'Drinking the liquid from the cauldron? What was that, just having a nice brew up were you?'

'Yes,' I seized on this. 'It was tea. We came out for a picnic.'

'In *November*? In the dark?' He pretended to shake a leg. 'Jingle jingle, my darling. Try again. Because I've got pictures, love, photos of the candles with the blood and everything, and pictures of you sweet little girlies sitting there doing your thing with them.'

Now my palms had started to sweat and I could feel my heart rising up in my throat. 'It's a free country,' I started again, but he made a quick jump across the snow and grabbed my arm so suddenly that I couldn't speak any more.

'No, it's not a free country. At least, this part here is *our* country, and it most certainly is not free for lesbian sluts to writhe around in, copulating with the forces of Hell.'

I almost laughed then, at the overblown ridiculousness of his hatred. Vivienne and copulating with the forces of Hell were not compatible images. But his hand was hard on my arm, I could feel each individual finger even through my multitude of sweaters and my good coat. 'What if we promise not to do it again?' I asked, my voice smaller than I liked.

'Yeah, 'cause you can always take the word of Satan's whores.' He began to walk now, dragging me backwards across the hard packed snow.

'What are you doing? I'm not going *anywhere* with you!' I skittered and wheeled alongside him, struggling for purchase but my boots had only nylon soles and slid unprotestingly across the wet surface. 'You can't do this.'

He inclined his head downwards. 'Think I can, darling.' He nodded again. 'This gives me permission to do pretty much whatever I want right now,' and I saw the metal sheen and grip of a hand gun, jutting from his pocket like a lethal erection.

'What . . . where are you taking me?' I tried to dig my heels in but my feet just slipped out from underneath me and his crocodile-jawed grip got tighter on my arm as he used it to hold me up.

'Putting you somewhere. Somewhere you'll be safe until I come back for you.' Now he stopped walking but kept pulling until I was dragged right up against him. 'I've got uses for you yet.' His spare hand came into view, gun casually between his fingers as though it was nothing more than an accessory. He ran his thumb over the barrel like you might stroke the palm of a sinisterly familiar hand.

I started to struggle, yanking back against his hold on my arm. I could smell his body, his hair, an age-old cigarette on his breath. I tried not to notice, not to feel the threat of the swelling in his groin or the insolently possessive way he put the gun barrel under my jaw and tipped my face up to force me to look him in the eye. I couldn't breathe now past the terror tightening my airways as he forced my body to turn slowly in front of him and squealed as I felt the gun drop, his hand move across my body, dipping and diving, until he increased his grip with a jerk that almost broke my arm. 'Shut up. I'm just looking for . . . ah, there we are.' My mobile appeared from my pocket for a second and then vanished into the depths of his clothing.

'You can't do this!'

'Yeah? You think?' His tongue became visible, poking from the corner of his mouth like a little hard-nosed rodent. My fear seemed to be exciting him or at least fuelling some twisted fantasy. 'Because *I* think you need to learn some manners, girlie. Need to learn your *place*.'

My heart rose and rose until I thought it was going to come out through my ears and I could taste the bitter swell of adrenaline on my tongue. 'And where would that be, exactly?' It barely came out, a mere whisper, but I said it and then felt proud, even though my tongue had clacked with dryness over my teeth as I had.

He pushed his face against mine, so close that I could see the chip in his front tooth and my nose pricked with the rancid scent of wet wool from his coat. 'Underneath me, darling, that's where.' And then he laughed, a harsh spit-spraying laugh that sent flecks of phlegm onto my cheek and he dragged me forward again, tightening his grip on my arm again until my fingers went numb.

Eventually we stopped in front of a small wooden hut, the kind the farmers use to keep their pheasant feed in and my abductor took a key from his pocket. 'We'll be nice and quiet in here,' he said, as though showing me to a hotel room. 'No one ever comes out here, except Michael, and I was wondering what to get him for Christmas.' He swung round suddenly and touched my face. 'Might be the first year he gets an *un*wrapped present.'

Even my skin backed up at the feel of his finger on my cheek. It crept tighter to my bones while I swallowed a sudden flood of saliva and tried to keep myself from vomiting.

The padlock opened and the door swung inwards. 'But then, wouldn't want you freezing to death before Mike gets a go at you. He likes his girls warm and lively; now me, I'm not so fussy. In you go.' A shove and I overbalanced, toppling into the little hut and banging my knees on the ground. The man was right behind me, a silhouette of evil in the doorway, blocking the light, my air, my escape, his elbows angled oddly until I realised what he was doing — flipping his coat aside to get access to his zip.

I screamed, just once, a weirdly throaty noise as though it came from a nightmare, heeling myself backwards on the muddy floor until I was tight up against the far wall, splinters rasping at my neck. My fists clenched and I worked my back up the timber as I fought my shaking legs to let me stand, let me fight, while my brain begged me to lie down, play dead, stay still, and breathing and gagging had become the same thing.

Into the rough quiet a two-tone tune exploded like a gun-shot in a mausoleum and the man swore then began fumbling his coat back into place, grabbing through the pockets until he came up with a phone. 'Shit. What do you want?' A squawk-back of answer. 'Yeah. I guess. Okay, I'm on my way.' Two seconds later I was alone, the man gone without a word to me, the door was relocked and I was left perched awkwardly on the muddy floorspace, bile souring my tongue and my breath broken in my throat. I looked around. There was no window, the only light in the hut came from under the door in a narrow slice and the air smelled of birds and plastic.

After a few frozen seconds I gave in to tears. Pathetic, I know, but it seemed appropriate and gave my body time to get over the shaky, shocked feeling. Then, after a moment's consideration — I didn't want to find that he'd only walked a couple of yards and could shoot me through the wood — I hurled myself at the door in case, by some fluke, he hadn't locked it properly, or I could burst free. But the door opened inwards. Even if I'd been heavy enough to break the hinges, I would have had to be on the other side of it. After that I yelled for a bit, kicking at the door in the hopes that some passing ramblers might hear me and come. They didn't. When my throat was sore and my eyes were stinging, I slumped down on the claggy earth floor and wondered what I was going to do when my captor came back for me.

Getting the element of surprise, grabbing the gun and fighting like a bitch was my only option. I felt a bit weak and silly that I'd let him get the drop on me so easily anyway, especially after I'd recognised him. And who was this bastard anyway? What axe did he have to grind with anyone doing whatever they wanted in these woods? So what if my best friend was black? So what if we *had* been prancing about, invoking Beelzebub? So fucking *what*?

But really. What *was* I going to do? What had so nearly happened hadn't felt like something I could talk my way out of. My bum was numb and my back ached at the awkward way I had to hunch. The hut was only about six feet square and I couldn't stretch either out or up. And what was Kai's involvement with these men? Did he share their cause? And how long had I got before the guy came back, possibly with his friends?

I indulged myself in another kicking and screaming session, but although it relieved my feelings a bit it didn't attract any help. The hut was too deep into the woods, too far from any footpaths, and Barndale was too remote for there to be hope of anyone wandering past. My heart skidded again as my generalised fear threatened to spiral down into hysteria and I was suddenly struck with the thought that this guy might come back, rape me, murder me and no one would know where I'd gone. I'd just be . . . gone. Nicholas, my parents, Meg, Cerys . . . would they be left forever wondering, forever hoping that I might turn up?

I lay down on the floor with my face against the gap at the bottom of the door and felt a small draught move my hair. Tears fell hotly, running down into the ground as I lay there feeling stupid. Helpless and stupid. Wishing I still had my mobile, some way of signalling to the world that I was here.

Come on, Holly. You're noted for being able to talk your way out, or deal, or . . . *think*.

I cut the self-pity loose and crouched up. The dim, snow-tinted light showed that, apart from half a bag of mouldy-looking grain, the hut contained one wooden pallet with an unopened plastic sack of fertiliser on, two bits of string, a big metal tin that had probably once had something useful in but now contained only a few damp-looking matches, and the wrapper off a Mars Bar which told me I could win a ticket to the 2006 World Cup. Great. I sat on the edge of the pallet with my knees uncomfortably bent double and dug in my pocket. I'd nicked the last of Cerys's glucose tablets so I wouldn't starve, and could probably manage to scrape some snow in, so I wasn't going to spite my captors by being nothing but a freeze-dried corpse when they eventually came back for me. I crunched a tablet, the sweet taste contrasting horribly with my circumstances, and thought.

It was strange how the prospect of being raped and murdered concentrated my mind, and the melting sugar on my tongue swam around my senses, combining with the free-sky blue of the fertiliser bags until an image clicked into my head. Sweet smoke, lots of attention . . . Ooh. All that hanging about on film sets might finally be useful. Fertiliser and glucose. I'd been on set for one spectacular bitch fight between two rival costume guys, where one had bribed some of the backstage boys to build a smoke bomb and set it off in the other's trailer . . . I'd seen how it was done. All I had to do was replicate it and I could set up a smoke signal that should be visible to anyone in Barndale Woods. With luck they'd at least come to find out what was on fire in such damp conditions . . . Well, what was the alternative? Sit here in this damp, chilly little hut until I got terminal rheumatism or raped at gunpoint? I think I'd go with the possibility of blowing my own head off, thanks.

So I did what I'd been shown how to do. Bearing in mind I'd seen it done by professionals, who'd measured everything and observed all the correct safety procedures, it went surprisingly well for an amateur event, right up until I was trapped in a hut full of sugar-smelling smoke, with a load of burning wooden pallet. The draught came swirling under the door, sucking in oxygen and driving the smoke up and out through the holes in the roof. The fire went out and I started coughing, my breath squeezed out past roughening soreness in my throat as the smoke billowed past me. It stank.

Just then I heard a sound outside the hut. A soft footstep. I stopped breathing. Tears streamed from my eyes as I tried to hold the coughing for long enough to hear what was going on out there, no voices, just the sound of someone being quiet. A brief, exploratory shake of the door, and I barely had time to ready myself before an almighty grinding, splintering sound and the door came flying back into the hut, bringing half the frame with it. I ducked past the smoke, kicked out at the coat-shrouded and hooded figure behind it, and ran. Felt my foot connect with a groin but barely had time to register the grunt of pain as my attacker went down and I was running. Racing headlong into the forest, the snow dragging at my feet, tipping me into drifts that I almost burned my way out of with fear; no idea of where I was going or how many I was escaping from, just head down, panic-stricken running as fast as my smoke-congested lungs and my snow-braked boots would allow.

I sprinted for as long as I could, muscles stretched with fear and my hearing supernaturally alert for the sound of gunshots or pursuit. Ran, weaving through the trees, until with my chest groaning and wheezing I slid down into a hollow surrounded by huge oaks and filled with the cast-off leaves of centuries. There I collapsed. My ribs ached, my legs had no strength left in them and I had the horrible feeling that I'd run back towards Dodman's Hill rather than away from it. I lay flat, on top of melting snow and surrounded by plastic sheeting and loose earth, gasping as quietly as I could.

After a few minutes, when my breathing had eased, I heard a voice.

'Holly?' It was a cautious whisper.

'Kai!' *Kai?* What on earth was he doing out here?

'Where are you?'

'Down here,' I threw a meagre handful of leaves up into the air. It was the only act I had strength for. 'In this hole.'

'Jesus.' There was a moment of scrambling activity on the lip of the depression, then Kai appeared, gingerly sliding his way down to me, bent in half. 'How did you get here?'

'I ran. I was in a hut and . . .'

'Yeah. You kick like a mule, you know that?'

'That was *you*? With the door?'

Kai winced and rubbed a tentative hand across his pelvis. 'Which is why it took me so long to follow your tracks through the snow. Whatever happened to asking questions first?'

'I thought you were him! I thought he'd come back with the gun to rape me and if I didn't get out first chance I had then I probably wouldn't ever get away,' I let the words splurge, coasting on relief and spare adrenaline.

'Ssshh.' Kai put a finger over my lips. 'He might still be around, and if I can track you, he can. Can you walk?'

I gave a half-hysterical giggle. 'Better than you probably.'

'Come on then.'

'Where?' I found myself digging my feet into the loamy compost. 'You just said that guy might be still around. I don't want to . . .'

Kai faced me and smiled. It was a rather grim smile. 'We'll go back to the Old Lodge. You said you'd come and see Cerys this morning, didn't you?'

'Yes, but . . .'

'Holly, I need to talk to you. And I want you where I can see you when I'm doing it. Or, at least, both your feet.' He glanced at his groin and let out a little *pfffft* sound. 'Bloody hurts.' He started moving, hit his stride and I might as well have stood on the beach and shouted at the tide for all the notice he took of my protestations. In an echo of my previous abduction his fingers were curled around my arm in an unbreakable grip and he was dragging me along.

'Please don't hold on to me.'

Without speaking he broke his hold and held both hands up, fingers spread. Showing he meant no harm, or was it annoyance? I didn't care. My limbs were trembling with

188

relief and unaccustomed exertion and I couldn't keep up now without him towing me. I began to lag.

'Hurry up.'

'There's still two feet of snow lying here and I'm not wearing seven-league boots.' It probably sounded sharper than I'd meant. Panic was only just now seeping out of my blood. 'Just because you've got abnormal legs . . .'

He surprised me by slowing down. 'Sorry. I want you somewhere safe.'

'But . . .'

'We'll talk when we're under cover. Now, come on, we don't want them coming back and tracking both of us down. Can you run again?'

'I don't know.'

A cautious, cool hand slipped over my wrist. His fingers wound through mine tentatively. 'How about if I help?'

'It's worth a try.' I took a deep breath and kept up as, dodging from large tree to large tree like Wile E. Coyote, and slipping and sliding like really bad Dancing on Ice contestants, Kai raced me through the woods until we came upon the reassuringly gargoyle shape of the Old Lodge. He yanked me through the front door and we fell in a panting, messy heap on the hall floor.

'Wow. Olympics here we come,' I said, leaning forward to try to get rid of the stitch. 'Mind you I'm not sure the four mile ski-drag is an accepted sport yet. Perhaps we should appeal . . .'

'Holly, I know you're in shock, but please shut up.' Kai was puffing too, I was glad to see. All those years of debauchery had clearly left him no fitter than I was. 'We need to talk.'

Cerys shouted down from upstairs. 'Holly, is that you? You coming to say hello, or what?'

'She's talking to me for a bit,' Kai called back, and there was a moment's pause.

'Oh. Oh! Right, yep, get it, you go for it girl. And don't take any of his bullshit, he fancies you something chronic so you get your demands in first.' Her door opened and her voice became clearer. 'I'm up to my ears in here in shit and background noise, so you two let loose and get it out of your systems, and then come in and give me a hand. Oh, Zac, no, not again . . .' and the door closed.

Kai and I closed our mouths, looked at one another and grinned, then realised simultaneously that our hands were still joined, and there was a moment of slightly embarrassed dis-entwining. 'Kitchen?' I asked, trying to pretend that it hadn't been at all awkward.

'I think so.' He led the way and went straight to the kettle. 'And tea, for some reason.'

I didn't say anything. I watched him starting to make tea, being domesticated and comforting, even though I now knew he was the kind of guy who kicks in doors. And my inner feminist protested wildly, but it was nice to be able to sit, hands clamped between my knees to stop them from shaking, tears worrying away at the back of my throat, and know I was safe because of this man. The man who'd also driven through near Alaskan blizzards to find my brother, the man who'd been there when I'd needed him. My opinion of Kai Rhys had changed quite a lot since I'd met him.

He filled the kettle and came to sit on the stool beside me. 'Right. That talk.'

'What are we talking about?' I cleared my throat of the lump of shock and tried to ignore the fact that he'd put himself so close that our legs touched under the table.

'Look.' He stared at his hands and twisted the ring on his thumb. 'Those guys.' A deep breath. 'Holly, you're caught up in something . . . Look, what I do, it's . . .'

'You're a journalist.'

'Yes, but more than that. I'm an in-ves . . . come on, play with me here.'

'Not right now,' I said tartly, and he smiled. 'You're an investigative journalist. And a bastard.'

'In a nutshell. But — I've got the knack, teasing out the stories, and when I moved in here and found out about . . .'

'Why pick on here to live?' I could feel his arm against mine, see the slight prick of silver earring behind his hair. I was too aware of him, that was the problem. 'It's the back of beyond.' I was shaking. Delayed reaction, or just Kai? Didn't know, couldn't tell.

A small shrug. 'Because . . . when I was found, underneath the Daily Mail there was a small scrap of a local paper, the Gazette and Herald. And I always wondered, was it meant as some kind of clue? Was it something she did subconsciously to lead me here? But . . .' another shrug. 'It was something. Something I felt I had to follow. Anyway. Even though I didn't move for work . . . more to get away from it . . . I came here, and there was this bunch.'

The kettle shrilled and he stood up. Carried on talking with his back to me and I wondered if it was deliberate, if he was making himself busy. 'Oh, they're nasty. They've already kicked a lad so hard he's still in hospital. Ruptured his kidneys because they caught him and his boyfriend in the woods. The boyfriend legged it, luckily, went and got help but they hadn't seen anything, just masked shapes coming out of the trees.'

'So, how do you know . . . ?'

He brought two mugs to the table. 'People talk, if you know the right people. And I wondered, you know, about these guys, about what it was that they were doing up there in the woods, what was so important that they had to walk around with guns and scare the shit out of anyone who moved off the official footpaths. I had a good idea, but I got it confirmed by some — well, not friends, but people. But, you know, hearsay is no proof, so . . .' As he passed me my mug he touched the back of my hand with his thumb.

I wrapped both hands around the reassuringly hot china and stared into the downward spiralling of the swirling liquid. My insides felt as though they were spiralling down after it. 'So what has this got to do with me?'

He sat back beside me again. 'Holly. I was watching. I've got a telescope set up' — a wave towards the stairs — 'on the roof. Keeping an eye on Dodman's Hill. And then I saw you getting grabbed.' His breathing stuttered and his words broke.

'You've got a telescope on the *roof*?' I drank some tea, giving myself time to feel my way around this conversation. 'Wow. Seriously pervy.'

A sudden sharp grin. 'Yeah. 'Cause those courting couples are tearing their clothes off and shagging up there in their thousands, what with it being the middle of winter and fifteen degrees below freezing.' He raised his mug and his hand was shaking almost as much as mine. 'I came down off that roof so fast that Cerys actually thought I'd fallen down the stairs. You can ask her if you don't believe me.'

'And why wouldn't I — Oh.'

His eyebrows arched. 'Today you kicked me in the bollocks like you meant it.'

'I didn't know that was you! Why didn't you shout out or something, instead of Bruce Willis-ing it?'

'Couldn't be sure it was you in there. It could have been one of the guys, could have been anyone. Why weren't *you* shouting?'

'I did. No one came.' A ridiculous moment of weakness caused a few tears to attempt a mustering in the corners of my eyes.

'I was out, hunting through the woods and I couldn't find you and I . . . and then there was all this smoke, I heard the coughing and reckoned someone was in trouble. What were you trying to do, by the way? You looked like you were trying to kipper yourself.'

'It was a smoke bomb,' I wished my voice had been steadier. A sentence like that ought to have carried more conviction.

'A bomb.' His mouth twitched.

'Why is that funny?'

'Oh, it's not.' He reached out as though to touch my hair, but let his hand drop. 'You are a very remarkable woman, Holly Grey. And I want you to trust me. No, it's more than that.' His hand went to his own hair and raked through it with a kind of displaced frustration. 'I *need* you to trust me.'

'Why? Why is it so important?'

He stood up again now and began pacing around the kitchen, hands thrust into his pockets like he wanted to stop himself touching anything. 'You and I. It's . . . When you came to Leeds and you were *there* and I realised . . . everything is getting deeper than I'm used to. I'm not great at handling this kind of thing.'

'You can say that again.'

A momentary look. 'Yeah, coming from Ms Emotional Fluency. Look, Holl, I saw that guy grab you and I was terrified. I mean really, flat-out shitting myself. That *means* something to me, the fact that I was so scared for you, it showed me that I — well, goes without saying, Cerys, obviously, and probably the twins too but nothing like it was with Merion. Do you see?'

'Obscure is your first language, isn't it?'

He stopped and turned around slowly. His earring was tangled in his hair and for some reason I couldn't tear my eyes away from it. 'Something is happening, something big, something that feels like elastic stretching between us, snagging us, not letting us go. Something I'm bad at.' Kai put both hands flat on the table and leaned towards me. 'And I don't like being bad at things.'

'Yesterday I saw you talking to the Ginger Man outside, in the woods. I thought you were part of whatever it is that they've got going on.' It came out way too fast, like I was ashamed of having thought it. Maybe I was, a little. 'I thought, maybe, you'd set me up.'

He snapped back away from me like I'd hit him. 'Jesus. God. You seriously thought I'd . . . Woah.' He went back to the pacing, up and down the flagstoned floor like he was on rails. 'This is hard to get my head round.'

'I don't think it any more.' My voice was a bit feeble. 'When you kicked in that door . . . I mean, after I knew it was *you*, I realised you couldn't have.'

'Not just couldn't, Holly.' Kai spun on his heel at the furthest extent of his travel and headed back. '*Wouldn't*. Jeez, woman, I know I'm a journalist but I do have *some* scruples. Is that why you wouldn't stay last night? Because you thought I couldn't be trusted?'

'No. I don't know.' But I did know. Knew that, all along, Kai had been my ally. That I'd used my trumped-up suspicion of his meeting to try to keep him at arm's length, *because I was afraid of letting myself get close.*

'I've been trying to work my way in, yes, trying to get them to trust me. I need . . . I want to blow their whole operation open, so I've been trying to get on the inside.' He closed his eyes and rocked his weight from side to side. 'The job has come first with me for so long. I should have told you, I should have explained, but I don't know how to do it. I want you' — he held up one hand, palm up — 'and then there's work.' He held up the other hand. 'And I don't know how to run it all together. I've never had to. You're the first.' He took one step closer. 'You're the first, Holly,' he whispered.

'You,' I started, but my mouth had gone dry. I licked my lips and saw his eyes follow my tongue. 'So you're investigating those guys?'

'It's drugs, Holly. Okay, yeah, so maybe I used to drink too much, used alcohol to block stuff out and make life a bit easier, but not drugs. Never drugs. I know what they do to you, I've seen . . . And these guys . . . they're running a nice little operation, preying on people in the towns around here; the desperate, the poor, people with no hope. They're shipping the drugs in and then cutting them down so far that they make a huge profit and . . . I can't stand back and let it happen. They don't know I'm a journalist, they see the image and they reckon . . . they think I'm a big time dealer. I've told them I can cut them in on some deals in the city, stuff that will make big money rather than selling to the under-belly of North Yorkshire, and they're all over it.' Kai cleared his throat and looked away from my mouth. 'I tried to warn you off, Holly. Didn't want you getting mixed up in any of this shit.'

'I could go to the police and tell them that one of these blokes threatened me with a gun and locked me in a shed.'

'But there were no witnesses.' Kai looked a lot happier to be talking solid facts rather than wading about knee-deep in emotions. 'Your word against his. And they've got friends, people who would warn you off ever pressing charges with more than a *threat* of violence. His name's Andy, incidentally. Ex-military.'

'Why would anyone believe him over me?'

Kai stared at his hands. 'They've got stuff on you. Pictures of you and your friends doing "magic". They've probably Photoshopped the Devil in by now too, all prepared to use it against you. Proof that you've been up to no good in the woods, that you might want to get *them* locked up to keep the woods to yourselves.'

'Oh.'

'Yep.'

'Why do you do it, Kai? Why not stick to reporting on celebrities and digging the dirt on facelift clinics and stuff like that?'

Kai straightened up suddenly and I had to tilt my head back to keep watching his face. 'The way I grew up, Holly, I saw a lot of good people go to waste. Losing their chances and their hopes and eventually losing themselves . . . and I fucking *hate* it. Don't blame them, for some people there's nothing else, no real life, nothing to look forward to, why not take something that makes it all easier, let it all go over your head? But it's the bastards that get behind it, the ones that make all the money, those are the ones I want to bring down, anyone who's *caused* that kind of misery, the ones that make their millions on the back of others with no future. The ones that make sure it stays that way, the ones that top up the sales pool every so often with some free samples or cut price deals; the *bastards* that laugh and take the money . . . Does any of that make sense? I'm sorry, I tend to get a bit soapboxy when I talk about work.'

'No. You're . . . I think it's great.'

'Really?' Kai leaned back, propping his body against his arms. I tried not to look at the muscles working under the skin, or the way his tight T-shirt gave definition to his chest. 'Most women find it a bit freaky that I hang around with people on the edge of the law.' Thoughtfully he reached his arms above his head in a long stretch, curving slightly backwards until his hair brushed his shoulder blades. It made him look like an erotic statue and then the thought struck me that he was posing for my benefit. I dragged my eyes away, protesting madly, and stared at the surface of my tea instead. It wasn't nearly so interesting, but it kept my blood pressure within European-legal limits.

'So you're trying to catch this lot in the act?' I said, to the table.

'Yeah. But I wanted them to stop hassling you, which is why I tried to talk to Michael. To persuade them to leave you alone.' He came back over to where I had to look at him. 'I didn't think I was giving them ammunition. I was a jerk.'

'A journalist.'

'Not *quite* synonymous, but I see where you're going with it.'

'No, I mean, you were doing your job. Doing what you thought was right.'

He put both hands on my shoulders and his thumbs caressed my neck. 'Thanks for the justification, Holl, but it wasn't right. I should have told you what was going on.' I let the subtle movement of his fingers relax me a fraction. 'I haven't learned to balance it, work and—' His fingers stilled. 'Like I said, you're the first.' There was a sudden slowing of the world, even the dust hanging in the air between us stopped moving. My heart seemed to beat half-time. 'Holly. I think there's something going on here. Something I don't think I've ever been in the right place for before. I see you and how you are with Nick and something inside me just kind of . . . vibrates.' He put one hand out. It was shaking. 'I'm falling, Holly.' Through treacle-thick air he swam towards me.

The artificial gravity began to affect my limbs. Arms too heavy to lift, legs like molten weight and truth was forced out of me by the nearness of him. 'I don't know, Kai. I don't know what this is, and I'm scared.'

'Hey. Past master at terror.' A finger moved like silk over my skin. 'Or is it some unfinished business that's really frightening you? Something to do with Nicholas?'

'Nick is going, Kai. He's talking about moving in with Cerys . . .'

The finger continued to stroke, barely touching me. 'Yeah. My daughter talks to me, you know. Tells me what's happening.' The stroking stopped but the fingertip hesitated, trembling, against my neck. 'And that's worrying you, because of us? Because you're losing your barrier against caring for someone else?' His hand rose, cupped the back of my head.

'I'm worried about *everything*.'

'Then let it go, just for now. Because I think everything just became very, very different for both of us.'

'But Cerys . . .'

'. . . is carefully not listening. You wouldn't want to waste her dedication, would you, Holly?'

This was something else. I could feel it in every molecule in the room, it was in the edge to his voice, that little catch of his words that made them sound as though everything was for me. When he held out his hand I found myself rising to take it, feeling his fingers close around mine and pull me into his warmth until his mouth connected with mine. Unspoken, another dimension, a deep connection, stretched between us, like wire.

I held onto his hand as he led me upstairs. From Cerys's room I could hear the sound of a lullaby as she sang to the twins, probably louder than was commensurate with actually putting them to sleep.

'It's okay,' Kai whispered, 'I can't even hear the twins cry from my room.'

I wasn't sure if he was reassuring me that Cerys wouldn't hear us, or that we wouldn't have to listen to her singing. The Welsh facility with music appeared to have skipped that particular generation.

Once inside his bedroom door, I stopped. 'Kai . . . I don't know if I can do this.'

He turned around and looked at me, that deep, hard look he did sometimes that felt as though it reached right inside my head. 'You're scared. Of me?'

'Of the situation.'

His fingers brushed my face. His thumb ring was cold. 'Can you tell me?'

'When you said your relationships were short and intense . . . well, I don't do them at all.' I tried to read his expression but it was hard, those yellow eyes reflected emotion back, they didn't let it out. 'Hence Aiden and the whole fuck-buddy thing. I've never really had a proper . . . anyone I could talk to.'

A steady breath. 'Do you have many friends, Holly?'

I dropped my eyes and scanned the wooden floor for something to focus on. Anything to distract me from that looking-glass stare of his. 'Of course! Meg and I have been friends since my family moved back to Malton. We were at school together and . . .' I stopped. My eyes traced round and round a knot in a floorboard lost in a loop of memory, 'and she's known me a long time.' Wow, that floorboard was just thrilling to look at. Round and round and round . . . 'Can we not have this conversation now, Kai. Please.' And I forced my eyes up to meet his darkening stare.

'Then say it.'

'Say . . . ?'

'Tell me this isn't just some fly-by-night thing, that you don't just want my body for an hour, a weekend. That I'm different. Because I want . . .' He dropped his hands to my arms, sliding along to my wrists, my skin bunching under his touch. 'I want it to be different.'

I watched his hands moving as though the touch of him was somehow separate to the sensations he was causing and

198

my stomach lurched downwards as I tilted my head to see his face. 'You are definitely different,' I whispered. 'And . . .'

'And?'

'*And I want you.*'

His hands moved from my arms to my shirt, unbuttoning so slowly and carefully that it was all I could do not to knock his hands away and do it myself. 'Oh Holly,' his words blew warm over my skin. '*Holly.*' He dropped his mouth and kissed me with the same edge as he spoke, thoughts, feelings all on that knife blade that cut through these moments. Everything was sharper, the rush when he touched me, the head-whirling sensations of his mouth on mine, as though life had suddenly come into full focus.

We fell onto the bed, reckless and hungry. I yanked at his T-shirt, trying not to lose his mouth while I dragged it off over his head and skimmed my fingers over his chest, glorying at that first sight of his naked skin. Under his clothes his body was lean as a racehorse, fuzzed with dark hair between his nipples and down across his stomach, and he clearly knew how to use every inch of it. His mouth knew how to tease, *where* to tease, turning up new erogenous zones with relentless expertise, his hands stripping my clothes from me with such subtle ease that I didn't realise they'd gone until I felt his cool skin against my own. And his fingers — well. They could pinpoint with almost military accuracy those places guaranteed to make me shiver and gasp.

He was a slender powerhouse. Every inch of him — and there were quite a few — was under control, carefully paced and placed for maximum effect. And when he seemed to consider that he'd done all he could with my outlying regions, he moved to lie above me, hair brushing against my shoulders and eyes burning a hole through my soul.

'Okay?'

He was looking into the liquid core of me, watching me float about as though my body was so many tectonic plates swirling over a molten heart.

'*Mmmm*, Kai . . .'

His mouth came down. 'Ssshh,' he whispered when he raised his head again. 'I'm just getting started.'

'Wow.'

'Oh yes,' the grin was wicked. 'In the words of the song, you ain't seen nuthin' yet.'

Slowly at first, achingly slowly, he moved into me, resting his weight on his arms, looking into my eyes, his pupils so huge that his eyes were nearly black and then they descended like twin shooting stars until his face was against mine and his hair traced the contours of my skin. 'Still okay?'

I just groaned, feeling the weight, the hardness, the sheer intensity of him.

'Good.' And then he let rip. Over and over and he didn't let up, didn't stop for breath, pinning my arms above my head with one hand, reaching between our bodies with the other, a wave of motion and power and force until his eyes closed, his rhythm faltered and I was arching under him, reaching, stretching as the arch broke, fell, dropped through the maelstrom, plunged screaming into the quiet depths where he was waiting.

'Oh,' I was nearly speechless. 'That was . . .'

He turned towards me. 'That was the beginning,' he said, 'because I think I'm in love with you.' His face was so solemn, so shadowed that it was almost frightening. 'I don't know where it came from, I don't know how it's going to go and it terrifies me, but all I can tell you is,' he leaned forward and kissed my mouth softly, 'this feels nothing like what's gone before.'

We lay in silence for a while. Outside the rain started up again and rinsed more snow from the woodland floor, hopefully concealing the fact that our footprints ran from the shed straight to Kai's front door, while underneath the covers, Kai's hand found mine. 'You okay?'

'Stunned, I think. All of this. None of it is what I wished for.'

Kai twisted himself up in the sheet to sit up. 'And would you have? If you'd known, would you have wished for me?'

He folded those devastating long legs into a yoga pose under the covers.

I looked at the naked torso above me, and ran a finger down his ribs. 'Maybe. But I didn't know. I didn't know that it could feel like this. I've always kept feelings out of it, never let things get complicated . . .'

A single raised eyebrow. 'Complicated? Why should this be complicated? You've not got a large angry husband tucked away somewhere, have you?' His hand left my arm and he was suddenly climbing out of the bed, pulling on his clothes, dragging his shirt on over his concave belly and muscled shoulders. 'You'd better go and talk to Cerys. Any minute now she's going to run out of alternate lyrics to "Twinkle Twinkle, Little Star".'

'Are you all right?' I watched him hook an earring back into place and comb his hair straight with his fingers.

'Yeah, yeah. Great. Why?'

'Because you look like you're getting ready to run. It's okay. I'm not going to hold you to some lifelong commitment just because we, well, because we've done this.'

The eyes came down to look at me properly now and their narrow goldenness took me aback again. 'What if I want you to? I thought . . . I've had no practice at this, you know? I . . .' He waved a hand at his chest, '. . . I *feel* it, but I don't know what to do about it. I told you I want this, Holly.' His expression was hot. 'I want *us*.'

'That's partly what I meant when I said it was complicated. I think you need answers first.' I struggled upright to watch him. He'd frozen in the middle of the room like a stag at bay, shirt half way to tucked in and the buttons of his jeans still undone.

'Answers?' He sucked in a deep breath. 'I *give* the answers. That's what I do, why I write, so that I can deal with the cryptic bastard of a crossword that the universe has thrown at us all.'

'Before you can let yourself have anything which might be long term you need to stop dealing with problems and let yourself find a solution.'

'To what?' His eyes had cooled now, they were hard and reflective like yellow diamond.

I stood up and rested my hand against his chest. I could feel the convulsions shuddering inside, the emotions he was trying to hold down. 'To who you are, Kai. Isn't that why you've never really formed a relationship? Because you don't know who you are, where you come from? You need to meet your mother.'

'Shit.' He folded down onto the bed, head bent. '*Shit.*'

'I'm sorry.' I knelt down in front of him but he ducked, keeping his expression hidden.

'No.' The word was muffled. 'You're right. Of course you are. I need . . . some kind of closure before I can start living my life properly, I know that. I *know* that,' he repeated, words tight as though his teeth were clenched. Then his head raised and two hell-bound eyes met mine. 'But why does it have to be so fucking *hard*?'

'Kai.' I had to repeat his name twice more before he looked at me properly again. 'It's okay. You were right, I am starting to realise that all that one-night-stand stuff . . . it's shallow and pointless and my way of avoiding the issue.' I let my gaze wander away from him, across the room, taking in the grim coldness of the light, the mawkish sight of a soggy robin on the balcony rail. 'I know it. Maybe I always did. And now even more so.'

'Now that you know I'm stupendous in bed, you mean.' Sharp humour, but something.

'Yeah, now I know you're hung like a stallion,' I agreed. 'Which is what matters, of course. But I'll be there. If . . . *when* you decide to meet her.'

He looked down again, quickly, letting his hair hide his face. Then he nodded, one short movement, dragged in a deep breath and blew it out. 'I want to know that I'm not — That it wasn't because of me. That's all. No excuses, no reasons. I just want to know that I'm not—' The merest trace of a sob, lost in sudden, violent movement as he leaped up and paced towards the window, fingers busy on the buttons of his shirt. 'And I'm not the only one who needs closure, am I?' He spoke with his back turned, body almost pressed against the glass.

'Sorry?'

Now he spun round, head tilted as though his world view needed adjustment. 'You and Nicholas. You need to forgive him for not being the perfect big brother, Holly.'

I found I was dragging at the bedcover, pulling it across my nakedness. Putting back that barrier that I'd kidded myself had come down. 'I don't understand.'

'You need to think about it.' Kai spoke gently, although his voice was still uneven. 'I can't make you see, Holly. I'm not in the right place myself to be dictating how anyone's life goes. And besides . . .' Again, that breaking note, 'I'm not really the person to talk about forgiveness, am I?' A quick, mood-changing flick of his head, a grin and he opened a drawer and threw me a shirt. 'Here. Go prancing around the house in this. Although if Cerys asks for details, I hope you'll have the decency to fudge over the anatomical stuff.'

Okay, I thought to myself, well, I'm right behind that emotional flip. 'I'm not sure fudge will cover it. I might have to toffee as well, possibly chocolate coating and a layer of coconut too. It is pretty big.'

'Hey, what's your best friend like?'

I thought for a second, then threw a pillow at him.

CHAPTER TWENTY-ONE

Okay. This is different now. You're so close that I can almost touch you and I'm putting up all these walls to keep you away from me, but I'm still . . . God, I'm still writing these letters. So part of me wants you to know me and the other part . . . the other part is fucking terrified. But now it's not just us that's different, it's my whole life. For the first time I'm making room in my heart for someone. Or, I'm trying to. 'Course, there's part of me that's saying this is stupid, I should keep her away — it's all going to end the way it always has ended, tears, recriminations, me pouring all the pain into my job and my writing. Never standing still long enough to feel anything. But she . . .

The prospect of meeting you isn't about you. It's about me. I want to know you, or . . . I want to know who you are but really I want to know me. Where I came from, how I came to be. And I want it straight, no justifications, no excuses. No hiding. I just want to know. And then it's over, this whole life I've built on sand, because I shall know. Whether I'm from doctor or digger stock. No more late-night fantasies. You'll be tearing away the plaster that's lain over an old, old wound, ripping it off and letting the air get to it, get to me, show me who I am. Then I can go on with life, I can start to settle.

And I want that. Holly is . . . for the first time, she's the woman I want to be with. I don't know how it happened, suddenly she was here, touching my heart. When she listened, just sat there and listened to me talk, about you, about the past . . . and she saw. She watched me open up for the first time in my life, talk about what all this meant to me — all the shit that I've kept hidden, kept away from the other women, the ones that just wanted the image . . . And it makes me cry, over and over again, the fact that I couldn't live, couldn't be who I was, because I had to protect myself from their pity. Had to be in control of it all. Never let anyone in, never let anyone see that at the heart of me was this big, empty nothingness, because how could I know what lay inside me, when I didn't even know who I was?

Now I'm ready to share myself with someone else. But first I have to understand . . .

CHAPTER TWENTY-TWO

I stood on the edge of the field and watched Megan chasing after Rufus. He was treating it like a game, waiting for her and then dodging away just when she thought she'd got close enough to snap his lead on. 'You could help, Holly,' she said crossly, sprinting past me for the third time. 'Head him off.'

'Nicholas, head him off.'

'She asked you. And anyway, it might wake Zac.' He jiggled the buggy containing a sleeping baby.

'I thought that was Freya?' I looked at the bundle, double-wrapped against the chilly wind and wearing a pink knitted hat.

'Cerys wants to avoid gender stereotyping. Don't you?' He called over his shoulder to Cerys, who was sitting gingerly on a bench, rocking a rainbow of blanket, bootees and mittens.

'Yeah. Plus he's been sick on everything else.'

I went and sat next to her, blatantly ignoring Megan's increasingly desperate accelerations. 'So, you're off tomorrow.'

'*Mmm.*' Cerys wiped her face with a gloved hand. 'I'm going to miss you. Please come and visit as soon as you can. I need to go now, I can't stay forever, I'd cramp your style too much.'

'What do you mean?'

A snotty giggle. 'Oh come on. You and Kai carefully keeping your hands to yourselves. Half the time I needn't be there when you come over, you spend the whole time looking at him like you want to eat him. I don't know why you don't just fuck it out of your systems.' She winced. 'Ow. It even hurts to *mention* sex. That can't be right, surely.'

A quick, bright blush crept up my face. 'I don't, do I?'

She nodded. 'Yep. What are you waiting for? Move in with him, Holly, he needs you. Well, he will when I'm gone; how are you at ironing?'

'I don't iron.'

'Oh. Oh well, I'm sure you have other talents.' Cerys nudged me. 'Did he appreciate them the other day?'

'I don't know what you mean.' The blush had reached my hairline where it clashed almost audibly with my hair.

'Holly, you came in to talk to me wearing Kai's shirt and no bra. You'd either just got out of his bed or you'd decided to let your inner slut run free. *And* he was singing all morning and, while I don't usually appreciate karaoke Muse, it was great to hear him so happy. But since then you've been all hands-off.'

Almost, I thought, and the blush deepened. 'We want things to go slowly. Not to rush anything.' And besides, collectively we had more issues than The Times.

'Bollocks to that.' Cerys didn't seem to have anything to follow up with, so we sat in quiet contemplation for a moment, appreciating the comedy potential of a small, chunky brunette chasing a huge athletic dog.

Eventually Nick, being a gentleman, gave in. He got up and went over towards Rufus, clicked his fingers and then patted the dog's head. Rufus sniffed at his hand for a moment then stood, stock still, with a look of incredulity on his face.

'How did you do that?' Megan snapped the lead on and Rufus, instantly contrite, plodded alongside her rolling his eyes and trying to look at his own teeth.

'I gave him a toffee. It's all right, it was a vegetarian one.'

Rufus crouched down and tried to shove his paws in his mouth. 'Well, at least it worked. We're supposed to be going over to see Vivienne this afternoon, and I didn't want to have to cry off because I couldn't catch my dog.'

'Are we?'

'Yep.'

'It's not another "commune with the mother earth in the hopes that some idiot bloke tops himself" is it? Or are we still trying to find men for Isobel and Eve?'

'I'm not sure. She says there's news, not sure if it's good or bad, but we ought to go and express our solidarity.'

'And we ought to get back and finish packing.' Cerys wound her arm through Nick's. He'd already been mistaken for the twins' father twice, which he quite enjoyed even though it made Cerys laugh until she was nearly sick. 'Kai is keen to get rid of us as early as he can tomorrow. I can't *think* why.' She rolled her head towards me. 'Can you, Holly?'

'Can't imagine.'

'It's going to be great. Just think, Peterborough.'

My heart raced at the thought of him being so far away, but I kept my voice light, didn't want to scare him. Couldn't really believe that he'd go, not like this, not *really* go . . . 'Er, Nicky, you do know that Peterborough isn't the same as Los Angeles, don't you?'

'Don't care. It's somewhere new. Somewhere different.'

'Come on then Holly. Let's take Rufus home and then we'd better go in your car to Vivienne's. He did something nasty in the boot of mine yesterday and I can't get the smell out.'

'Yeah, all right.' I kissed Cerys, hugged Nick and touched the twins' cheeks. 'I'll come over and see you tomorrow. Before you . . . go.'

'Making sure we leave the premises,' Cerys began pushing Freya's buggy over the muddy field. 'Doesn't want us hiding round the back and sneaking in when she's deep in a bit of literal how's-your-father.'

'That whole wishing thing has really worked out for you, hasn't it?' Megan sounded a bit forlorn. 'Your "excitement". Is he really . . . you know . . . *exciting*?'

'He's a lovely man. A bit confused about things, but lovely.'

'Better than Aiden?'

'Meg, *the Creature from the Black Lagoon* would be better than Aiden. Kai is . . . something else. On a completely different scale. Totally . . . just wow.'

'I always thought . . . one day, you and Aiden . . .'

'. . . and Aiden's friend and *his* friend, and his friend's girlfriend. No, Megan, I was never going to end up with Aiden.' We walked back to Megan's little flat with a docile Rufus striding along between us.

'Take no notice, I'm just jealous it didn't work for me.' She reached down to fuss Rufus's head, although she didn't have to reach very far. He turned his eyes up to her.

'But it did.'

'Oh yeah, I'm being worshipped by *invisible* men. Just my luck.'

'Meg, look at him.' I pointed to Rufus. He was still staring at her face, ears rising and falling like a comedy puppet's. The string tail wagged when she glanced down. 'If he isn't worshipping you like a goddess, then I don't know what it looks like. He's devoted to you.'

'But . . .'

'Did you specify it should be a man?'

'Can't remember,' she said sulkily.

'He adores you utterly. You can do no wrong. Even when you shout at him, he won't leave your side. To him you are God.'

'I wanted a man.' But her fingers curled around the knobbled top of the dog's head and ruffled his ears. He beamed.

'And I was kind of inclining more towards winning the lottery. I think, maybe, we should have been more specific.'

'Next time,' Megan began, but I stopped walking and put my fingers in my ears.

209

'No, no, no, lalalalala, I can't hear you. No next time. Never, ever again am I doing anything as stupid as a wishing spell.'

'Not even if the others want to? Okay, maybe you're right, maybe Rufus is my wish come true.' He looked up at the mention of his name and his dark eyes were ablaze with love. 'But nothing seems to be happening for the others. They might want a rerun.'

'Count me out.'

'Isn't that a bit selfish?'

I turned to her. Her brown eyes were wide and childlike, she was cute and innocent and guileless. 'Pissfuckingwank,' I said, and strode off towards my car, not caring whether she joined me or not.

After a further brief tussle with Rufus to get him to go into the flat alone, she came and sat in the passenger seat. 'I'm sorry,' she said. 'I didn't mean it. I know you're the least selfish person there is.'

'Huh. We'd better hope that there's some breaking news on the wishing front then, because selfish or not, I am never again going anywhere near anything more magical than the Harry Potter films. And even then I'm going to watch from inside some kind of protective circle.'

Vivienne opened the front door to us, and as usual we were the last of the group to arrive. 'Holly and Megan!' She sounded as though she were announcing the Queen and Prince Philip. 'How wonderful that you're here.'

'Well, you did ask us to come.' Megan draped her coat over the sofa next to Eve. Eve herself looked a little smarter today. She'd had her hair cut and coloured so that it curled softly around her face. I thought her clothes looked new too, but didn't like to mention it.

'Oh yes, things are definitely starting to happen.' Vivienne clasped her hands to her lack of bosom, twisting them around one another like someone trying to squeeze the last toothpaste out of the tube. She looked perkier too. She'd lost the grey roots under a new scarlet tint, her skin was less pallid and her make-up seemed to have been done with a surer hand.

I wondered if the local hairdresser had a two-for-one offer on.

'He's lost everything!' Vivienne announced proudly. 'The business, the company car, all those little perks associated with the job. Isn't it wonderful? We'll see how Miss Busty from Accounts likes him now, when there's no sporty little Audi for her to show her breasts off in!'

Eve made a face. 'But what about your lovely cottage?' She waved a hand around. 'All your beautiful things?'

'Maybe the cats will get repossessed,' Isobel whispered in my ear. She hadn't sneezed once since we'd come in, so perhaps they already had been.

'Oh, they can't touch anything here, it's all in my name,' Vivienne airily shook her head. 'But Richard is losing everything, which was the point of the spell. Soon he'll be forced . . . I mean, he'll see no other way out. Once the tax people start looking into his affairs, asking all those wretched questions . . .' She tailed off, a rather sinister little smile shuffling its way across her mouth. 'I think we'll have biscuits today. I have a packet of Belgian Chocolate cookies put away for just such an occasion.'

'She keeps biscuits for the day her husband is driven into penury?' I sat next to Eve. Isobel and Megan went to help in the kitchen. At least, Isobel went to help, Megan would go anywhere if there was a Belgian Chocolate cookie at the end of it.

'Ah well. She's taking it as a sign that the spell is starting to work for her.' Eve moved her well-upholstered bottom further along to make more room for me. 'And I have a little news in that direction myself.'

'Eve, you dark horse!' I stared at her in amazement. 'The man of your dreams?'

She nodded, then looked down shyly at her swollen feet. 'Oh, but it's *such* early days yet, I hardly want to say anything in case it all goes wrong.'

'I thought you had a bit of sparkle to you,' I said admiringly. 'Well, good on you, Eve. What's he like? What does he do? Or is he a retired millionaire who can keep you in luxury?' I surprised myself by hoping that this was the case.

'My lips are sealed.' Eve did the statutory mime.

'Well, I hope we get to meet him.'

'Oh, I hope so too. Maybe, in a while.'

'What's his name?'

But Eve shook her head and did the 'lip-zip' mime again. But her eyes shone with humour and anticipation, so whoever he was, he was doing her good.

That only left Isobel. 'I hope Aiden wasn't horrible to you the other day,' I said as she came in laden with a tea tray. 'Thanks for letting him out.'

'No, he was a perfect gentleman.' Isobel poured tea and Megan put a rather depleted looking plate of biscuits on the table. 'Quite sweet, really. Very cute too, Holly. You certainly have a good taste in men.'

'So, any news from you? Any men hell bent on making you the centre of their world?'

She did comedy-disappointment-face. 'Sadly, no. But it's all right, like I said. I'm coming to think that I'm better off without one. Mum and Dad are talking about making the house over to me and going off to live in Australia when Dad retires next year, and between work and redecorating, I don't think there'll be time for a man.'

'They're not like horses, you know. They can manage to do most things for themselves, men.'

'Oh, you know what I mean. I want to be able to remodel the house without having anyone distracting me. I'm taking an evening class,' she added proudly.

'In not being distracted? Gosh. That's a bit specialised isn't it?' Megan dunked a biscuit in the hot tea and dribbled consequent chocolate down her chin.

'In interior design. It's an old cottage we've got, sixteenth century, and I want to do it up as close to the original plans as possible. If it works I'm thinking of starting up my own business, sort of fifteen-hundreds' bed and breakfast.' Now I came to look at her, Isobel was looking better too. Her acne seemed to be clearing up finally and her hair had extra shine. It might not have been her wish coming true but she clearly had a new lease of life.

'Pallet and pottage?'

'So, Holly. I take it that you didn't collect my candles and go straight to the police?' Vivienne sat opposite Eve, a poised cup and saucer on her lap and a cat staring down from her shoulder.

'Ah. Yes. Been meaning to talk to you all about that . . .'

On the way home in the car Megan finally lost her boggle-eyed expression. 'He *held you at gunpoint?* And *locked* you in a *shed*,' she said wonderingly. 'And Kai rescued you?'

'Only technically. I was well on the way to rescuing myself, but the bomb went out. Good grief, that's a weird sentence.'

'God, Holl.'

We were silent again for a bit, watching the hypnotic windscreen wipers fighting the downpour. It had begun to rain with a vengeance and going anywhere at the moment was a bit like sailing the Atlantic. 'It was frightening,' I admitted at last. 'I got taken in by the whole "looking sexy" thing, and by the time I realised that he was as mad as the Planet of Spoons, it was too late.'

'Handsome is as handsome does,' Megan nodded wisely. 'And I was thinking about what you said before. About Rufus. He *does* treat me like a goddess, and it's my own stupid fault for not being more specific with my wish that I've got a big hairy dog instead of . . . well.'

'A big hairy man?'

'Yes, that. But then, I have met more men since I've been walking Rufus than I ever did at work. It's not noted for its straight male demographic, British Home Stores but it's amazing how many people will come and talk to you when you're out with a dog.'

'There you go then. You've got your wish, but just obliquely.'

'Obliquely? Those are pillars, aren't they?'

'Obelisks, Meg. But maybe that's the price we're paying for doing the spell with all those weird photographs and bits cut out of books and things. I mean, my excitement is very odd, and then there's Nicky's wish . . .' I had to explain the whole 'girlfriend with big tits' thing then and Megan didn't stop sniggering all the way back to her flat.

'It does serve him right a bit,' she said. 'But it makes you wonder. If it's all gone, um, *oblique*, then what about Vivienne? And Eve? And why hasn't anything happened to Isobel?'

I shook my head. Things were moving in such mysterious ways that they were positively heading the Ministry of Silly Walks, but was it just my imagination? Would everything have happened this way anyway? Were we all guilty of falling for the, very human, desire to be able to put the universe into order? Or . . . I felt the fairy-fingered tickle of wonder rise up my spine . . . was there really more to this 'magic' than I realised?

'I've got an address.'

'That's nice. So much better than the old no-fixed-abode thing which, I have to say, wasn't really working out for you.'

'Ha.' Kai swept a load of crumbs off the table and then gazed around in search of something. 'Have you seen the vacuum cleaner? Cerys must have left it — I'd have noticed if she'd tried to smuggle that back to Peterborough, surely?'

'With the amount of stuff she had? I doubt it.'

'What did she do, stuff it in a giant condom and make Nicholas carry it up his backside?' Kai opened a cupboard and peered inside. 'And there's pickled beetroot in here. That *has* to be Cerys, I hate the stuff. God, I miss her.'

Not as much as I miss Nicholas. My hand still wandered to the telephone receiver every morning, my heart thumped whenever I saw a text from him ping onto my phone. It felt like a death in the family. Knew I had to let him go, to let him make a life for himself, ashamed of how it felt . . . Ashamed of the blank hours, hours I had used to spend running up to his flat to make sure he'd eaten, washed his clothes, taken his meds; it was only now that I was realising how many of those hours there had been.

'What's this address then?' I tried to distract him, well, both of us. We were still skirting around our relationship like a couple of deserters from a battlefield trying to avoid capture.

'From the PI in Leeds. Strange, really.' He sat down on the newly uncrumbed table, putting his feet up on one of the stools and picking at a thread on the knee of his jeans. 'She only lives a handful of miles from here. Think, I could have walked past her in the street without knowing.'

'So, what's the next step? Do you write to her, or what?'

He stopped picking and stared down at the floor. 'No. She wants to see me, well, I'm not giving her any time to prepare, I want to see her as she *really is*, not as she'd have me see her. Does that make sense?'

'Isn't it a bit unfair on her?'

'I don't think I have to be fair. I think I'm entitled to be as fucking *un*fair as I feel like.' He kicked his feet off the stool and stood up, opening cupboards at random and slamming doors.

I watched him for a moment as he turned his fear and longing into anger and activity. 'When do we do it?'

'Soon,' his voice was muffled in the boiler cupboard. 'Yeah. Soon. Before Christmas anyway.'

'That's only a couple of weeks away.'

'Yeah. Maybe New Year. Or . . . Oh, here's the vacuum. Jesus, more beetroot, what did she do, bath in the stuff?'

'It makes you go orange.' I didn't want to think about Christmas. With Ma and Dad so far away in Scotland, the last few years it had been Nicholas and me, with the occasional addition of Megan if her dad and step mum had taken off on another cruise. I'd shopped and cooked and we'd gone to midnight Mass and it had all been a bit . . . thin, somehow.

215

Nick couldn't drink on his medication and I hated drinking alone, so we'd sat stone cold sober and eaten fruit cake neither of us liked. Now Nick was going to have his first true family Christmas with Cerys and the twins and her mum and dad who, apparently, adored him and I was here, looking down the barrel of the festive season alone. Kai had only mentioned Christmas once, in the context of how much he was looking forward to escaping it by working on a piece about Afghan rebel fighters in their native habitat.

'Before Christmas might be best. She'll spend Christmas knowing that she's got a granddaughter and two great-grandchildren.'

'Come on, Holl, you're behaving as if she's been in stasis since she gave me away. She's probably had a bunch of children and loads of grandkids and I'll just be one more, tacked onto the family like some kind of prosthetic.'

'You don't know that.'

'No. I don't.' He stopped slamming around and stood in the corner, resting his head against the wall with his back to me. 'I am so, so bad at this.'

'I don't think it's something you can practise.' A little bit tentatively I went over and touched his shoulder. I had to stand on tiptoe to do it.

'I meant, forgiveness. I know, deep down, that it probably wasn't her fault, that she didn't want to . . . to leave me, but then I think about Cerys. You know she got pregnant by accident? She and her boyfriend' — he spat the word as though it was the same as *steaming pile of shit* — 'had only known each other for a matter of weeks. And then she's having twins and he's having second thoughts. But she never, *never* considered giving them up.'

'Kai.' I ran my hand up and down his arm. 'Thirty-six years ago the world was a different place.'

'You don't know.'

'No, but I did history at school,' I said sharply. 'You can't make any judgements until you know, that's all I'm saying.

Yes, Cerys kept the twins, but she's got a rich, successful journalist for a supportive father, and a nice mum and an extra dad who were both behind her all the way, and her own flat . . .'

'Bought by her rich, successful journalist father,' Kai put in, but he was sounding a bit more cheerful now.

'You see? Not exactly life on the breadline for our Cerys.'

'Cerys would toast and eat the breadline.' He turned round now, biting his lip. 'I am such a jerk, Holly. A screwed-up, cowardly jerk.'

'You forgot self-pitying.'

'Oh yeah, that too.' He traced my cheek with a finger. 'Why do you hang around with me?'

'I'm after your money.'

'Ah. Thought that might be it.' He smiled and I tried to keep my knees from wobbling. 'How about tomorrow?'

'How about what tomorrow?'

'We go and find my mother.' Now his look was challenging, as though he was expecting me to bottle out.

'Okay, yeah. Right. Fine.'

'Holly.' Kai grabbed my wrist. 'Don't go home tonight. Stay. Please.'

'Kai, she's your mother, not a man-eating hyena, this isn't your last night on the planet.' I felt that I had to be sensible for both of us.

'Are you regretting the sex the other day?' He let go of me suddenly. 'Is that it?'

'God, *no*. And, if you remember, it was me who told you to sort your head out before you started any kind of relationship.' I watched him flip his hair nervously, tap his ring against the table edge, twitchy and edgy.

'I know. I . . . We don't seem to have talked. I mean, properly talked, about anything. About us. I admit, I freaked a bit with all these feelings crashing down around me, all stuff I've never felt before and don't know how to handle. But, there you are, still. Like this kind of constant. And that's something I've never managed to keep, Holly, constancy. I had ten years of it, and I took it for granted then, but . . . I couldn't hold it, and now I don't know how to . . . I've never looked for it in any of my relationships, I thought transience was all there was.' He put his hands either side of the sink and leaned forward, seeming to be looking out of the window, but really looking inside himself. Those strange, yellow eyes lost focus and he went very still.

'Are you afraid you're going to blow it?' I asked softly. 'Because I am.'

A flick of the head and he was looking into me again. That intense stare that twisted my stomach and made my heart slide sideways in my chest. 'Yes.' It was a whisper, barely even that. 'Yes, I'm afraid I'm going to blow it.'

'One day at a time, Kai.' It took all my concentration not to tear his shirt off. There was something purely sexual about his look, and yet something deeper than sex, something that spoke to my soul. 'Let's take it slowly. You do what you have to, to keep your head straight, and I'll do what I have to.'

His eyes were suddenly alive, moving like flame, darting across my face to my lips, down my neck and back up again. 'I want you to stay, be with me tonight, keep me from backing down, backing out, running away, because that's what I want to do too.'

'Don't run from me, Kai.'

He touched my face, ran a finger down where his eyes had already licked my skin. 'At the moment I'd be lucky if I could walk.' Mouth followed fingers following eyes, and then we just let the hormones do the communicating for us. He pushed me up onto the table, rucked up my skirt and, with a suddenness that made me inhale like hiccups, he was inside me.

I tried to speak but he kissed the words away, kissed me till the kitchen spun, moved until the air went black and sparks rose, fanned to fire and then burned to embers. And then did it all again. Finally he lay above me, boneless and wordless, damp hair in both our eyes. 'Good, yes?'

218

'Oh, yes.' I stared at the ceiling cornices, chuckling demons and something that looked half-man half-pig. '*Yes*.'

He pulled me up into a sitting position next to him. 'Let's not leave it so long next time, yeah? In fact, let's do this a *lot* more.'

'Hey now, don't get reckless.' We let our legs dangle off the side of the table. 'One of us is going to have some work with the Dettol before we have dinner.'

'So you'll stay then?'

I looked at him, dark hair counterpointing those eyes and stubble-scattered cheeks. 'What, turn down a man who makes love to me on the kitchen table? Do I look mad?'

'At the moment you look flushed and very, very sexy.' He kissed me again, long and slow. 'And now Cerys is gone, I'll make love to you all over the house if you want.'

'Only if *you* want.'

He gave me the most evil grin and pushed my hand down. 'Oh yes, I want,' he said. 'See?'

'Where do you get your energy from?' I closed my fist and he closed his eyes.

'Same place as you.' It was a groan, not real words. 'I sold my soul to the Devil . . .'

CHAPTER TWENTY-THREE

'Do I look all right?' Kai asked for the hundredth time. 'It's not too . . . you know, scruffy?'

'You look gorgeous, as you well know. That poor waitress nearly dropped the coffee pot, can't you tone it down a bit?'

'How does one tone down one's natural sex appeal?'

'Well, *one* could try not wearing jeans that are quite so tight, for a start.' I rubbed a patch of steam off the café window and peered out onto the street. Outside, another shower blustered down the road, sweeping a week's worth of newspapers before it and depositing them in a pile of leaves and chip shop debris. The little town where Kai's mother evidently lived was clearly not having a good day — everywhere looked grey and underpopulated and the cobbles which lined the main street looked treacherously shiny.

'You didn't complain this morning,' Kai blew in my ear. 'In fact, I distinctly remember having to get dressed twice.'

'That was your fault, with the . . .' I made a general gesture which pretty much indicated his whole body, 'and the leather jacket and the earring.'

'I just want to look good.'

'Kai, she'll know you're successful. Bin men don't wear Prada.'

He rested his elbows on the sticky table. 'Funny, having to tell your own mother your name.' Now he looked out through the smeared condensation. 'I've been here loads of times. I had the Jeep serviced over there,' he jerked his head. 'Never knew she was here, this close.'

'No reason you would.' I looked at his empty cup. 'Are you ready?'

'Yes. No.' He held his hand up. 'Look, I'm shaking. What kind of a way is this to behave?'

'A natural one.' I gathered up my bag and kicked my high heels back on. All right, I admit it, I'd dressed up to meet Kai's mother. Not that she'd be looking at me, of course, she'd be struck blind by the glamour of her son, who was working the battered leather jacket, long hair, silver jewellery thing to death. But I wanted her to . . . what? Think me suitable? Not assume that I was his minder? To those ends I'd worn a black jacket and skirt, with heels and matching bag and I'd put my hair up. I looked like I was off to a high-class funeral.

He watched me without moving. 'I'm going to introduce you as my girlfriend,' he said. 'It won't freak you out too much, will it?'

'I think I can cope.' I shoved a fiver under a saucer. 'You look like an entrant in Britain's Next Top Model.' He still wasn't standing up. 'Kai, you don't have to do this if you don't want to.'

'No, I do.' Now he stood up and blocked out what little light was coming in to the tea shop. 'I really do. And I have to do it in the next ten minutes, because I think that's as long as my breakfast is going to stay down.'

'Hey.' I grabbed his hand. 'Come on. You never have to see her again, if you don't want to.'

'Yeah, I know.' A weak smile brought a little colour to his face and a shine to his eyes. 'I've faced the Mujahideen and been less scared.'

We walked along the street up the hill towards the twelfth century castle ruins that lay picturesquely overlooking the town. 'This is it,' Kai stopped outside a white-painted little house which fronted straight onto the road. 'Seventeen. God, Holly.'

'She might not even be in.' I stared at the innocent window, framed by cream curtains. 'There's no lights on.'

'Well, she'd better be, because I'm not coming back.' He braced his hands on his knees, leaned down and took two deep breaths. 'Okay. C'mon Rhys, you can do this.' Then he knocked, knuckles sounding hollow against the door.

I watched him slip from scared civilian into journalist mode. He set his face against disappointment and dismissal, narrowed his eyes, drew his mouth into a line. His back straightened and his shoulders squared. He gave me a tiny wink. And if I hadn't known it was all an act of massive bravado, I would have been impressed. But I did, and I knew how fragile he was under it all.

There were footsteps. We could hear them through the door, shuffling towards us, the tapping sound of a stick against a wooden floor. Kai's eyes widened, his head came up and I thought for a second he was going to run, but he stood his ground, although I could almost see his heart beating through his jacket. The door opened.

'Bloody hell,' I said, but I needn't have spoken at all. They looked at each other.

'David,' said Eve, softly. 'I would have known you anywhere. You look just like your father.' Then she noticed me. '*Holly?*'

'I repeat, *bloody hell.*'

There was a moment of three-way staring. 'You know David?'

'It's Kai. Kai Rhys,' Kai said sternly. 'Holly is my . . . we're together.'

Eve couldn't take her eyes off him. 'David,' she kept saying. 'You found me.'

'Do you think we could come in?' I asked eventually. 'I'm afraid he might fall down if we stay out here.'

'Oh! Oh yes, I'm so silly, come through. There's so much . . . so much . . .' Limping ahead, she led us through to a neat, cream and white living room. There was a fire blazing in the hearth and Cash in the Attic on mute in the corner. It was tidy and clean and, I noticed, there were no photographs of family anywhere. 'Oh. I can hardly believe it. David . . .'

'Kai.'

'I'm sorry. Of course, Kai. And the accent.'

'I was born in Wales. Oh, you know that.' He sat down and clamped his hands between his knees, and only I knew it was to stop them shaking. 'You were there. Briefly.'

And then he started to cry and she started to cry and it was only by excusing myself to go and make some tea in the midget kitchen which adjoined, that I managed to prevent myself from bursting into tears as well.

Eve's kitchen was as neat as her living room, and her tea canister contained tea, unlike mine, which held matches. There was a small packet of fancy biscuits in the cupboard, but since the cupboard contained little else, and the fridge was down to half a pint of milk and three eggs, I left them there. On one of the shelves was a brown medicine pill bottle and I read the label while the kettle boiled. Made three cups of tea and carried them through to find Kai sitting on the floor, knees under his chin and his arms wrapped around his legs, like he'd tied himself into a parcel. No one was speaking, the only sound was the crack and spit of the fire and the deep tick of an old clock on the mantelpiece.

I handed Eve a cup and listened to it rattle as she took it. 'You must have so much to talk about,' I said into the uncomfortable silence.

'I don't know where to start.' She looked at me helplessly. 'There's too much to say.'

'Well, let me give you a starting point.' Kai wouldn't look up. 'How about, who the *fuck* am I? Who was my father, what happened there?' His eyes met mine for a second and I was taken aback by the desperation I saw there. 'What *happened*,' he repeated, his body starting to shake inside the leather jacket. He pushed a fisted hand into his mouth and I heard his teeth connect with the silver rings as he tried to stop himself crying by biting down.

'I grew up . . . My parents . . .' Eve's words faltered as her throat juddered. 'Well, no, that's unfair on Mum, it was Dad, really. Mainly. He was a bit . . . narrow minded, I suppose. Strict. I was his little girl, his princess.' She blinked hard as though her eyes couldn't believe this man twisted around himself on her living room floor. 'Didn't want me to have boyfriends or wear make-up, or go out with friends, you know . . . protective. That was all.'

I could think of other words to describe that kind of behaviour, but none of them mattered now.

'I worked in Pickering, in a care home for the elderly. It was . . . nice. I used to sit and chat to the residents about the old days, they used to tell me their life stories, it was, yes, *nice* and a job that dad approved of. Not much chance of meeting any eligible men, you see, not when you spend the day with the over-eighties.' She smiled at her joke but Kai was looking at the end of the world and couldn't muster so much as a deathly stretch of the lips.

'But you did.' I felt I had to keep everything on track. My job to be the responsible one. 'Obviously.'

'I . . . He came on a delivery, laundry, I think. Gorgeous boy, dark hair and those *eyes* . . .' She bit her lip. 'Da — Kai, you look so much like him' A wobbly half-smile. 'Do you always look like this, by the way? The leather and the earring and things? Or is it for my benefit?'

Kai's head came up. He'd drawn blood on his fingers and I felt my heart triple-time. 'No,' he said. 'No. *I* ask the questions.'

'Kai,' I touched his face. He took hold of my hand, and gripped like a child afraid of falling.

'It's okay,' he said, either to me or himself. 'It's okay. I can do this. Holly . . .'

'It was only the once. In the potting shed in the gardens, while I was supposed to be putting up the Christmas decorations. And then, of course . . .' Eve gave a tiny shrug that encompassed a world of terrible decisions. 'I didn't dare say anything at home. Dad would have . . .' another little shrug. 'And I didn't have any money, or anywhere to go, no friends to take me in . . . *please*, David, please try to understand.' She reached out and tentatively touched his shoulder, a touch he either couldn't feel or ignored.

Instead he looked up at me, as though this were my story. 'Holly, I need to . . . can you give us some time?'

He needed to fall, I could see that. To drop into this whole new relationship without a safety net. 'Yeah. I'm going to pop out and get some milk,' I replied to his unspoken plea. 'Back in a sec.'

I walked up and down the main street a few times, popped into the little Co-Op and bought milk, eggs and some bacon to replenish Eve's sparse stores. Watched the Christmas lights swinging in the chill wind, saw some children racing down towards the river, gloved and booted against the rain, hand in hand and laughing. To occupy some more time I watched them, obviously a family group, making paper boats and setting them afloat on the meltwater-swollen beck at the bottom of town, then following their progress by running down to the bridge to stand and watch to see whose boat came underneath first. Two brothers and a tolerated little sister, annoying and adorable in equal measures, hero-worshipping her older siblings, accepting their taunts when her boat floundered, and cheering when she beat them.

This was how it was *supposed* to be. For the first time in the twenty years since Nicholas's illness had manifested, I allowed myself to feel the loneliness, the *wrongness* of growing up with my brother the way he was. In that sleetwashed medieval street I stood watching a group of children play, and I cried. The cold rain mimicked my tears sufficiently for my unhappiness to be invisible and, as the children yelled and laughed and splashed one another I remembered my childhood and the way it had ended.

Kai was right. We were alike, he and I, and that was what drew us together. We'd both been cheated out of a proper childhood; he by the double loss of parents and me by having to become responsible for my brother. It was why Kai saw through my capable, coping exterior to the damage that lay underneath. The pragmatic, realistic outer shell that I'd had to adopt to deal with Nicholas, because my parents couldn't. Because he'd had to develop his own outer shell, to cope with abuse and with the lack of love. *We were the same . . .*

Kai. Back in that little house, discovering his mother — *Eve*, wow, turn up for the books — confronting his own origins. I shook the tears away from my eyes. He needed me, and he needed me capable, managing, able to deal. The last thing on earth he needed was for me to break. I sniffed hard and did a couple more turns of the streets to let the redness subside from my eyes and until I could put the puffiness down to the ferocious wind. When I judged that I looked sufficiently brimming with self-control, I went back.

Kai was alone, pacing up and down the little room like a wild animal that's just recovered from the tranquilising dart. He was running his hands through his hair and shaking his head as though trying to escape from something that kept following him. 'Are you all right?'

'I don't know. I . . . it wasn't what I thought, Holly. I've been so *bitter*, for so long, and now I don't know how to feel, what to think.'

We heard Eve's slow descent of the stairs long before she came back into the room. 'Oh, Holly,' her eyes were full again. 'It happened. It was all real. I was beginning to doubt, and then I got the phone call and, I knew. *It was all real.*'

'I'm sorry?'

'The spell.' Eve's eyes were alive, she'd lost the stooped posture, the frail look. 'Look at him, Holly. He is what I

226

wished for. My David. Here.' She held something out to Kai. 'I kept it beside my bed. All these years.'

It was a photograph, a blurry colour shot which slowly resolved into a picture of a tiny, smeared face. The eyes were open, mere slits in the clearly yelling face, but even so the pale colour was unmistakable. 'Me.'

'Yes. I carried that camera around for the whole of the last three months, just to be sure . . . I took a couple, but my hands were shaky and this is the only one that came out.'

'But I thought you wished to meet the man of your dreams?'

Eve's eyes were red, not my brief moment-of-self-pity red, the kind of red you get from crying forever. 'I used to dream of a little boy running to me with flowers in his hands. Then I dreamed of a man coming up to me and saying "I'm David".' She put her soft hand on mine. 'I can stop dreaming now.'

Kai was studying the photo, under the window where there was more light. I drew Eve into the kitchen and began unpacking the shopping. 'Eve, he's going to need time, you understand that.'

'Of course.' Eve lowered her voice. 'Tell him it doesn't matter if he never wants to come again. Just knowing — knowing he's out there, with you, that's all I ever wanted.'

'I'll come back.' Kai's voice from the other room made us both jump. 'How can I not? I need to know who I am. You are the only one who can tell me.' His voice dropped. 'The only one.'

'Do you have more family?' I looked around as we went into the hallway. There were no photos there either, only a small oil painting of a constipated-looking cat.

'No.' Eve said sadly. 'I never married. I trained as a nurse once Dad died, took early retirement and bought this little place. I've always lived around here and this is where my friends are.'

I nearly dragged Kai out into the rain, which had turned to hail in our absence. He was rigid and had that frozen kind

227

of expression you usually see on trauma victims. 'That was my mother,' he whispered. Then he turned to me and wrapped me in his arms. 'Fucking, fucking crazy.' For a while we hugged, his body warm against mine, a defence against the weather.

'Kai,' I began carefully, 'why don't we invite Eve over for Christmas?'

He even stopped breathing. Stood still in my embrace with his shoulders set. 'What?'

'You saw the place. She's on her own, she's not got much.' And I wouldn't tell him about the heart pills in the cupboard, her breathlessness, her swollen ankles. He'd just found her, if he thought he might lose her again soon, God knew what he'd do. 'We could give her a great Christmas.'

'Ah. Now you're acting like I owe her something.'

'Well, you do, sort of. She found you. Or, at least, she put the mechanism in place to find you, and now you know that she loves you. You weren't just thrown away, Kai. Eve did what she thought was best for *you*. The only thing she could do. And, in that kitchen . . . the cupboard was nearly empty. And we've got each other. And besides,' I swallowed. Wanting something for myself was harder than I'd thought. '*I* don't want to spend Christmas on my own.'

'Oh. *Oh*. Shit, sorry Holl! I didn't even . . . oh shit.' He dragged his fingers through his hair again, which made him look like a mad Rock God. 'Stupid. I'm sorry.' He pushed me away so that he could look in my face. 'Told you I'm crap at this relationship thing. Never had to plan, see, no one's ever wanted to be around long enough. And no one has ever wanted to spend Christmas with me, so I've always worked, gone somewhere where Christmas is meaningless. It helps,' he added.

'Hey, no going for the sympathy vote.'

A grin. 'Sorry. Again. So, what, the whole nine yards? Tree, pudding, presents? Can you cook?' A hot look. 'And will you dress up as Santa?'

'Only if you promise not to ravage me. Well, not while anyone is looking.'

'Making no promises, Holl.' We started to walk back to the car, not feeling the sleet or the cold wind any more. 'Christ. Can't believe it . . .' He stopped, pulled me across and kissed me hard. 'And my *mother*. Fuck. Starting to feel like a real person here. Talking of which . . .' he stood back so that he could look me in the eye, 'you've been doing some thinking of your own, haven't you?'

Those yellow eyes were almost hypnotic when he did that straight stare. No wonder he was such a good journalist — with his empty silences and his stage-magician's magnetic gaze. 'I . . . sort of . . . when I was walking. How did you know?' I gave him a suspicious frown. 'You don't read my mind as well, do you?'

He moved and pulled me tightly against him. I could feel his heartbeat, even and steady. 'That's the first time I've ever heard you say "I don't want" about something. First time you've ever dared really say what you feel?'

And my mind was suddenly full of Nicholas, frightened of the world, scared of its inconsistency and unpredictability. The need to keep him calm, to be the one stable thing in his terrifyingly unstable existence. 'I . . .'

'You need to let go, Holly.' Kai's words were coming from deep inside him, I could feel them, feel his heart speed up as he realised what he'd said. 'Sometimes . . .' he sighed, 'sometimes shit just happens. No one's fault, it just does. And the only way to truly get over stuff is to let go.'

'Can you?' My voice was a bit muffled by his jacket. 'Let go?'

Another sigh. 'She did what she thought was best. She didn't know . . . *Shit*.' One hand came away from my shoulder and raised, from the quick motion I guessed he was wiping his eyes. 'I can try. I have to.'

I took a deep breath and shuffled myself a step back. Change position, change the subject. *Change*. 'Having a real Christmas does mean you have to buy presents though. And a turkey. Not something that you'd have to do much in Afghanistan, I shouldn't have thought.'

'Ah. Didn't think of that.' He fussed with his jacket, raising his collar against the sleet, adjusting to the new topic, gladly, it seemed.

'And a tree, and lights, and cards, and . . .'

'All right, I'll go to bloody Afghanistan, if that's what you want!' We looked at each other and grinned. 'Are relationships always like this?'

'Dunno. I'm not exactly Ask the Expert, am I? Going out with the kind of wanker who thought he was God's gift to women because he stuck his arse out of the bed to fart does not make me fit to answer questions like that. And anyway, I'm still boggle-eyed by the fact that *Eve* is *your mother*. Talk about a dark horse. We all thought she'd got some grizzled old solicitor-chappie tucked away and that was what was making her all dewy-eyed. Turns out it was getting the news from the PI that you wanted her address.'

The Jeep was sitting alone in the car park. Everyone else had gone home, it was getting dark and the sleet was beginning to freeze. Kai started the engine and then sat, holding the wheel but making no attempt to drive away.

'She — *Eve*, told her family she'd got a temporary job in Wales, came to Anglesey and stayed in a B&B so that no one would know. She gave birth sitting in a ditch and then wrapped me in some newspaper and left me where she knew someone would come along.'

'It wasn't because she didn't love you,' I said softly. 'It was never that.'

'I know. She had no one to help her, no one to support her and she didn't dare tell her father . . . She kept my picture,' his voice was wondering, 'all these years, she kept my picture.'

'And now her wish has come true.' I smiled to myself. 'Obliquely.'

'What, like pillars?'

'That would be funny if I didn't know you had a bigger vocabulary than an entire set of Encyclopaedia Britannica.'

'Let's go home and I'll show you what else I've got that's bigger . . .'

'You're sex mad.'

'It was you that brought up sex. I was going to show you my greenhouse.'

'Just drive, Rhys.'

CHAPTER TWENTY-FOUR

'I want to stop the spell.'

I stared at Vivienne. 'But I thought you said it *couldn't* be stopped. In fact, I distinctly remember you told me . . .'

Vivienne wasn't listening. Her fingers wove a complicated pattern through the fur of the cat which sat smugly on her lap. 'It's gone too far. I never meant—' A deep sniff. 'I suppose you think I'm vindictive, don't you?'

'No. Well, yes, a bit. Your wish did seem a touch drastic.'

'Twenty-five years Richard and I were married.' She stared over my head at a patch on the wall where brighter paper showed that a picture had hung until recently. 'I suppose we took one another for granted really, what with his job and the children and everything.' Her scarlet head nodded solemnly. 'And then he was gone.'

'So,' I took a deep breath, wanting to get this straight in my head. 'You wanted him to suffer and now you're having second thoughts?'

'I'm wondering if I wasn't a little bit hasty. No, not hasty. *Mmmm.*' A thoughtful pause, until the cat butted at her hand. 'No. He was wrong to abandon me, of course he was. But since he left I've discovered a whole new lease of life, what with our little *group*, and Isobel is getting me a part-time job in the hospital. Oh, nothing grand, pushing a trolley round the wards but it's better than sitting at home all day. And Eve, she's become such a good friend, we speak on the phone most days. All of this is something I never had before, when my life was so regulated by Richard and his comings and goings. Maybe his leaving did me a favour. Plus, I have this place . . .' Her eyes briefly unfocussed, wandering to the gap on the wall again, as though this was habit. 'He put everything into my name just before he went.' A quick shake of the head against possible softening, adding, 'Probably to stop Miss Busty getting her hands on it.'

'So Eve told you about Kai.'

'Oh yes.'

'Right. Just wanted to sort that one out. And you know that Kai and I are . . . ?' I waved one hand. It wasn't really indicative of 'banging like a barn door on a windy day' but it was the best I could do.

'Lovers, yes.'

I opened my mouth to correct her, but didn't.

Vivienne pushed the cat off her lap and it stalked off, doing its best to look as though leaving had been its own idea. 'I wanted him to suffer, Holly. He'd hurt me so deeply, shrugging me off as though I meant nothing to him, that I wanted him to know how it felt to be at rock bottom.' She touched my arm lightly. 'I'm nearly fifty, you know.'

'Prime of life,' I threw in gamely.

'It's old to be starting again. But I can, I will. I shall meet someone else, one day. I can see that I do have a future, even if that does start with pushing the book trolley around a geriatric ward, and I no longer want Richard to . . .' She looked at me and her eyes were sunken under swollen eyelids. 'His whole business is gone, and I know how much he loved that company. Everything he ever did was for his work, he put all of himself into it, his time and his energy, and I resented it, Holly. I hated his job as if it was his mistress, because that's how he treated it, like someone more exciting than I could ever be. And now he's lost it.' She dropped her eyes to her hands, which fidgeted in her lap. 'He's suffered enough.'

'But now it's all running out of your control?'

Vivienne stood up slowly. She seemed to have aged suddenly. 'But the spell has worked for everyone else, so well. You have your Kai . . .'

'He's not "mine".'

'No matter. You and Kai are together, Megan has the dreadful Rufus who, as you pointed out, adores her far more than any man could ever do. Eve has met her David again and Isobel — well, Isobel seems to have back-pedalled on her wish. Maybe she's realised that men aren't the great catch they seem to be when you don't have one. Now I'm afraid of what the spell might do to Richard.'

I restrained myself from saying 'you should have thought of that before'. 'I'm sorry, Vivienne. If there's anything I can do . . . ?'

Vivienne gave me a cautious smile. 'Ah. Well. That is where I need your help, Holly, and this is why I asked you to come alone today.' She carefully moved a tabby cat from the top of the dusty piano and retrieved a book which it had been lying on. 'I'd like you to do a charm to keep Richard safe.'

'Me? Why me? I never even . . .' I had been going to say that I never even believed in any of the magic nonsense, but a quick audit of the results made me bite my tongue. 'I mean, I never even knew it could be done.'

Vivienne turned the pages of the book, causing little puffs of dusty air to swirl into the room like exhalations from a tomb. 'This is the book I used.'

I took the book out of her hand and began riffling through the pages, reading passages at random. It mostly seemed to be full of things about 'freeing your inner creativity' and 'addressing the earth as mother'. There wasn't a single spell in it, although there was a recipe for a thyme and parsley dressing which looked rather interesting. 'But there's no spells in here.'

'No. It encourages a — how shall I put it — a freestyle approach to magic.'

'You mean you *made it up*? All those horrible things you had us looking for?'

'The book says that the more esoteric the ingredients one requests, the more intense will be the thought put into making the wish work.'

'It's a mind trick,' I said, almost admiringly. 'You make people focus on what they want, so anything they get looks like it's the result of the spell. That's actually quite clever, Vivienne.' Then I frowned sternly. 'But it's a con.'

'No. Lives have changed for the better, Holly,' She tapped the book. 'Because of the spell.'

'So why do you need me to do the charm? If you created the spell, isn't it your job?'

Vivienne wore the expression you might give a five-year-old who wanted sweets for breakfast, patient but ever-so-slightly 'you're being stupid'. 'I can't change my own wish. I know how it works, you see, how it's done. But someone else can change it for me.'

'But you created the spell in the first place! Why can't you create another one to counteract it?'

'Because it's all suggestion.' Her lower lip trembled. 'I need someone else to "suggest" to me! And you do have access to the warlock's house, which I believe . . .' her voice went a little faint and she cleared her throat. 'No. I really *do* believe that house is the source of some kind of magic.' Her voice was stronger now. 'Please, Holly.'

'I can't do magic.' I said in a dull voice.

'But you can! Just look at the way the spell is working for you.' She put the book very firmly into my hands again, even though I'd tried to leave it on top of the piano. 'Just think magic. Be creative.'

I gave her possibly the most unmagical look ever. 'Sparkly party wings and fairy dust?'

'If you like.' She seemed happier now, as though devolving responsibility was enough. 'But please make it soon, Holly.' A moment's thought. 'Although, perhaps, not *too* soon.'

'Right.'

'Just do something, anything, a little ritual. Anything you do in that house will magnify . . .' Again her voice tailed off and she blinked quickly. 'Yes. The warlock's house will make the spell work,' she said, with that heavy certainty of tone that people use when they're trying to talk themselves into something.

I found myself being escorted firmly to the front door of the little cottage. The sun was setting behind Dodman's Hill and the shadows of the forest stretched and flexed across me as I started the car and turned the heater up to maximum. Two days until midwinter, and it hardly seemed worth the sun getting started in the mornings — it had barely climbed past the treetops and there it was sinking again. I sat for a moment and let the warming air blow over my feet; Vivienne's cottage was picturesque but lacking in the centrally heated areas. I found myself wondering about Richard, her ex. It seemed very *convenient* that the cottage and everything in it was all in Vivienne's name, particularly from a man whose company had just shot down the tubes, presumably with at least a little warning. Why hadn't he at least tried to sell it before they split up? Why had he adopted such a complete hands-off policy with regard to his ex-wife? Maybe he really had been having an affair with the large-breasted lady in Accounts, as Vivienne suspected, but the whole thing smelled of old fish to me.

I drove round to Megan's. Although she probably wouldn't have a perspective, as such, she could usually manage a lateral angle on things. Today, however, her angle seemed to consist of lying down and trying to stretch an arm underneath the sofa.

'Oh good,' she said as I walked in. 'You're taller than me, see if you can reach it.'

Obediently I lay down and reached under the green veloured monstrosity that she'd bought on such an enormous discount that it was unmissable, even if the result made it look as though she'd been cursed by leprechauns. 'What are we grovelling under here for?'

'Rufus dropped his ball and it rolled under.'

I looked sideways and found a huge, grey head almost up against mine. An anxious eye rotated towards me, containing a world of ball-related worry. 'Okay. Failure doesn't seem to be an option here. He might eat me.'

'He just wants his ball.'

Luckily my fingertips managed to touch something and I groped it forwards until it rolled out. There was a snapping snatch by my ear and Rufus lay down, obviously considering himself whole once more.

'Get him a bigger one,' I said, standing up and trying for dignity whilst covered in dog fur and dribble.

'Oh he's got a bigger one. He prefers that one.' Megan sat down and riffled Rufus's fur. His look was pure adoration which I didn't understand — I was the one who'd got the damn ball back. 'Why did you come round? Not that I'm not grateful, but I thought you were busy doing the couple-thing with your grandad. Not your *personal* grandad, that would be odd and besides he's Scottish, but the grandad-journalist guy.'

'Thank you for that clarification, Meg, and I must introduce you to Kai soon, because you've obviously got some very strange ideas about him. Anyway, I came round to talk about Vivienne.'

Megan bounced in her chair. 'Ooh, is there some badass gossip? Is it the husband, has he finally done a solo car-park-dive?' I explained Vivienne's new position, and Meg looked disappointed. 'Oh, pooh. She's gone all obligay on us, hasn't she?'

'Oblique, and it's not really oblique if you change your mind, I don't think. But now I've got to come up with a charm-type thingy so that I can tell Vivienne I've done it to protect Richard and, oh God, I've just thought, it's nearly Christmas and we're going to have to do something soon because Eve is coming to us for Christmas and . . .' I realised I was hyperventilating and on the verge of tears, 'I haven't even done any shopping yet.' And then I had to explain about Kai and Eve and the whole David thing.

'Wow. So you've not so much gained a grandad as gained a mother-in-law as well. That is quite fast going, for someone who didn't even want a man in the first place,' Megan said, a little tersely. 'I thought you said you were happy as you were?'

'I was.' I leaned forward earnestly and Rufus gave me a warning look. 'Really, I was. But then it all suddenly seemed so shallow, all the unconnected sex and always getting up and leaving, never taking the time to build anything that might become more permanent. Even when I thought that was what I wanted. But Aiden showed me that it couldn't go on, that if I wanted any kind of real life I had to commit to something, and then, there was Kai, all black leather and silver rings and the most terrific arse . . .' I stopped and let the thought of the rangy writer fill my head. 'And I think I might be in love.'

'You must be. You've gone pink.'

I fought the memories of long hands on my body, hair in my eyes and sweat pooling. 'Bit warm. Anyway. Better, you know, pop off. Now I've filled you in.'

'I thought you might have come round to tell me you were having a Christmas party! I mean, I'm going to Dad's and Barbara's this Christmas so I won't be here on the day, but we ought to do something . . . Hey, what about us all having a midwinter solstice kind of thing? All us witch-girls? Midwinter is meant to be pretty auspicious, isn't it?'

I raised an eyebrow. 'Okay. So you don't know what oblique means, but you're prepared to bandy words like auspicious about?'

Megan hid her face in Rufus. 'What can I say? Patchy education.'

'Obviously. But you might be onto something. Midwinter, yes. We really *ought* to put on a bit of a show for that, shouldn't we?' I pulled my jacket back on. 'I can feel a plan coming on.'

'What sort of plan? Remember your last one, when that man thought we were blokes in drag? Anyway. I'm off out with Rufus. We've got a play date with a greyhound.'

'Same one, or are you putting it about in the hound department?'

'Same one. Cute owner, fast dog, keeps us both busy.'

I left her brushing Rufus. She clearly wanted to make a good impression, because she was giving the dog a centre-parting, like a werewolf Little Lord Fauntleroy. I toyed with the idea of going back to my place, which was beginning to look a bit uninhabited, but settled for popping in to pick up some clean clothes and the post, and heading back to the Old Lodge.

Kai was in the living room, on his laptop. He'd got a pencil clamped between his teeth and his fingers were travelling at near warp speed over the keys.

'You have discovered the delete button, haven't you?' I pointed to the pencil. 'You really don't need a rubber.'

'Ha. Gave up smoking last year. Still get the cravings when I write. Working on my story about the lads in Barndale Woods.' He rattled away at the keyboard a bit more. 'I've had a whisper that they're moving on. Probably something to do with you . . .' He shot me a quick look over the pencil. 'Locking you in that shed wasn't the smartest thing to do. They think they've got you intimidated over the witching thing, but they don't know if you'll stay quiet forever. So . . . getting away, good move, as far as they're concerned. Bearing in mind that they think dealing drugs is a pretty clever way to make a living, so . . .' A shrug and he chewed the pencil end, staring at the screen. 'I'm going to have to be quick. Do something to drive them out into the open . . . If I could find where they've got the stuff it would be a start, but . . . there's no cohesion, no narrative. Bugger. Anyway.' He looked up at me, eyes gleaming. 'Not your problem. How was Vivienne?'

'She wants me to do a charm.' I flopped onto the sofa, and then had a moment of good feeling that I was at home enough here to flop.

'Intriguing. Tell me.'

I rested my head on the sofa arm and told him. He spat the pencil onto the chair, he was laughing so much, and, when he heard that the whole spell thing had been made up, I seriously feared for his internal organs. Since meeting Eve he'd come down a little and lost some of the darkness that had surrounded him, even though he was still protesting a bit about the whole 'spending Christmas' thing. Kai was nicer relaxed, less edgy and easier to live with. Not that I was living with him, you understand, oh no, we were feeling our way into this relationship, creeping forward incrementally and trying to adjust to having someone who cared.

'I'm wondering what you're going to come up with for this charm,' Kai calmed down enough to be able to speak, and took up the pencil again. 'Are you going to make it obscure, or is it going to be a bit more down-home simplicity? I hear it's amazing what you can do with two boiled eggs and a feather.'

'It's amazing what *you* can do with a feather.'

His eyes were suddenly hot. 'What can I say, I'm a talented guy.'

'Ain't that the truth.' We looked at one another for a few moments. He was tapping the pencil between his fingers, playing it along his thigh. 'And stop doing that. We've both got work to do.'

He tipped his head on one side. 'You worried we're going to use up all the sexual mojo we've got going on?'

I shrugged.

'Hey, Holly, it doesn't wear off you know. We make love. It's never been that for me before, *never*.'

'But we don't know, do we?' I burst out, jumping to my feet with a suddenness that made my ears sing. 'Neither of us has ever managed to sustain anything that's lasted longer than face paint! How do we know that we're not going to get sick of the whole thing in a couple of weeks, and then you'll sod off back to Hurgleflurgle-stan and I'll . . .'

'You'll what?' He stood up, carefully balancing the laptop on the chair. 'What, Holly?' A fingertip traced my cheekbone, tipped my chin so that I had to look him in the eye.

'I'll be left alone,' I whispered. The hair on my neck was prickling at the way he looked at me. His eyes were sincere but guarded, as though he was shielding himself against my words. 'Nick's gone . . . If you go, what's left? I used to think I liked being alone but . . .'

'You liked being alone, or it was *easier*?'

I had a quick flash of memory. The attempts I'd made when I was younger to reconcile dating with Nick's unpredictable demands, the so-called 'boyfriend' who'd insulted him, the men who'd come and then gone again when they'd realised that I was always going to put my brother first. Always *had* to put him first. 'Oh, none of it was easy,' I half-whispered. 'None of it.'

'Holly,' my name was an outbreath. A sigh. 'Talk to me.'

Fury whiplashed me, an anger I rarely let myself feel these days, and absolutely *never* let out. I bit my lip until it bled in an attempt to trap the words behind my tongue. 'Nothing to say.'

'It's hurting you to keep it all inside. Please. You're safe, I won't get hurt like Nicholas, *I* won't run. Just tell me, all those things you won't even let yourself think.'

His hair smelled of gooseberries and his eyes had softened in colour to a kind of creamy amber with vast, dark centres that I couldn't stop myself staring into. 'You need to let yourself feel, Holly. Before you can really let me in, you need to let the anger out.' His hand moved, traced down the back of my neck and rested on my shoulder. 'Make room for other emotions.'

Something about the gesture made the rage flick its tail again and this time I let it. Leaned in to the solid warmth of the big Welshman and felt the heat rise. 'He . . . he was fine when we were kids!'

A slow nod. 'Yeah. Took him at adolescence?'

'Nicky was twelve, almost to the day. I remember . . .' A wet weight pressed the back of my eyes. 'I came in from school and he was upstairs, I went up to see him and he . . .' The hand on my shoulder squeezed. 'He was standing by the window talking to someone who wasn't there.' My voice tailed off into a cough. There it all was again, the pain, the uncertainty, the *fear* . . . 'And my parents wouldn't believe . . . they thought it was just a phase, attention-seeking . . . even when he . . . and I had to be the good one, the steady one, I had to keep him safe and look after him and keep him calm and never lose my temper or be difficult or unpredictable or . . .' I stopped and sucked in some much-needed air.

'Or have a life.' Kai bent and looked me in the eye. 'It wasn't his fault, Holly.'

'I *know*!' I let myself shout now. 'I know all this! And my rational brain says it's fine to go out and have a life and fall in love and not always have to be there for him but . . .' The rock in my throat let a few tears escape past it. 'But my heart couldn't do it. Couldn't do the double act, sensible, together Holly for Nicholas, no emotional overload, no recriminations, and yet be able to feel . . . really *feel* and react and throw itself into something. I've spent so long looking at the dark from this side, Kai' — the tears bubbled through and stroked a line down my cheeks — 'from *his* side. I don't know if I know how to feel from the other side.'

He caught my hand. 'That's perfectly understandable, Holly. Drifting along, taking care of Nick, turning a blind eye to all the rest of life because you cast yourself in the position of carer.'

'But maybe it's more than that. Maybe it's not Nick, maybe it never was. What about if it's just *me*? If I can't ever feel anything real for someone?' His hold on my hand tightened for a second then released as I moved away. 'I'm sorry, Kai. This wasn't a good idea.'

'What wasn't?'

'This. You and me.'

Suddenly his hand was back, gripping at my wrist so tightly that little electric shocks fired up to my elbow. 'No. No, Holly.

I won't let this happen. I will *not* let you turn your back on this, on us, on a relationship just because you feel guilty.'

'I do not feel guilty.' I twitched my arm in his grasp once or twice, but he didn't let go.

'Oh, I think you do. Guilty that you resent your brother for who he is, and guilty that you hate him for what he's made you into — someone who can't show emotion for fear of what will happen.'

'I . . .' Then everything stopped. A huge barrier rolled away from a part of my heart that I'd been ignoring, the part that I'd hidden behind sibling duty and responsibility; concealed so carefully that I'd been able to fool myself into believing that it didn't exist. I remembered those children playing by the river, the teasing, arguing relationship between them. The *normality*. 'I didn't mean to,' my voice was a whisper. 'I never wanted to hate him. I *love* Nick. But sometimes . . .' The horrible secret corner of myself curled inwards as the light of realisation shone upon it and I began to cry. 'Sometimes it's too much.'

'Holly.' Kai folded himself around me. 'No more protection, strip it all away and look at what's happened. It's the only way to let yourself get over it, I should know. Look at who did what and why . . .'

'*He should have been my big brother!*' The words came from my ten-year-old self. '*He* should have been there for *me*! But I had to always be there for him, protecting and standing up for him and not losing my temper or being irrational or any of the other things that ordinary *real* people do . . .' Hot hard sobs welded my ribs together. 'It's not *fair*,' wailed that ten year old girl, who'd had to take the responsibility for her brother when she should have been playing with dolls and riding ponies. 'It's *not!*'

Kai held me so tightly that my reluctant tears rocked both of us, resting his chin on the top of my head and using that long body to absorb the power of my resentment against my brother, a resentment I'd never allowed myself to be aware of until now.

CHAPTER TWENTY-FIVE

I don't need to do this any more. Weird that, huh? After all these years, these letters are now redundant. I can say this to your face, if I want to, but old habits won't die unless you shoot them in the head and . . . yeah, I guess these serve a function. Stuff that maybe I wouldn't say, couldn't say to you. Jury's out as to whether I'm even going to show you this pile of writing . . . maybe I'll get a book out of it, hey, there's a thought. 'Writing to my Mother' . . . but then there's the pat little ending to get over, 'and we met and we liked one another and the previous thirty-six years of misery and wanting and lonely nights and sabotaged relationships were all forgotten'.

Won't happen. I'm preaching forgiveness and opening up and catharsis and all to Holly but it's harder than you'd think to let go of all those years. They stain you so deep that it's part of your soul, part of who you are, me and her. I've been made into this social outsider, this guy who stands beyond the crowd and watches and I don't know that I'm ever going to be allowed to come into the firelight, while she . . . Holly . . . she's spent so long protecting herself from that pain of having someone she loved turn underneath her from fun brother to this guy she's had to protect from the world . . .

But together — ah, together we are something more. She takes the pain away. Somehow, being with Holly makes me feel that, hey yeah, I deserve a life. Spent so many . . . so many years believing that I was this lowlife piece of shit, something even a mother couldn't love. So, QED, anyone who loved me must be fucking deranged, need a lesson in never trusting, never loving, and, oh yeah, I gave them that lesson.

And now I see what I did, how I humiliated those women to try to bring them down to my level. To show them how it feels to be less than human, to be this discarded, worthless thing not worth loving, not worth even so much as casual pity, and I'm sorry. I thought I was doing it to get myself away, give them a lesson in objective reality — don't get attached to this guy, he's no good — but what I really did was try to make them feel just one tiny atom of what I felt.

Okay, so I'm shit on a stick. But Holly doesn't care. She knows what I did, she knows why. I'm not saying she understands, but she tries to. From the first she's seen through the image and she's not scared, even when I peel back the layers to show her what's underneath it all. And I love her for it. Love her for her struggle to come to terms with the fact that she's stifled her life for twenty years to care for her brother. Love her for the way she's letting her inner craziness come up from where it's been weighed down with the pragmatism and the logic. You know something, I even think she's starting to believe in all this 'magic' stuff? Mind you, even I am beginning to wonder . . .

CHAPTER TWENTY-SIX

It was absolutely dark. The kind of complete darkness you never get in a town, where even during a power cut there's people with lanterns and candles and generators. This was the dark of the deep countryside or, as Megan put it 'like being inside a water buffalo'. I've no idea why it would be darker inside a water buffalo than any other ruminant, but that's Megan for you.

Somewhere below us an owl boo-hooed, and an unconvinced blackbird twittered, a pheasant clattered sky-wards to my left and I grinned to myself. Underfoot the ground was still boggy, and every step felt like walking through undigested dinners, but the air had lost that shrapnel-feel of snow and settled down into a rain-tinged mildness. My right hand was loosely clasped in Megan's, she in turn held Vivienne's. Eve and Isobel were likewise joined to us, as we stood in a row on the hilltop and waited for the dawn. We must have looked like a set of paper cut outs, silhouetted as we were on the crest of the rising ground, joined hands outstretched, braced to meet the coming dawn.

'So, you performed sex magic as a charm?' Vivienne tugged at Megan's hand until she turned and Vivienne and I were drawn face-to-face. 'That was very enterprising of you, Holly.'

'What *exactly* did you do?' Megan's grin was visible even in the dark. 'I mean, was it complicated or did you go for the easy stuff?'

'We . . . look, it was a charm, all right? We . . . said words and stuff.'

'I bet you did.'

I gave Megan a shove and whispered, 'It's only for Vivienne's benefit.'

'So you didn't do "sex magic" with your man?'

I thought of the gentle way Kai had held me, the curative power of his kindness when we'd made love amid the tears and the pain. 'Well, it was pretty special.'

'And that's all? It's just sex?'

I pulled my hand out of hers. 'It was a charm. I was doing Vivienne a favour, and now at least I've put her mind at rest.'

Megan nodded. 'Good thinking. A bang with results.' She went quiet for a moment. 'So, if you've done the charm, why are we up here waiting for the sunrise?'

I sighed. 'Because it's the solstice.' I said enigmatically and turned to face the horizon. I had hoped for something symbolic, the golden glow of sunrise perhaps, but in Yorkshire in December you settle for what you can get, and we got a bleak, bleaching of the darkness to the east, a roil and bluster of cloud barely splitting enough to let a pale pink come through.

'That colour would make a lovely blouse,' came Eve's voice, very matter-of-fact, making Megan giggle.

'Ssshh. Think solemn,' I whispered at them out of the corner of my mouth, but I could feel Megan's hand shaking as she tried to stop the giggles. Nerves were making us all hair-trigger and a touch hysterical. At the end of the line I could see Isobel jigging from foot to foot desperate for the toilet and Vivienne's body a little hunched over by the weight of contrition.

'Sorry. But we're not going to be long, are we? I don't know how long that rope will hold Rufus.' We'd tied him up outside the cottage, Meg didn't trust him either inside or to be left in the car, since he tended to eat soft furnishings and pee against anything upright.

The air lightened still more. A few birds began to get the idea and sleepy twittering broke out in selected trees, a whirl of rooks took to the sky and began a noisy bickering above us as they climbed on the early-morning breeze. I could see the faces of the women now, all a little high on what we were doing. 'He'll be fine.'

A nod and I dropped Megan's hand, walked a few paces forwards and held my arms up into the air. It was a huge coincidence that at that moment the sun broke free of the horizon and let the first rays trickle along, illuminating me nicely. Behind me, Megan was humming 'Oh, What a Beautiful Mornin'', and I would have kicked her if that hadn't meant shattering my illusion of serenity.

The sunlight brushed the tops of the trees below us and I let my eyes drop from scanning the heavens to peering through the forest. A ratcheting drone told me all I needed to know. 'Brace yourselves,' I muttered. 'Here we go.'

The first bike broke cover. It jetted towards us in uneven spurts caused by the cloying mud. As it reached the bare hilltop, another shot up behind us, with a third zigzagging up the path until three bikes rode a circle around us, staying just the far side of being offensively close. All three riders were hooded and helmeted, their machines bearing no number plates or identifying marks apart from a rather amateurish double B insignia painted in black on the dark red of the petrol tanks.

I stood my ground, keeping my eyes on the gradually spreading patch of sunlight at my feet. It smelled of moss and crushed grass and was nicely stable, and all the while I could hear that ghastly buzzing and the sound of the women behind me grouping together. Vivienne and Eve had been in on the plan, but I'd kept it quiet from Isobel and Megan. Isobel,

248

because I was afraid she'd panic, and Megan because I was afraid that she'd come armed, and now they were a collective of fear and scared reassurances stamping a defensive circle at my back.

For a few moments it was an impasse. The bikes rode around us as though we were a wild west wagon train and they were some kind of native attack force until I was afraid that this was all they were going to do. Scare us then ride for the hills. But then I realised, incrementally, the circle was growing smaller and tighter. The riders were herding us closer together, almost up one another's tailpipes in their attempts to stop us breaking free. The smell of exhaust fumes was dizzying. I fought the urge to go round, to try to keep my eye on any one rider, and let them circle. I stood still and waited.

It didn't take long to come. From an inside pocket, while the rider steered single handed, the shotgun appeared, unfolding its length into the winter sunrise like Death's calling card. Okay. Now we're in business.

'Are you going to shoot me?' I shouted above the engines. 'Go on then.'

'Nah. Too easy.' The voice came muffled through the black balaclava. 'Too traceable. One thing I've learned, if you're gonna do something, make sure it leaves no marks.'

'So?' I was moving now, keeping him in my line of sight. 'What's on the agenda for today? Locking me up in some shed again?' *Keep him talking* . . .

The bike dropped to the ground, engine whining until it stalled in a flurry of blue smoke, and he stepped towards me across it. The gun barrel waved at the group of scared women. 'I'm thinking something more up close and personal. What I should've done to you last time, straight off. Thought I'd save you for later, y'see. Big mistake, should've done you there and then. And after that, your wog girlie here is going to find out what a white man's cock is really all about. And if this lot even so much as *think* about shopping me — well, I know where you all live, don't I?'

Vivienne squeaked. The two remaining bikes had idled to a standstill behind us. I could feel the eyes, watching and waiting behind the helmets — those unidentifiable helmets. 'Okay,' I said.

There was a visible double take. 'What?'

'I said okay. Go on, do it.' And then I made my mistake. Let my eyes flick upwards, beyond the muddy circle to the lone tree which guarded the edge of the path where it entered the forest. To the man standing underneath, arms folded across his chest and legs braced.

'Shit, she's got company!'

'It's fucking *Rhys*!'

Sunlight flashed on the gun barrel, arms came from behind and locked me down. Isobel screamed. Eve gave a grunt, there was a sound like a kick connecting and then a muffled swearing but the arms didn't loosen. They tightened and I couldn't breathe. There was the smell of sweat and leather, the unpleasant moistness of a damp biker's jacket pressed to my face like thick skin, no air and the ground falling away beneath me.

The mud hit the back of my neck like a slap and I began to struggle beneath the man holding me down, writhing and biting and jerking my head. But it was too late.

'He's over there!' A shout and then the abrupt violence of the gun firing which cut the noise into nothingness for a second. When I could hear again, it was panic. Eve was moaning, a kind of tearless crying, and the three men were arguing.

'You fucking moron. You weren't supposed to *hit* him!'

'I was trying to scare him off.'

'You shot him.'

The arms released me and the weight of my captor moved suddenly as he climbed to his feet. 'Nah. I was pointing at his feet, not his fucking head.'

A sudden punch, which I heard rather than saw, which sent a body landing next to me on its backside. 'You *fucker*. What do we do now?'

The three men started swiping at one another, helmets cracked together and jackets creaked and tore, sounding like mating time in a leather furniture showroom, as fists and arms flailed and connected. I struggled to my feet and stared across at the body lying underneath the tree, then I started to run with my feet skidding, three steps forward and one step back until I reached Kai's fallen shape hunched and huddled across the roots of the leafless oak.

'Kai! Oh God, don't be dead, please don't be dead!' I reached out and took his hand, but it flopped inertly onto the earth. I grabbed his shoulders and shook. 'This wasn't supposed to happen!' My tears fell onto his pale, chilled skin and ran down into his hair. 'Don't do this to me, Kai Rhys, you bastard, don't die on me!' My voice dropped to a whisper. 'Please. Don't let me lose someone else that I love.'

'You should always start this kind of conversation by looking for the exit wound.' Kai's voice was so level and its tone so coolly amused that I found I was looking around for the ghostly shade that spoke. 'That was your first mistake.' His eyes slipped open. 'And the second was telling me you love me.'

I suppressed the startled noise that rose. 'But . . .' was all I could manage. Then I slapped him on his shoulder. 'You're alive.'

He closed his eyes again. 'Well, yes. But it makes a much better ending for my piece if someone shot me, don't you think? Besides' — a cool hand rummaged inside his jacket and brought out the tiny, but very powerful camera — 'I've got it all. In all its megapixelled glory.' He shook the camera gently. 'It does sound too, y'know. Borrowed it off my photographer.'

I opened my mouth a couple of times but words refused to come out. They were forming a disorderly queue in my brain though. 'You . . . are such a . . . *journalist*,' I managed.

'When I saw him point the gun I decided to take a dive. Better all round if he thought I was out of things. Besides,' a lazy drift of his fingers pointed to the gang fight that had

251

erupted on the brow of the hill, where the rest of the girls had long since been left to their own devices, 'they'll do all the hard work for me.'

'But . . . I thought . . . where are the police? I thought you had the police watching through your telescope?'

'They're on their way.' He tapped his ear. 'I'm Bluetoothed up the wazoo. They've been watching all right. All we need now is to find where the drugs are before one of them gets them all shipped out and the case is dropped for lack of evidence.' He pointed again at where two of the men had a third down on the ground and were explaining to him where he'd gone wrong, with the teaching aids of both boot and fist. 'Of course, that has yet to dawn on these morons.'

Eve was doubled over, sitting on a muddy outcrop and rocking. 'She thinks you're dead too,' I said, gazing at her over the trio of scrapping helmets.

'Yeah, resurrection will have to wait until the police get here. It's only them thinking they've killed me that's keeping their minds off you lot. If I were you I'd get those ladies off the hill and somewhere safe.'

'But . . .'

His lips rose to mine and the words I'd been about to say vanished in hot breath and heartbeats. 'Kiss of life. If anyone asks,' Kai whispered, letting his head drop back onto the mossy ground again. 'Now go.' He tapped his earpiece again. 'Police are on their way. You and the girls vanish off to Vivienne's place, I'll catch up with you there.'

'Won't there be questions?'

A manic grin. 'Probably. And I should warn you that I am going to lie outrageously.'

'Well, you are a journalist.'

I headed back. Vivienne was leading everyone down the path towards her cottage, carefully not turning around to watch the increasingly bloody fight, which I managed to circumvent by tracking around the hilltop. As I dropped below the skyline, I heard the crackle of radios and the heavy-booted running of several men in police-issue footwear, then the gunning sound of a motorbike engine.

'Shit!'

'What?' Megan panted alongside me for a second, chest bobbing like two buoys on a choppy sea.

'One of them is trying to get to the drugs.'

'There are *drugs*? As in, little plastic baggies being sold in nightclubs? I thought you said they were poachers!' she puffed.

'I may have been a little economical with the truth.' I stopped running, Meg's words kicking an idea into the front of my brain. 'And I think I know where they've put the stuff.'

'But Holly . . .'

'I wished for excitement, remember?' I wheeled away from her and headed down over the lip of the hilltop into the wood, splashing through runny mud, keeping one ear on the rattle of the motorbike engine which sounded as though it was heading along the dry ground on the ridge.

Heading out through the woods to the gully where I'd hidden after my escape from the shed. To where, it had just dawned on me, there had been an awful lot of plastic sheeting and loose earth, just the kind of thing you might expect to find if someone had, for example, wrapped and buried a load of drugs, in the middle of nowhere, where no one ever went.

I tripped over my own feet as I ran. The bike engine was just ahead of me, so I kept going, following the sound, although my memory for places — honed by years of having to keep a mental image of locations in case of sudden need — told me that the gully was in the bottom of the valley and the bike was still running along the ridge. Suddenly the note of the engine changed, I saw the mossy outline of the innocent-looking shed where I'd been trapped just in front of me and realised that the bike was being ridden directly down the slope. I took a deep breath and sprinted amateurishly through the leaf mulch, slipping and sliding on the debris with the sound of the dirt bike whining in my ears.

Kept going, on through the trees. There was still a covering of snow on the floor of the forest, but all footprints were long gone. I had to run navigating by instinct, fear, and the vague memories that had formed as I'd hurtled through the trees afraid for my life. I found the gully the same way I had last time, by sliding down into it, rolling and jolting with my legs out in front of me and my shoulders catching on roots and branches, and I just had time to duck behind one of the low-growing ivy-covered bushes that littered the slope before I heard a bike drop with a dying drone. The engine cut out and there was a sudden green silence, broken eventually by a crashing slide as one of the men — I didn't know which of them I'd been chasing — came plunging down the slope, broke his fall by grasping at a stump of elder and swung around to start digging with both hands in the side of the hollow, tearing plastic and swearing loudly and emphatically.

I didn't think. I leaped out from behind my cover and confronted my nemesis, Big Ginge himself, who was pulling small white blocks from the earth, dusting them off and slipping them inside his leather jacket. 'The police are on their way,' I said, making him jump and drop one of the packets. 'They're just arresting your mates.'

'Then I had better hurry, hadn't I?' He was still helmeted, so the words were slightly muffled by his restricted cheeks, but his visor was open to show that he didn't look even slightly worried. 'And you had better stay out of my way.'

'No.' I went to push him away from the drugs but he was solid and wrapped in leather and my full-body charge just ricocheted off him and left me sliding through the mud. 'I'm not letting you go.'

A sigh and the final pack slid into the pocket. 'You have no choice.' And he turned around and hit me hard on the side of the head with his fist, almost unthinkingly. As I sprawled down, vision clouding, I saw him start to zip up his jacket and head back towards the fallen bike and I had the sudden, horrific vision of these blokes getting away with it, of Kai's face if he realised he'd failed to stop them. I grabbed and got hold of an ankle clad in neopropylene and, as my vision started to clear, I pulled.

Big Ginge slithered in the mud and went down, knees first, onto the ground. Packages fell from his jacket and he swore again, began groping around trying to replace them, while I held on to his leg and kept pulling in an attempt to stop him from moving. He started to kick, loosening my hold and catching me in the ribs with his foot. Breathless, I let go and he kicked me again, rolling himself until he could get purchase to stand. 'Stupid *fucking* women,' he stood over me now. I tried to get another hold on him but the mud sucked me down and my buzzing head and blurry vision meant I couldn't see well enough to get a proper grip. I shook my head but it made things worse, the bushes and trees that lined the sides of the depression began to swing and nausea grabbed at my stomach. My heart had begun to pound, panic-fuelled, now that the adrenaline of the chase had worn off, and I was beginning to realise that I might have made a *really* stupid mistake. 'Should have just shot you when we had the chance.'

And then he kicked me in the head. The world went black and all I could smell and taste was blood but I could still hear, and what I heard was a sudden scratchy dashing sound, a snap and my ginger captor screaming 'No, get it off, get it away!' and then a low, growling, grunting sound. After a pause so long that I wondered if I'd passed out, there was the sound of running feet and lots of voices in a cacophony of yelling, and snarling, but the kick wasn't followed up with any more bodily violence, so I curled myself into a little ball of pain around my aching head and let myself drop into unconsciousness.

CHAPTER TWENTY-SEVEN

'Wow.' Isobel gently touched the side of my face. 'Does it hurt?'

'Only when I breathe. Or eat.' Two days had seen the bruising turn from red to black, one of my eyes was still swollen shut and my jaw looked as though a three year old had been let loose with a painting set on it, but I was getting better. 'Or sit, stand, lie down and talk.'

'Oh, Holly.'

'And here's the hero of the hour!' Even Vivienne looked pleased as Megan entered, dragged by Rufus. 'If Rufus hadn't got loose and gone chasing after you, who knows what might have happened?'

I could have sworn that Rufus winked at me, but since I could only see out of one eye myself I might have been mistaken.

'None of us knew where you'd gone, you just vanished off the face of the earth.' Eve said. 'Dav — Kai was quite beside himself. He wanted the police to leave those thugs and go looking for you. Although, quite probably, he might also have wanted them to arrest me for flouting the unspoken rule of motherhood, "You shall not cover your adult son in kisses, however much you may have feared he'd been killed." I thought he'd die of embarrassment. Where is he, by the way? I thought he was coming with you?'

'He's down at the police station giving a statement.' I took an almost-warm cup of tea with my slightly trembling hands. 'I wish I was there with him.'

Eve gave a smile that was three parts relief to two parts romance. 'You two are so in love, it's wonderful.'

'Actually I want to hear how he's talking his way out of all this. He's going to be generating more bullshit than a field of cows seeing the vet arrive.' I let a slow, warm smile spread onto my face. 'He's really great in action, Eve.'

Megan gave a filthy snigger. 'And you've seen him in action a lot, haven't you, Holl?'

'Shut up.'

The telephone rang and Vivienne answered it, while the rest of us emptied the cooling teapot and ate the supplied biscuits. Isobel touched my arm.

'Holly, there's something I need to tell you.'

'Go on then.'

She looked quickly over her shoulder. Eve was grinning to herself, a grin that was entirely unwarranted by the choice of soggy options left in the unwelcoming biscuit tin. Megan was still snorting the kind of laugh which comes with over-furnished comfort and crap snacks, and Vivienne was busy exclaiming into the phone. 'Not here. Somewhere private.'

I raised eyebrows. Isobel's cheeks had a pink dab in the centre, like embarrassment, but her eyes were shining. Her hair gleamed more than usual and the spots had almost gone. 'Why? What is it?'

A coy, sideways look and her mouth opened, but our conversation was severed by Vivienne shooting towards the television set in the corner of the room.

'*Shh!*'

We all looked at one another. Being hushed like a room full of five-year-olds wasn't really in our brief.

'Why?' Megan asked.

'That was my daughter on the phone.' Vivienne fumbled with a remote control, fiddling with buttons, trying to find a channel. 'My husband . . . my *ex*-husband, is on TV.' The screen flipped between yet another Top Gear repeat and a cookery programme.

'He's the Star in a Reasonably-Priced Car?' Megan looked confused.

'No . . . damn thing . . . Channel Four. It's always hard to find on this set.' Vivienne pressed a few more buttons and the graphics of a new quiz show flicked up. '"Cash for Questions". I've never seen it.'

We watched as the camera panned the audience. 'Which one is him?' Isobel leaned close to the screen.

'He's there somewhere. Emily said she saw him . . . oh!' Vivienne collapsed onto the stool that Eve had vacated in order to rummage through the biscuits. 'He's there.' Her eyes widened. 'There. Not the audience. He's a *contestant*.'

The camera came to rest on a nondescript middle-aged man, chunky round the jowls, wearing a hand-knitted sweater and looking a bit shame-faced. 'Bastard?' Eve said, experimentally.

'No, he . . . oh, turn it up, Megan, please.' Vivienne straightened on her perch and we all watched in silence as Richard Bentley was introduced to an audience which seemed to be made up of pensioners on acid, judging by the gales of laughter raised by the presenter's feeble attempts at humour.

'Oh, Holly,' Vivienne turned to me, her eyes shining. 'The charm worked. It really worked! He's all right!'

'Must have been some sex,' Meg muttered, but everyone shushed her.

And then the quiz began. Fairly straightforward in format, it consisted of Richard being given money for each correctly answered question, and losing it for wrong answers. The cash, and forfeits, rose as the level of difficulty went up and I found that I was hugging a cushion as I watched, biting the careful piping around its edges to stop myself crying out in frustration.

But eventually Richard came to the final question. He could choose to answer — trebling his current winnings and scoring himself a massive financial prize, losing it all if he was wrong — or to take what he'd got so far and run.

'Take the money!' Vivienne pounded the screen with a slipper. 'You lunatic!'

'Gamble!' shouted Megan, and I had to stand quite firmly on her foot to shut her up. Vivienne's eyes were nearly popping out and I hoped she didn't have a history of high blood pressure, because the studio clock was ticking down to Richard's decision in a way guaranteed to cause a coronary in susceptible viewers.

'I'll gamble,' he said, into our collective intake of breath. The camera closed in on his face. 'But first I want to apologise.' The slick presenter knew good TV when he participated in it, and stood back, allowing Richard full access to the camera banks. 'Vivienne, if you're watching, I did it all for you. I *had* to leave, to stop you getting dragged into the God-awful mess that my life became. I thought you might have known . . . worked it out from the fact that I'd put everything into your name just before the bank foreclosed on the business loan. But if I win here tonight then so many of my troubles will be over. I hope you can find it in your heart to forgive me the pain I caused you, and that we could at least try to be together again.'

'Questioned good and hard and then put out of his misery.' I'd half-whispered it, but Vivienne heard and whipped her head around towards me. Her eyes were fixed, over-bright, as though she was holding tears under her lids.

'Oh . . . He loved me. All the time, he loved me.' Red-clawed fingers raked at her hair. 'He wasn't finding himself, he was protecting me.'

'I wouldn't want to find myself wearing a jumper like that,' Megan said, matter-of-factly.

'I knitted it. Three years ago. He's wearing it as a sign that everything he says is true, he really does want me to take him back.'

'If he wins.' I felt a bit of an old sourpuss. 'Then he can pay off a lot of his debts. Buy himself out of bankruptcy.'

'It's like that film, Slumdog Millionaire,' Isobel added. 'Winning the quiz gets him the girl!'

'He hasn't won yet,' Eve reminded us.

'But I'd take him back anyway, the old fool.' The tears were there now, spreading onto Vivienne's make-up like flooding pools. 'Win or lose, it doesn't matter. He never needed to protect me, he should have just told me the truth! I would have been there for him, no matter what.'

The final question came, dropped into a hushed audience. 'For the final gamble, Richard Bentley, can you tell me — who, or what, is Messier 81?'

A sudden sound beside me. Vivienne was sobbing quietly into cupped hands. I patted her shoulder awkwardly. 'Don't worry,' I said. 'Bankruptcy gets paid off eventually. And you might not have any money, but you'll have each other.'

She raised her head and I was surprised to see no trace of tears now. In fact, she was laughing gently. 'He knows the answer, Holly,' she whispered. 'He *knows.*'

Megan and I raised eyebrows at each other. Faith was one thing, but . . .

'It's a galaxy. A very distant galaxy.' Richard answered firmly, decisively, and the audience cheered wildly as the big red tick that signified a correct answer flashed up onto the screen.

'When we first married, Richard was studying astronomy. He wrote a dissertation on spiral galaxies, I remember having the notes lying around the place for weeks! I used to tidy them up, and he'd just go and get them straight out again, said he knew exactly where everything was, even when it was piled up on the floor . . . Messier 81 was one of his favourites. He gave up astronomy because he had a family to support.'

Vivienne couldn't stifle the laughter any longer. 'He thought there was no money in it.'

As we watched the huge numbers racking up on the winnings readout, we all started to laugh.

I cleared away the teacups, pouring stagnant tea down the kitchen sink, listening to the atmosphere in the living room becoming more relaxed by the second. Vivienne had broken out the plum wine and I suspected I was the only person who was going to be fit to drive soon, and I only had one operable eye.

Oh, and Isobel, who came into the kitchen with me, elbowing the door closed, but helping me with the dishes without speaking. When we'd washed and dried the final crockery, I turned to face her. 'Okay, now you can spit it out. What is it that you feel you have to tell me?'

Isobel let her hair hang over her face. 'I don't know if I can, now.'

'Is it anything to do with the spell?'

A pause and then a slight nod. 'I think so. At least . . . I don't know.'

'You're the centre of someone's world?' I looked behind me. Given the way the spell had worked for the rest of us, this probably meant that Isobel had become a supermassive black hole into which we would all be sucked.

Now pale, Isobel nodded. 'I know he was your friend, and it shouldn't have happened but . . . he was there.'

'Whoa, hold on, back up a minute.' I held up a hand to stop the cascade of meaningless words. 'Start again, but slower. Who are we talking about here?'

Isobel blinked. 'Oh, sorry. Did I not say? Sorry, my brain's a bit scrambled these days, what with . . . oh, I see. From the beginning. Well, it was Aiden, obviously.'

I leaned against the draining board in a sudden state of flop. 'Aiden?'

'When you asked me to go round and let him out of the handcuffs.'

'Ah.' A quick memory of a naked, and overly-eroticised Aiden thrashing about chained to my bed. 'Oh. Oh my God! Aiden — I should have thought. I am so sorry Isobel, I would never have sent you if I'd known, if I'd thought . . . God. Did you go to the police?'

She stared blankly. 'Why would I do that?'

Suddenly shocked into awkwardness, I shrugged. 'You know, sexual assault? But, how, if he was handcuffed — did he go for you after you let him out? Oh, this is all my fault, I should have made him wait, I was only trying to be humane about it and not leave him for too long and I should have thought, I know Aiden, what he's like and he must have seen you as—'

'He didn't. He barely noticed me at all, just like everyone else. But then — something happened, something changed, I don't know what. Maybe it was the spell. He was talking about how he didn't really know why he'd come down from Scotland, didn't know what he'd been thinking about to turn up at your door, and I just, sort of, listened, and he was . . . But when I told him, you know, about being a virgin and everything . . . He was very gentle, very sweet and kind. And, oh, Holly,' a rapturous smile crossed her face, 'it was *fabulous*. Better than I'd ever imagined.'

'You *wanted* it?'

'Oh yes. I've read the books and stuff but, they never really make it clear, you know? So when he — Well, he was naked and everything and — Holly, do you have any imagination at all?'

'As far as Aiden's concerned, I try not to have. So, let me get this straight, you're dating him now?'

'Dating?' Isobel frowned. 'No. Why would I do that? Besides, he's gone back to Scotland, hasn't he?'

'But you said—' realisation tapped on my shoulder and let incredulity come in as well. 'Oh God. Isobel. You mean you're *literally* the centre of someone's world . . .'

She gave a shy smile. 'Due in the middle of August, actually.' Protective hands crossed over her lower stomach. 'And everything going well.'

I flopped further, until both my elbows rested in a pool of water. 'Oh, Isobel.'

'And the oddest thing is, my parents are delighted! Can't wait to be granny and grandad, and I'm still going to get the house next year, although obviously the makeover is going to have to wait until this little one is at least walking.' Another half-hug around her middle. 'And it's going to be fantastic. Only I wanted to make sure you were all right with it, what with Aiden being your friend first, and then, if you could possibly tell him because I don't know how to find him. Oh, it's all right, I don't want anything from him, but I think he should know he's going to be a daddy, don't you?'

I tried to put the image of Aiden, leather trousers and reckless sex addiction, into the same context as the word daddy, and failed oh-so-miserably. 'I can try,' I said feebly.

Kai turned up, accompanied by three policemen who all looked as though they topped up their salaries by playing extras in The Bill. Eve hugged him, tentatively.

'Wow. Policemen aren't just getting younger, they're getting better looking,' Megan whispered, tossing her hair and pouting at the nearest one. 'Why have we never thought about committing crimes to find a boyfriend?'

'Because I didn't want one, you're too intimidated by authority and we'd probably have got interviewed by the last remaining Gene Hunt on the police force,' I whispered back, pretending to be immune to the glamour cast by the uniform. Kai winked at me from across the room and mouthed 'You're a Ladies' Walking Group' over everyone's heads, which, with his height, was kind of a given.

'We're a Walking Group,' I said to the blondest, youngest and, it had to be said, most attractive, of the policemen. 'We were . . .'

'Taking an early morning stroll, when those ruffians accosted us.' Vivienne finished for me. Obviously, hearing that Richard still loved her had given her a brand-new, and paradoxically old-fashioned, vocabulary. The police wrote everything down earnestly, even when we elaborated rather more than was necessary, while Kai stood leaning against the wall and smirking, particularly when I mentioned my abduction at the hands of Big Helmet himself and managed to make it sound as though I'd escaped through my own ingenuity rather than by sending smoke signals and nearly asphyxiating myself.

'So I do have to ask why you didn't report all this at the time?' Mid-hair-and-attractiveness-policeman asked.

'Because they were threatened,' Kai managed to involve himself without anyone telling him to shut up. 'Holly told me, and I advised her to keep quiet, unless there was enough proof to stop the lads coming after them for revenge.'

'They were going to say that we were witches, and they'd seen us doing black magic on the hill, with blood and stuff.'

All three policemen rolled their eyes. 'Well, I guess it's not surprising what drug gangs will come up with to keep people off their turf,' said the one I was presuming to be a recent import from a big city. 'Unless you actually *are* witches, of course.'

There was an inordinate amount of laughter at this, some of it rather shrill and desperate, and Kai managed to cause the interview to be terminated without seeming to do anything at all. When the door closed behind the last one, I stared at him.

'You seem to know a lot about handling the police. Anything you need to tell me?'

'The ability to manipulate the police is a skill learned during a very misspent childhood. Give them Occam's razor, nicely sharpened, and the event is as good as over.'

'What?' Isobel frowned.

'Basically, you give them the simplest explanation which seems to fit the facts, and it takes a very keen copper to go looking for anything more complicated.' Kai twisted his thumb ring for a bit, so as not to look at us.

'But they have the candles!'

Kai grinned. 'Not any more.'

'You broke into Drug-Dealer Andy's house and stole the candles? And the pictures?'

A small shrug and the smile went secretive. 'Something like that.'

'Then we were fortunate that we have you on our side, Mr Rhys.' Vivienne, still possessed by the soul of Jane Austen, patted his shoulder. As she touched him, the floor of the living room seemed to swirl momentarily, the walls flowed and there was the brief sense that the world was a notional place. A second later everything was as before.

'Did anyone else feel that?' I swallowed the giddiness and gave my head a little shake. 'Or is it those tablets the doctor gave me — they're absolutely enormous. I'm not one hundred per cent certain which end I'm supposed to be putting them in and I'm sure they're made for horses.'

'A discharge of energy,' Vivienne said. 'The spell ending.' Several cats ran in from the kitchen, stared at us accusingly and stalked, bristle-backed from the room again. 'You see? They sensed something.'

Isobel sat down hard. 'I thought it was me. I get dizzy sometimes. That, and I can't bear the smell of Dettol.'

'She's pregnant,' I muttered to Megan, who widened her eyes until she looked like a mad cow.

'*Really?* But . . . I thought she said she was a virgin . . . Oh, *surely not* . . .'

Before she could start crossing herself and kneeling, I pinched her elbow. 'The spell wasn't that good. She's just not a virgin any more, which seems to have been her desired result, oh, that and the baby.'

We all looked at one another, feeling the weight of statistical likelihood pressing on us. 'And we all got what we wanted,' Megan voiced what we were all thinking. 'All of us. That's pretty incredible when you think about it.'

'One dog, one returned husband, one adopted son, one baby and . . .' I hesitated. Kai was looking at me out of those yellow eyes with an expression that was impossible to guess the meaning of, 'and one journalist,' I finished, going for the safest option. 'But was it really magic?'

A long arm slipped around my waist. 'Maybe belief is all there really needs to be.' Kai smelled of fresh air and his skin was cold as diamond. 'Belief and love. Because that's what this spell did, if it did anything, it showed that love doesn't have a simple definition. Except in our case, of course. Which is where my carefully crafted theory falls down.' The arm gave me a squeeze.

'I said I loved you because I thought you were dead.' I leaned away slightly.

'So? I'm twice as easy to love alive.' He closed the gap and whispered in my ear, 'I move about more, for a start.'

'You are so smug.' But I couldn't even manage to sound really annoyed; my breath had thickened in my throat and maybe there was some residue of self-imposed magic in the air because I suddenly wanted to kiss him, with the implied possibility of throwing him across a sofa and ripping his clothes off with anything capable of exerting sufficient grip.

But not in front of his mother, of course.

CHAPTER TWENTY-EIGHT

Hey, mum. This is just for you. A kind of PS, if you like. The rest of the stuff I showed you, yeah, that's making the book — being a journo has some advantages and one of them is knowing a load of guys who're all fighting over the rights. Even Holl isn't going to get to see this. She's read the rest. Made her cry. But this one — this is 'your eyes only'.

It's not always going to be easy, what we've got. I know you want to rush straight into 'mother and grandmother' mode . . . all that shopping you did for Cerys and the twins? Christ, never seen so many M&S bags in my life, but, yeah, I understand. You might not be around forever, want to make up for not being there up till now . . . yeah. Understood. But. You can't buy love, guess you know that. You have to earn it. Just be there, mum. That's all I ask. Just be there. For them, for me, for Holly.

This time last year . . . wow, when I look back it's like everything's changed. Then I'd just fucked up my life with Imogen in ways that made Christmas in a war zone look peaceful. Now I've got a family, a real love, I've even got a bloody Christmas tree and a turkey — what the fuck is that all about? And you. You were always like this bogeyman in my head, you know, this creature who left me as soon as she could get away, and now I know you were just a scared kid — it's like I'm reappraising everything.

And it's going to take time. But I think we can do it. I never thought I'd love a woman, but I love Holly. So, just maybe I can learn to love you too.

Like Holly says, maybe there is something in this 'magic' after all. Or maybe it's just us, offloading responsibility onto some 'spell' shit. Either way, we're doing okay. Dealing with life, working things out.

Which is another kind of magic really, isn't it?

CHAPTER TWENTY-NINE

Christmas day brought a surprise visit by Cerys and Nicholas and the twins.

'We thought we'd come over and eat all your chocolate, and then go back to Mum and Dad's and eat all theirs,' Cerys stripped the outer layer of clothing off the twins, like a very experienced ape peeling bananas.

Nick hugged me. 'Thanks for the books, Holl. Not sure when I'm going to get time to read them, though.' He waved a hand at the twins.

'That's why I gave you books. They don't go off.' I found my arms suddenly full of Freya, touchingly dressed in a stretch-suit that I had given her. 'So, how are you both?'

'I'm ninety per cent tits, and he has his moments,' Cerys carried Zac through into the living room, pausing only to grab a handful of dates from a bowl on the side. 'Other than that, we're good.'

Nick rolled his eyes. 'Yeah, I've had a couple of not such good days, but we're pretty busy, you know? Not a lot of time to be anything other than running from place to place and mopping.' He smiled at me, relaxed and happy. 'Honest, Holl, there is a *lot* of mopping.'

'I can tell.' Freya had dribbled down my arm. 'She's worse than Rufus. But prettier, obviously,' I added quickly. 'Not so, you know, sticky.'

'Nicky! Can you get me the changing bag?' Cerys called through. 'And find out where he's hidden the chocolate!'

Nicholas gave me the grin again. His hair was growing out of the self-trimmed-fringe-and-mullet style he'd always had, and with his blue eyes not pulled into their customary wary squint, he looked less like a careworn elf and more like a pin-up.

'Nicky, eh? Looking good, bro.' I patted his shoulder.

'Yeah. I know,' he said, enigmatically, gave me another, rather secretive, grin and went out to the car to fetch another mule-load of child-paraphernalia.

Kai and Eve returned from their tour of the house and greeted Cerys with delight. Eve was still getting her head around the whole having a family thing, but she had embraced the idea with considerable enthusiasm and already carried pictures of the twins in her purse. Kai was . . . well, he was working on finally being someone's son. I couldn't exactly say that he'd welcomed Eve with open arms, but he was doing his best, and getting better at it with each meeting. Cerys was so fuddled with new-motherhood that Kai's somewhat edited revelations about the existence of her grandmother had been taken on board with barely a murmur.

'Hey Kai, if you are *any* kind of decent human being you will have chocolate somewhere. Holly, tell me he's got chocolate somewhere, before my life becomes not worth living.' Cerys poured Zac into the unresisting arms of his great-grandmother and necked the dates. 'I am permanently starving, but I'm losing weight like a Slimming World champion, I guess that's the advantage of breastfeeding, please don't hate me.'

'I know where all the food is, I bought it. Kai still hasn't quite got a handle on Christmas,' I said, pulling a tin of biscuits out of a cupboard. 'He's a bit out of practice on it.'

'But he's getting plenty of practice with you.' Cerys levered the lid off the tin. 'And it's not just the sex either, is it?

Oh, come on, Holl, I've seen his face, the way he looks at you, he almost seems normal when you're around.'

'Oy, don't take all the shortbread,' Kai himself appeared, helping Nicholas to lug two changing bags and a rolled up changing mat into the room. 'And, for your information, madam, I'm as normal as they come.'

Cerys opened her mouth. I could almost see the single entendre hovering, then she noticed Eve and pursed her lips tightly.

'Holly and I are working on it,' he said conversationally, 'but I think she's still got issues.'

'Well of course she has.' The words came from Nick, on his knees on the rug, unfurling the twins' activity playmat under the Christmas tree. 'She's spent all her time looking after me and going out with twats.'

'Nicholas!' I covered Freya's ears. 'Children present.'

'Stop trying to change the subject, Holl.' He straightened up and flipped his lengthening hair from his eyes. 'You know it's true. You only went out with disposable gits. You've never had a proper boyfriend, a nice one.'

'I never wanted one,' I stared at this new, assertive version of my brother.

'I think you did. Deep down. You just hid what you really wanted behind the sex, so you never had to deal with them rejecting you. Because you always put me first, didn't you?'

'No, I . . .'

Kai's eyes were like two cinders against my skin. Burning. I couldn't meet them.

'Holly. I think you need to talk to Nicholas.'

Eve cleared her throat. 'I think the pudding is boiling over,' she said. 'In the kitchen.'

'Yes.' Cerys slid Freya from my arms. 'In the kitchen. Pudding. Boiling over. Yes.' She nudged Kai.

'What? What pudding . . . oh. In the kitchen. Yes.' And the three of them managed the most unsubtle 'leaving them

alone together' manoeuvre in the history of sibling relationships, with Freya's rather traumatised wails being cut off by
the slam of the heavy oak door as they sealed themselves in,
away from any fallout.

'As a matter of interest, and before this goes any further, *is*
there a pudding?' Nick asked, folding his arms across his chest.

'There is. In the microwave.'

'God. I hope Cerys doesn't find it.' He ran both hands
through his hair, leaving it exotically tousled. 'Look at me,
Holly.' Reluctantly I forced my eyes onto his face.

'It's okay. Whatever you want to say, I can take it. Honestly.
Whether it's the meds or just having a new life . . . I'm doing all
right. Just, you know, don't shout or anything.'

I looked at his newly squared shoulders, his cool pale
eyes that still moved too much to be normal but held a new
expression of responsibility. 'I'm sorry, Nick.' I whispered the
words. 'I'm so sorry.'

His lip curled. 'Oh yuks, sister dear. Is this Christmas
bringing out some horrible sentimental streak?'

'No. I just needed to say it. For myself, more than you,
you daft bugger. I held it against you, you know, your illness.
All these years, looking after you . . .'

'I'm sorry too, Holl. For what it's worth.' A shiver of his
upper body as energy struck, but he held it down. 'We both
crapped up each other's lives a bit, didn't we?'

I stared at him. 'What?'

'Look at me.' He held his arms wide and turned a slow
circle, like a circus pony. 'Look. Yeah, I'm a weirdo, up and
down like a vicar's nightie . . . hold on . . . sod it, doesn't
matter . . . but I'm doing it. Capable of a real life out there in
the big world. Looking after twins, looking after Cerys, when
she'll let me, the daft cowbag; who'd have thought? Thirty-
two years old and I'm finally getting to see what a real life *is*.
And, yeah, okay, there's a lot of other stuff going on, better
meds, being older, all that cognitive behavioural shit but . . .
who knows what I could have done, could have been, if I'd

just broken away sooner.' He stopped turning. Angled his body towards me. 'You made life easy for me, Holl. So I stuck with it. Never had to face it, never had to be *absolutely definitely positive* that I'd taken my meds, because, if I didn't? Well, you'd pick up the pieces, sort me out, prop me back up again until I could get on top of it all. No imperative to take care of myself. Whereas now,' another slow whirl, 'now I'm my own responsibility. And *I* have things to take care of.'

It was like looking at a stranger. This marble-skinned man with eyes like a faded sky was no longer my brother. Why had I never asked how it felt to be him? To have his life micromanaged by his younger sister, unasked, unwanted? We'd resented each other equally but we'd carried on with our lives amid our resentments, hating yet loving, struggling to make the best of everything. 'If only I'd known . . .' I whispered.

Nicholas put his arms around me. It was the first time I could ever remember my brother hugging me. It had usually been me hugging him, and even that had had an element of restraint about it. 'Hey, we all just do the best we can with what we're given,' he said. 'And you got given me. And, let's face it, you made a pretty good job of me, really, Holl, but now it's time to get out there, yell at a few people. Kai can take it if you lose your temper with him or chuck a few plates, and it might be nice for you for a change, not to have to be reasonable all the time.'

All I could do was nod. My one good eye had flooded with tears, and the squinty, bruise-stained one was watering in sympathy. Nicholas let me go, walked to the kitchen door and opened it. Freya's wails billowed out. 'Your turn, Kai,' he said. 'It's like relationship tag here today.'

Kai came towards me. 'Okay?'

I nodded and the tears pattered down onto my neck. 'Yes. You were right, we needed to sort things out between us.'

'And now you have?' At arms' length he stopped. 'Have you forgiven each other too?'

I sighed a deep breath out and moved into his arms. 'Yes, I think we have.' And, as though the spell was giving a last gasp, the earth shook. Like a horse ridding itself of an irritating fly, like a leaf flicking off a raindrop, the floor beneath my feet twitched. And I realised how things went from here.

'I think the turkey might be done,' I stretched myself up on tiptoe against his body. Reached up and tangled my fingers through his hair. 'And we don't want dinner to burn, do we?'

'Is that some kind of metaphor for "I love you and I want to live with you"?' Kai took half a step forward, so that I was pressed hard against him, feeling his heart beat against my skin through our clothes.

'No, it's practicality. *This* is I love you.' And I dragged his head down so that our mouths met in a kiss that singed the needles off the tree. 'And yes, I do want to live with you, even in this gothic woodcarver's nightmare of a house, and even with your job, which is a thousand interesting deaths waiting to happen. It's you, Kai. I want you, whatever else comes with you.'

And as we fell into a stomach-rolling, heart-stopping kiss, I heard Cerys's voice echo from the kitchen. 'Thank God, she mentioned dinner.'

THE END

ACKNOWLEDGEMENTS

The staff, students and parents of Lady Lumley's School, for their unfailing encouragement and their delight in my successes, particularly the Science department — Robbie, Jo, Katie, Peter, Faye, Mark, Sam, Chris, Tom, James, Fran, and particular thanks to Heather for 'Rufus'. Sorry about all the smoke bombs, guys, don't worry, most of it will sponge off . . .

All my wonderful friends at the RNA, for laughing in all the right places and generally not minding me behaving like a six year old at an 'all you can eat' cake party.

My brilliant editor and everyone at Choc Lit, for . . . well, the 'six year old' comment pretty well covers them too.

And TMMQ for . . . now I come to think of it, I behave like a six year old quite a lot, really.

THE CHOC LIT STORY

Established in 2009, Choc Lit is an independent, award-winning publisher dedicated to creating a delicious selection of quality women's fiction.

We have won 18 awards, including Publisher of the Year and the Romantic Novel of the Year, and have been shortlisted for countless others. In 2023, we were shortlisted for Publisher of the Year by the Romantic Novelists' Association.

All our novels are selected by genuine readers. We are proud to publish talented first-time authors, as well as established writers whose books we love introducing to a new generation of readers.

In 2023, we became a Joffe Books company. Best known for publishing a wide range of commercial fiction, Joffe Books has its roots in women's fiction. Today it is one of the largest independent publishers in the UK.

We love to hear from you, so please email us about absolutely anything bookish at choc-lit@joffebooks.com

If you want to hear about all our bargain new releases, join our mailing list: www.choc-lit.com/contact

www.ingramcontent.com/pod-product-compliance
Lightning Source LLC
Chambersburg PA
CBHW011453170626
46814CB00009B/3035